Racing Hearts

Grace Newman lives in Los Angeles with her husband and their dog, Daisy. Originally from Gloucester, Grace grew up as an avid Formula 1 fan and has had the pleasure of watching Jensen Button and Lewis Hamilton win the World Driver's Championship, which is where her love of the sport was born.

RACING HEARTS

GRACE NEWMAN

hera

First published in Germany in 2025 by Knaur

This edition published in the United States in 2025 by

Hera Books, an imprint of
DK Publishing, a division of Penguin Random House LLC
1745 Broadway, 20th Floor, New York, NY 10019

The authorized representative in the EEA is Dorling Kindersley Verlag GmbH.
Arnulfstr. 124, 80636 Munich, Germany

Print ISBN 979 8 217 25311 1
Ebook ISBN 979 8 217 25351 7

Printed and bound in Great Britain by Clays Ltd, Elcograf S.p.A.

Look for more great books at
www.herabooks.com | www.dk.com

1

To the women who are overlooked, underestimated, or told it isn't their place—this one is for you.

Chapter One

Georgia

"Pole position, baby!" Mel yelled into my radio as I settled into the driver's seat of my Formula 1 car. "Let's show those boys how a Formula 1 race is won, yeah?"

Through my mirror, I glanced at my brother whose car was in second position on the starting grid. Henri wanted this Spanish Grand Prix victory as much as I did, and he wasn't going to make this win easy for me. His cold text messages earlier this morning showed just how frustrated he was to get second place in yesterday's qualifying. Sarcastically telling my brother he should have practiced more *probably* wasn't the best choice of a response, but this was my first time qualifying on pole this season, and I wasn't in the business of apologizing for my success.

I stared up at the lights that danced above the F1 starting line, taking a deep, calming breath.

One light.

Two lights.

Three lights. The distinct smell of engine fumes crowded my senses as I continued to breathe deeply, steadying my heart rate.

Four lights.

Five lights. Lights out.

Without hesitation, I squeezed the throttle and launched into the first corner, determined to defend my first-place starting position from Henri's aggressive overtaking tactics. Our cars jostled for the lead, tires sliding as we fought for control.

So, it's gloves off then, is it, Henri?

"Careful on tires, G," Mel mumbled through the radio. She wanted these tires to last. Defending position from other drivers tore away the rubber grip, but like hell was I going to let my brother overtake me on lap one. The Barcelona-Catalunya circuit required two pit stops, and the longer you could make the first set of tires go, the better the second half of your race would be.

Lap after lap, I maintained my lead, my car gliding through the track with precision, edging just slightly away from the rest of the cars behind me. At around lap seventeen, the Hermes team called Henri into the pits first, his tires worn thin from his attempted overtakes. My brother had never mastered the ability to conserve his tires. Two laps later, it was my turn to veer off the track and into the pits.

I exited the pit lane clean, heart still pounding, only to see a bright purple streak fly past me. My heart sank as I watched the other Hermes driver pass me by.

Luca Rossi.

"Of course, I come out behind Luca," I muttered under my breath. Memories of last week's tense battle flashed through my mind. He'd refused to give up the racing line to me, a line that I'd clearly won, and his arrogance had sent him into the gravel, ending his race. But now Luca was in front of me, and he was undoubtedly going to make me pay.

For an entire lap, I shadowed his every move, analyzing his trajectory, searching for weaknesses. But each time I lunged, he defended his line, refusing to let me by. Even if it wore down his tires.

"Asshole! We're not even racing each other!" I screamed inside my helmet, glad the radio feed was off. Considering Luca had qualified in sixth place, he should have been more worried about saving his tires to battle it out with Lily and Éliott—not me. Defending your position wasted lap time.

My attempts to overtake him at various corners were thwarted, but in a moment of slight misjudgment, Luca drifted too wide on a turn, giving me the inside line, and I was not going to back down. I braked late, turning in sharply forcing Luca to yield, which he wisely did.

Luca had learned his lesson: Georgia Dubois didn't back down from fights, she won them.

Finally, after maneuvering through the other cars, I'd easily returned to first position, my car gripping the track with absolute perfection with my newer tires. A second pit stop was completed with utter precision, and by lap forty-nine, I'd put ten seconds between me and my brother, an excellent buffer. My body tingled with adrenaline that sent a fire through me. Imposter syndrome had been my biggest weakness this year, and after each lap, its grip on my heart was fading.

At the start of lap fifty, Mel popped on to the radio. "Yellow flag and safety car. Accident close to the pit entrance."

"Shit! Just my luck to get a safety car this close to the end."

Five races into the season, and Lady Luck never seemed to be on my side. A restart with the safety car meant all the

F1 cars would be forced back together, eliminating that beautiful ten-second gap between me and my brother. All of the work from the first half of the race was down the drain. With the yellow flag in play, the next five laps felt like utter agony as I drove behind the safety car, weaving as best I could in an attempt to keep my tire temperatures up. For cars meant to go 200mph, driving this slow in a race was nearly impossible.

"Track is almost clear. Race is about to restart," Mel announced.

Henri was right behind me now, probably singing his victory speech in his helmet. When it was safe to restart, I led the group of cars off again, but as I rounded the next corner, I felt my wheels spin, making me go wide. A rookie mistake.

"Fuck!" I yelled out as Henri's car zoomed past mine, his tires hugging the track as he overtook me in one fell swoop. I knew I hadn't kept my tires' temperature up during the yellow flag, and cold tires were impossible to control.

There was no response from the team, and undoubtedly Mel was assessing the situation from the pit wall where my race engineer and leadership sat. My tires were wearing, and we couldn't risk a blowout.

I drove behind Henri for another ten laps, and as I entered the penultimate lap, I was still trailing a second and a half behind my brother in second place. Time was running out for me to catch up, and my heart was pounding so hard it felt like it would break through at any moment. This was Valkyrie F1's first real opportunity to win a race, and with each passing second, that dream of being the first women-run team to win a Grand Prix was slipping from our grasp. The jaws of defeat started to wrap around my heart, but I gripped the steering wheel harder, forcing the dread away.

Formula 1 champions didn't give up, and come hell or high water, I was going to be this year's F1 champion.

Isabelle's voice came on the radio like a thunderclap. "Georgia, only one and a half laps to go. Fuck the tires. Punch it."

Had my team principal just told me to *fuck the tires*? A staunch variation from the tough, determined, *take-no-shit* approach that she was known for, but I knew there wasn't another option, not if I wanted to be on the podium's top step.

If we'd all been thinking straight, Isabelle would have told me to play this safe. We shouldn't be risking a blowout on used-up tires, not when P2 was full of valuable points. Points we desperately needed.

But we hadn't come to Barcelona to place *second*. After dominating free practice and qualifying, we knew this was our race to win, and no man was taking this from me, especially not my brother, F1's beloved golden boy.

I increased my pace, and after another turn, my window of opportunity appeared. Henri had made a mistake on the apex in front of me, his tires sliding slightly off the racing line, causing him to lose time.

"Yes! Yes! Yes!" I screamed. Half a second stood between me and Henri, and all I needed was to reach a passing zone where I could gain an advantage on his car. I flew past another corner and saw the next passing area come into view.

It was now or never. The flap on the wing of my car opened, and to my surprise, I easily flew past my brother's Hermes car. The sheer speed of my Valkyrie in a straight line was unmatched, and the race lead was mine again.

"Final lap, G." Mel's voice was almost a whisper over the radio, and I knew the entire team was holding their breath while they watched. With no more laps remaining, there was nothing they could do but silently cheer me on.

I started the last lap, hitting the racing line with such ease I almost didn't recognize myself while I defended another lunge from my brother's car. As I rounded the final corner, the long-awaited checkered flag came into view.

"Come on, Georgia," I whispered to myself, "you can do this."

Focusing on the black and white cloth straight ahead of me, everything else faded away. The roaring of the crowd, the small hum of the radio feed—the world around me fell silent as I felt that familiar rush of adrenaline surge through my veins the moment the flag was behind me.

But this time was different. This time I had crossed the line *first*.

My radio was full of joyful yelling, but their words were fuzzy and muffled. I took a moment to look up at the large screens, watching my bright blue car on the grandstand TVs.

"Wh–what was th–that?" was all I could utter back as I heard distant screaming and cheering through the radio, the sound of the crowd roaring so overpowering that I couldn't hear Mel's voice.

Warm tears formed in my eyes, and I knew my body was registering my win, even if my brain was struggling to catch up. Mel's voice popped back on, and I finally felt the pent-up rush of tears trickle down my face, like a dam that had been blown wide open. The sadness, the excitement, the *fear* that I had bottled up inside me came pouring out as all of the emotions that I had forced myself to hide since Valkyrie F1 Racing had signed me as their lead driver could finally be released.

I was the first woman to win a Formula 1 race in forty years.

Pulling into the pit lane, I turned off the engine and stepped out of the car, my knees sinking to the ground as I hugged my front left tire with all my might. My brother's hand landed on my shoulder, and I could feel it vibrating from his excitement.

"Congrats, Peaches, I'm so damn proud of you!" my brother yelled over the roaring crowd, his voice almost completely drowned out by their deafening cheers. At hearing the affectionate nickname he'd given me when we were young kids, I smiled back up at him.

Even though I had passed Henri on track in what I'm sure the media would deem a "*tense battle between siblings*," I could see the look of love and happiness for me in his eyes as he grabbed me and pulled me toward him. Henri knew what this meant for me, and when I'd joined F1 we'd made a deal: when the race ended, so did our rivalry.

Behind Henri I saw a familiar body emerge from the group of parked F1 cars. As soon as my brother saw his teammate, Luca Rossi, he let me go.

"Luca!" Henri frantically pointed at me. "We got another member of the F1 winners' group!" Henri ignored the slight pinch I gave him.

Luca walked toward us, taking off his helmet before running his hands through his dark, wavy hair. His large brown eyes were red and full of exhaustion, but that didn't stop a sly grin from inching onto his face.

"Congrats, Dubois." He leaned in, the smell of his pine tree cologne was overwhelming. His soft eyes and beaming grin might have fooled my brother, but I knew there wasn't a bone in Luca's body that was happy for me. "See," Luca motioned his arm toward the roaring crowd, "looks like you *can* win a race without bullying someone off the track." Sarcasm dripped from his voice like poison from a fairy tale's apple.

The nerve of this man. "For the last time—" I spat out, stepping into Luca's space. Henri slipped between us, giving us both a wide-eyed, panicked look, a reminder that some discussions should be kept out of the public's eye.

"For fuck's sake, keep it together," he hissed. Luca looked down at my brother, and then back at me, slapping on his infamous Cheshire cat grin as he patted me on the back in a move that felt more patronizing than praising.

Fucking prick.

"Ignore him. Let's go celebrate," Henri whispered, before leading me to the post-race weigh-in. Looking back, Luca was still standing there, his gaze locked on to mine with a silent glare that spoke volumes, and I knew this battle between us was far from over.

After a quick stop in the cooldown room, Henri and I were ushered to the podium celebration where bottle upon bottle of champagne was sprayed over both me and my race engineer, Mel, who had joined me as the winning team's representative. She was the first female racing engineer to stand on the podium, and I knew this was equally special for her. Mel had fought to be here just as much as I had, and for the first time in Formula 1 history, there were *two* women on the podium. Drenched in champagne and smelling of sweat, I smiled back at Henri, giving him one last hug before running down the paddock and back to my team, who were waiting for me with more popped bottles of champagne and open arms.

"Congrats, Georgie. That's P1, first place! Well deserved!" Nora called out as she practically strangled the upper part of my body. My media manager undoubtedly had the toughest job on the team, and yet she wore her assignment with the world's bravest face. The Formula 1 paddock could be on fire and Nora would still announce, "*At least it's warm in here!*"

"You know what I think this win deserves?" I chuckled, a little hint of mischief playing on my face, which I could tell Nora noticed by the slight arch of her brow.

"You still have to do media duties. Don't even ask."

Worth a try.

Win or lose, there was never a reprieve from the Lion's Den—my affectionate name for our contractually obligated press conferences. After every race, the top three drivers were forced into a special dog and pony show full of ruthless questions, lest we be fined thousands of pounds by the FIA, Formula 1's governing body.

I glanced at Isabelle, the Valkyrie team principal, who flashed me a small smile as she *casually* waved, like we hadn't just made history as the first women-run team to win a Formula 1 Grand Prix. And yet in all my time of knowing her, Isabelle had smiled maybe three times, so I was honored that my race win was one of them.

"Alright, time to go show the media that you are the *star* we all know you to be!" Nora gave my shoulders a squeeze as she gently pushed me toward the garage's exit, like she wasn't convinced that I would attend the press conference without some coercion. To be fair to her, if I could've gotten away with feigning an illness to get out of media duties, I would have.

Still, today I'd made history. *We'd* made history.

And for the first time, these journalists were going to have to acknowledge Valkyrie as a winning team. As championship contenders.

Or so we hoped.

Chapter Two

Luca

"Fuck!" I slammed my racing helmet down on the sofa in my driver's room before letting my hands sift through my hair in frustration. Another terrible race where Henri had almost sailed away with a victory, while I struggled to keep my points scoring position.

"Knock, knock, can I come in?" My father opened the door, taking a seat on the plush couch before I could object.

"No point in knocking if you're going to barge in anyway."

His clenched jaw told me he didn't appreciate my sarcasm, but quite frankly, I didn't appreciate his intrusion. I didn't care if my father was a former three-time World Champion for Hermes; my private driver's room was my sanctuary, and he didn't have a right to barge in whenever he wanted to, even if the rest of the team allowed it.

"Luca, we need to talk."

"Oh yeah, about what?" After finishing sixth place out of twenty earlier today, I knew exactly what my father wanted to discuss. Four grid places between me and my golden-boy teammate, Henri. To my father, any place that wasn't directly above or below Henri was a failure. It didn't matter that sixth place brought points to the team; it simply wasn't good enough.

"Luca." His stern voice snapped me out of my thoughts, and I turned to face him as I plopped onto my other sofa. His disapproval was so overbearing I could practically taste it, like soured milk in my coffee. "Luca, I need you to get serious here. What happened today?"

"I just couldn't get the tire temperature right." *Not a total lie.*

"We worked on this earlier, had a strategy around the race start—"

"Well, sometimes strategies don't play out during a race."

His piercing gaze felt like a knife to my heart. "Luca, you're fifth in the championship while Henri is leading! And Georgia, if she keeps driving like she did today, she's going to quickly catch up to him, leaving you further behind."

"Well, it would help if the stewards actually did something about Georgia's aggressive driving," I muttered.

"Enough!" The sound of my father slamming his hand on the coffee table echoed throughout the room. "Enough of the whining, Luca. Georgia takes risks, and those risks have turned into rewards. Those were championship-winning moves, something you could learn a thing or two about if you watched her race instead of complaining to the media."

I bit back the retort that threatened to spill from me, instead opting to stare out of the small window. Pointless was an understatement when it came to arguing with my father. Considering he was famously known for *his* aggressive overtaking tactics, I knew he lauded Georgia's driving style.

To him, that's how a driver became a champion.

My father sighed in frustration, his eyes fixed on mine. "Luca, your existing contract with Hermes is up after this year, and we don't have a renewal signed. They could easily swap you for another driver. We need to fix your driving, and quickly, or you're going to get replaced by the team."

"Don't you mean *we* might get replaced?" It was always a team effort with my father until I was losing.

"Luca—"

"What are Hermes going to do, replace me with our reserve driver, Anthony? He's barely capable of finishing an F2 race, never mind an F1 race."

"It's exactly that kind of cocky, arrogant attitude that is going to get you kicked off the team," he scolded. "You're running on borrowed time, son. It's not just your pathetic performance this season, it's your image in the media. Your blasé attitude toward driving is making the team's sponsors reconsider their contracts. After the yacht incident over winter break, I can only keep your name out of the papers for so long."

By my age, my father had won three world championships. My biggest achievement? I'd managed to steal a yacht off the coast of Spain… and get caught.

"Maybe Hermes *should* just give Anthony my seat—"

"Luca Michael Rossi," my dad cut me off. "For fuck's sake, I don't want to hear that crap come out of your mouth again."

I pointedly avoided my father's gaze, wishing for a moment that I had asked my mother to attend this race. After my embarrassing qualifying yesterday, I'd told her not to bother. Both my parents didn't need to watch me disappoint them.

"Sometimes the car just doesn't click with me," I sighed.

"Then you need to work harder. Like Henri."

Because my fucking teammate was so perfect.

Every muscle in my body tensed at hearing *his* name. Last year we'd had a good relationship, a friendship even, but this year the team had made it clear that Henri was their number one driver, their priority, the future of Hermes Racing. My only job was to not crash the car and make sure Henri won, not the other way around. Why bother trying to win if Hermes were just going to take it away from me?

"What does the golden boy bring to the team that I don't?" I crossed my arms, before sarcastically adding, "Definitely not good looks and charm…"

"Dedication," my father deadpanned, ignoring the sarcasm oozing from my body. "Henri cares more about his *professional* life than his *private one*. Something you could stand to learn from him." My father didn't give me a chance to respond before he slammed a photo onto the table with such force my water bottle flew off.

Shit. I knew that photographer from a few nights ago was a tabloid journalist. I grimaced. There, sitting on the coffee table, was a less-than-flattering photo of myself draped over not one but three women at a party that even I knew I shouldn't have attended so close to a Grand Prix.

"Feel free to profusely thank me for shelling out tons of money to have this destroyed…" I peeked at the photo before sheepishly looking up at him.

"Thanks—"

"I mean it, Luca. This is the last time I'm doing this. I don't know what's gotten into you. You used to love racing, but now… now I barely recognize this person sitting in front of me. Two years ago, you were second in the championship, and yet this season you're barely holding on to fifth place. Keep this up, and not only will Hermes not want you next year, but no other team will either."

Without another word, my father rose from the couch. He ran a hand through his graying hair, his lips pressed into a thin line, before striding out of the room. I slinked back onto my sofa cushion, grabbing the photo from the table. After giving it one last glance, I shredded it into pieces.

Chapter Three

Georgia

After sixty-six laps of white-knuckle driving at intense speeds, I should have felt calm. Steady. Triumphant. Instead, I was sitting in the center seat of the post-race press conference, gripping the edge like it might suddenly vanish beneath me. Not because I doubted I'd earned this spot—but because I knew exactly what came next.

Sitting in this chair was symbolic, the winner in the middle flanked by second and third place, but it also came with being the center of attention, something I was definitely not used to. Henri slid into the seat beside me with that insufferable mix of swagger and confidence, his face armed with a smug grin. He shifted his eyes, and I knew he was tracking my breathing, noticing the steady four seconds between each one, an exercise my therapist had suggested before media obligations to help relieve the anxiety that always accompanied these events. Like a gnat at a picnic, press conference anxiety always felt impossible to get rid of.

I never understood why my body reacted this way—heart racing, palms slick, breathing unsteady—the moment I sat down in a press chair and the stage lights turned on. Here I was with my first ever F1 win, but with each passing second, all I could focus on was the feeling of my profusely sweaty hands and blurring vision. That, and the creeping dread that any words to tumble out of my mouth were never quite what I wanted to say—or what the media wanted to hear.

Henri leaned over, his voice just low enough not to carry. "You've got this, Georgia. Just grin and bear it, yeah? They're not going to be too tough on the *winner*."

"As long as they don't ask me something stupid like '*Should we have more women in racing?*' I'll consider it a victory," I grumbled. A crowd favorite from this group of journalists.

"Just keep it civil, please." Henri shot me a warning look. At the start of the season, the media had dubbed me "Sissy Dubois," a somewhat rude but boring nickname referencing the fact that I was the sister of fan-favorite Henri Dubois. By race three, I had become "Sassy Dubois"—which was definitely worse. Apparently, correcting reporters during press conferences did not make you friends. No one liked a know-it-all, especially not a female one.

I flashed my brother a small smirk, turning back to face the bright lights that were shining directly into my eyes as I fought to keep my breathing level. *In. One. Two. Three. Four. Out. One. Two. Three. Four.*

A hushed silence grew over the room, and a question broke me out of my breathing pattern.

Time for the vultures to descend.

"Georgia, congrats on your first win with the new Valkyrie F1 team. It must feel thrilling to be the first woman to win a Formula 1 race since 1980. How do you feel?"

It's an easy one, Georgia, I reassured myself. After years of practicing this answer in the shower, this one I had locked down.

Ignoring my trembling hands, I answered, "Phenomenal."

I spared a glance at Nora, who was standing at the back of the room, motioning with her left hand for me to continue as her right hand massaged her forehead in silent frustration.

More words, Georgia. I chastised myself. *You've got a whole dictionary full of them.*

But for some reason, getting them out was a near impossible task.

"Yeah, umm, it was… great." More silence surrounded me. "Very… cool?" Hearing a low laugh next to me, a poorly hidden grin stretched across Henri's face.

"Just cool?" the press officer prodded, his voice filled with amusement. "How *lucky* do you feel to finally have a race win?"

"Not lucky at all," I said flatly. "I earned this win." The journalist's scrunched face told me he didn't appreciate my dry tone, which was fine since I didn't appreciate him implying that I'd won out of *luck*.

Deep down I knew what everyone wanted from me, from this press conference. They wanted a fairy tale. A teary monologue about how shocked and surprised I was that I'd finally won—that a *woman* had finally won in this *man's* sport.

But I wasn't shocked or surprised, and I definitely wasn't *lucky*. It was hard work from me and the team that pushed me over the finish line first. Night after night, I studied every inch of the circuit until I could drive it in my sleep. I memorized every corner, every braking point, every curb down to the millimeter. While Henri and the other drivers were out grabbing dinner or pranking each other, I was on my simulator at home or the office.

Thinking back to my pathetic media training, I swallowed the urge to scream, throwing on a big smile to help ease the awkwardness, but Nora's wrenched face told me I'd failed. She was standing at the back of the conference, her expression willing me to continue, but before I could muster another word, the journalist had already moved on.

"So, Henri, I saw you and Georgia had quite the battle at the end. How did it feel to be beat out by your sister?"

"It was great! Sorry... it was very *cool*!" Henri winked at me. "My sister is an incredible driver, and that Valkyrie F1 car is fast as lightning, especially in a straight line. Disappointed I couldn't keep up with her, but it's hard to fight with that kind of talent. Plus, I knew if Georgia beat me, I could guilt her into buying the drinks tonight, so it's not all a loss." Henri smiled, earning himself a few laughs from the crowd.

Show-off. Press had always come easy to Henri.

After a few more engineering and strategy questions for my brother and the third-place driver, another hand shot up.

"We noticed after the race, Georgia, there was some tension with you and Luca Rossi. Are there still hard feelings after last week's race?"

Of course they'd noticed. *Just fucking great*.

Taking a deep breath, I stared at the back of the room, willing myself not to say what I actually thought about Luca Rossi—that he was a sore loser with more excuses than podiums. That he'd blamed his failure on my "bullying" overtakes instead of owning the fact that he'd driven like a jackass.

But I didn't have a legacy to fall back on. No famous father. No powerful name. No one was there to save my seat if I slipped up.

"We're both professionals racing in the world's most competitive motorsports championship." My voice was astoundingly level for how heavily my blood pressure was racing. "Tensions can be high, but I'd like to think we can leave our track disputes on the track."

A subtle dig. Sharp, but safe, and just under the threshold of what would have Isabelle hauling me into her office for one of her infamous lectures. While Luca could sling around his complaints no problem, the one time I opened my mouth about his aggressive lunges, I had no less than five articles about my "*whining.*"

The big thumbs up from Nora gave my confidence a boost.

Another journalist cleared their throat. "Georgia, I hear Valkyrie aren't leaving for Miami until Tuesday. Do you have any shopping plans for your day off tomorrow?" I fought hard not to roll my eyes. Henri had spent ten minutes answering questions on suspension upgrades, but I'd managed to snag me a tried-and-true classic: a question about shopping.

"This is a race week, which means I'll be back on the simulator tomorrow and studying the track all week." I resisted the urge to add, "*You know, professional athlete stuff.*"

"Practicing *all* week? No minibreak after your *well-deserved* win?" The incredulous way he said *well-deserved* assured me he didn't believe it. If this were a race, the yellow flag would have just turned into a red one. "I figured you would have a shopping spree organized or a photo shoot with a makeup brand?"

"Seriously?" I snapped. "Did you ask my *male* counterparts if they intend to spend their few precious days off before a Grand Prix shopping?" Heat bloomed on my cheeks. After five races, I could count how many engineering questions I'd been asked on both hands with fingers to spare.

"Well, you know—" Before Henri could finish his attempt to save me from myself, I cut him off.

"I've never raced in Miami. In fact, no one has raced this new track layout. I need to focus every spare moment on learning it if we're going to win next week. If Valkyrie wants to win the championship, there's no time for a day off. Today's win doesn't mean that the championship fight is over; it means it's just begun."

The journalist's face looked as if I had just told him pigs could fly. Then, finally, he sat down. A wave of relief swept through me.

Almost done, Georgia.

Another hand shot up, and Michael Clifton, the F1 commentator, nodded for Frank, an Upland Media press officer, to ask his question.

"Georgia, congrats. So, tell me, now that you're a race winner, I bet you're beginning to see the World Driver's Championship in your view. Must be nice to be the first woman to win in several decades." My body immediately tensed, and I cautiously nodded, already knowing what was about to be thrown my way. This was the intro I fucking hated before the question that I despised.

Please don't ask it. Please don't ask it, I silently begged to whatever God was listening, although based on how all of my press conferences had gone this season, I suspected I'd probably pissed Her off in a past life.

"Do you think it's time to see more women in racing?" *Ah, there it was.*

My brother let out an almost inaudible gasp next to me, and I couldn't help but smirk. If there was one thing the journalists were good for, it was this question. A full preseason and several races later, the men in the room never failed to softball this question with a patronizing grin, like they were just dying for me to say, "*Actually, I think women should get back to the kitchen where they belong.*" Notably, they never asked the other male drivers. Just me and my teammate Lily.

Unable to keep my frustration bottled up any longer, I let out the most exasperated sigh, matched only by my rather noticeable eye roll.

"I think we all know the answer to that question, Frank, because you ask it every race. Did you think my answer changed in the span of a single week?" Nora was waving in the background, her finger crossing her throat, signaling for me to quit before I said something I couldn't take back.

But it was too late. "Sassy Dubois" had been released, and the silence was deafening. Apparently, the cure for my anxiety was arguing with sexists. I glanced over to Henri for help, a gleam of desperation hanging in my eyes, but his face told me I should have followed his earlier advice to just grin and bear it.

"Obviously, I want more women in the sport. If we had more women, maybe you would all stop asking about my *love life*, or my *menstrual cycle*, or my *racing bra selection* during our interviews because I wouldn't be the shiny new toy to harass."

Silence.

Thick, uncomfortable, no-one-meets-my-eyes silence engulfed the room.

Ten minutes ago I could barely get a word out, and now I sounded like a raving lunatic. But that was the thing about anxiety—it was a constant battle between not being able to utter a coherent sentence and ranting my inner thoughts through a rambling tirade. No in-between.

Shit. Isabelle was going to kill me.

Michael Clifton put his hands up, a large *everything is fine* grin plastered across his face. "Right! Well, thanks for that, Georgia… We wish you the best of lu—uh, we wish you the *best* in Miami. As always, folks, we'll see you next time in sunny Florida!"

Before Henri could make a snarky comment, I was already out of my chair, bolting toward the exit. Nora took off after me, her long legs frustratingly allowing her to catch up. When we burst back into the Valkyrie F1 hospitality suite, Isabelle's expression stopped me cold. The smile she'd worn an hour earlier was gone, replaced by a look that said she was already halfway through writing my obituary. She motioned for me to join her in her office with a sharp flick of her finger. The moment I stepped inside, my confidence from before had withered.

"Before you say anything, I know I should have just answered with, '*Yes, of course, I want more women in motorsport, blah blah blah.*' But I couldn't do it. Not this time, Isabelle. The male drivers get engineering questions, and I get questions about shopping? It's degrading and, quite frankly, their questions are becoming morose and repetitive," I started to argue.

Isabelle didn't respond. She didn't even look at me, just typed aggressively on her keyboard, not caring to spare me a glance.

Feel sorry for whoever is getting that email.

When she finally deigned to give me her attention, she pointed toward a chair. "Georgia, I appreciate that the press are morons," Isabelle started, her piercing green eyes slicing me open, "but unfortunately, change in a male-dominated sport isn't going to happen overnight, so it's our job to help guide them. Slowly. Carefully. Losing your temper in front of the media only plays into the 'hormonal' hothead stereotype they're trying to stick you with."

"But I *finally* won." My voice cracked with frustration. "Why can't they just see my talent?"

"Because life isn't fair," she snapped.

I looked down, picking at my fingernails, wishing the floor would open and swallow me.

Isabelle sighed, softer this time. "The media and sponsors aren't looking at your talent. They're looking at your sassy attitude. And the more successful we become, the more desperate they get to prove it's a fluke. Or that we're cheating. That a women-led team couldn't possibly deserve to win in Formula 1. Crusty old men don't like being embarrassed. And Valkyrie F1 has embarrassed the hell out of them. The FIA don't want us here. The legacy teams don't want us here. And the press? They're doing exactly what the establishment wants: baiting you. One bad quote at a time."

Isabelle's words were hard to digest, even if they were true. I wanted to argue. Wanted to scream that it was the twenty-first century and it shouldn't be this way. But the truth was the best defense was to just keep *winning*. To keep giving the team the success they deserved.

"I know," I said finally, shoulders slumped. "I'm sorry. I'll work on it for the next race and get some answers prepped with Nora."

"Good. Because like it or not, Georgia, F1 is a sport where money talks louder than talent. Talent doesn't buy engine parts. It takes *money* to build a race-winning car. We're not backed by a car manufacturer or billionaire's trust fund. Our future depends on sponsors, and sponsors want polished, media-friendly, brand-ready drivers. You and Lily are two of the most talented racers on the grid, but if you don't sell the dream, they'll take their money elsewhere."

And there was the crux of it all. More sponsors meant more money. More money gave us better car upgrades and builds. It was simple math, and as my race engineer liked to say, "the math doesn't lie."

I nodded, knowing there was no reason to further the conversation as I turned to leave the office. Regardless of how the press conference went, I was now a Formula 1 winner, and the fight for the World Driver's Championship was on.

Chapter Four

Georgia

Just before seven p.m., a loud banging rang through my hotel room, causing the eyeliner I was *perfectly* applying to slip.

"Shit!" I exhaled a groan. "Coming!" As soon as I opened the door, Henri and Éliott burst into the room, a champagne bottle in Éliott's hand and chocolate cake in my brother's.

"Nice raccoon eyes," Henri chuckled, and I gave my brother a quick shove, lunging for the dessert.

"Bring this all the way from Monaco in case I won?"

"No, I brought it in case *I* won," he laughed, lifting the cake above my head. "But since you did, I figured we could *share*."

Behind my brother stood Éliott, Henri's best friend, who over the last couple of years had truly become one of my closest friends. Éliott was a ray of sunshine on the darkest days. While Henri offered more tough love, Éliott offered solidarity. He understood what I was going through, and even though we were competitors on different teams, his loyal support had been unwavering over the last five races.

"Georgie Pie." Éliott smiled. "So fucking proud of you today!"

Grinning, I waved them inside, handing over spoons as we flopped onto the suite's leather couch. Éliott popped the bottle of champagne, pouring us each a glass from the kitchenette's mismatched glassware.

"Figured we had to get a pre-drink in before we head out to celebrate your win tonight!" But as Éliott clinked his glass with mine, he flickered his eyes to my brother, and I knew they had an ulterior motive for being here. Like a cloud brewing before a storm, the mood of the room darkened slightly.

"So…" Henri started, awkwardly poking at his cake.

And there it was.

"What did Isabelle have to say?"

I stuffed my mouth was a large chunk of icing, chewing painfully slow as I stalled for time, but neither of them broke eye contact. Their gazes were expectant. Almost like they'd spent the late afternoon planning this intervention.

Or been told to by Isabelle.

"She was displeased, *obviously*. This year has been financially tough, and the team has been struggling to get sponsors. If we don't secure this big Maison de Klotho sponsorship deal soon, the team could be put up for sale. The embarrassment of the only woman-owned team failing, it puts added stress on the team. Added stress on me."

"And she thinks your sharp tongue isn't helping?"

I shot him an irritated look. "Apparently, the phrase '*there's no such thing as bad press*' isn't actually true."

"I don't get it. You're a brand-new team featuring the only female drivers on the grid. Why is the team struggling to get sponsors?"

"Oh, Henri. You sweet, naïve golden boy." Even Éliott uttered a disbelieving scoff at my brother.

Henri groaned; he hated that nickname, even if he knew it was true. The motorsports world adored my brother. Tall, handsome, charming, and fast—sponsors loved him. He was the package all teams wanted in their athletes.

"Look at the logos on your car, Henri. It's companies with *male* CEOs and *male* executive teams who like to watch *men* race fast cars. Name one company on your car that is run by a woman." Henri's face was tense, and I watched my brother mentally go through his list of sponsors: oil companies, private investment firms, IT infrastructure companies, not a single one with a female CEO. "Motorsport is predominantly watched by men, sponsored by men, and run by men."

A concept that had never occurred to him. It hadn't needed to.

"What's going on with the Maison de Klotho sponsorship? Any more movement on that?" he asked.

"They're interested." I stared at my plate. "We need this to come through. They're one of the largest fashion houses in the world. They see the growing female fanbase, but we still have to show them we're worthy of sponsoring." I exhaled, my eyes fixed on the dark, velvety chocolate sauce that swirled on my plate. "I need to show them that I'm worthy of sponsoring."

"It's a team effort, Peaches..." My brother started.

"But *I'm* the team leader, the number one driver. A big part of this burden rests on *my* shoulders."

"I guess just raw talent doesn't get you sponsors these days," Éliott sighed, dusting a few crumbs off his pants.

"Sponsors want charm and the ability to sell; talent is just a nice bonus." The unfortunate truth with any sport. It was like the media expected me to be a social butterfly in front of the press simply because I was a woman. Silent dread filled me as I took another bite of cake, the sudden dryness making it hard to swallow.

I had the talent, but the charm? I'd spent years mastering my ability to hide from cameras, a not so helpful skill when your team's survival depended on being the center of attention.

"I know you try to understand, Henri, but I just can't explain how being in front of the press makes me feel. I hate being put in front of people I don't know, only to be asked the same ridiculous questions every week. I feel like a monkey at the circus, on display for everyone to see."

"But Georgia—"

"I just want to race," I said softly. "It's all I've wanted to do since Dad took us to see our first Monaco Grand Prix." As young kids, we'd fought to be lifted onto our father's shoulders, desperately trying to catch the action of the Monaco Grand Prix below us. It was how we'd fallen in love with racing.

"I eat, sleep, and breathe racing, and yet when I say that in interviews, I'm considered *obsessive*. I must constantly practice to keep up with the tracks, but I can't practice too much or I'm *boring*. I'm supposed to be a team leader, but whenever I give advice, the media labels me as the *bossy* driver. It's a never-ending bout of criticism. I'm just a 25-year-old who wants to race fast cars with her friends."

Éliott grabbed my hand for a moment, giving it a small squeeze, and Henri, to his credit, sat quietly and listened to me rant, his kind hazel eyes watching me like they hung on my every word. A few tears rolled down my cheeks, and Éliott reached into his pocket, handing me a tissue.

"You're not obsessive or bossy, Georgia, but maybe when the media asks if you plan on doing something other than racing, you don't tell them *more racing*?" He gave me a small, pleading laugh, trying to soften the blow.

"I'm a professional athlete who wants to win the most competitive driving championship in the world. I'm pretty sure if the press caught me shopping before a Grand Prix, they'd roast me for not being focused on the race."

"It's more that—" Henri started.

"No! Valkyrie hired me to win the championship. These women depend on me. The other drivers might be open to spending time visiting Disney World before next week's race in Miami, but I want to be the first driver to win on this new track layout. I'm not going to put the Valkyrie mission at risk because I want to go gallivanting around the US before a race."

Henri laughed, raising his hands in defeat. "Alright, alright. I get it. Look, Peaches, we just want what's best for you, yeah? That's all. I finally get to race with my sister, and I don't want that to end after a season. We're here to support you."

"Would some paddock gossip about Luca make you feel any better?" Éliott asked with a smile, nudging my brother who gave him an annoyed eye roll. Considering Éliott knew my past with Luca, he was always a little too eager to gossip about my brother's teammate, a trait I very much appreciated.

I downed my champagne, holding out my glass for a refill. "Obviously, yes."

Henri sighed begrudgingly, pouring a second refill into his glass, before topping up mine. Even though Henri found his teammate rather infuriating, his unwavering loyalty to Hermes usually stopped him from oversharing the team's drama.

"Fine. Just before I headed over here, I heard my team principal and Luca's father whispering in Francesco's office. They were discussing Luca's… reputation. One of our largest sponsors is threatening to back out, and the team hasn't renewed Luca's contract. With his dad being a former World Champion for Hermes, the team are willing to cut Luca some slack, but there's only so much they can do about his crumbling reputation."

"Hah, good luck to them," I sneered. "That man is incredibly cocky and self-absorbed. He's always hitting on the women's F1 Academy drivers, which is just insulting. He shows up each week with a different woman on his arm, just like the *playboy* everyone thinks he is. I mean, the man commandeered, no, I'm sorry, *stole* a yacht, and all he got was a wrist slap," I grumbled. "I give one-word answers at a press conference, and I'm made out to be a villain accused of bringing down motorsport. Luca Rossi *literally* steals a boat and gets a headline. I could start my own online magazine with the amount written about me."

"Geez, Georgia, tell us how you really feel." Henri looked taken aback.

"Oh, please, you complain about him all the time."

"I know," Henri admitted, "but you have to also consider the intense pressure he's under."

"And I'm not? Life's just a walk in the park for me, huh?"

Éliott shot Henri a look that said *drop it*. "I think what Henri is trying to say is having a World Champion as a father, especially one like Michael Rossi, that's not something anyone can live up to. It can't be easy."

My head started to spin. Not three hours ago Luca was staring me down after the greatest achievement of my life, and here were my brother and friend, *defending* him.

"Imagine how *amazing* it must be to have a father who was a three-time World Champion," I retorted, throwing my finished plate down onto the coffee table. "The racing advice alone is invaluable, and yet he can't even turn that into a podium finish. No, let me rephrase that, Luca doesn't *want* to turn that into a podium finish."

Frustration bubbled in my throat, making it hard to get the words out. All week I'd heard about how it was my fault that Luca was run off the track during last week's Grand Prix, even though the stewards had ruled in my favor.

But I was used to this sort of criticism. From a young age, I'd never backed down from a challenge. At each karting race I'd fight tooth and nail with the boys, never relenting, and I wasn't going to stop now, no matter how much they whined.

"Last week Luca was late to the apex. I earned that overtake fair and square. But all Luca could talk about was *my* aggressive moves. He's incapable of accepting that his poor performance is from his pathetic driving. Plus, he—" I caught myself, shaking my head as I caught my breath.

"He what?" Henri asked, arms folded. Éliott shook his head behind my brother.

"Nothing." Best not to go there. Henri and Luca were teammates, and my brother had to deal with him on a daily basis. Sometimes it was better to leave the past alone, especially since there was enough in the present to determine my feelings on Luca.

"I think someone sounds a little jealous," Henri teased. His champagne glass did nothing to hide his sly chuckle.

"Oh, come off it," I laughed, giving my brother a shove. "Luca is full of so much talent, and if he wanted to, I bet he could beat either of us."

Henri looked at me incredulously. "Let's not get ahead of ourselves…" he laughed. "Now, I gotta go grab my jacket from my room. No more talk about this, yeah? We're celebrating your win together, that's all that matters. You and Éliott good to meet downstairs in five?"

Henri reached out and pulled me into a warm embrace, and as I leaned into his hug, I felt a sudden sense of calm envelop me. "See you in a few."

As soon as the door clicked shut, Éliott plopped next to me on the couch, an expectant look on his face.

"Don't start…" I warned.

"You need to tell him," Éliott chided. "What Luca did to you was shitty."

"What am I going to say? Three years ago I said yes to a date with your teammate, behind your back after you told me not to, and then he didn't show?"

Éliott's faced softened. "You sound a bit unhinged when you talk about him, but you're not. I mean Luca has so much potential, it's enviable. I'd kill to sit in a Hermes seat."

I nodded, my heart aching for him. He'd worked so hard, but after being dumped by Rennen, the other top team on the grid, he'd ended up at Aether Racing, a perfectly fine team, but with no real chance at winning races. The talent in Formula 1 was enormous, and yet so much of the race was decided by the quality of your car. Quality that came from sponsorship money.

"Don't let this become a feud. The media are already circling, and it's now painfully obvious that there's bad blood between the two of you." Éliott grabbed my purse, handing it to me. "But enough about Luca. Victory was yours, and you earned it."

Taking my black clutch from his hands, we made our way from the hotel room to the elevator, with me fumbling with my bag along the way as I frantically looked for my room key while Éliott trailed behind.

"Blasted thing, always disappearing…"

Suddenly, my body collided with something tall and hard. Before I could lose my balance, a strong hand grabbed my waist, pulling me forward. Without thinking, I put my hands up to steady myself, making contact with a chest that my romance books would describe as "*built from solid muscle.*" Then I caught a whiff of his cologne, a musky scent of lilacs and pine trees. When I looked up to see who had saved me from falling on my ass, the first thing I noticed was his Cheshire cat grin.

Luca *fucking* Rossi.

"You know, if you wanted to get this close, you only had to ask," Luca said with a wink and voice much too sultry for my liking. He made a show of letting his eyes rake up and down my body, and I suddenly felt naked. I quickly straightened my dress, forcibly removing Luca's hands from my waist.

"Luca, flattering yourself as always, I see." He just grinned in return as he followed us into the elevator, offering Éliott a quick head nod as he watched us curiously. Luca's stare burned into the back of me, but I refused to face him out of fear that I would make eye contact with the Italian race car driver. With bright brown eyes, dark hair that always seemed perfectly styled, and a sultry Italian accent, it didn't matter that Luca was undoubtedly the most handsome driver on the grid, he was also the most insufferable.

"You know, Georgia," Luca said suddenly. "I think you should have told the journalists in your press conference that racing is *a man's sport*. Would have at least made that press conference interesting." I scoffed at his sarcastic tone, putting my hands on my hips.

"Unfortunately, we don't all have a rich daddy willing to pay off reporters," I deadpanned. "Speaking of… commandeered any more yachts recently?"

"Why, interested in becoming a pirate, *amore*?"

I clenched my fists, doing my best to avoid eye contact.

"Believe it or not, I'm not exactly turned on by criminals."

"Well, you do have the reputation as the *boring* twin for a reason," he snickered.

Pompous asshole.

"With the number of messes your PR team cleans up, they should call themselves a maid service," I retorted.

"And your car should be turned into a tank with the number of fights you pick each week." Even Éliott couldn't resist letting out a small chuckle.

Luca: 1. Georgia: 0.

Fortunately, before either of us could respond with something we'd probably both regret, the elevator dinged and I quickly bolted out, practically running to my brother. The faster I got away from Luca Rossi, the better.

"Hey, Luca," Henri called out behind me, "thanks for joining. It'll be good to have another Spanish speaker with us. It's not like Peaches paid attention during school." I immediately shot my brother a dark glare.

"Surely Luca has better plans tonight, no?" I asked a little too quickly.

What was Henri playing at? Not ten minutes ago I'd made my feelings clear, and now Luca was joining us like we were some big happy family?

"Don't be silly. I can't think of anything better than celebrating our race winner," Luca crooned, and I internally cringed, keeping a smile plastered on my face. I couldn't mask my disdain during press conferences, but with Luca, I had no problem concealing my emotions. Letting him see how much he got under my skin would mean he'd won, and I couldn't have that—both on and off the track.

Chapter Five

Luca

I had zero intention of accepting Henri's invitation tonight, but after seeing several photos circling around social media showcasing the tense standoff I'd had with Georgia earlier today, I figured showing up would help quell the rumor mill—and my father's anger.

Inside the Barcelona club, we slipped past the velvet rope and into the exclusive VIP section. I scanned the room and quickly spotted my best friend, Edward, ordering at the bar. Sandy hair tousled to perfection, white shirt unbuttoned far too low, this was classic Edward to a tee.

He waved me over with the subtlety of a man who'd already had two drinks. "Well, look what the cat dragged in," Edward teased. "Surprised Daddy Rossi let you out to celebrate tonight with that sixth-place finish." I rolled my eyes, before pulling my old teammate into a hug.

"Apparently, it would look bad if I didn't celebrate the first woman winning in decades." And I hadn't exactly told him where we were going.

"Well, then here's to Georgia's win." Edward's eyes sparkled with amusement as he handed me a cold beer, but before I could clink my glass with his, another pint met mine, spilling some of its beer onto my shoes. I glanced up, instantly recoiling as I looked straight into the eyes of Anthony Walker, the human embodiment of mediocre white privilege with a trust fund, and my other looming problem in Formula 1.

Why Hermes had signed the inconsequential, untalented American to be our reserve driver in case Henri or I was sick was beyond me. Georgia had wiped the floor with him in Indy Car and F2. But somehow Anthony had managed to bag our reserve driver slot.

Actually, I knew why. His dad had more money than God. Formula 1 might be the pinnacle of motorsport, but it wasn't immune to the scent of money. Unfortunately for me, Anthony had made it painfully clear to just about everyone he'd ever met that he was gunning for my seat.

"Anthony," I groaned. "I'd say it's good to see you, but my mother didn't raise a liar."

"And apparently your father didn't raise a race winner," he snickered back.

I had that one coming.

"That's rich coming from someone who's doing their third stint in F2," I retorted. Like most drivers in Formula 1, I'd won my first F2 season. Twenty-six racers competed in the junior league, but typically, only one seat was available each year in Formula 1 and the competition was fierce.

"Well, they do say third time's the charm." Edward gleefully collided his glass with mine, causing liquid to spill all over his shoes.

Anthony inched toward me, the scent of smoky Scotch wafting from his breath. "Laugh all you want, Rossi. By the end of this season, I'm taking your F1 seat. No doubt you have another screw-up in your future."

My fingers tightened around my glass. I'd have loved nothing more than to rearrange his smirk. But Edward, ever the peacemaker, clapped a hand on my shoulder and steered me toward a booth in the back before I could do something I'd regret. Swallowing my pride, I opted to ignore Anthony. After this afternoon's lecture from my father, the last thing I needed was a bar brawl with my teammate.

I slinked into the booth, chugging half my beer in frustration. Edward's gaze was fixed on me with curiosity. From his wide eyes, I could tell he wanted to discuss something important.

"Yes?" I finally asked.

"Your mom texted me today…"

"My mom?" I scoffed. "What are we, ten?"

"Luca, she told me about the fight with your dad. She's worried about you. You didn't answer any of her calls."

"Maybe because I didn't have anything worth saying."

"Come on, Luca. The party? That photo?" Edward shot me a frustrated look, one that told me to cut the crap.

Join the line of people disappointed in me.

"I know I shouldn't have been there, Ed," I muttered. "But it took the edge off all of this stress. Everyone wants me to be the second coming of Michael Rossi, and I—" I stopped, staring into my beer. "I'm not him. Just because he was a World Champion doesn't mean I will be."

"You know," Edward's voice was low, "you don't have to race if you don't want to." Edward looked around the bar, as if he was afraid my father would appear from the shadows and scold us for his blasphemy.

Sighing, I shrugged my shoulders. "I don't know what I want anymore." My eyes drifted across the bar, locking on to Anthony who was currently charming a group of girls with stories probably stolen from my interviews. My blood boiled inside at the thought. "Scratch that. I *know* I don't want to give my seat to fucking Texas-Oil-Money Anthony over there."

Edward raised his glass in agreement. "I hate that guy. How Georgia ever dated him is beyond me."

"Georgia dated Anthony?" I asked, aiming for casual but landing somewhere much closer to *too interested*.

His eyebrow lifted, but he appeased me. "They kept it quiet. His dad sponsored her team in Indy. She didn't want anyone thinking she got her seat because of him. Henri told me it was serious—for a while. They broke up last year. I don't know why. Must be hell for her seeing him around."

"Well, well, well," I smirked, "turns out Racing-Is-My-Entire-Personality Dubois and I have something in common: we both can't stand to be around Anthony." I leaned back in my seat as I feigned shock, my hands waving in the air. Edward rolled his eyes, shaking his shaggy head.

"You're such a prick to Georgia," he grumbled.

"She starts it—" I argued.

"More like she finishes it." Edward smirked, clearly pleased with himself.

I rolled my eyes, choosing not to take the bait. "You know, I was sort of surprised at Georgia today."

"Surprised that she's bad at media? I mean, I guess considering Henri's so good—"

"No," I cut him off. "I'm surprised that after dating Anthony, she's moved on to another driver. She doesn't strike me as someone who'd date a rival."

"Excuse me, who is Georgia dating?" Now it was Edward's turn to be overly invested in the gossip.

"Earlier today, I saw Éliott and Georgia come out of her room together; she was practically wrapped around him."

Edward let out a loud snort. "Really?" He considered me for a moment. "Nah, no chance they're dating. Henri would have Éliott's head on a spike if he made the slightest move after his sister… I think." Edward wagged his finger, adding, "And I suggest you take that advice to heart. Georgia is off limits."

"It'll be a cold day in hell before I date Georgia Dubois," I scoffed, although the words didn't taste as satisfying as I'd imagined them to be. Several years ago, I'd received that same warning from Henri, but that hadn't stopped me then.

Something else had.

As I placed my empty glass on the counter, I caught sight of a group of women who had managed to sneak into our reserved VIP section. A perfect distraction.

"Well, since I've already been scolded by my parents once today, I might as well make the most of a free pass." Nodding toward the women at the bar, I gave Edward a wink followed by a thumbs up.

"Glad to see you took our talk to heart!" he yelled after me as I made my way over.

I caught the attention of the bartender and ordered another beer, leaning against the counter as I sized up the group of women nearby. Just as I was about to strike up a conversation with a pretty brunette in red, a familiar voice caught my attention.

"I'll have a gin and tonic, please." Turning to my left, I noticed Georgia rummaging through her purse. "Ugh, of course, I left it," she grumbled, waving at Henri and her teammate, Lily, as she frantically tried to get their attention.

"Put it on my tab," I called out to the bartender as he handed her the drink. Georgia glanced at me with a hint of suspicion, gnawing on her lower lip with uncertainty as she continued searching for her lost wallet.

"I can buy my own drinks," she mumbled.

"Can you?" I glanced pointedly at the contents of her purse, now spread across half the bar. With her slightly red cheeks, I had to admit, Georgia looked adorable as she fumbled through her embarrassment.

"Thanks," she said sheepishly. "I'll buy your next one. Well, if my wallet ever turns up."

"Nah," I said with a wink. "This one's on me. A pretty girl like you shouldn't buy her own drinks." Georgia scoffed as she took a sip of her gin and tonic, scrunching her nose in disgust.

"Please tell me that line doesn't actually work."

"What do you think?" I asked, leaning in to watch her reaction.

Her sapphire eyes widened, just slightly, but she didn't move away. Instead, she crossed her arms, gaze steady and unimpressed. From this close, I could see the small creases around her eyes as she frowned at me, could smell her lavender perfume. A stray strand of hair was caught in her soft eyelashes, and I had a sudden urge to gently tuck it back behind her ears. But before I could so much as blink, a familiar, unwelcome voice oozed into the space between us.

"Well, what do we have here?"

Fucking Anthony. I inwardly groaned as he approached us, a tauntingly amused look on his face. Stepping back,

Georgia straightened her skirt as she nervously took another sip of her drink, chewing on her straw before setting it down. She looked uncomfortable as she searched for a way out of this conversation, cornered by her ex-boyfriend and rival.

Wonder who she hates more? I mused.

Just as I thought she was going to slink away and pretend that she hadn't heard Anthony, Georgia stepped closer. Her body pressed against mine like it belonged there, her hand slipping into mine. When she looked up, her smile was sunshine-level sweet. Like I hung the damn moon.

"Just hanging out with Flash." Georgia grinned, not caring to look at Anthony. Caught off guard at hearing my racing nickname, I returned her large smile, casually putting my hand on her waist, pulling her closer. Georgia's lips curled into a satisfied smile as her eyes pleaded with me to play along.

Fuck it, I thought. *Who am I to turn down an opportunity to get on Anthony's nerves?* I pulled Georgia closer to me.

Her brow twitched for half a second, like she couldn't believe we were doing this, before plastering a sickly-sweet *I'm in love* smile back on. Noticing the lack of space between us, Anthony's eyes watched Georgia's hands softly caress mine. Her breath smelled of pink champagne, and I was almost enjoying this laid-back, tipsy version of Georgia. Five minutes had gone by, and she hadn't mentioned my yacht incident once.

"And here I was thinking we broke up because you wanted to focus on your career," Anthony sneered.

Georgia let out a pretend gasp. "Really? I thought it was because you slept with every woman that batted an eyelash your way." Without missing a beat, she turned to me and whispered loud enough for the nearby girls to hear, "I thought being exclusive meant I was the only one doomed to see his dick."

The group next to us erupted in quiet snickering.

Anthony watched my arm tug Georgia closer. A frustrated look danced in his eyes while he assessed the two of us. My fingers softly rubbed up and down her waist in soothing, circular motions, and to my surprise, Georgia rested her chin against my chest.

"With how *boring* you are in bed, you're delusional to think that Luca isn't getting some on the side," Anthony scoffed as he crossed his arms, still assessing the two of us with narrowed eyes. Georgia flinched, just for a second. And for reasons I didn't want to examine too closely, that tiny reaction made something sharp twist in my chest.

Pushing Georgia aside, I stepped forward, blocking her from Anthony's view. "Funny thing, Anthony, women aren't lousy in bed if you know how to make them scream." I leaned in, eyed locked on to his. "And, wow, is Georgia a screamer."

He opened his mouth to fire something back at me, but before he could, I felt Georgia's surprisingly soft hands on my cheeks, turning me toward her. Her eyes flickered down to my lips and she licked her own, her teeth grazing her bottom lip.

And then Georgia Dubois did the unexpected.

Gentle lips met mine in a soft, tender kiss that I knew was full of uncertainty. My eyes flickered to Anthony, whose face was full of satisfying rage. With our two drinks forgotten on the counter, I wrapped my arms around her waist, deepening the kiss. She arched into me, her hands sliding from my face to the back of my neck, fingers threading through my hair. It was slow and maddening and somehow felt awfully *real.*

Anthony was probably still standing there fuming, but I couldn't bring myself to care. All I could think about was the taste of Georgia Dubois—gin, pink champagne, and something I knew I'd crave long after this moment was over.

My hand skimmed her back. Her nails grazed my skin. I swore the room disappeared.

Fuck, why is this the best kiss I've had in years?

Finally, she pulled away, breathless, cheeks flushed, eyes wide with the realization of what we'd just done. "Wow, um, sorry… I don't know what came over me," she gasped, still trying to catch her breath. Georgia looked mortified—and gorgeous with her embarrassed pink cheeks. I had the sudden urge to kiss her again.

"Glad to be of service," I said, still catching my breath. "Always happy to get under Anthony's skin."

She snorted, grabbing her drink. "Can't believe I ever dated that guy."

"Well, you can't be perfect *on* and *off* the track."

She scoffed, rolling her eyes at me before quickly marching back to her teammate Lily who was already fanning herself and mouthing something absurdly dramatic.

"Hey, Georgia!" Both she and Lily looked up at me. "You're welcome to come scream in my bed anytime!"

She flipped me off without missing a beat. But she was smiling. And not the fake PR smile Valkyrie had clearly taught her.

A real one.

And I'd be lying if I said it didn't do something to me.

Chapter Six

Georgia

I could count on one hand the number of times I'd been as drunk as I was on Sunday. And two days later, I was still paying for it. By the end of the night, Henri and Éliott seemed more intent on seeing who could buy the most rounds of champagne, a battle that decidedly had been won by neither, considering no one could remember past round five.

When I woke up on Tuesday morning—head pounding, stomach queasy—I knew the flight to Miami would be hell. Doubleheaders were the worst. No time to recover. No time to process. Just fly, race, and repeat on a new continent. Formula 1 didn't care if your will to live left your body somewhere over the ocean.

By Wednesday morning, after a restless, sweat-soaked night in the Miami humidity, I was starting to regret every decision I'd made since Sunday. Including not cranking the AC. The loud banging on my hotel room door did nothing to help with my headache.

Groaning, I wiped the sweat from my forehead before opening my hotel room door to an overjoyed Lily, grinning like a Disney princess high on sunshine. My teammate practically had sun shining out of her ass at any point of the day, and while she'd become one of my closest friends over the last year, her ability to see sunshine and rainbows everywhere was rather infuriating.

Especially when it felt like the surface of the sun in my hotel room.

"Georgia! Have you checked Instagram?" She barged in, tossing her race bag on the floor like a hurricane in designer sneakers, a gleeful smile on her face.

"No, not yet. Why?" Lily looked at me like I was the insane one, not *her*, impeccably dressed in a matching skort and Valkyrie polo, all ready to go two hours before we had to be at the paddock. Her makeup had been applied meticulously, her hair in a perfectly styled ponytail that said both effortless and copious effort. Impressive for seven thirty in the morning.

I, on the other hand, looked more like I'd been hit by the team bus.

"It's *all over* social media! A British tabloid released it this morning!" Lily squealed.

"Released what?" I crossed my arms as I frantically tried to think back to what the media could possibly be harping on about now.

"It's all anyone is talking about!" Her eyes were fixed intently on her phone screen, not bothering to look up at me.

"Lily!" I waved my arms dramatically in the air, trying to capture her attention. "Released what?"

"Oh, sorry!" She shoved her phone into my hands, and it only took one glance for my heart to sink into the pit of my stomach. Staring back was a photo of me and Luca from Sunday, our lips locked in a *very* heated kiss. My fingers were intertwined in his dark, wavy hair, while his arms were wrapped around me, holding on to my lower back. Even though the image was slightly blurry with the zoomed-in angle, there was no denying it was us.

"What is th-this? H-how did they get this ph-photo?" I stuttered, panic creeping into my voice.

"Someone at the bar must have took it?" Lily shrugged. "Do you seriously not remember?"

Flashes of that night hit me as my mind tried to piece together the hazy memories from that night. The adrenaline rush after crossing the finish line, the celebratory drinks at the bar, and then Luca. His brown eyes, the way his hand felt on the small of my back as he leaned in close. It was all coming back in flashes, each one more incriminating than the last.

I groaned, burying my face in my hands. "I remember enough. God, Isabelle is going to kill me."

No, worse, she was going to lecture me on my stupidity and then kill me. We were meant to be putting on a professional front; making out with a rival during a champagne-fueled rage didn't exactly scream maturity to sponsors.

"What! This is great, Georgia! Hell, people all over the comments sections are saying how your obvious hatred of one another must be a ruse, which is… better than what they were saying yesterday. I mean, who doesn't love a romance featuring the sister dating her brother's teammate?" Lily shimmied her shoulders like a mom who'd had too many mimosas.

Snatching my phone from the charger, I scrolled down my Instagram notifications. Hundreds of notifications had poured in, and while Nora managed my social media account, judging by how many unread notifications I had, she hadn't been able to keep up this morning.

Lily looked over my shoulder, pointing one out. "Oh, look at this one. '*Damn, Luca could have anyone, and he chose Georgia? She must be cooler than I thought.*' Aww..."

"I am cool!" I muttered. A word I had been using far too much recently.

"If you have to say it so much, is it true?" Lily grinned, giving herself a pat on the back.

I rolled my eyes, flinging my phone onto the couch. "This is ridiculous," I scoffed. "I got caught making out with another driver on the grid, and with Luca Rossi no less. That's so embarrassing and unprofessional!"

"Who cares who you're sleeping with? You're a grown-ass woman. You can sleep with whoever you want."

And this was why I loved Lily. Even in her sunshine-fueled state, she approached life with such conviction, even if it wasn't realistic. Life was full of injustices, ones that we had to navigate on a daily basis, as Isabelle liked to remind me.

I shot Lily a look that told her to get real. While the male drivers of the grid certainly did their best to test this theory, I couldn't possibly imagine what kind of double standard the press had in store for me.

"Well, it's irrelevant; I'm *not* sleeping with Luca."

Lily raised a brow. "Why not? He's a snack."

"Sure, if you're into cocky party boys," I shot back.

She smirked. "Kiss looked pretty real to me."

To be honest, in my champagne-fueled state, from what I could remember the kiss *felt* pretty real. Luca's lips were incredibly soft and inviting, but a kiss like that could never happen again, not with the paddock's biggest party boy who was having issues with his own sponsors.

He'd had his chance.

"I only kissed him to get on Anthony's nerves," I bit out. In the moment, it had been the only thing I knew would wipe Anthony's lurid grin off his face.

Hearing a buzz from my phone, I opened it to see a text from Isabelle.

> **Isabelle:**
> F1 offices at 8:30. Conference room 3.
> Don't be late.

"That Isabelle?" Lily asked and I nodded.

"Time to get ready for my execution," I sighed. "Thanks for coming by, Lil. Say nice things at my funeral."

–

As soon as I walked into the Miami paddock, I headed to the F1 offices where I noticed Luca standing outside the two white double doors of conference room 3.

Great, I'm going to get yelled at in front of Luca, I moaned to myself.

With his much-too-tight Hermes team shirt that showed off his arm muscles, his thick hair blowing in the wind, and his club master Ray-Bans, Luca looked more like a movie star than a racer. Which was fitting, since he walked around the paddock with an ego of someone who had won several Oscars, instead of a racer who could barely get on a podium. He acknowledged me with a curt nod and then proceeded to shift his weight from one foot to the other while the two of us stood in deafening silence.

"So," Luca said coolly, finally breaking the ice. "Did you spend your one day off on your simulator preparing for this race like you promised the media in Barcelona?" His question was a taunt and a trap, one that I refused to fall into.

"Did you spend yours planning which influencer to seduce?"

"Why? Jealous?" I hated how seductively he winked at me. *Cocky prick.*

"I'm not interest—"

"Interested in dating?" He cut me off. "Why doesn't that surprise me." I didn't have time to reply before Isabelle popped her head out of the conference room doors.

"Why are you both just standing there? Come in!" Of course, Luca hadn't even bothered to knock. Groaning, I brushed past him, taking a seat at the large conference table in the center of the room. He just grinned as he trailed behind me, sliding off his sunglasses and ruffling his hair like we had just walked onto *his* movie set, not a dimly lit, damp room.

Sitting at the table were Francesco, the Hermes team principal, who wore a stern look on his face, and Matteo, Luca's manager. Not long after I sat down, Nora came into the room and sat next to me, like a dutiful soldier flanking her general—or a prison warden guarding their prisoner.

"So, anyone willing to tell us why we've been summoned?" Luca stared at his watch as if he had somewhere to be. I glanced at Isabelle, who just frowned disapprovingly before shutting the door.

"Before I begin, I want everyone to know that what we're about to discuss is not to leave this room." Isabelle stood at the head of the table, arms crossed with pursed lips. "This wasn't an easy decision, but after chatting with Francesco and our respective sponsorship teams, both Valkyrie and Hermes think what we're about to propose is the best course of action. I know neither of you will be pleased with this idea, but I truly believe this will help boost both of your images with the media and, more importantly, your sponsors."

I stared at Isabelle intently, trying to decipher her cryptic words as I tapped my fingers on the table.

"Right, I'm going to cut to the chase since we're all very busy. Georgia and Luca, you've both been struggling with your respective media images, and if you keep going down this path, the two of you could risk losing your seats. There's only so much bad press the teams can handle, especially when it affects our finances." She paused, eyes darting between us to gauge any reaction before continuing. "So, after much discussion between our two teams, we've decided on a new PR strategy to help the two of you boost your reputation. I'm sure you've both seen the overwhelming response to this morning's tabloid photos that were released in the European press." Isabelle ignored my loud groan, instead pulling out a couple of articles she'd printed, planting them on the table.

The first page showed an article from the *Daily Reporter* whose title read, "Inside Formula 1's Newest Power Couple." Beneath the headline was a photo of me and Luca from last night, but this time the photo featured me with my hands on Luca's chest, staring up at him like he was some sort of God.

"Great, so there's multiple angles of me and Luca," I muttered sarcastically.

Luca leaned forward, snatching up the article to examine it more closely. His brow furrowed as he scanned the page, lips pressed into a thin line. After a moment, he tossed it back onto the table with a scoff.

Isabelle hesitated, which was never a good sign. She never hesitated.

"Spit it out," I demanded. *So much for brevity.*

"Look, I don't care what you and Luca do in your personal time…" I groaned at her inference that Luca and I would ever be sleeping together, but she just shot me a look before continuing. "However, those photos of the two of you have proven to be *very* popular with fans, so because of this, we've decided that we want you two to enter a… sort of… PR relationship." Before I could stop myself, I started to laugh, albeit a bit uncontrollably, like a jack-in-the-box that had just been released.

"You want *me* to start dating *Luca*? Hilarious, Isabelle. We have one stupid kiss at a bar," I waved my hand toward the printout of me and Luca, "and now you think everyone is going to believe that we're dating? What is this, revenge for my press conference last week?" I spat out.

She didn't flinch.

"This isn't revenge, Georgia. This is the *solution* to your bad press conferences," Isabelle said cautiously. The longer I stared at her, the faster my heart started to race as I realized that she was completely serious. "Luca works the media like it's a second sport," she continued. "He knows how to spin a headline, how to charm a reporter. And you, Georgia… well, let's just say that's not your strength. Pairing you with someone like Luca will shift the narrative. You'll get softer questions, better coverage, and if this relationship looks even halfway real, the FIA will start putting you two in joint press conferences. He can help you. This morning, we've sold more Dubois shirts than we've sold all month."

"Because I won a race last week," I stated.

"Really? Then why did the sales only start piling in this morning, after the photos dropped?"

Fucking hell, was that true?

"Let's face it, Georgia. We love you, but the fans and sponsors… haven't connected with you." A polite way to say they didn't like me. "I hate to say it, but those paparazzi photos with Luca have put you on the map."

Before I could formulate a response, Luca finally stirred—only for Francesco to shut him down with a raised hand.

"Luca, your playboy image is putting several of our sponsorship deals at risk, most notably our tenuous Helios Sunglasses deal. They are looking to up our exclusive deal this year, but with all your partying and… yacht commandeering… they aren't sure you're the best person to represent the brand. Dating Georgia will give you the legitimacy you need and credibility that you are a serious driver and not just in it for the social perks." Luca loudly scoffed but said nothing to defend himself, likely as stunned as I was.

"No one is going to believe this!" I yelled, frantically gesturing between me and Luca. I barely believed this. "You think a few paparazzi shots are enough to convince the grid that Luca Rossi and I are dating?"

"That's where we'll need Henri," Nora chimed in. "Fans will believe that with him being your brother's teammate, you've all been hanging out more and more over the last few months. One thing led to another… and now here you are."

"The other drivers will never buy this!"

"Which is why we need the two of you to *really* sell this," Isabelle sighed. "Like it or not, the funding for both your seats is at risk."

The room closed in around me.

"This is fucking ridiculous!" My foot stomping made me look more like a toddler throwing a tantrum than a grown woman, but I was too far gone to care. "I'm not doing it. I won't. If that means giving up my seat, so be it. I'm one of the best drivers on this damn grid, and it is ludicrous that this is what it takes to stay in Formula 1. When did we stop giving a shit about talent?"

I didn't wait for an answer. My feet had already carried me to the door, and before I knew it, I was sprinting out of the offices and toward the safety of my private driver's room, tears pouring down my face. I slammed the door, collapsing against it as I curled into a ball on the ground, my arms wrapped tightly around my legs.

This can't be happening. This can't be happening, I repeated over and over. My mind raced as tears cascaded down my cheeks. I obviously hadn't meant it when I said I would quit. The truth was, I would do just about anything, even start a PR relationship with the grid's cockiest driver, to keep my Formula 1 seat.

Even if he had just spent the last week fanning the flames of my career.

I heard a knock on my driver's room door, and from the sharp tapping, I knew that the group had sent Isabelle. She had a strong and distinctive knock, one that no one could deny entry to, no matter how angry you were.

"Go away, Isabelle!" I shouted through my tears.

"Georgia. Let's talk." Her voice was low and soft. Against my better judgment, I opened the door.

"Don't get comfortable," I said spitefully. Isabelle gave me a stern look that told me she didn't appreciate the bitterness as she sat on the couch.

"Georgia, I know this sucks, and I know it's unfair. You've fought twice as hard as the men on this grid to get here. And I've seen you fight, every damn step of the way. When we launched this team, you were my first call. I wanted you. Not just because of your speed. Because of your grit. And I still believe in you. But Valkyrie can't survive without funding, and you can't win a championship without a seat."

She paused, letting that sink in.

"Lily manages the press like she was born for this. It's part of the reason we picked her. I knew your competitive drive would complement her light, easygoing personality. But you're not Lily, and that's okay. We hired you to win a championship, and I still believe you can. But this PR thing? It's the cost of keeping that dream alive."

Isabelle finished and moved toward my massage table. She wrapped her arms around my shoulders, giving me a gentle hug. I took a few moments of silence to compose myself, wiping away the tears that were falling from my eyes.

"But why Luca?" I sniffled.

"Because he needs this too," she said confidently. "The photos already sold the fantasy. Plus, with Francesco being my cousin, and the Hermes team principal, it'll be easy for all of us to manage the relationship and keep this secret."

I took a long, shaky breath. "Do you truly believe this is my best option?"

"Yes," Isabelle replied simply. "If I could have found something better than having to endure Luca Rossi visiting our garage for the next several months, I would have found it." There was the hint of a smile in her voice, even if her expression didn't change.

"Fine. But the moment my sponsorship prospects start to improve, we're ending this."

"Agreed." Isabelle extended her hand like we were about to shake on the deal of the century.

As if on cue, I heard another knock on my door. Nora popped in, cautious and smiling.

"Come on in, Nora," I groaned. She bounced in with that eager PR energy and handed me a pink Lisa Frank folder covered in sparkly dolphins, no doubt to represent Miami.

"So, what's the plan then?" I didn't need to tell Nora the obvious. Of course, I had agreed to this ludicrous plan. My F1 seat was too important. The mission to get women into Formula 1 was too important.

"We'll take it slow. This week in Miami, we'll do some small dates. Tomorrow, we'll have you and Luca head to dinner. Nice and easy. Hermes have agreed to let you pop by Luca's garage a couple of times this weekend, and they'll *accidentally* catch you on their social media."

"I'm not kissing Luca if I get onto the podium." Even if he was a pretty good kisser, *never again*.

"No one's asking you to do that." While Nora didn't say *for now*, it was implied. The moment any driver made it on the podium, the media frantically searched for their significant other, desperate to capture that special moment.

"And I refuse to wear his stupid purple team jersey. I have my *own* jersey." Nora's lips curved upward, but she nodded her unspoken agreement.

"This weekend is about sowing the seeds of the relationship and getting the fans excited. They're going to love you dating F1's most eligible bachelor," she laughed, trying to soothe the tension. "Details of this week have all been put into your Miami outline so you know when and where you are expected, starting with a dinner date between you and Luca tomorrow."

Nora smiled at me as if she was proud of all this nonsense. I opened the folder, sifting through the pages as guilt started to eat at me. My screw-up with the media wasn't just affecting me, it had now given Nora an extra job as my personal assistant and "relationship manager."

"Alright, it's decided," Isabelle stated matter-of-factly. I stood too, grabbing my team sweatshirt from the back of the chair.

No need to say anything else. If I had to fake date Luca Rossi to save my career and my team?

Fine. But this time?

He was damn well going to show up.

Chapter Seven

Luca

When I left the conference room, I was fuming. This charade had my father's stink all over it. After the yacht incident, he'd made it very clear that if I didn't "get my act together" he would take matters into his own hands. And judging by today's ambush, he'd decided to make good on that threat.

I stormed into Hermes's hospitality suite, only to find both of my parents sitting calmly at a bistro table, sipping espresso like they hadn't just orchestrated a coup over my life.

"A little heads-up would have been nice," I grated out, pointedly glaring at my father.

"If I'd warned you then you wouldn't have gone to the meeting," he replied evenly, not even bothering to look up from his paper.

"Tell me, why Georgia Dubois?" I paced in front of their table, not waiting for a response. "I don't think she's even capable of having a conversation that isn't centered around tire temperature or fuel loads." My teammate's sassy sister might be one of the most beautiful women in the paddock, but even that couldn't redeem her dull personality. Or the fact she couldn't open her mouth without talking about racing—or my father.

"Good, maybe she'll teach you something, and then you'll be better suited to answer *actual* questions about the car," my dad retorted. I resisted the urge to roll my eyes. I'd been a Formula 1 driver for much longer than Georgia, and I was well versed in the car's setups.

My mother gestured for me to take a seat as she poured me an espresso. "Now, Flash, don't be rude. She's doing you a favor, and I think you'll find that there's a lot more to her than meets the eye." I sneered at the insinuation that Georgia was doing *me* a favor. She needed this as desperately as I did, but my mother was the kind of person who couldn't speak ill of the devil himself.

My father finally set the newspaper down, his jaw tight. "Georgia is an excellent racer. Her talent makes her brother look like a rookie, and her passion for the sport is that of a champion. I'm hoping some of that rubs off on you. She reminds me of *me*, back when I was winning championships."

"Great, exactly what I want, to date my father. Lucky me." Judging by the slight twitch of my father's jaw, he'd had just about enough of me.

"Luca, you're doing this," he said flatly.

"And what if I refuse?"

He didn't even blink. "Then maybe I'll let that paper print that horrific photo of you from a week ago."

"Michael!" My mom gasped, and from my father's wince, I knew she'd just kicked him under the table.

"No, I've had enough of this. You've got one shot to fix your reputation, and this—" he gestured broadly "—is it. Clean image. Steady girlfriend. Legit teammate. And maybe, maybe, a second chance with Helios Sunglasses."

My father's words hung in the air, heavy with disappointment and frustration. I couldn't meet his gaze, instead focusing on the intricate patterns of the tablecloth, tracing the swirling leaves and vines with my eyes as a small ounce of shame crept in.

Shame I deserved.

He leaned forward, and I looked up at him, his eyes narrowing as they locked on to mine. "Honestly, Luca, if you didn't want to be saddled with Georgia, then you shouldn't have been photographed kissing her last weekend. What was going through your head? I can see the tabloid headlines now the first time Georgia has a bad race: '*Playboy driver breaks the heart of F1's newest female race winner.*' You'll be crucified in the papers if you don't do this, son."

There was no denying that my father was right. While the journalists had been nothing but cruel to Georgia, they still loved the *idea* of having a female driver on the grid. My father could only save me from so many clickbait stories, and I wasn't sure if he would even bother trying to save me from this one.

My father took another sip, watching me over the rim of his espresso that had likely gone cold by now. "It's time you learn what an honor it is to be a Formula 1 driver, something that you've clearly forgotten. Back in my day, we weren't drivers because it meant we could date the latest TikTak model. We did it for the thrill of feeling the wind in our faces as we stood on the podium in victory."

"That's how low you think of me, hmm? That I just do it for the Tik*Tok* models?"

His accusation lingered in the air. Somewhere over the last year, that burning desire to get into the car every weekend had vanished. An inconvenient truth I knew I could never say out loud—not if I wanted to keep whatever fractured part of my relationship with my parents I had left alive.

I shoved up from the table, seething. "Fine. I'll do your stupid stunt, but when this ludicrous plan backfires, just remember that it was *your* idea. Doesn't bother me, I don't give a fuck either way." Snatching my espresso, I stormed off to the driver's room, which now felt more like a padded cell than my sanctuary.

I slammed the cup down, flopped onto the leather couch, and ran both hands through my hair.

"Whoa, aren't you gonna knock first?"

Startled, I immediately spilled coffee down the front of my jeans.

"Fuck. Edward! What are you doing here? In *my* driver's room?" Edward tossed me a towel, and I made quick work of wiping up the hot coffee that was staining my trousers.

"Your mother let me in." Edward shrugged. "Said you could use a friend after a tense morning meeting."

"Oh really?" I drawled. "How nice of her. Did she also tell you about her *betrayal*?"

"Come on, Luca. Dating Georgia won't be that bad. Hell, after the impressive response to today's tabloid article, it's sort of a good idea. The fans love the two of you."

"*Et tu, Brute?*" I tossed the damp towel into my laundry basket and fell back onto the couch, facing Edward with my arms crossed. He joined me on the opposite end, propping his grubby feet up on my coffee table.

"Let me guess," I muttered scornfully, "you're here to talk me into it."

Edward glanced at me, his brow furrowing slightly. "Well, from what I can see, you don't *really* have much of a choice."

"Thanks, Ed, just want I want to hear." He shot me a sympathetic look, his eyes softening as he leaned forward.

"Luca—"

"Save it," I snapped, waving my hand dismissively. With the number of lectures I was getting today, it felt like I'd been enrolled in school. "I know I have to do this. My father made that crystal clear. Georgia and I are splashed across every tabloid, and my phone has been blowing up all morning. If I don't do this, the press will crucify me. Dating random girls is one thing, but breaking the heart of the newest female driver on the grid? Any remaining sponsors I have left will run for the hills."

Edward leaned back onto the couch, crossing his arms over his chest.

"You know my father had the nerve to say that dating Georgia would help with my *driving.* I can fucking drive an F1 car, Edward. I have countless trophies sitting in my cabinet at home from the last five years, but why bother trying to win when Hermes prioritizes Henri? I mean, in Australia, I was running in second, ahead of Henri, and they still demanded I move aside for their precious number one driver. Not that my father gets that, considering he *was* Henri when he was racing for Hermes."

"Luca, I'm sure he didn't mean it."

"Oh no, he did." My voice cracked, and I turned away, blinking hard. "He thinks I'm in it for the social perks, as everyone likes to say. Like I had a *choice*, as if racing wasn't forced onto me since I was a child. Why does it even matter if I like the social perks? Am I not allowed to have fun?"

I reached over to the side table to grab my water bottle, but my attention was immediately drawn to a fallen picture frame. My stomach sank as I recognized the photo of me and my dad at one of my early karting competitions, another reminder of the racer I *used* to be. Edward noticed my distraction, inching closer to look at the photo.

"Your dad talks about that track often," he remembered. "You used to love racing, Luca. What happened?"

I set the photo back in place, brushing off the dust. "When I was a kid, I wasn't a Formula 1 World Champion's son." My voice was barely above a whisper. "I was just Flash, the kid who loved to go fast."

"And now?"

"Now I'm Michael Rossi's disappointing failure of a son. The son of Hermes's most *beloved* champion, who finishes *behind* his teammate." I tried to laugh, but it came out thin and bitter. "You know, last week someone in the press accidentally asked Henri about how wonderful it must be to have a Formula 1 champion for a dad? I'm so embarrassing, even the press can't believe *I'm* Michael Rossi's son."

Edward put a reassuring hand on my shoulder. "I hate how we're forced into all of these painful press interactions. I'm sorry that happened. You aren't a failure, Luca. It's a new week, a new race. Hermes signed you because you're talented, and there's still time to show them that you're worth investing in, too. Or even better, maybe show another team that you're worth their time. There have to be other teams interested in you."

"Hah," I snorted. "As if my father would ever let me race for someone other than Hermes."

Why would Hermes want to invest in an almost 30-year-old racer when they had an up-and-coming 25-year-old star as the lead driver? If I was lucky, I had maybe another three-year contract before all the teams considered me washed out.

I was still stewing in that grim thought when Edward, in true Edward fashion, cut through the spiral with a smug grin. "You know what I think?" He leaned in like he was about to tell the world's biggest secret. "I think by the end of this season, you and Georgia will actually be dating."

I scoffed so hard I nearly choked. "Pretty sure Georgia would rather crash into a barrier during Monaco than date me."

He held up his hands. "A thousand euros says I'm right."

"Look, if you want to lose some money, who am I to stop you? Deal."

Edward shook my hand with unwarranted determination.

"Hopefully, there's a softer, more complacent Georgia," I added, "or this media training they're expecting me to give her is going to be near impossible."

"Well." Edward sprung from the couch, downing the remainder of his coffee. "If anyone can teach Georgia how to become a charismatic, egotistical asshole, it's you, Luca!"

I grabbed my dirty towel and threw it at him, but he was already out the door, cackling as it hit the floor behind him.

Chapter Eight

Georgia

"Georgia, are you there?" Standing behind my hotel room door was Lily, shit-eating grin included.

Ah, so Isabelle had decided to fill her in.

"Thought I'd check in," she said in a voice that sounded like it was dripping in sweet caramel. "Make sure you're ready for your first *date* with Luca tonight." Tonight marked the official start of my public relations romance with Luca Rossi: part media stunt, part horror movie.

"I'm just dandy, Lily. Managed to win myself that boyfriend the press are always so worried about," I muttered sarcastically.

For months now, the media had been obsessed with my love life. Apparently, it was both appalling that I wasn't dating, and scandalous that I might be. Lily snorted, helping herself to a cup of coffee before plopping down on my sofa.

"Keep your head up, Georgie. Who knows, maybe under that rugged, dark, handsome exterior, you might find something you like about Luca Rossi." Grabbing a cushion from my couch, I hurled it in her direction.

"The only thing I imagine I'll learn about Luca is that he is exactly as insufferable as I imagine him to be."

Lily's look told me she was not entirely convinced by my performance.

"If I'd known we'd be given handsome boyfriends if we sucked at media, I would have started swearing at reporters weeks ago," she teased.

"Happy to swap if you'd like." I had no doubt she'd love to take me up on that offer, and I gave her shoulder a friendly shove before straightening a crinkle in my dress.

"So, you're wearing *that* tonight?" Lily smirked at my outfit, and I knew we were both thinking the same thing. Wrapped in this royal purple dress, I looked like a Hermes present.

I nodded. "Nora dropped this off earlier."

"Wearing Luca's team colors on date one… *spicy*." I flipped her off before giving myself one last solemn glance in the mirror.

A second knock rang through my hotel room, but I didn't need to open the door to know who was standing on the other side.

"Georgia? You there?"

I gritted out a frustrated groan as my brother's voice echoed through the hotel room, knowing full well that he'd also dropped by to observe my misery.

"Nice dress," he chuckled.

Ignoring his amusement, I motioned toward the couch.

"Just wanted to pop by and see how you were doing. Big night. First date and all." He took a seat next to Lily on the couch, the two of them now fully settled in like they were waiting for a reality show confession cam.

"Hermes booked us a little table at a Cuban restaurant on the water. Ninety minutes of Luca and I trying to survive each other."

"Just try to talk to him about something *other* than racing," Henri teased.

"Oh yeah, like yachts? Piracy?" The thin line of his lips told me he fully intended to ignore my pettiness.

"Maybe ask about golf? He's very good." My brother shrugged.

"Sure, let's talk about the slowest sport in the world as we race in the fastest." Henri and Lily both flashed me a couple of glares. "The only thing Luca and I have in common *is* racing. I don't see why it's so taboo to talk about it."

Over the course of the season, it felt like the moment I opened my mouth about racing, Luca was headed toward the nearest fire escape.

"Well, just don't drone on about his dad. I know Michael Rossi is your hero and all, but Edward told me they got into a huge fight yesterday. Half the garage heard it."

Perfect, another issue I had to dance around tonight.

"Come on, Georgia," Lily chimed in. "I know you and Luca don't have a close… well, *anything*… but hey, if you're going to fake a relationship with anyone on the grid, at least they picked the most attractive driver. There's no denying it, that man is sex on wheels—literally."

"Can we not talk about my teammate in that way?"

Lily just smirked, licking her lips exaggeratedly. Henri looked like he might physically combust. If there was one thing Lily was exceptional at, it was getting under my brother's skin.

"Regardless, I'll be there for the planned coffee date on Sunday before the race," Henri insisted. "You aren't in this alone, Peaches."

"Thanks. I need to head down. Supposed to meet Luca downstairs at seven."

Lily snickered, glancing at the time. "It's five past already."

"Cheer up, Georgia!" Henri pulled me into a warm hug. "This'll get easier."

-

When I arrived downstairs, I spotted Luca at the entrance of the hotel, leaning against his purple Lamborghini. He was engrossed in his phone, scrolling through it absent-mindedly. He looked up the moment I cleared my throat, his eyes sweeping over me from head to toe, lingering just a second too long. If I hadn't been acutely aware of him at that moment, I might have missed the slight darkening of his eyes.

"Georgia, good of you to show," he said dryly.

"Can't put a time on beautification, Luca." I casually looked at my watch. I was only ten minutes late.

The drive to the restaurant was quiet. Uncomfortably so. I wondered if he remembered that night in Monaco, the date he bailed on. I thought about bringing it up. But then we pulled up to the restaurant, and the moment passed.

After so many years, it didn't seem worth bringing it up. We were such different people now.

Luca handed his keys to the valet and hurriedly opened my door. Offering me his hand, I reluctantly took it, if only because getting out of a sports car that low to the ground with heels was next to impossible. The Italian casually brushed off my mumbled thanks, and we followed the hostess to our table.

Curious eyes watched us as we trailed through the restaurant, and I suddenly felt Luca's hand gently resting on the small of my back, commanding me forward. The soft touch sent a jolt of electricity down my spine as goosebumps appeared.

Traitor, I reprimanded my body.

We took our seats at a small, intimate corner booth at the back. If Luca noticed everyone's prying eyes, he didn't show it. Instead, he dove straight into the menu, clearly starving from a full day of training. Truth be told, if I wasn't so anxious, I would have been equally ravenous. Within minutes, a waiter approached and asked us for our drink order.

"Sparkling water." Luca looked at me as if I had just ordered poison.

"We'll take a bottle of the merlot," he added. The waiter described the daily specials, then left us to peruse the extensive menu.

I drummed my fingers on the polished wooden table. "I don't drink during race weeks. Well, not until *after* the race." Luca stared at me like I'd just told him the earth was flat: dumbfounded.

"If we're going to survive this hoax," his lips curled into a smirk, "you might want to reconsider that habit."

God, he was infuriating.

Luca snapped the menu shut, edging closer to me. "You know, it's your fault we're in this mess."

"My fault?" I shot back. Just as I shifted, Luca casually slung his arm over my shoulder, anchoring me in place. He wasn't entirely wrong, but like hell was I taking all the blame.

"You're the one that leaned in for the kiss."

"Well, you didn't exactly pull away," I retorted.

The nerve of this man.

Luca's grip on my shoulders tightened and his fingers traced slow, teasing circles on my arm. His gaze bored into mine, intense and searching, lips curved into a sly smile as he leaned in closer, his warm breath tickling my skin. To the average onlooker, we looked like a couple casually having an intimate conversation, not a bickering pair of rivals.

"What are you doing?" I hissed, attempting to shake off his firm grip.

"Being your boyfriend," he said, straight-faced. "You know, what you wanted last Sunday, when *you* kissed *me*." Luca licked his lips as he continued to stare down at me with intensity, and for a moment, I wondered if he'd even thought about our kiss. Wondered if he'd also felt that electric pull between us back in Barcelona.

Probably doesn't even remember it. A thought that left me with just a tad bit of disappointment. Ever since Luca had abandoned me in Monaco several years ago, a part of me wanted him to know what he'd missed out on.

"So, tell me, how does Éliott feel about this little arrangement?" Luca looked incredibly pleased with himself, like he'd unearthed a deep, dark secret.

"What the fuck does that mean?"

Luca's voice was casual, but I could tell he'd been wanting to ask about it. The assumption that Éliott and I were dating was a common one, and quite frankly, it drove me bananas. As my brother's best friend, he was a constant staple in my life, and I wasn't going to forgo his friendship because the press couldn't comprehend a woman and a man being friends.

"You two seem awfully close."

"Luca, I'm only going to say this once. Éliott and I are friends, and considering you and I aren't actually dating," I declared, my voice steady as I locked eyes with him, "it's not any of your fucking business."

He threw his hands up in mock surrender, but the glint in his eye said *noted*. "Fine, fine, just remember who you're supposed to be dating in public next time Éliott comes around."

I ignored the dig, pulling out my phone. "Nora's created some 'getting to know you' questions for us so we can be prepared for future interviews about our *relationship*."

Luca said nothing, continuing to caress my shoulder as he stared at me with his dark brown eyes. He had a way of pulling you in, like a deep, entrancing abyss that seemed to swallow every coherent thought. His rich voice basically oozed charisma, and I felt more like a fisherman being sucked in by a siren, than a woman in control.

He nodded for me to continue, and I cleared my throat. "Besides racing, what is your favorite thing to do?" I had to stifle my groan—*how morose*—as I kept myself composed. We needed to know these things if we were going to sell this stunt. Luca let out a dismissive laugh, and I shot him a sharp look, making my disapproval clear.

"I golf," he mumbled finally. Raising my finger, I motioned for Luca to continue, but I knew the battle was lost when the waiter arrived with the wine, pouring us each a glass. I begrudgingly moved mine to the side, staring at it like it was a ticking time bomb about to explode at any minute. Truthfully, I wanted nothing more than to gulp down the delicious merlot.

Just one sip wouldn't hurt, right? Luca watched me like a hawk circling its prey, his lips curling into a smug grin.

"Goody Two-Shoes," he teased under his breath, and it took all of my will not to chuck the wine in his face.

"So… golf?" I prodded. Luca raised a single eyebrow, taking a sip from his wine glass. "You… do it often?"

Good one, Georgia. You don't sound like an idiot at all.

"Yes."

It felt like an eternity as Luca and I stared at each other, his arm still casually resting on my shoulders before he shifted his eyes to a nearby table full of diners not-so-subtly photographing us. I thought back to my brother's earlier comment, and I scratched my brain, trying to remember just one fact about golf. Something about birds, eagles maybe?

Nothing.

Well, I tried. Sort of.

Luca leaned in. "You know, if this one is too hard for you to answer, we can skip it." He winked.

Prick.

"I like to paint. Your turn." Shoving my phone at him, I nodded for him to read a question.

"You paint? Really?" Luca sneered with disbelief.

"Why is that so hard to believe?" Probably wasn't the best time to tell him all of my paintings were of race cars.

"Didn't know you knew how to do anything other than race. Or, you know, run people off the track."

Of course, he managed to get that dig in.

"That's rich coming from someone whose dad is a three-time World Champion. How amazing it must have been to be able to race with him whenever you wanted, get all that priceless advice from his experience. Loving racing isn't a crime, Luca." His face tightened, just for a second. One breath. But I caught it.

Then came the grin, a smooth recovery.

"Well," he paused, his eyes darting to the tables around us, ensuring our conversation wasn't being secretly filmed, "since we're dispensing free advice, here's something to consider. Perhaps when the journalists ask what else you're doing on your days off, you say *painting*?"

"Why on earth would the journalists care that I paint? They barely care that I race."

"Because, believe it or not, fans actually like a well-rounded person. Why do you think our silly social media videos of us cooking, playing golf, or doing literally anything other than racing go viral? It gives the fans a way to connect with us." I stared at Luca, very much wishing that we weren't so close to each other, as I nervously bit my lip, contemplating his advice.

Painting had always been a stress relief for me. Even as a racer in F2, I'd kept up my private art lessons, not wanting to let that creative part of me go. But for some reason, sharing that with everyone else felt impossible. Not only was it the one private part of my life I had left to myself, sharing it with the world felt like I'd give them one more reason to judge me. One more reason to say I wasn't focused on the championship.

Sensing the awkward silence between us, Luca grabbed my phone, opting to read another question. "Oh, come on," I heard him mutter before clearing his throat. "Your favorite color?"

"Gold."

"To symbolize all your winning?" he sneered.

"Jealous?"

Luca didn't even bat an eye at my response. "Mine's purple." He raked his eyes over my dress. "And I have to say, I like it even more after tonight." Winking, he gave my dress a pointed look.

I was going to murder Nora after this dinner.

"Your favorite color… is the color of your team car?" I asked incredulously, doing my best to ignore his cocky grin.

"Like yours isn't *actually* Valkyrie blue."

The air quotes he'd put around "Valkyrie blue" irked me to no end, but I kept my face neutral. Quite frankly, I suspected I'd sound *stupid* admitting that my favorite color was the color of my team car and after hearing Luca say purple, it turned out I was right. Before I could continue to pat myself on my back for my pettiness, Luca slid the phone back to me.

Searching for one that wouldn't give me heartburn, I finally whispered, "Favorite movie?"

"Who wrote these stupid questions?" Luca groaned. "No one is going to ask us about our favorite movies or favorite pasta or favorite song. We aren't children."

"My favorite movie is *Pride & Prejudice*," I said nonchalantly.

"Never seen it." Not surprising. Luca didn't strike me as someone who watched romantic movies about two enemies whose love was an uphill battle. He struck me as a *Terminator*, *Transformers*, *Godzilla* sort of guy. Lots of action, pretty girls, little plot.

Luca grabbed the phone, frantically scrolling through the questions before shoving it back into my hands. "Forget the list. Here's something I *do* want to know." His tone shifted just enough to make me wary. "Every time Henri talks about you, he goes on and on about how funny and 'darling' you are." I did my best, once again, to ignore the air quotes. "Why can't you be like that in front of the media?"

All at once, I had a million things cross my mind, a million things that I wanted to say. I should have said that when I went into press conferences, it felt like the wind was being kicked out of me. Or, when I approached the media pen, my palms got so sweaty that I struggled to focus on anything but the drops of sweat dripping down my face. How my quick remarks weren't meant to be snippy, all I wanted was for the interview to be over so I could retreat to the ease of my garage.

How I had suffered from anxiety since I was a child, but because my brother was so outgoing, my incredibly loving parents didn't know how to deal with my emotions. How it took me turning twenty before I was able to seek professional help. But I couldn't let Luca know any of that.

Show the enemy no weakness.

"The same way you can't stop yourself from partying or stealing yachts," I said cooly. "It's in my nature."

Georgia: 1. Luca: 1.

Chapter Nine

Luca

Like all Formula 1 races, Friday in Miami was dedicated to free practice sessions, which consisted of rigorous testing at the start of the Grand Prix weekend. After a grueling couple of sessions and several engineering meetings, I traipsed back to my driver's room filled with exhaustion, disappointment, and quite frankly a shit ton of embarrassment.

Another horrible practice session.

Just as my head hit my sofa's pillow, my manager popped his head in. "So, how was it?" Matteo had a large, expectant grin on his face.

"Free practice was fine."

He narrowed his eyes, giving me a disapproving grunt. Considering he'd never asked me about my free practice sessions before, I knew what he was really asking about.

"Dinner was fine." Fine was a nice way of putting it. Every offhand jab about my party habits or inherited privilege had been on a loop in my head all day. Somehow, her opinion mattered more than any headline ever could. And I hated that.

Matteo stepped inside, closing the door behind him. "Well, the photos of your *fine* date look phenomenal." Before I could protest, he thrust his phone into my hands with a look of triumph. "Look at this photo of the two of you!"

The image that greeted me wasn't what I expected. A candid shot of Georgia and me at the restaurant, mid-laugh. Her head was tilted slightly toward mine, her eyes scrunched with genuine amusement. And there I was, mirroring her expression, looking more carefree and happier than I had in ages. In the picture, we looked like a couple deeply in love.

Not like the bickering rivals that we actually were.

"Pretty good, huh?" My manager looked rather pleased with himself.

I shoved the phone back at him. "It's fine."

"Georgia and Nora will be stopping by soon," Matteo added, already halfway out the door. "Smile for the cameras."

Before I could tell him exactly where he could stick his cameras, I heard her voice.

"Hiya! Is Luca around?" Georgia's bright tone rang out through the garage, just as calculated as it was casual. "We were just walking past and thought we'd say hi."

My team principal grunted as he nodded, but before he could summon me over, I waltzed out of my room and into the garage, pulling Georgia into a warm embrace. Her eyes widened in surprise, but the initial stiffness in her shoulders melted away as she relaxed, returning the hug. A sudden flood of comfort filled me. For all her icy exterior, Georgia's hugs were inexplicably full of warmth.

"How did free practice go, *amore*?"

Georgia brushed imaginary lint from her pants, avoiding eye contact, cheeks tinged a faint pink.

So, she liked the nickname. *Noted*.

Georgia shrugged. "Car felt good, but the heat was draining. Hoping we get some rain; would make it cooler."

We chatted awkwardly—small talk, rehearsed smiles—while one of the Hermes social media interns not-so-subtly filmed us from across the garage. A reminder as to why both teams felt it necessary to add this inconvenient stop into our busy schedules as drivers.

Finally tired of awkwardly standing in the way of the mechanics doing *actual* work, I put my hand on the small of her back and led her further inside, pretending to give her a tour of the garage as the social media intern followed us. A tour that felt positively ridiculous, considering her brother had raced here for years.

When I opened the door to my driver's room, Georgia let out a surprised gasp, and I knew exactly what she was thinking. On the other side of this wall was her brother's room, a room whose disheveled nature rivaled a war zone.

"Not all men are slobs like your brother." Chuckling, I motioned for her to take a seat on my sofa. She wandered in, trailing a finger along the spotless counter before dropping onto the couch.

"Good to see some men can pick up after themselves." Probably the best compliment she'd ever given me. "So, now that it's just us, how did your free practice *really* go today, Luca?"

Considering lap times were public, she knew exactly how it'd gone. That I'd managed to barely squeak out a sixth-place finish in the second free practice. Part of me wondered if she was trying to remind me of my failures. My father had spent the better part of the afternoon berating me with ideas, I didn't need them from Georgia as well.

"Well, you can't win them all." My joke sounded stiff, and she didn't say anything. "I see you and Henri are like a hundredth of a second off each other. No shocker there," I added, trying to sound breezy as I collapsed onto the far end of the couch. I kept my eyes on the window, anything but the pity on her face.

"The Hermes car has great pace this weekend. I'm sure you'll find it in qualifying."

I thought Georgia was going to add, "*if you put in the effort*," but she kept the light smile on her face. No biting remark, no smug grin. Just a steady confidence in her voice that almost sounded like belief.

"Perhaps." I shrugged.

"You should watch Henri's free practice laps." Georgia immediately held up her hands in protest at my disgust. "I know, I know. Just hear me out. You know that area of the track by the bridge? It's more elevated than it looks on camera. The camber is higher than you'd expect. Henri is losing some time because he's religiously taking the racing line." She paused, clearly second-guessing herself, but I nodded for her to continue. "As you go around, take your car off the line just a bit during qualifying tomorrow. It might help you if you time it right."

She was nervous. I could see it in the way she wrung her fingers, the tension etched in her shoulders. Which meant she actually cared what I did with her advice. Georgia had a sharp eye for detail and a knack for spotting subtle nuances on the track. In this case, my father was right, I probably did have a lot to learn from Georgia.

I let the words settle, playing the line through my head. It was, to be fair, a clever idea.

"Not a bad idea," I said finally, and Georgia relaxed enough for a soft smile to slip through. "You watch *everyone's* free practice laps?"

"You don't? Learned that tidbit from your da—" She hesitated, choosing to look out the window instead of finishing the sentiment.

"So, why are you helping the enemy win? Francesco paying you more than Valkyrie?" I gave her arm a slight, teasing squeeze.

Georgia smirked. "What can I say? I'd like some actual competition tomorrow. And if you could keep Henri on his toes, that'd be an added bonus too."

"Who knew Georgia Dubois was so devious?" I laughed, before leaning in closer. "So, since we're sharing advice… I saw this morning's press."

She groaned, rolling her eyes like it physically pained her. "For whatever reason, this morning's journalists were so focused on my ability to race in the heat, that you'd think I haven't raced in the US during the summer before."

"While it's certainly fun watching you battle it out with the press like a dutiful general, have you considered just joking with them?" I suggested. "They're so worried about you being able to face the heat, just tell them you eat chilis for breakfast."

"Wh-who on earth would believe that?" she scoffed.

"It's not about them believing you, Georgia. It's a joke." She looked about ready to combust at my idea. "Find yourself in an uncomfortable situation? Make 'em laugh. Divert the attention elsewhere." Georgia looked skeptical but she didn't dismiss the idea.

Progress.

"Joke with the lions *before* they eat me, got it."

"See, just like that." I grinned, pointing finger-gun-style.

A knock on the door startled both of us. "Georgia, you're needed back at Valkyrie!" the voice called out.

"Best you head back. I'm sure you've got *tonssss* more practice laps to watch."

Georgia scoffed, smoothing out her team jacket as she stood up. "Right, yes, see you Sunday for the coffee date. Good luck in qualifying."

We made our way out of my driver's room and to the Hermes' back exit, but before we could exit, a dark chuckle caught my attention.

"Well, well, well. Georgia, collecting consolation prizes, are we? I see the paddock's most *unexpected* couple has finally gone official." I didn't need to look at the person to know who was behind me. Only one person could master that sarcastic, southern drawl.

Anthony.

Georgia balled her hands into fists at her side, but before she could step forward, I pushed her slightly behind me, squaring up to Anthony. At six-one, I lorded over the five-six American driver, but to his credit he didn't back down, continuing to gnaw on his apple as he sized up the two of us. His confidence reeked of someone who believed they held all the cards, and every part of me wanted to knock him down a few pegs.

"What can I say, Anthony, just couldn't hide my excitement any longer. Snagged me the best racer on the grid, don't you think?" I gave Georgia's hand a quick squeeze in a show of affection.

Anthony ignored me as he stepped closer, his eyes searing into Georgia's bright blue orbs. "Really hopping from driver to driver, I see."

I felt Georgia's entire body bristle beside me, but her voice was ice-cold calm. "Well, much like cars, Anthony, even boyfriends need upgrading."

He ignored her. "What does Éliott think about you having a new boyfriend?" I felt her falter. Not much, but enough to notice. Enough to piss me off with that same anger I'd felt back in Barcelona.

Edward had insisted that her relationship with Éliott had been platonic, but something about Georgia's death grip on her pants told me she'd heard that theory from other people.

Or they'd actually dated. A thought that made my stomach sour more than I appreciated.

"Who do you think set us up?"

The words came sliding out of my mouth, and Georgia immediately gave me a questioning side-eye. Our press teams were going with a loose story about us 'falling in love' during her garage visits to her brother, but I couldn't help the sly words leaving my mouth in an effort to put Anthony in his place.

Anthony raised his brows in mock delight. "The ex set up the new beau? You might want to be careful who you introduce her to, Rossi."

"For the last fucking time, he was not my—" Before Georgia could finish her thought, I dragged her out of the hallway, leaving Anthony's smug face behind.

"Gah!" Georgia screamed as soon as we were outside. "It was one fucking time!"

Her cheeks were bright pink, her eyes blazing. But just as quickly, her face shuttered again. Calm, collected. Only the way she wrung her hands betrayed her.

I really wanted to ask about her explosive comment, but now didn't feel like the time to satisfy my curiosity.

"You okay, *amore*?" I asked gently. "I should have made sure that Anthony wasn't around." Georgia shifted uncomfortably, and I could tell she was searching for the right words.

"I knew I'd see more of him when I agreed to this." She looked down at her feet, then back up at me with something close to vulnerability in her eyes—something she clearly hated.

"Look, I'm only going to say this once, so savor it. Whatever happened between you and Anthony doesn't matter. He's a joke. You? You're going to be a fucking World Champion. Let him rot in mediocrity."

She nodded before glancing at her phone which had been buzzing since we'd left my driver's room. "It's Nora. She's been ringing me nonstop. Look, I gotta run, but I'll see you Sunday. Good luck in qualifying tomorrow."

She started to walk away, but just before she turned the corner, I called after her.

"Oh, and Georgia?"

She glanced back over her shoulder.

"You're welcome to come test this upgrade anytime!"

She didn't reply, except for a single middle finger in the air.

Chapter Ten

Georgia

"You look like the sun is literally shining out of your ass. What's with all the yellow?" I asked as Nora waltzed into my room, dressed in a bright yellow bucket hat and matching pants. Her happiness was a complete contradiction to the dread that all but consumed me this morning.

"Thought I would try and bring the sunshine in case Miami brought rain, but now I fear it worked too well. Heard today's race is going to be over 100 degrees," she moaned. "Speaking of which, you feeling ready for today?"

The question I'd been dreading since my horrendous qualifying yesterday.

"Frustrated I'm starting eighth."

Embarrassed was more like it. In Saturday's qualifying, a piece of debris had gotten lodged into my car's floor, forcing me to retire from the final session early. An eighth-place starting spot was a disaster for my race today. Didn't matter that the debris lodged in my car wasn't my fault, there was no changing my qualifying position.

The brutality of Formula 1.

"Well, I'm sure you'll make your way to the front in no time."

"I'm sure the team will have no problem letting me pass Lily on track," I grumbled sarcastically.

I was pleased that my teammate had gotten fifth in qualifying, but Valkyrie wasn't going to just wave me by past her if she was having a good race. Lily had a chance for a podium here, and I'd have to earn my pass.

Nora either didn't hear the sarcasm or chose to ignore it. "So, I forgot to ask... did you happen to ask Luca any of the questions I wrote during your date? We should subtly slip some of those into your interviews today. No doubt they're going to ask you about your relationship." Nora waved her hands at me, and I made a point not to look up from my phone. "Georgia!"

"I learned he likes the color purple." *The worst color.*

"Really?" Nora shimmied her shoulders with unhinged giddiness. "Good thing I put you in that purple dress then."

"He must have thought he'd died and gone to heaven!" Lily called out from my doorway.

I flipped her off without looking up. "Doubt it."

Neither of them seemed convinced, and before I could protest, Lily thrust her phone into my hands with a look of triumph. "Ye of little faith! Look, a new photo of your *date night* came out this morning!"

A warm blush crept across my cheeks despite my best efforts to appear indifferent. Luca's arm was draped casually over my shoulder, his lips brushing close to my ear as if he was sharing an intimate secret only for me.

"Date didn't look that bad," she added with a wink.

"Alright, enough of you," Nora laughed, shooing Lily out of the room. "Time for Georgia's coffee date!" Leaning in close, Nora looked like she was about to reveal a top-secret plan. "Okay, so when we get to the

Hermes hospitality suite, you need to be all cheeky and ask Francesco if Luca is there."

"Why wouldn't Luca be there? He's a *Hermes* driver and it's the *Hermes* suite on a race morning."

Ignoring my barb, she added, "And then Luca will come out with your brother, and you'll have a little harmless pre-race chitchat, blah blah blah. Try to throw in something that isn't racing related."

"You do realize the only thing Luca and I have in common *is* that we race cars."

The truth was, I talked about racing with Luca because it was the only thing we shared. His idea of a Tuesday night involved yacht parties with influencers and an open bar. Mine involved sweatpants, an F1 simulator rig, and whatever romance novel Nora and Lily forced into my hands.

Nora straightened her bucket hat. "Well, I'm sure you can find something else to discuss!"

"Never stolen a yacht before, so that one's out."

She didn't dignify that with a response. "Come, let's get this pre-race date over with so we can get back to focusing on the whole reason we're here. Your race win!"

–

Every time I visited the Hermes hospitality suite I was left completely in awe. The gleaming marble floors, floor-to-ceiling windows, and framed portraits of past champions oozed old money and sixty years of Formula 1 history. Just past the entrance, I spotted Luca and Henri tucked away at a small table in the back, mid conversation. Luca, ever the strategist, already held two cups of coffee.

Smart man. If he had drinks ready, we could shave at least two minutes off this awkward encounter. If there was one thing I suspected we could agree on, it was that every minute we didn't have to spend together was a win.

He looked up, grin already in place, his Hermes team shirt soaked through from the Miami humidity. The tight spandex clung to every inch of him, highlighting a body that absolutely did not deserve to belong to someone so insufferable. I could make out every curve of his chest and the cut of his abs.

Stop. Staring. Georgia. Didn't matter that Luca basically looked like a sweaty, handcrafted statue from the Italian Renaissance era, he didn't need any more of an ego boost.

Suddenly, Luca had his arms wrapped around my waist, and we were locked in a large, sweaty embrace. I could smell the salt on his skin as he tugged me closer, pressing my head against his muscular chest. He gave me a tight squeeze, which I might have *secretly* enjoyed if he wasn't soaking wet from the sweltering heat.

That was a lie. I enjoyed it anyway, a fact I decided to shove into a deep, dark place. No one had accused me of being blind, just of being bad at media.

Luca let me go, motioning to a chair next to him as he handed me my cup of coffee.

I looked into the cup, and before I could ask, Luca whispered, "Don't worry. Not an ounce of cream or sugar."

Just how I liked it, which left me with a hint of surprise.

He turned toward Henri with a theatrical sigh. "Look who came to steal our racing strategy!" He took a sip from a purple mug that had his team number etched into the side.

"Don't be silly, we don't steal *losing* strategies over at Valkyrie."

Luca huffed out a laugh at my quip, one that almost seemed genuine, but Henri didn't seem quite so amused. He was very touchy about Hermes F1 strategy—or lack thereof, as he often bemoaned.

"Nice of you to visit us this morning," Henri proclaimed, giving my arm a squeeze that was accompanied by an "*I'm sorry you have to do this*" smile. I made sure my cheerful grin screamed, "*This is your fault for inviting Luca to that party.*"

"Well, when Luca boasted that Hermes's Italian coffee was better than our French roast at Valkyrie, I knew I had to give it a try. You know how I feel about anything *Italian*."

Luca cocked an eyebrow at that jab but said nothing. Instead, he scooted closer, draping his arm along the back of my chair. His fingers began tracing gentle circles on the back of my neck—an unconscious tic I was beginning to recognize. Over the last few days, it had become increasingly obvious that Luca's love language was touch. At first, I'd thought the hugs were just for show, but I was starting to realize that they did carry some meaning for him.

Henri topped off my coffee ever so slightly, before leaning in closer. "So, Georgia, I hear that Luca has you to thank for our front-row lock out today."

"Oh?" I narrowed my eyes at my brother, trying not to let my curiosity show.

"That advice you gave me yesterday, *amore*, was quite useful." Luca leaned in with a lazy grin.

No part of me believed that he was going to listen to the advice I'd given him after free practice. But somehow, Luca had managed to squeeze out second place on the starting grid. Oddly enough, I felt more pride than frustration toward him. He might be Hermes's number two driver, but Luca had immense talent, as shown by his large collection of Grand Prix trophies from the last eight years.

As much as *I* wanted to win, I hated watching another driver suffer through the kind of dry spell Luca had been enduring all season.

"Glad to be of service," I muttered. "So, you going to use any more of my racing secrets to knock my brother off of his high horse and steal his victory today?"

Luca's face told me exactly what he thought about my rhetorical question. If I thought it was unlikely that Valkyrie would let me pass my teammate Lily on track, there was no chance in hell Hermes was letting Luca pass their golden boy in today's race. Hermes had made it clear that Henri was their number one driver with Luca in the supporting role. Sometimes I wondered if that was why Luca never seemed to try during races anymore, wondered if he felt like it was pointless because the team prioritized Henri winning.

Without thinking, I placed a quick, sympathetic hand on his thigh. His muscles tensed for a split second beneath my touch, but he didn't flinch, just smiled. "It doesn't matter who stands on that top step, as long as it's not Team Valkyrie."

How incredibly diplomatic of him. I had no doubt that, deep inside, Luca wanted to crush my brother in this afternoon's race. In F1, your teammate was both your best friend and your worst enemy.

"Well, we Hermes boys will have to stick together today." A pointed reminder from my brother that Luca's job was to help defend Henri's first-place qualifying position.

Rolling my eyes, I internally prayed to anyone listening that I could turn my eighth-place start into a win so that

I didn't have to spend the rest of the evening listening to Henri and Luca boast about their success.

Nora appeared behind me, her subtle wave a polite way of saying, "*Wrap it up.*" I drained the last sip of coffee and stood, patting Henri's head with a wicked grin. "Gotta run, but see you boys at the podium celebration. I'll be the one on the *top* step."

Henri snorted, standing up to give me a hug, before nudging me toward Luca, with a meaningful look that said, "*Hug your boyfriend.*"

Hesitating for a moment, I awkwardly draped my arm around Luca's waist, giving him a half-hearted side hug. He coyly laughed, wrapping his arms around me as he pulled me flush against his chest. He was wearing that cologne again—the one that smelled of lilacs and pine trees. Eyes closed for just a brief moment, I let myself drink it in before quickly opening them, backing off from Luca. Despite his propensity to get under my skin, he truly had this ability to give you a hug so warm and inviting that it made you think you'd been best friends for several lifetimes and not enemies for a few years.

"Right, better get back. Stealing first place won't be easy. Need to go prepare!" I flashed my brother a sly grin, pointedly ignoring his *colorful* language.

-

"Alright, time to get in the car, G. Race is about to start," Mel yelled into the garage.

I hoisted myself into the driver's seat. A bead of sweat trickled down my temple as I clipped my radio into place and tugged on my gloves. Just before pulling down the visor, I gave my water pouch a quick squeeze.

God, I was going to need this.

The sun blazed above, relentless and unbothered, and I pulled up to the eighth spot on the starting grid, my heart racing with adrenaline. The start of a Formula 1 race always felt like being at the top of a rollercoaster just before the thrilling drop. Magical was the only way to describe it.

The first light went red, followed by four more.

Then lights out.

In a matter of seconds, I had advanced two places due to poor starts from the cars in front of me. The first few corners were chaos—heat shimmered off the asphalt, tires screamed, and the blur of liveries jostled for position. Another car retired just ahead, overheated, most likely.

"Fourth place, G. Order is Henri, Luca, Lily. Let's push," Mel called into the radio.

"Roger." I tore another cover off my visor. "It's real hot in here, Mel. Everything okay?" I mumbled into the radio.

"Car is fine."

"Doesn't feel fine." The heat was a slow, choking grip around my chest. Struggling to focus, I squinted at the road ahead, my hands gripping the steering wheel as I pushed through the sweltering heat. I went to suck on my drink pouch, but nothing came out.

Oh, fuck. This was not the race for my water to break. I debated on mentioning it to the team, but there was little anyone could do at this point.

Just grin and bear it, Georgia.

By lap forty, I had closed the gap between me and Lily, with my car practically tailgating hers. "Tell Isabelle I have the faster race pace. Lily needs to get out of the way if she's going to drive this slowly." Not one of my finer moments, demanding to be let past my teammate, but I knew I could overtake her, even with the draining heat.

"Hold," was all Mel responded.

"No, tell Isabelle that either Lily gives me the position or I'll take it from her."

Isabelle had made it clear that while I was the lead driver, she wasn't about to take podiums away from my teammate, even if I needed the championship points.

To my surprise, Mel popped back with good news. "Lily has been instructed to give you her position. Make it quick." As soon as the track opened up, I swung wide, passing her on the straight, and bolted into P3.

"Thanks." Regardless of how embarrassed I felt from my outburst, I was P3, and Luca was only five seconds ahead of me. With my fresher tires, there was still time for me to catch up to the pace set by the Hermes drivers.

Beads of sweat dripped down my forehead and stung my eyes, my helmet feeling heavier with each passing second. Despite the intense heat and increasing exhaustion, all I could think about was catching Luca's car, but as I closed the gap between us, my vision began to blur and my head throbbed with pain, making it hard to concentrate on anything but my racing heartbeat. I reached for my straw out of pure instinct and got nothing, again. My lips and mouth were completely dry, yet so much salty sweat was dripping down my face, I felt like I'd just taken a swim in the ocean.

"Ten laps to go." I pressed the radio button to respond, but no words came out. "G, you slowed down last lap. All okay?"

No. Opening my mouth, I tried to get something out, but I couldn't find the words to tell her how I was feeling, didn't want to embarrass myself on international TV by admitting I was failing to keep up with Luca because I couldn't stand the lack of water.

Or the heat.

The journalists had spent Friday and Saturday commenting on my heat exhaustion, and now all I could think about was not letting them be right.

"Gap is now three seconds." Her tone told me she already knew I wasn't going to close it. No one said anything on the radio after that, and I knew the team had accepted that I was going to finish third.

"Last lap. Can you push for the fastest lap? Henri currently holds it." Getting "fastest lap" gave me an extra point in the championship, and every point mattered.

"Fuck it, Georgia, let's push," I mumbled to myself.

Focusing on the track, I let everything else fade away. The humming of my engine was the only sound I could hear, the blur of colors as my car sped by the jam-packed grandstands the only sight I could see. After an excruciating race, I was flying in what was probably my best lap of a Grand Prix this season. I might have been blinded by the heat, but I would be damned if I was going to let my brother take this one tiny victory from me.

As I slid past the finish line, Mel popped on to the radio. "That's P8 to P3, G, and fastest lap. Stellar race in this dreadful heat! Unfortunately, Lily had an issue with the battery which forced her to DNF. Race order is Henri, Luca, you."

Well, at least I didn't have to feel guilty about passing Lily.

It wasn't the race win I'd hoped for, but I was proud of the achievement. Pressing the radio button, I went to congratulate the team, but as I opened my mouth, a wave of intense nausea hit me. The adrenaline from the final lap had run its course, and I suddenly realized how intensely ill I felt.

"Yeah… uh… thank… the team…"

My voice was barely audible. No doubt the pit wall took my words as an indication of how upset I was about losing, but truth be told, I was surprised I could get anything out.

I pulled into my P3 parking spot, the cheers of the crowd a distant hum behind the pounding in my ears. Henri was already up on his car, fists in the air, playing to the cameras.

For a second, I just sat there, my hands gripping the seat belt, trying to will my body to get out of this car.

Don't faint in this car, Georgia. Don't let this race be for nothing. I had to make it to the weigh-in station, or I knew my race wouldn't count.

One hand made it to the halo. Then two. I pulled, hard, launching my body out of the cockpit with whatever will I had left. My feet hit the ground like cinder blocks. I forced myself toward the weighing station, nodding at the officials, barely hearing their congratulations. A staff member tore off the slip and handed it to me.

I wasn't sure if I ever actually took it, because all I could focus on was my buckling knees.

Well, shit.

Chapter Eleven

Luca

"That's second place, Luca!" My engineer called into my radio, before passing it to my father who had managed a spot on the pit wall.

"A 1-2 finish for Hermes. I couldn't be more proud of how you drove today, son."

Proud. A word my father hadn't said to me in over a year. My body tingled at hearing it over the radio, like a spark bringing a fire back to life.

As soon as I climbed out of my car, heat slammed into me like a concrete wall, but I ran toward my mechanics, giving them a large group hug. They'd earned this second place, too.

Across the paddock, Henri was basking in the chaos of celebration, lifting his helmet for a victorious fist pump, his crew practically vibrating with glee.

But something was missing.

Someone was missing.

Georgia wasn't with him.

A pulse of panic fired through me. Before I even realized I'd moved, I was running toward the weigh-in station. That's when I saw her—standing unsteadily, her helmet in one hand, the weight slip fluttering from the other like a leaf in the wind.

She swayed.

"Georgia!" I shouted, just as her knees buckled.

I caught her before she hit the ground, her body collapsing into mine. Georgia's limbs dangled limply as I lifted her up, her head lolling against my chest. Sweat glistened on her pale forehead, her gold hair plastered against her damp skin.

"Georgia!" Henri's panicked voice broke through the noise. Before he could reach her, I gently scooped her up in my arms, letting her head rest against my chest.

"Medical tent. Now," I demanded, clutching Georgia tightly to me as I sprinted toward the medical tent with Henri in tow.

"It's likely heat exhaustion," the doctor said as we crashed into the tent. "Or heat syncope from lack of water. Let's get her flat; she'll come to in a moment or two."

I laid her down gently, brushing damp hair away from her face as the medic began his assessment. Her eyelids fluttered, mouth moving sluggishly.

Henri pushed me out of the way, and I begrudgingly let him take my place next to Georgia on the cot. As much as I hated leaving her side, she needed her brother more than she needed me in this moment.

Henri grabbed my water bottle, putting it to her lips as he demanded that she drink slowly. Her eyes fluttered open, and the moment her beautiful blue eyes locked on to mine, relief flooded me. A few drivers had experienced heat syncope throughout the weekend, but there was something different about watching Georgia endure it. It made my stomach twist, head spinning with frustration.

And anger. What had Valkyrie done?

"How is she, doc?"

Isabelle and Nora came bursting into the tent, both pale and wild-eyed.

"How much water did Georgia have in her car?" I asked suddenly, and Isabelle turned to me, shock—and a hint of frustration—written on her face.

"The water device broke. Georgia didn't let us know."

"How could you not have checked it?" I demanded.

Georgia shot her hand up, and I turned my attention to her. "Luca, it's fine. I should have said something. Let's not make a big deal about it." Her eyes begged me to quit it, but the more I stood there watching her sip slowly at the water bottle, the more anger bubbled to the surface.

"It's not fine, Georgia, you fucking fainted!"

She made a move to get up, attempting to swing her legs off the bed, but Henri put his hands on her shoulder, stopping her.

"Peaches, what the fuck? Luca is right. You passed out. You're going to lie down for a bit," he insisted.

Ignoring her brother's demand, Georgia sat up, waving the doctor over. "I'm fine. Just give me a few minutes, and then I'll join you both in the cooldown room." Henri scoffed at her insistence, lightly pushing on her shoulder to stop her from getting up.

"This is insane, who cares about the stupid podium, Georgia?" Henri was now standing, his arms on both hips as he stared down at his sister like a mother scolding a child.

"I do." Georgia's voice was strong, and as she took another sip of water, the color in her face started to return. "All week the media have been commenting about my ability to race in this heat, but I did it. I finished in third after a dismal qualifying, and like hell is anyone stopping me from getting the podium celebration I deserve because of a little heat exhaustion."

The defiance in Georgia's eyes was nothing short of remarkable, and no one said anything as Nora and Isabelle stared at her with some disbelief.

But this was what made Georgia such an accomplished racer, what made her *special.* Nothing stopped her from accomplishing her goals; and like hell was she going to give the media more fodder to come after her.

And truth be told, if it was me, no one would be able to stop me from collecting my trophy either.

"How about this," the doctor suggested, putting his hands up in defeat. "Give it another five minutes. Recovery for heat syncope is quick. Georgia, head to the podium celebration, but I expect to see you back here for more fluids after it's all finished." The doctor dumped another hydration packet into my Hermes water bottle. "Here, take this water and hydration packet with you."

The F1 stewards had surprisingly pushed back the podium celebration. We made our way to the cooldown room that held the winners before the podium celebration. Georgia was already there when we walked in, perched on the edge of a bench, one arm lazily fanning herself while the other gripped my water bottle like it was a lifeline. Her racing suit was peeled halfway down her torso, tied around her waist. The flush hadn't fully left her cheeks, but she was upright, alert, and still looked like she could take someone's head off if they offered her sympathy.

A blast of cold air brushed against my face, but it did little to alleviate the oppressive heat that clung to my skin. I was still in my racing suit, and the longer I stood in it, the more desperate I felt to escape. I unzipped my suit, peeling off my damp shirt without thinking, tying my race suit around my waist. I tossed the fireproof spandex shirt onto a chair, sighing in relief as the cold air hit my skin.

Georgia's eyes were locked on me, gaze skating slowly across my chest before jerking back to her water bottle like she'd been burned.

My brows lifted, a slow smirk curving across my mouth.

Henri crossed his arms, pointing to the chair next to me. "Put your shirt on, there's cameras in here."

"Spoilsport," I muttered, tugging my shirt back on, but not before catching another quick glance from Georgia.

"Alright, you're on," the steward said, leading Georgia out first, and then after a few more seconds, motioned for me to join her on the podium. Walking out to the roaring crowd, a feeling of invincibility washed over me, something I hadn't felt in a very long time. I looked to my left, and Georgia was waving down at the fans, blowing a few kisses to her mechanics. It was impossible not to smile at the genuine laughter on her face. Impossible not to admire the strength it took to get up on that podium.

When Henri got his trophy, we all huddled in for a group photo.

"Right, Dubois, you ready?" I winked at Georgia, and before Henri picked up his bottle of champagne, the two of us were spraying down her brother and his Hermes race engineer with the cold liquid.

This was my favorite part of being on the podium. Rivalry forgotten in the euphoria of champagne, deafening crowds, and the satisfaction of knowing we'd survived another Sunday. The three drivers up there, for just a few moments, had a special connection filled with pure, blissful joy.

My father and mother waved to me from down below, and that feeling of warmth that I used to have as a kid, it felt like a small piece of that was returning. The moment I walked down, my father grabbed me and pulled me into a hug.

"Amazing work today, son. How did you know Georgia wasn't well?"

I barely had time to answer before reporters swarmed us. Flashes exploded in every direction. Matteo shuffled in quickly, steering me toward my private room while we left my father to face the cameras. Not one more word about my race. Not a nod to the way I'd defended P2, or nearly closed the gap on Henri. The small light from the podium celebration seemed to fade, as a reminder of my position on the team came back to me.

I walked into the room and threw my trophy onto the sofa. Matteo's voice pulled me out of my fog.

"Luca," Matteo said as he handed me a towel. "How *did* you know Georgia wasn't okay?"

I shrugged. "Luck, I guess."

"Luck? Really?"

I didn't answer. Couldn't answer. Because truthfully, I couldn't articulate how I knew. I'd felt it in my gut, the way you feel a storm before it breaks. Something wasn't right.

"Fine, keep your secrets." Matteo picked up the trophy to admire it. "Anyway. Nice driving today. Really. You know, Rennen approached me after the race."

I blinked. "Why?"

He looked uneasy as he placed the trophy onto my coffee table. "They're interested in you."

I scoffed. "Don't waste your time, Matteo. Hermes is where I belong." I tried to sound more convinced than I felt.

Matteo looked like he wanted to press, but something in my face stopped him. He exhaled slowly and stood. "It doesn't hurt to have a conversation, Luca. But it's nothing we need to talk about now. Get changed, press conference is in a few."

As the door shut behind him, I continued to stare at the trophy. The room felt hotter than it should with the AC blasting, and that feeling was bubbling back up—the one where no matter how hard I fought or how well I drove, things around me would never change.

Rennen F1 wasn't going to happen.

Michael Rossi, three-time World Champion for Hermes, had no intention of watching his son wear another team's colors. Hermes was his legacy.

As far as my father was concerned, I was going to die in his shadow.

Chapter Twelve

Georgia

Once the podium celebration was over, I was moved back to the medical tent, and after some more fluids, I was beginning to feel like a new person. The podium celebration had breathed new life into me. Getting up there and being able to accept the trophy, it gave my critics less fuel to the raging fire that seemed to be my racing career.

Or so I hoped.

"How do you feel?" Isabelle called out from behind me.

"Much better, thank you."

"That was an excellent race today. You showed great pace, and I'm sorry we didn't prepare you enough as a racer. Next time, tell us when there's an issue. The championship isn't more important than your safety." Her words hung heavy. It wasn't often Isabelle admitted fault, and I didn't take the apology lightly. I nodded slowly, searching her face.

"Well, thankfully Henri was quick to bring me in here."

"You mean Luca," she corrected.

I blinked in confusion. "Luca?"

Pausing, I closed my eyes, trying to remember the events that had led to the medical tent. I remembered my vision blurring, my hands trying to grip the halo. I'd somehow made it to the weigh station. And then, as things were going dark, a familiar scent of lilacs and pine trees surrounded me. Where did I know that cologne from?

Then it clicked. It was *Luca's* cologne. Somehow, he'd sensed my desperation and had been the one to catch me as I fell.

But how did he know?

I sat up a bit straighter, swinging my feet off the edge of the cot. The thought of him noticing my distress before I had even started falling unsettled me. A strange warmth bloomed in my chest, one that had absolutely nothing to do with dehydration.

"I-I need to th-thank him," I said suddenly.

"Well, fortunately, you'll be able to do that at the press conference. Starts in thirty."

Of course it does. Lucky me.

When fighting for the podium celebration, I knew that it meant I'd have to show up for the post-race press conference. Hell, I suspected even if I didn't make the podium celebration, they'd still have dragged my unconscious body to the stage just to show all of the journalists that they were right.

Isabelle grabbed my hand, as if she sensed the war going on within me. "You earned third place, Georgia. P8 to P3 is something to be proud of. Make sure the lions know that."

–

The press conference room was buzzing with reporters, cameras flashing and voices discussing the race. I strode into the crowded room, spotting Luca sitting at the table up front, his hands clasped tightly together as he chatted with Henri.

"Thank you for today," I said softly, handing him his water bottle. Luca grabbed it, his fingers gently brushing against mine before twisting off the cap and peering inside. "You should finish what's in here."

Nodding my thanks, I took a seat next to my brother as I took another sip from the bottle.

Henri leaned over, whispering, "Hermes water bottle looks good in your hand."

"Oh yeah? Are you going to give me your seat next year?" I winked, earning me a light chuckle from Luca.

Before Henri could fire back, the lead press officer, Michael Clifton, jumped in with his introductions. The journalists started with typical, safe questions. Tire management, pit stop strategies, temperature regulation. All the greatest hits.

When the conversation shifted to temperature, one of the broadcasters turned his attention to me, and I knew it was time to pay penance for today's performance.

"How's it feel, Georgia, to be on the podium with your brother?" Always a soft question before they delved into the humiliation.

"Truthfully, it doesn't matter who is on the higher step, being on the podium with my brother is a dream come true." Henri gave me an enthusiastic high five, which I awkwardly returned.

"You looked pretty rough at the end there—how are you feeling now?"

Ah, there it was. I knew the media were all itching to dig into this, like a bunch of grave robbers, they couldn't let this stay buried. Turning to Luca, he flashed me an encouraging, toothy smile, and I knew what I had to do.

Divert. Make them laugh.

"Yeah, you know, I probably shouldn't have indulged myself in all of that delicious, spicy Cuban food this week," I joked with as much lightheartedness one could muster after passing out in front of thousands of people. "There's only so much heat a girl can handle."

Can't believe I just said that.

Henri gave me a slow side-eye. Luca, however, let out a real chuckle, his shoulders shaking as he leaned back slightly in his chair.

"All jokes aside, it was a tough one today. The water device broke in the car, and the lack of water definitely got to me."

Nice and easy, Georgia.

"Well, we're glad you're okay." The journalist paused, and I did another breathing count, trying to soothe the tension in my shoulders. "But I have to ask, since there's a big push to get more women in F1, do you think your heat sensitivity has anything to do with your body not being able to handle the pressure in the same way?"

He forgot to add "*as the men*," but I knew it was what he meant. I stared at the reporter blankly. Angered, yet unsurprised.

So much for the joke idea. Just as I was about to throw Luca's suggestion out the window and give the guy a piece of my mind, a thick Italian accent caught me off guard.

"Did you not just hear Georgia? It was the lack of water. What does that have to do with being a woman?" The voice was rough and laced with frustration. I turned to the right, and saw Luca leaning back in his chair, arms crossed with a pointed glare.

"You know, we all struggle with water consumption in the cars. Our water contraptions break, but we have to press on." Henri spoke up, attempting to clear the tension that had settled into the room.

I cleared my throat and locked eyes with the reporter. "It feels worth mentioning that Lily was able to complete 98 percent of the race without passing out, so I would say no, it has nothing to do with my gender."

A reminder to the vultures that another woman sat on this grid. Lily had been phenomenal today, and she so rarely got the credit she deserved.

"I learned about my limits this weekend, but even with the lack of water, I still came in third. That's what matters. But I can assure you, next race I'll be back better than ever. I mean, after eight years of missing out on the Monza podium," I said, shooting Luca a sideways glance, "someone has to show Luca how to win at his home race."

The room chuckled, a few even applauded, but Luca didn't take his eyes off me. That Cheshire cat smile was back—dangerous, effortless, infuriatingly attractive.

"We'll see about that, *amore*. We'll see."

Chapter Thirteen

Georgia

"*Damn, the make-up sex must be amazing. Georgia and Luca totally had us fooled into thinking they hated each other!*"

Lily nearly let her phone slip from her grip as she keeled over, laughter echoing through the halls of the Valkyrie offices. She was deep into the social media comments on my latest post—a congratulatory nod to Luca that Nora had insisted we publish.

Groaning, I rubbed the creases in my forehead. "Why are the comments so obsessed with my and Luca's sex life?"

Lily flipped her auburn hair gleefully, still reveling in her social media finds. "Because, as I keep saying, that man is sex on wheels. Not that you've taken him for a spin yet."

"It's been one week! We're barely even official!"

She gave me a look so exaggerated it deserved its own Oscar. "Which is a whole seven days longer than I would have taken." Her eyebrows—and entire body—were practically dancing with excitement. "I can only imagine what the teams have in store for you this week, considering it's Luca's home race."

After the whirlwind of Miami, we finally had a week off between races. A precious week to regroup and dissect what went right and, more importantly, what went wrong, before heading to Monza. But as the week dwindled down, I knew it was time to address the elephant lurking in the room.

If Miami was the appetizer to our relationship, Monza had to be the main course.

Nora poked her head out of the conference room, her voice echoing down the corridor. "Hurry up, you two!"

Lily entered first, and her high-pitched shriek should have been my cue to retreat back to the safety of my office. But before I could make my escape, Isabelle was ushering me into the brightly lit conference room.

The moment I stepped inside, I understood Lily's shriek.

On the massive projector screen, clear as day, was a photo of Luca—shirtless, muscles glistening with sweat like a goddamn Greek statue carved by the sun itself. And there I was, standing beside him, staring up with what could only be described as the dumbest, most star-struck grin I had ever worn.

Kill me. Actually, launch me into the sun.

Laughter pulled me out of my shock. Lily was cackling like a schoolgirl as she stared at the boardroom's TV. Mortified didn't even come close to describing how embarrassed I felt. I prided myself in being a serious, level-headed racer. I had spent my entire career cultivating a reputation as a competitive rival to the male drivers—not a swooning 25-year-old girl ogling an attractive athlete.

"Take a seat, Georgia," Nora announced sweetly, like she wasn't broadcasting my embarrassment in 4K.

Snickering, Lily added, "She would, but she's still trying to peel her eyes off of Luca's abs."

Huffing out a groan in annoyance, I took a seat across from her. The screen displayed the infamous post, the comments overlayed in bold text beneath it.

"Glad social media is talking about my ogling," I grumbled. "Lucky me."

"Oooh, look at this one!" Before I could protest, Lily proudly held out her phone. "It says, '*Looks like Georgia Dubois has moved on with a new driver in the paddock, Luca Rossi, son of famous F1 champion Michael Rossi. Sources tell us that rumored ex-boyfriend and fellow racer Éliott Simon is fuming at the match.*'"

I dragged a hand down my face. "I'm sure Éliott will love that."

That rumor had been haunting me since F2. Heaven forbid a woman have a platonic friendship with a male driver. If Éliott and I had so much as shared a coffee, the press turned it into a candlelit dinner with matching tattoos. That was part of why I hated this fake dating idea, it almost gave validity to their gossip.

Nora cleared her throat, trying—*and failing*—to hide her smile. "Right, well, needless to say, things are going great in the social media department. Fans are *loving* the two of you! His catching you before you hit the ground? Absolutely priceless. Defending you from the journalist during the press conference? The cherry on top." Nora clapped her hands together, her face lighting up into a large grin.

I rolled my eyes, forcing a half-smile that barely masked my bubbling irritation. Luca might have fiercely defended me in front of the media circus, but I'd also stood up for myself. Not that anyone mentioned that in any of the post-race articles. Apparently, when I defended myself, I was being combative. But when Luca did it? He was my hero.

A woman defending her honor wasn't nearly as interesting as a man doing it.

"Alright," Nora continued. "Miami was an incredibly successful teaser for the fans, and due to this, Luca's manager and I have decided to move up the timeline a tad."

A knot of apprehension twisted in my stomach. "How much is *a tad*?" With this being Luca's home race, I knew that they'd want this relationship to be front and center.

Nora hesitated, never a good sign. "Next week, you and Luca should be more public in the paddock..." The uncertainty in her voice made my spine stiffen. I leaned forward, waving for her to continue. "It's time for us to go official. As far as fans are concerned, you've been dating since before Barcelona. For this race, you need to properly look like a couple. Do things like hold hands, attend a couple of events together, take photos with one another," Nora said quickly, and I knew she was silently praying I hadn't heard her. There was a brief moment of silence as everyone watched me with bated breath.

"Fine." *Not that I had a choice.* Nora let out a sigh of relief.

Monza wasn't just any race. It was *his* race. Luca's home soil—a chance to show off and potentially win in front of his home crowd. Outside of winning the championship, a racer's "home race" was the crown jewel of their trophy collection, but it also meant you had to put on a special dog and pony show. At these sorts of races, everyone was laser focused not just on you, but your family, friends, and relationships.

This wasn't going to be a casual PR stunt. This was going to be a spectacle, and there was no hiding from it.

"Excellent! I'll email you the rest of your itinerary. Oh, and just one more thing." She said it far too casually for the chaos she was about to unleash. "Hermes are booking two rooms next to each other for Monza. Since it's Luca's home race, fans will expect you guys to be all *lovey-dovey*. Didn't make sense to have you in separate hotels."

My head snapped up. "Separate rooms, right?"

After his rescue at the Miami race, my feelings on Luca had softened, but that didn't mean I wanted to spend every waking moment with him. Hanging out with Luca might not seem quite so terrifying, but I still needed *some* personal space.

"Yes, yes," Nora assured me.

"Shame," Lily piped up. "Sharing a room with Luca means you'd get to see him shirtless again. And we all know how much you *loved* it the first time."

Lily avoided my shoe as I hurled it across the room.

Chapter Fourteen

Luca

The Miami Grand Prix had been my best race of the season. After I swallowed my pride and listened to Georgia's advice, I found myself second in qualifying. Turns out watching Henri's practice sessions was invaluable advice, not that I'd admit that to Georgia. While there was no hope of convincing the team to let me pass Henri during the Grand Prix, for the first time in a long time, just being on the podium felt like a win.

Sitting in the brightly lit conference room at the Hermes headquarters, I waited for the rest of the social media team to arrive so they could debrief me on how they planned to *ruin* my home race weekend with a ramp-up in Georgia's and my relationship. I kept reminding myself that the sooner my reputation was back on track, the sooner I could be rid of my parents' meddling in my personal life.

My father waltzed in, patting me on the back as he stared at me like the sun shone out of my ass. A sure-fire way of telling me he wanted something.

"What a great race, Luca. Rescuing Georgia like that? Genius! And then defending her at the press conference? Very proud," he congratulated, kissing the tips of his fingers like a chef who had just finished an award-winning meal.

I forced a smile, ignoring the twist in my stomach. Not a single word about the race itself, my *actual* achievement from Miami. In my father's eyes a good racing result wasn't going to fix my reputation or the damage I'd done to the Rossi name, but rescuing Georgia? Now, that was priceless PR.

Ridiculous memes of me wearing a cape, holding Georgia like a superhero, had surfaced all over the media. While Edward found them to be hilarious, I found the whole thing to be almost insulting. I wasn't Georgia's hero, I was just a decent human being.

"I'm not going to leave a driver who is suffering. Plus, that journalist is an asshole in press conferences. I've been wanting to put him in his place for a while."

Did everyone think so low of me that no one expected me to help her?

Henri, sitting across from me, shifted awkwardly. "How *did* you know something was wrong with Georgia?" There it was: the quiet frustration in his voice. He wasn't upset with me. He was upset with himself. That he hadn't been the one to notice.

"I just knew." A teasing grin crept onto my face. Henri flipped open the purple folder in front of him, but I could see that the pages were upside down.

Pretending to read. Avoiding eye contact. Classic Dubois pride.

Matteo clapped his hands, garnering both of our attention. "The fans are loving this relationship. Monza is going to be a great race to go fully public. In fact, Georgia has thought of something fun to start the week off!"

"*Fun?*" I choked on my coffee, some of it spilling onto the table. "Oh, do tell?"

"Georgia thought it would be nice to do some karting at that local track you used to love."

Of course she did.

"Let me get this straight. You want me to go *karting* with the few days I have off before my home race?" I narrowed my eyes at Henri, my voice filled with accusation. "Can your sister do anything that doesn't involve racing?"

"What's wrong with karting? Sounds fun." The genuine confusion on my teammate's face reminded me why he also drove me up the wall.

"I don't see why the entire week has to be consumed with racing," I demanded.

"Because it's a fucking Grand Prix week, Luca!" The unwavering firmness in my father's gaze made it clear that escape from this situation was utterly impossible. "It'll be a good media day for you both. End of story."

There was no doubt in my mind of who'd *actually* thought of this idea.

With each inhale, my chest tightened, and I tried to focus on anything but how heavy my head felt. Exhaling, I tried to get out from under the suffocating feeling that had overtaken my throat. It felt like a hand had wrapped itself around my trachea, and all I could do was watch as it squeezed the life out of me. Matteo and Henri's voices faded into the background, and I closed my eyes, sinking deeper into my chair as I hoped to silence the roaring screaming in my head.

Get it together, Luca.

I forced a breath in. Then another.

Matteo's voice cut through my thoughts, and I slowly opened my eyes. "And who knows, maybe if you get on the podium, Georgia will give you a little congratulatory kiss."

Henri bristled next to me, his face no longer smiling. "Let's not get ahead of ourselves," Henri said dryly, and my jaw clenched at his condescending tone.

Was I not good enough for his beloved sister?

"Don't worry, mate, no one wants to kiss your sister less than I do." It was a joke—mostly. But Henri didn't laugh. His expression stayed hard, unreadable. Something flickered behind his eyes, but I couldn't tell if it was relief or insult. He didn't want me to kiss his sister, but he was clearly offended on her behalf.

"Oh, another thing, you and Georgia will have adjacent hotel rooms so we can easily get footage of you two coming and going from the paddock."

I couldn't resist stealing another glance at Henri, his arms crossed over his chest. The number one benefit of dating my teammate's sister?

Watching Hermes's golden boy squirm.

While Henri had agreed to go along with the idea to help his sister, he'd made it clear he wasn't particularly thrilled it was me. After one of our practice sessions in Miami, I'd overheard him grumbling to Edward about how he'd wished Valkyrie had picked Éliott. Apparently Éliott was more trustworthy than I was, a comment that hit a little deeper than I cared to admit.

"Cheer up, Henri. Maybe I can steal some Valkyrie secrets from her room." Annoying Henri was probably not my smartest move, considering I'd likely need my teammate's help to win in Monza.

But the twitch of his jaw was incredibly satisfying.

"Why would you be in my sister's hotel room?" Henri challenged.

"Oh, I can think of a few reasons why a *boyfriend* would be in his *girlfriend's* hotel room."

Henri shot me a warning look, his lips tight with frustration. "Don't push it, Rossi."

No promises.

Chapter Fifteen

Luca

"Fuucckkkk!"

My tires screeched as I slammed on the brakes too early, causing my go-kart to skid into the grass. Georgia's kart zipped past me and there was no way I could catch her. After another five laps, I crossed the black line that signaled the end of the race and drove my kart into the pit stop station. Probably should have been a little embarrassed that Georgia had beaten me, but I was so over this press day, I couldn't find it within myself to care.

"You hit the brakes a little too hard back there!" Georgia called out. I narrowed my eyes at her rather large, sickening grin as she hopped out of her kart. Climbing out of my own car, I rubbed the grease from my hands onto my pants, giving her a curt nod.

"Show-off," I grumbled, trailing behind Georgia as we made our way to our press day lunch. Taking a seat at the table, I politely waved at the owner who took that as his cue to come over, much to my dismay.

"Luca Rossi at my karting track!" Antonio gushed. He eyed the two of us like we'd fallen from the heavens. "*Grazie!* I am just so happy to have the two of you here. I couldn't believe it when Hermes called and asked if you could enjoy a nice rest day at my karting track!"

"Rest day" was one way to describe today.

"We're happy to be here," Georgia smiled. "I used to love this track as a kid, the twists and turns are so fun. One of the best karting tracks in Europe."

"Indeed, thanks for having us, Antonio. My father told me to say hello."

He clapped his hands, his face bright as I mentioned my legendary father. "Well, I'll leave you two to it. I'll be over with some sandwiches in a few, hmm?"

Georgia and I nodded our thanks, and I reached for my water glass, taking a small sip. Her face lit up with a bright smile as she watched the ongoing karting race.

"I haven't been karting in so long..."

"Really?" There was no hiding the disbelief in my voice. "Figured when you weren't on your simulator, you'd be on a karting track outside Monaco."

"Just haven't had time this year." She shrugged. "I'm looking forward to the small break after Monaco."

"... so you can go do more racing?" As soon as the words slipped out of my mouth, I almost regretted my snide tone.

Georgia scrunched her nose. "I do *other* things."

"Ah yes. Like paint," I teased.

She made it too easy.

"Keep up the attitude, Rossi, and I might just drag you to an art exhibition when we're in Monaco." Her smug face told me exactly how uncultured she thought I was, and I almost wanted to take her up on the offer just to prove her wrong.

"Good. It might be nice for us to be seen doing something other than racing."

She scoffed, but said nothing else. My point had been made.

Antonio returned with a tray of sandwiches piled high with prosciutto, mozzarella, and fresh basil. Absolute heaven.

Georgia reached for one immediately. "So, any movement on the Helios Sunglasses sponsorship?" she asked between bites.

"No," I sighed. "Not surprised. To make matters worse, Anthony's dad has offered Hermes some additional funding if the Helios Sunglasses contract doesn't come through."

I couldn't bring myself to mention the requirements, although I suspected Georgia could make an educated guess as to what they were. There's only one reason the father of a wannabe driver would offer millions of euros to a team.

Georgia sighed. "I can't imagine his terms being worth it. The team would get more money from having a second driver scoring in the top ten and getting points for the team than taking Anthony's family money. The fans aren't going to accept a subpar driver, not from Italy's oldest racing team."

Every time a driver scored in the top ten, the teams got points which turned into money at the end of the season, but I knew I'd have to do a hell of a lot better than one second-place finish to replace the funding they would get from Anthony. I needed to keep getting on the podium.

"So," she said, wiping her hands on a napkin. "Feeling ready for Monza this week?"

No.

"Yup," I lied, emphasizing the "p" at the end.

Every mention of Monza made my chest tighten, but of course, it was all anyone wanted to talk about. I knew I couldn't admit the truth, couldn't tell her how terrified I was of the upcoming race. How I'd barely slept this week.

Of all the drivers on the grid, I hated the idea of Georgia knowing my weakness. She was strong and confident—she reminded me so much of my father. Fear had never been his weakness, and it certainly wasn't hers.

Georgia assessed me with another blink. "How does Antonio know your father?" she asked finally. A better subject change; she learned quick.

"I used to race here a lot as a kid. It was my favorite track, and my father brought me here anytime he had a spare weekend." My throat tightened as I choked on my words, hating how small I sounded.

I looked out at the track, blinking against the bright sun, and there it was: my childhood. The podium where I'd stood at age seven, beaming up at my father while he clapped like I'd just won a world championship. Some of my best memories with my father were at this karting track.

I could still remember that feeling of watching my dad cheer me on. That look of pride in his eyes. In Miami, I'd had a taste of that euphoria again, a reminder of what it was like to win. Part of me wanted more.

"Why did you enjoy this track so much?" Georgia's question brought me out of my haze.

"It's like you said, the twists and turns are fun. Plus, it was close enough to home, so my father and I were able to race here together whenever he had a break."

"I noticed a photo of you and your father in your driver's room, is that from this track?" I nodded, once again taking a moment to gaze out over the active karting race.

"I used to love it here," I said finally.

"Used to? Well, sounds like we have some work to do then."

Before I could spiral further into my own head, a loud voice boomed through the space.

"Who is ready to get their ass kicked?" Edward pulled me into a hug, my neck in a chokehold as he ruffled my hair. Behind him stood Lily and Henri, the two of them shaking their heads at his antics.

"Wha-what are you doing here?" After the exhausting morning, relief surged as Edward stood in front of me, grinning away like a buffoon. His dimpled smile was a welcome sight, even if it came with my teammate.

"Thought I'd come kick your ass on the karting track before doing it in Monza," Edward laughed. "Dragged these two along so they can watch me dominate!" He nodded his head over to Lily and Henri, who were still standing there with amused looks.

Of course, they're here to race. And just like that, the relief was gone.

"I'm always down for any chance I can get to show you boys how to win," Lily chuckled.

"Right." Georgia clapped her hands, motioning to the four of us. "The track is ready for a little *friendly* competition." She stuck her tongue out at Edward, who returned the favor.

"Friendly my ass," I muttered. As if five professional Formula 1 drivers could have a noncompetitive race on a track.

"Aww, come on, Luca, scared of a little competition?" Edward laughed, and I felt myself relax slightly at his beaming face. It was hard to be upset in his presence, and part of me suspected Georgia knew that when she'd invited him.

"Fine. If you all want to get in some practice losing before you do it again this weekend, then don't let me stop you."

Georgia stepped forward. "To make things more interesting, I was thinking we'd select the starting order the old-fashioned way: rock, paper, scissors."

Did the paddock's most serious and competitive driver just suggest we substitute a qualifying session for a silly game notoriously known for its randomness?

"You're serious?"

"We don't joke about rock, paper, scissors, Rossi," she said solemnly, although she couldn't stop a grin from crossing her lips.

One by one, hands flew, but the final round came down to me and Georgia.

"Alright, Rossi, on three." We both raised our fists.

"One, two, three!" Our hands shot out simultaneously, Georgia with paper and me with rock. She let out a triumphant cheer, pumping her fist in the air.

"Don't get used to it, Dubois!" I yelled after her. "That'll be the only winning you'll be doing today." She waved me off before heading to her kart.

After another quick water break, and some strategic photos of the five of us friends chatting, Antonio ushered me over to the lane entrance.

"Good luck, Luca!" He handed me a small, carefully wrapped gift, his face beaming. I peeled back the layers of gold tissue paper, and my chest tightened. Inside was a black-and-white photo of a little boy, holding a trophy much too big for him, standing next to his father. The smile on Antonio's face was blinding. "It's you and your dad, over two decades ago. I remember that day. You'd won the race by pulling off some daring pass, and afterward, your father told me he knew you'd be a Formula 1 driver, just like himself."

"Wow. I can't believe you still have this," I whispered.

That particular race win had been incredibly special. Holding that trophy as a young boy, I wanted nothing more than to be a Formula 1 driver like my father.

He clapped his hands on my shoulder. "Now go teach those Monégasque drivers a lesson, hmm?"

"*Sì*." I nodded, slipping the photo into my racing suit where it rested close to my heart.

I made my way to the starting line, getting into the second-place starting position.

"Alright, first one around the course twenty times is the winner!" Antonio called out as I settled into my P2 spot, flickering my eyes to Georgia, whose car was just slightly ahead of mine. When the final light turned green, I pushed the pedal to the floor and shot forward, launching off the second-place line. The track's curves, once familiar, now felt like home again.

Twist. Brake. Accelerate. Slide.

Georgia was right. Racing here on the winding track, it was just *fun*.

After the tenth lap, I could hear Henri's engine roaring behind me. Ignoring him, I continued to focus on Georgia as my kart crept closer to hers on each lap, chasing her down like a cat taunting its prey. By lap fifteen, I was practically on top of her, but I let my kart simply rest beside hers, knowing that with each lap, Georgia would be second-guessing her moves, wondering why I hadn't passed her.

As soon as I slid into the penultimate lap, I knew it was my time to shine, my time to remind them all that I was still a force to be reckoned with.

Approaching a sharp turn, I seized the opportunity I'd been waiting for. I dove to the inside, my kart hugging the track's edges as I braked hard and late. The tires screeched in protest as I slid past Georgia as we went side by side. The moment I felt the rush of fresh air in front of me, I knew I'd overtaken her. I shot past her, grinning like an idiot as the checkered flag waved in the distance. Crossing the line first wasn't just satisfying, it was joy. Pure, uncomplicated, childhood joy.

I yanked off my helmet, hair damp with sweat, and threw both arms in the air before taking a deep bow. Considering I was behind all of them in the *actual* championship, I probably shouldn't have looked quite so smug.

"No need to be *too* impressed with my victory," I teased, taking a second bow.

Georgia marched up to me, pointing her finger at my chest, but I just continued to smirk at her sour face. I knew Georgia would be upset with my pass, but seeing her steaming in front of me made that move even more delicious. She'd had her fun for nineteen laps, but like hell was I going to let a Monégasque win on *my* track.

If I thought she was cute when she smiled, she was even cuter standing in front of me, face red with her ears practically on fire.

Forget cute. Furious Georgia was gorgeous.

"That move was *dangerous*, Luca!" I let out another laugh at her ferocity, pulling her flush against my chest as I wrapped her in my arms. Kissing the top of her head, I gave the photographer an opportunity to sneak in a quick, intimate photo. Georgia let out a small groan, but I was pleasantly surprised when she leaned in, resting her head on my chest. If I was a betting man, I would have sworn she was smiling.

"You're cute when you're being a sore loser," I whispered, earning me a huff. She pulled away, flashing me a small grin in return, and I couldn't help but beam back at her.

"Feel like I just got sandbagged." Even through her groan, Georgia couldn't hide the growing smile on her face. There was something adorable about watching her struggle between her frustration at losing and her willingness to admit she had lost gracefully, at least in front of the camera.

"Correction. You *did* just get sandbagged," I smugly corrected, although the smirk on her face told me that while I had won the race, she had won something else.

"So, I guess spending the afternoon karting wasn't such a bad idea after all?" Georgia looked like the proverbial cat who had got the cream.

Cocky, beautiful, annoying.

"We'll see if you still feel that way after I make you go golfing with me next week." My retort did nothing to wipe the cocky grin off her face.

"Now where has *this* Luca been all season?" Edward had his hands on his hips as he stared at me in disbelief.

"What can I say? Couldn't let a bunch of non-Italian drivers win on my turf."

"I don't think even the great Michael Rossi could have defended that pass," he snorted. "Toying with Georgia like that? Thought I was watching Michael Rossi out there!" He nudged me playfully in the ribs, his eyes crinkling with laughter.

"I guess the apple doesn't fall too far from the tree."

The words came out easily, and for a brief moment, they felt right.

For months, I'd convinced myself that racing just wasn't for me anymore. That the dread I felt getting into the car was proof I didn't belong in one.

But after another few races around the track and a round of beers at a local bar, I considered that perhaps that was just an easy excuse, because as much as I hated to admit it, today had been *fun*.

Chapter Sixteen

Georgia

"Okay, spill, how perfect was the karting date?" Even over the phone, I could feel Nora's eagerness for all the juicy details. As much as I wanted to hang up and slink into my bed after a day of travel, I needed the lowdown on the podcast recording event with Luca tonight.

"Honestly—" and I knew I was going to regret saying this "—it was fun, better than expected."

"Oh?" I could hear her crooning on the other end of the line.

"Luca noticeably spent the morning sulking, but after his vicious win, he definitely loosened up." When Luca's dad first mentioned the idea to me, I was excited, until Luca showed up with a miserable frown and bad attitude.

"Vicious win?" Nora giggled. "Georgia, it was *karting*."

I scoffed. "I watched the video of the race, and I'm pretty sure the bastard was toying with me! For almost ten laps Luca could have passed me but didn't, and then in the last lap he casually sailed by like he owned the place. Cheeky bastard."

I wanted to kick him for how dangerous that overtake was at the karting track, but when I saw his Cheshire cat grin and gleaming brown eyes, I couldn't help but smile back. The joy on his face was contagious, and after another three races, including a second win for Luca, he was all smiles and laughter. Inviting the other drivers had helped smooth over the tension. We were just kids again, doing a sport that we loved.

No requirements. No demands. Just *fun*.

"Well, let's hope he got that win out of his system, eh?" Nora laughed. "Don't need the enemy getting too confident."

"Yeah, it was nice to watch him and Henri race again. Luca has always been known for his late braking and strategic overtakes, but somewhere along the way, he's sort of lost that drive, that hunger to win..." Nora's silence made me realize I was rambling, and I quickly inhaled a breath to slow myself down.

"Sounds like you all had a phenomenal time. Love to hear it!"

"Let's not get ahead of ourselves. I still wanted to kill him half of the time," I mumbled back dryly.

"Well, that's an improvement on the usual 80 percent, so I'll take it," Nora teased. "Plus, it made for an amazing announcement post on your profiles. The picture of the two of you racing each other in those karts was just perfection." I could hear Nora kissing the tips of her fingers on the other side of the line. "Your post alone got almost half a million likes!"

"So Lily told me," I moaned. "Guess there's no turning back now." Not that I could exactly backtrack after the Miami fiasco.

"Keep your head up, Georgia. It'll be worth it in the end." Nora's voice softened, a gentle reassurance that seeped through the phone's static. "So where are you now?"

"I just reached the hotel room. One moment, I'm about to walk in."

Grabbing the key from my purse, I opened the door to my room, letting out a gasp of surprise. Sunlight poured in through the expansive bay windows, illuminating the elegant suite, which was filled with beautiful paintings and ornate furniture. Within the room were two bedrooms and a vast living room.

"Now this I could get used to!" I exclaimed, my voice echoing off the high ceilings. "I mean *two bedrooms*? Maybe we'd have enough money for next year if we cut down on the hotel budget." I threw my bag onto the plush sofa before I immediately investigated the large kitchen.

"You drivers always get the nicest rooms," Nora sighed. "Right, well, I'll leave you to it. Glad the karting wasn't a disaster. And remember, tonight is Luca's podcast taping, so we need to be on our best behavior."

As part of F1's initiative to pull in younger fans, they'd started interviewing the drivers before each of their home races as part of a new podcast series called *Home Stretch*. Each episode was recorded in front of a live studio audience full of superfans.

"Yes, yes," I grumbled, running a hand through my hair as I reluctantly agreed.

"Good, and who knows, you might even learn a thing or two?"

"Oh look… I'm going through… a tunnel…" Not my proudest moment, but I'd heard this lecture no less than three times now and it all boiled down to one thing: avoid becoming Sassy Dubois at all costs.

Glancing down at my phone, I noticed a new text message from Henri lighting up the screen.

Henri:
I'll drive us to the podcast recording. Meet downstairs at 7 p.m.?

Georgia:
See you then.

Stepping into the shower, I turned the knob until the water was just shy of scalding, letting steam envelop me. Eucalyptus wafted through the shower from the incense the hotel had left. For the first time in what felt like days, my muscles stopped buzzing.

"You can do this, Georgia. You can survive being Luca Rossi's girlfriend this week," I reassured myself, breathing in the warm, soothing steam.

The hotel room door made a loud bang, catching my attention.

Fuck, has someone broken in?

Panic surged as I stood naked in the shower, contemplating my next move. As a female athlete, I'd received countless harassing fan mail and social media messages, some with death threats, over the course of my career. Not everyone was thrilled that the sport was "letting women in."

Probably just Nora here to fill me in on some extras for the weekend.

I scanned the bathroom like it was a weapons locker and reached for the only viable object: one of my high-heeled shoes, the best I could do in the relatively empty bathroom. With only a towel wrapped around me, I stepped out of the shower with my shoe gripped tightly.

But as I walked into the living room, I saw something *almost* worse than a rogue fan: Luca Rossi in my hotel room, grinning like he'd just won the lottery.

"Well, hello to you too." Luca's eyes roamed unapologetically over my body. "I guess after Miami, it's only fair I also get to see *you* shirtless."

So, he had seen the photo. Fabulous.

"What the fuck are you doing here? I thought you were a stalker!" I screamed, retreating back into the bathroom. Poking my head out from behind the door, I motioned for him to explain himself, but Luca just leaned against the wall, arms crossed with an amused look.

"And what, you were going to bludgeon them to death with a shoe?" he snickered.

"Answer the question, Rossi!"

"Well, according to the front desk, this room is mine." Dropping his duffle on the couch, Luca added, "So, I think the question is, why are you *here*, in *my* shower?"

"This is my room, you idiot." Seething didn't begin to explain the emotion I was feeling.

"Well, looks like we're roommates, 'cause clearly my key card works." He motioned toward the door with his key like a buffoon.

"Absolutely not. No way. Not happening. Now, turn around so I can call Nora! And don't get comfortable. I'm sure she'll get this sorted."

He just chuckled and headed to his room, whistling away.

Frantic, I grabbed my phone and dialed Nora with the desperation of someone trying to win concert tickets off the radio.

"Nora, there's been a mistake," I said, my voice laced with panic. "Luca is in my suite! I thought you said these rooms were *next* to each other."

"Wha-what do you mean he's there?" From her tone, I could tell she was equally confused. "Let me call the hotel and get this sorted out."

The five minutes Nora had me on hold felt like a lifetime.

"Georgia, you there?" I picked up the phone so quickly it went flying out of my hands.

"Please tell me you have some good news," I begged.

"Unfortunately, Georgia, when the Hermes coordinator phoned to get the rooms next to each other, the hotel heard two rooms side by side, so they booked you a suite with two bedrooms in it, and with the Grand Prix this weekend, the hotel is completely booked..." She trailed off at the end, but truth was, I'd stopped listening after the word *unfortunately*. Hanging up the phone, I threw it down on my bed in frustration.

After taking five minutes to gather my thoughts, I threw on my pink dress that Nora had purchased for tonight and then marched into the living room.

"Alright, Luca, we need to set some boundar—" I opened the door to Luca standing before me, towel slung dangerously low around his hips, droplets of water trailing down his chest like the universe was mocking me. His dark hair was damp, clinging to his forehead, and the faint scent of soap and shampoo lingered in the air. His white towel was loosely draped around his waist, seemingly defying gravity as if a gentle breeze could send it cascading to the floor at any moment.

God, I almost wish it would, I thought as horror filled me at my own revelation. Luca popped his head up, a grin crawling on his face.

"Enjoying the view?" he asked, smug as sin.

I snapped my head away. "Put your clothes back on! This is a shared area in case you forgot." *Asshole.*

"And deny you the opportunity to get a *second* peek at your favorite racer? What kind of man do you think I am?"

"A man that's probably never been told to put his shirt back on by a woman, but there's a first time for everything," I hissed.

Luca made a show of grabbing his chest dramatically. "Oh, how you wound me!"

"No, but I could," I muttered, stalking across the room.

"Ah, yes, with your scary high heels." Luca grinned at my defiance, waltzing into his bedroom, where he disappeared for a minute before rejoining me, now wearing a pair of slacks and a purple polo, his dark brown wavy hair still damp from the shower.

I leaned casually against the wall, attempting to look as unbothered as possible while I picked at my fingernails. As he strolled past, he stopped, then pivoted, stepping closer. Without a word, he braced both hands against the wall on either side of me, boxing me in.

"If you play your cards right, *amore*, you might be able to see *more* of me."

His breath grazed my neck, and goosebumps chased up my spine. Gorgeous brown eyes stared deeply into mine. Warmth started to build, my legs trembling more than I cared to admit. Having Luca this close to me, his breath tickling my neck as he softly whispered, it felt like my nerves were being set on fire. Despite wanting to come up with something witty, all I could think about was how close his lips were to mine, how good that kiss was from a few weeks ago.

Get it together, Georgia.

I tilted my chin, forced a saccharine smile, and met his gaze. "Well, let's hope I have a losing hand then, because what I really want is to see *less* of you!"

He laughed, so deep and genuine that it startled me. Pushing off the wall, he gave me a wink as he headed for the door. Silence engulfed the room as he exited, his chuckling fading as he made his way down the hallway.

Chapter Seventeen

Georgia

"So, Luca, rumor has it that F1's most eligible bachelor is no longer single," Josh, the *Home Stretch* host, said slyly. After opening with a nice bio about Luca, his history of karting, and his entry into Formula 1, it was clearly time for the juicier details to unravel. Shifting uncomfortably in my seat next to Henri, I watched as Luca leaned into the microphone. Josh wiggled his eyebrows seductively, prompting laughter from the audience.

My brother gently elbowed my side, a reminder to drop the scowl.

"You heard that rumor, too," Luca grinned, "I mean, can you blame me? With a smile that gorgeous and talent that enormous, it was pretty easy to see that Georgia is someone special." The audience erupted into a symphony of oohs and ahhs, which Luca played into with a flick of his hand.

"I'm sure it wasn't easy getting her brother's approval, even if he is your teammate?" Josh gestured to Henri in the audience, who simply waved back with a crafty grin.

"Well, I was basically Georgia's biggest fan from the day she signed her F1 contract. I did my best to drop hints to Henri, but after preseason, I finally mustered up the courage to ask her out. My teammate sort of joked that if

I hurt his sister, he'd be sure to ram his car into mine—but I told him not to worry, Georgia would undeniably beat him to it. She is the faster Dubois after all." Henri scoffed, his arms crossed in annoyance, much to the audience's amusement.

Good grief, I thought to myself. *Had they practiced this?*

"You know, I have to say, we were all kinds of shocked when we saw those photos of you two after her race win in Barcelona. Not to be rude, but we didn't think you could pull a lovely lady like Georgia." A subtle insult if I'd ever heard one.

Just ask the real question, Josh, I mused to myself. *How did Georgia Dubois manage to bag dashing playboy Luca Rossi?*

If only they knew the truth.

"What? You saying she's out of my league?" Luca pretended to feign shock, an effort no one else in the crowd attempted to do. "You know, Josh, I was as surprised as you were. You see, the rest of the world sees her as this quiet racer who only has eyes for winning, everything else be damned. But the Georgia I know? It couldn't be further from the truth." My eyes flickered to the various exits as I contemplated which one provided the easiest escape in case I started to melt with embarrassment.

"Oh?" Josh motioned for Luca to continue. Charm oozed from Luca, and it was clear the audience around me was desperately hanging on to his every word. That was the thing about Luca, he really did have this uncanny ability to captivate your attention.

He leaned in closer to Josh. "Did you know Georgia loves to paint? I'm always telling her she needs to share her artwork with the fans."

My cheeks flushed red with embarrassment, but to my surprise, I heard a few whispers of surprise behind me.

"Georgia is incredibly talented, and I keep telling her she needs to share some of her artwork during the next Grand Prix." A silent dare from Luca.

Josh pointed at me, wagging his finger. "Well, then you'll just have to make sure we get a glimpse next race!" Luca looked awfully smug as he winked at me on stage.

I offered a polite wave and the most neutral smile I could muster, something between "*I love this man*" and "*I hope a rogue camera light falls on him.*"

"Now, Luca, let's talk about Miami. It was like you already knew she wasn't feeling well. Fans have speculated that the teams put a radio for you to chat inside the cars. Any truth to that?"

"Are they kidding?" I muttered, earning me yet another nudge from Henri. As if Valkyrie would allow me the extra weight so I could chat with my boyfriend. Who did he think this team was run by, middle school girls? The engineers weren't about to add in *relationship radios*. Luca shifted in his seat, trying to hide a bewildered smile.

"No, no, I don't need anyone hearing me chatter to myself throughout the race. I think I'd be deemed insane." His face slowly turned more serious, gaze fixed on his twiddling thumbs.

Henri leaned over, whispering, "Did you ever ask him why?"

"No." A pathetic answer, because it was all I'd wanted to do since Miami.

Henri furrowed his brow, unimpressed with my response. To be honest, I wasn't impressed with myself either. The cowardly part of me wasn't sure I wanted to know how Luca had figured it out, because I knew it would force the even bigger question: what else had Luca noticed about me when I wasn't paying attention?

But there was no avoiding the question now. Luca paused, his eyes flicking up like he was replaying something in his mind.

"When Georgia gets a podium finish, she immediately jumps out of the car, a huge smile on her face. Both of her arms go flying into the air, and she does this silly 'window washing' dance. It's very adorable. When she didn't hop out of the car and start doing her dance, I just knew something was wrong."

The room went silent, just the soft rustle of jackets and shifting legs in the audience.

"If there's something I know for certain about the Dubois siblings, it's that they're the first to congratulate each other. It doesn't matter who's won."

The audience swooned all around me, but I didn't move. Couldn't move, shocked by Luca's admission. Had he really noticed that about me? Thinking back to each race, I replayed all of the podiums in my head, thought back to each celebration.

Fuck. I did do that. The realization hit me like a ton of bricks.

Henri bumped my shoulder gently. Remembering to smile, I plastered one on before blowing Luca a kiss as I went through the motions of the dutiful girlfriend, all while contemplating how Luca had *actually* acted like a boyfriend in Miami. Not even my brother or engineer had noticed how unwell I was.

Just Luca.

"What a true gentleman," Josh preened. "Well, we're glad Georgia is alright, and we're looking forward to watching the two of you fight it out on the racetrack this weekend. This is our last question of the night, and then we'll let you go. Do you think your fights on track will affect your relationship at all? You're both title contenders this year. Has any animosity on the track spilled over to off-track drama?"

Luca didn't even hesitate. "Not at all. We're both fierce competitors on the track, that's true, but the fact is, every moment I spend with Georgia makes me a better athlete. Hell, even a better person."

The crowd collectively sighed. I narrowed my eyes at him, silently daring him to turn this heartfelt moment into one of his patented Rossi jokes. Anything to make these growing butterflies go away—anything to remind myself that Luca Rossi was nothing more than a fake boyfriend required to pull off this publicity stunt.

He threw me a coy smile before continuing, "Our fights on the track? They sharpen me. When we talk engineering over dinner, I learn. When we watch her favorite movie together—*Pride & Prejudice*, by the way—I find a calm that actually carries into my race weekends."

He paused for effect, that damn signature Cheshire cat grin sliding onto his face.

"Plus, the more fighting we do on the track, the more *making up* we get to do off of it. Let's just say, Josh, track fights definitely lead to late nights."

I buried my face in my hands, dying. Henri muttered something like "unbelievable" under his breath. The room erupted in a mixture of applause and laughter, followed by a standing ovation. Josh rose from his chair to shake Luca's hand, still chuckling.

Cocky, egotistical prick. I folded my arms, my eyes narrowing at Luca.

As the crowd started to disperse, Luca jumped down from the stage, calling out to me. "Like my interview, *amore*?"

"The only thing I'm going to be doing with my nights is sleeping," I deadpanned. "Nora is not going to like that one."

Luca snorted, his arms now wrapped around my waist. He kissed the top of my head as we waved at the departing fans who were eagerly snapping photos of us. His fingers softly massaged my neck, and I felt myself lean into his comforting hold, even though I was pissed.

Pissed that while Luca had ended his podcast with something ridiculous, the butterflies I'd felt a few moments ago hadn't left—they'd gotten stronger. Despising the womanizing, egocentric Luca was easy, but this Luca? This wasn't the Luca that I was used to.

I knew deep down that I was too much of a coward to face the possibility that another Luca was hiding under the one that had abandoned me on the date all those years ago, one that was perhaps observant, kind, and caring. A Luca who noticed my coffee order or the way I celebrated podiums.

Because if there was another side to him, then this whole week in Monza was going to be a lot harder than expected.

–

Back at the hotel, I kicked off my heels, flopped onto the couch, and told myself I'd only rest my eyes for a second. I probably shouldn't have had that second glass of wine at the after-party, but technically, the race weekend hadn't started yet, so I'd justified the rule break to myself.

I woke up groggy and disoriented with my dress halfway up my hips. A cough brought my attention to the doorway where Luca stood, a goofy smile on his face, and I frantically pulled my dress back down.

He strolled over, calm as ever. "Did you have fun at the podcast?" he asked casually, like we were two friends catching up. Here was Luca stalking toward me, pupils blown, the body language of a lion, and he wanted to have some casual chitchat.

"It was definitely amusing watching you lie your ass off."

Luca stood in front of me, gently stroking my cheek. The next thing I knew, I was in his lap, straddling him. His hands were on my waist, his body impossibly warm. My breath caught as his mouth hovered inches from mine.

"Who said I was lying?" he whispered.

Every part of me screamed to get up. Run. But I didn't move. Not when his fingers brushed the hem of my dress, feeling the lace hidden underneath. Not when he leaned in even closer.

"Should have talked about you even more," he said softly. "Definitely would've if I'd known you had this lovely little lace set on."

My breath hitched. "Maybe if you hadn't spent all day trying to annoy me, I would've told you I had a secret."

"Oh?" His eyebrow arched, interest clearly piqued.

My cheeks grew hot, and I gnawed on my lower lip until it was puffy. Part of me knew I should go to bed, but another part wanted to find out what it was like to have Luca's hands all over me, exploring every inch of me.

Why shouldn't I reap the rewards of this fake relationship? I contemplated. It's not like I could date someone else while

I was fake dating Luca. Plus, after the podcast tonight, I'd seen a different side of Luca.

Luca watched me chew on my bottom lip, and finally leaned in for a slow, passionate kiss, which I greedily returned. He gently let his hands work their way up and down my body until one of his hands began to fiddle with the waistband of my thong. He looked at me, silently asking permission to let his fingers play with their target, like a cat playing with its food before dinner. I eagerly nodded for him to continue, guiding his hand deeper as I licked my lips in anticipation. His fingers slid down as they started to slowly stroke where I desperately wanted him most. Feeling how wet I was, Luca let one finger tease its way into me. I moaned, trying to push my hips down further, but his other arm wrapped around my waist, caging me against him.

"Ah, ah, ah, not so fast," he smirked. I groaned in frustration, but Luca continued his teasing. He allowed me some reprieve when he sunk his entire finger into me and started pumping in and out. Even if it was slow and excruciating, it felt incredible.

My moans fortunately earned me a second finger, which Luca started to pump even faster. His lips ghosted mine while he eagerly watched my every expression, curling his fingers in just the right spot. I could feel myself careering toward an orgasm, and I started moaning louder.

"Oh, Luca… more… please…" I begged, a little embarrassed at how quickly I had fallen apart for him. Smirking, he slipped a third finger inside of me, enjoying the moan that escaped my lips.

"Fuck, you're such a good girl for me, taking my fingers like this," he purred into my ear. I'm not sure if it was his soft praises or the fact that he'd picked up the pace, but I was now hurtling toward a mind-numbing orgasm. Reaching my high, I screamed his name, tumbling quickly into intense pleasure as Luca helped me ride out my orgasm.

All of a sudden, everything stopped.

It felt as though my body had been thrust from a heavenly dream, and instead of being on top of Luca's lap in our shared living room, having just received an incredible orgasm, Luca was standing in front of me, quirking an eyebrow at me with a silent question, his cocky Cheshire cat grin on his lips.

Shit, shit, shit. Had I just dreamed that?

My cheeks were burning, and I knew I couldn't hide the panicked look on my face.

"Everything alright?" he asked, one brow cocked, voice deliciously amused.

"Um… yeah… of-of course, why wouldn't it be?" I responded far too quickly. "Just fell asleep on the couch while watching TV." Luca glanced at the television, which was off, and simply smiled before turning back to me.

Such a moron, Georgia.

"Of course, sorry I woke you. You were just calling out to… someone, and I wasn't sure if you were having a nightmare." If Luca had truly thought I was having a nightmare, he wouldn't have said that last retort with a grin that could have given the devil a run for its money.

I straightened up, mortified. "Was just dreaming about this weekend's podium."

"Oh, well, that makes sense as to why you were calling out *my* name then." He grinned. "Assuming you were congratulating me on getting first place?"

I don't think that, in the history of my twenty-five years, my cheeks had ever gone that red. For the first time in this fake relationship, I was absolutely dumbfounded. Still, I wouldn't be myself if I didn't make sure to get the last word in, so I got off the couch with as much gusto as I could manage and looked Luca right in the eye.

"Quite the opposite. I figured since your hands were *empty*, you could help me carry *my* trophy." Before he could respond, I headed straight for my room and closed the door loudly. Forget taking my makeup off, I wasn't coming out of this room until I absolutely had to.

Chapter Eighteen

Georgia

Morning came far too quickly. I sprinted out of my room to the bathroom, showered and changed as speedily as I could, then hurried back, lest I see Luca in the flesh—*or towel*—again. I wasn't sure what was more horrifying, the fact that I had a sex dream about Luca or that Luca had caught me having said sex dream about him.

The latter. It was definitely the latter.

Grabbing my Valkyrie bag, I headed to the elevator. "Please be empty. Please be empty," I quietly prayed to whatever deity might be listening. When the elevator dinged, I looked up at the open doors and realized one thing: I had *definitely* wronged someone in a past life.

There, standing in front of me, were Luca's parents. As soon as his mother saw me, she put her hand over the doors to stop them from closing as his father eagerly waved for me to join them.

"Georgia!" his mother exclaimed, and I did my best to keep my beaming smile plastered on my face. "You look dashing in this blue Valkyrie skirt. They really do know how to dress you and Lily."

"Morning," I responded casually, hopping into the elevator.

Luca's father flashed me a large grin as he patted me on the back. "We're glad to see you. Luca said you couldn't join us for breakfast. Something about you sleeping terribly? Hope you're feeling better."

Mortified was the only word that came to mind. I did my best to stop my cheeks from turning red, but I could tell I was blushing when Luca's mom tilted her head, looking at me with the same gorgeous brown eyes that Luca possessed.

God, this was going to be a long breakfast.

"Um, yes, all good, just needed a solid night's sleep."

How can I get out of breakfast with the Rossis? I questioned over and over again. In another universe, I would have died to have breakfast with three-time World Champion Michael Rossi. As a kid, I had his poster hanging on my wall, and now all I could think about was my steamy dream involving his son.

Kill me now.

Running through various scenarios, I tried to conjure up an excuse believable enough that it wouldn't insult their intelligence. Unfortunately, before I could think of an excuse worthy of Luca's endearing parents, the elevator opened, and his mom linked our arms, gracefully dragging me toward the restaurant. For a woman who knew our relationship was fake, she was certainly acting like it was real, but that was the magic of Lucile Rossi. It was easy to see how she'd spent the majority of her life as a television host; the warmth of her smile and voice was absolutely captivating.

We stepped out the elevator looking like we'd been friends for decades, not mere acquaintances.

"Luca! Look who we ran into," Michael called out cheerily. "Grab an extra chair, son."

I thought Luca might refuse his father's request, but after a couple of seconds of staring at me like a deer in headlights, he trotted over to the host stand and requested a fourth chair. His mother shuffled me into a seat and grabbed my bag, placing it underneath.

The host pulled up a chair, and Luca awkwardly sat down. There was a lot of pressure on him this weekend, and by the looks of his grim face, I suspected he wasn't prepared to have breakfast with his pretend girlfriend.

"So, Flash, looks like you'll have some real competition this weekend. Good! I look forward to an exciting race. That Valkyrie car has incredible speed, and your girlfriend clearly knows how to drive it," his father preened.

I felt my heart skip at the word girlfriend. I knew I'd be hearing it all weekend, but hearing it for the first time left me with a weird mixture of butterflies and dread.

Luca's face was the epitome of *just* dread. Staring at his dad with a stern look on his face, I could tell he was less than impressed.

Better get used to it, Rossi, I silently mused.

"Also," Luca's dad leaned in, his voice low, "I heard those photos from your excursion on Monday went over very well." Michael looked incredibly pleased with himself. "A great idea! I know Anthony's father has been sniffing around, making offers to Francesco and the Hermes leadership team, but this sort of good press is exactly what we needed, Luca."

Luca gave a vague nod of agreement, but his mouth was tight.

Michael turned to me with a gleam in his eye. "So, Georgia, I heard you let my son beat you on the karting track this week?"

I shot Luca a confused look, but he just continued to stare down at his yogurt cup with dedication, like it was a crystal ball willing to give him all the answers in life. Had Luca actually told his dad that I'd let him win? I wasn't sure if I should be offended.

Georgia Dubois didn't *let* anyone win.

"I think you've been lied to, Mr. Rossi," I chuckled. "I might have won a race in the morning, but Luca beat me fair and square in the afternoon, even if that pass at the end was vicious!" I elbowed Luca in the side, earning me a small, discerning smile from him before he went back to listening to his yogurt bowl's sound advice. "Plus, I'm not in the business of letting anyone beat me."

Michael let out a booming laugh. "Ahh, now that's the winning spirit we've all heard about!"

Luca flinched. His solemn eyes told me he was enduring this breakfast, not enjoying it, and for a moment my heart ached for him.

"How do you feel about today, Georgia?" his mom asked, pulling me out of my trance. His mother had such a calming air about her. Dressed in a beautiful red dress and lovely beige heels, she looked just as much the movie star as her son often did.

"Truthfully? Nervous. This is the first time I've arrived at someone's home race as their girlfriend, and while I know I shouldn't feel any different about walking into the paddock, part of me does." All morning I'd dreaded the media circus Luca and I were about to walk into. At a large event like Monza, our relationship would be front and center, there for everyone to comment on.

"I always feel so bad for the girlfriends," she sighed. "It's constant scrutiny: what they wear, how they speak, whether they're 'good enough' for someone the public doesn't actually know."

I tilted my head, surprised by the candor. "Exactly."

"Well, as far as we're concerned, you're walking into the paddock as one of the finest racers to ever step foot in a Formula 1 car. Your parents must be so proud." The compliment caught me off guard. I nodded politely, but the words hit deeper than I expected. Luca's face was blank, but his eyes betrayed something else.

Resentment? Shame? I couldn't quite tell.

"Well, that's very kind of you to say, but I know you're just as proud of Luca." Lucile's eyes sparkled as she looked at her son. No matter the tension in the air, her adoration for him was unmistakable.

Meanwhile, the pressure of being Luca's "girlfriend" at the biggest race of his career was beginning to chip away at my appetite. I poked at my oatmeal, suddenly unsure if I could stomach another bite. Luca must've noticed. He gently squeezed my leg, grabbing my attention, then leaned over, his voice low.

"You should have a little more breakfast," he whispered. "It's going to be a warm one today, and greeting all of *my* fans will be more exhausting than you know." He flashed me a small smirk, clearly trying to make light of the situation, which I almost appreciated.

"Georgia knows what she's doing, Luca," his father chastised. "Clearly whatever diet the team has her on is working!"

Luca didn't answer. He didn't even look up. He just moved his eggs around his plate like they were pieces on a chessboard. I took another bite of my oatmeal, almost missing the frustrated glare from his mother.

Were their interactions always like this? I wondered.

After a few more moments of watching him build an egg fort with his toast, I decided to break the uncomfortable chasm of silence that had settled.

"So, I'm curious, where did the Flash nickname come from?"

"Ahh, a good question," his father pondered, taking one more bite of his eggs before setting down his fork. "I wish I could say it had a long, riveting story, but it's quite simple, actually. You see, as a child, Luca was *obsessed* with go-kart racing, but his mother was always worried about him—even karts can be dangerous. So, in order to quell his mother's concerns, he would tell her before every race, '*Don't worry, Mama, I'll be back in a flash.*' An American slogan he had heard on TV, but it stuck with him. Before long, it had become the slogan the family adopted. The fans came up with the lightning bolt logo once he got into Formula 1, and it's stuck from there."

Across the table, Luca looked like he wished the story had stayed in the family vault. His spoon clinked gently against his bowl as he stirred what little yogurt remained.

"I can only imagine what a cute little momma's boy Luca was." I gave Luca a quick grin at my attempted jab, but Lucile just beamed at him with admiration, and he smiled back at her. For a moment, my heart warmed at their interaction.

"And tell me, where did Henri's nickname Peaches come from?" Lucile asked.

"Oh," I laughed. "Not nearly as good a story. My parents call me Georgie Pie, and as a kid we often visited America. One visit, we went to a peach farm in the state of Georgia, where Henri had his favorite peach pie and the silly nickname stuck after that."

"Oh, what a cute story! It must be so amazing to race with your brother." She smiled, and for the first time I noticed it: the dimple. Left cheek, just like Luca's. He might race like his father, but the face? That was all his mother.

"Undoubtedly two of the most talented drivers of your generation! Imagine having *two* children madly in love with racing," Michael exclaimed.

Luca slammed his spoon down hard enough to rattle the silverware. "Yep," he said, exhaling sharply. "A real dream come true."

Chapter Nineteen

Luca

My gut told me I should have canceled breakfast with my parents this morning, but after the excited text from my mother stating that she couldn't wait to see me, I couldn't bring myself to do it. The moment I saw my parents dragging an exhausted, slightly bewildered Georgia out of the elevator and toward the restaurant, every muscle in my body told me to run, make up an excuse that I had to be at the track early, because I knew this entire exchange would consist of my father gushing over Georgia, the daughter he wished he had.

And I was right. Breakfast was crucifying.

As soon as my father made that pointed comment, I knew I couldn't sit through any more of this charade. Watching him gush over Georgia made me feel sick to my stomach. He fawned over Henri every race weekend; I didn't also need to watch him do the same with the other Dubois twin.

"Well, breakfast has been great, but I think we best be leaving. Don't want to be late." I tapped my Rolex, hoping Georgia would catch the hint.

Please agree to leave, my eyes begged her.

"Luca, it's only eight thirty. You have another thirty minutes before—" my dad began to argue.

Georgia squinted, giving me a quick once-over. "Oh, no, this is my fault." She tugged at her jacket sleeve before realizing too late that she wasn't wearing a watch. "I told Luca I wanted to get in a tad earlier this morning, I like to meditate before it gets busy in the garage, but thank you for breakfast. We'll see you at the dinner later."

I shot her a grateful look, surprised that she hadn't put up a fight. I was sure that if Georgia had her way, she would have spent the morning grilling my father about his racing strategies, secrets he would have happily spilled to her. Henri had mentioned that his sister had a signed poster of my dad hanging in her apartment.

We quickly said our polite goodbyes before heading to the front of the hotel where my car was waiting for us.

"Thanks for agreeing to leave early. Didn't mean to take my dad's biggest fan away from him," I attempted to joke as we climbed into the car.

"It's no problem." Georgia flashed me a genuinely sweet, small smile, which I couldn't help but return. A blush flooded her face as she quickly glanced away, chewing on her bottom lip as she stared off into the distance, a casual smile on her face. She looked as if she was a million miles way, dreaming of something else, and I desperately wished I could slip into that head of hers.

"What's got you smiling like a little schoolgirl this morning?" I teased.

Georgia quickly replaced her smile with a frown, shaking her head. "None of your business, Rossi."

Truthfully that only made me more curious, but I put up a hand in defeat. She'd let me escape my parents early, least I could do was give her this tiny win.

"Fine, fine, keep your secrets."

Georgia's smile lingered a moment longer, her lips still etched into a soft curve, before she reached into the Valkyrie bag at her feet, pulling out her phone. "Nora instructed me to ask a few more questions if you're up for it."

Nodding in agreement, I motioned for her to go first.

"Here's a good one. When did you know you wanted to be a Formula 1 driver?"

Even though my eyes were glued to the road in front of me, out of the corner of my eye, I could feel Georgia staring at me.

Something about that question caught me off guard. As F1 drivers we all had this speech perfectly prepared, had all answered it countless times each year. But as time had gone on, my answer felt more and more crafted, and less and less genuine. Suddenly, that feeling I'd felt back at the Hermes offices overtook me again. It felt like an invisible weight had settled on my chest, squeezing tighter with each shallow breath I took.

Why was this question so difficult to answer?

I don't know if Georgia sensed my hesitation, but I appreciated her answering first.

"When I was five, our father took us to the Monaco Grand Prix. I remember it like it was yesterday. The cars were shiny and beautiful, the weather was incredibly sunny, and my father held me for most of the race, pointing out the different cars as he explained the racetrack. I knew in that moment that I wanted to be a race car driver, wanted to make him proud. Racing each weekend, it became more than just a hobby. It was a way for our family to spend meaningful time together. My parents sacrificed everything to get Henri and I into race cars, and now, each week, we get to pay them back in the best way possible."

There was a comfortable silence in the air as I pictured the image of sweet little five-year-old Georgia learning about the cars as they raced at one of the most famous tracks in the world.

She wanted to make her dad proud. My heart tugged at the thought. How could Georgia not make her parents proud? She was unstoppable this season. "*A real champion*," as my father liked to gush.

"You don't have to answer if you don't want," she offered quickly.

I shrugged. "I guess, since my dad was one, it was expected I'd become one, too."

Her pursed lips told me she didn't quite know how to respond—or didn't believe me, which was fair. Racers dreamed of competing in Formula 1. Until recently, racing the fastest cars in the world had been all that I'd wanted to do, but now? Now it felt more like a nightmare I was trapped in.

"If your dad wasn't a professional driver," she asked finally, "what did little Luca want to be when he grew up?" A good question, one that I had been too afraid to ask myself recently.

Had I always wanted to be a driver?

"I don't know," I said softly, thinking back to my childhood. "I really love to cook."

"An Italian that loves to cook, could you be more of a cliché?" Georgia teased, poking me gently in the side. "Well then, Chef Luca, here's a question that Nora keeps sending to me. Let's see if you'd pass the test: What's your favorite pasta?"

"I like maccheroni. It's a simple, classic Italian pasta. Easy to make, no matter the sauce."

"As in… mac and cheese?" Georgia's loud snort startled me. "Are you telling me that Luca Rossi loves *mac and cheese*?"

"No," I replied with mock offense. "I am telling you that Luca Rossi loves the classic Italian pasta maccheroni, which is an excellent way to eat a meat-based sauce." It was difficult to keep a straight face when Georgia was grinning at me with that radiant smile. Her laugh was something special; when she laughed, it was as if every part of her joined in. Her shoulders shook and her eyes sparkled as effortless laughter filled any open space. It was infectious being around Georgia when she laughed, and impossible not to smile back.

It made me want to do it more.

"I don't know, Luca. All I can picture is you shoveling copious amounts of mac and cheese into your face like a five-year-old."

"I wouldn't be caught dead making mac and cheese." I shook my head in disgust. "Next question?"

She scrolled through her phone. "Ugh, so sneaky of Nora. She wrote, '*Luca, what's something Georgia could do better in this week's press conference?*'"

I cleared my throat, maybe a little too eagerly. "Well…"

Georgia scoffed. "Oh, do tell. Please bestow your wisdom upon me, Luca, King of Journalists, First of his Name."

"Mock me all you want, Dubois," I teased. "I watched some of the conferences from the last few races, and I noticed something." My voice trailed off at the look of apprehension on Georgia's face. The press conference in

Miami had been brutal, and we needed to get things back on track.

"Yes?"

"I think for this week you should really focus on your body language. I hate to say it, but you kind of look like prey to these journalists."

"Ahh, so you want me to tell my anxiety to quit it?" Georgia said with a hard edge, crossing her arms tightly across her chest.

I cracked a smile, shaking my head. "No, *amore*, not at all, but I want you to at least try and think about your body language if you can. I just want you to *look* confident in front of these journalists. You're a successful F1 driver and it's an honor to be in that room with you. I want you to sit with your back straight, smile wide as you face them down. Even if you don't feel it on the inside, I think it'll help. I like to liken it to a black bear. If you look scary, it's probably going to leave you alone."

"You know a brown bear will chase you if you look intimidating," she deadpanned.

Such a know-it-all.

It was impossible to stop a smile from slipping onto my face. "I want you to show them that you're not to be underestimated. You're a predator on the track. Let that translate to press conferences, too."

Georgia didn't answer right away. Her lips were pursed, her eyes focused on the road ahead. "I'll give it a shot."

Better response than I was expecting. "That's the spirit."

A moment of silence passed. "So, Luca," she said suddenly, finally turning her gaze back to me. "I just wanted to thank you… for Miami." Her voice was soft and low, almost a bit unsure of itself.

"You don't have to thank me, *amore*."

Georgia took a sip from her water bottle. "No, I do. I don't know how you noticed that about me. Truth is, I don't think I've actually noticed that about myself..." Her voice trailed off.

In the moment, I hadn't realized how I knew Georgia wasn't feeling well. It wasn't until later, when I saw her doing the dance with Lily after a decent press interaction, that I realized. I'd always thought it was so cute, and I found myself each race looking toward her car first to see her doing the dance.

Before I could respond, she sat up straighter, pointing to the gates ahead. "We're here," she half-whispered.

The entrance to the drivers' parking lot was already teeming with a bustling crowd of guests. Pulling up to the gate, I flashed my Hermes pass as all feelings of relaxation vanished.

"And so it begins..." I wasn't sure if Georgia caught my almost silent whisper, but she nodded, and I wondered if she was also too scared to leave the safety of my car. The moment we stepped out and into the Monza spectacle, this relationship was solidified. More than Miami. More than Barcelona. Here, we were officially a couple.

"The fans love you, Luca," Georgia said finally. "You're going to do incredible this weekend." Her confidence shouldn't have surprised me. Georgia never showed weakness.

Putting on the biggest smile I could muster, I took a deep breath and stepped out of the car to the sound of deafening cheers, screaming, and applause. The crowd had grown around the barricades, craning their necks to get a glimpse of us. Georgia swung open the passenger side door and gracefully stepped out onto the sidewalk, her dark blonde hair swaying in the wind as she waved at the fans.

"Ready to walk down?"

She nodded. Her eyes focused on the growing crowd as I took her hand in mine. Our fingers intertwined effortlessly, and for a few split seconds, everything felt right with the world. The walk to the paddock entrance looked like a movie premiere, with fans clamoring over barricades to get selfies and our signatures.

"Georgia! Can you sign my hat?" A small, outstretched hand held out a blue Valkyrie cap. Georgia crouched, took a selfie, and added her signature to the hat.

"You know, I love to paint, too," the little girl whispered shyly.

"Oh, yeah?"

The girl nodded enthusiastically, her pigtails bouncing with each nod. "I told my mom that if I can't be a racer like you, then I wanna be the person who paints the cars!"

Georgia chuckled warmly, adjusting the oversize racing cap back onto the girl's head.

Once we reached the end of the cobblestone walkway, I leaned closer, whispering, "So, turns out the fans sort of like this artist side of you, huh?"

Georgia let out a soft scoff, but she begrudgingly nodded.

"You're a woman of many talents, *amore*. Don't hide that."

Georgia just shook her head, but the corners of her mouth betrayed her, curling into an undeniable grin.

"I know we've got a lot to do today, but thanks for giving me some time to chat with the Valkyrie fans. One of my favorite things about being a driver is interacting with the young female fans. Watching their eyes light up when I speak to them reminds me why Valkyrie's mission is so special. As women in motorsports, we can be more than grid girls—we're drivers, engineers, and team principals. I want little girls to know that."

"They do, Georgia," I insisted. "Every day you get in that car, you prove to the world that women can race with just as much determination and speed as anyone else."

Chapter Twenty

Georgia

As soon as I walked into my garage, Nora's nails were dug deep into my arm as she dragged me into the makeshift office hallway. "Georgie! How was the podcast taping last night?" she asked cheerfully, but I just gave her a look of disbelief that said, "*As if you didn't spend all night checking social media.*"

Before I could respond, Isabelle popped her head out of her office, waving us both in. There was no smile on her face, but the gleam in her eyes told me she was pleased.

"Good morning. Georgia, looks like you had a productive evening last night," Isabelle announced.

If she only knew how I'd ended it.

"Well, I have some excellent news! I just got off the phone with the clothing brand, Maison de Klotho, and they have requested a meeting with us next week in Monaco." Isabelle turned the computer monitor around, presenting the email to us both.

"Oh! My! God!" Nora screamed, prompting Isabelle to motion for her to quiet down. "Sorry, sorry," Nora quietened. "But this is amazing!"

"It's just a meeting," Isabelle added, "but still, it's a step in the right direction for us. If we keep up the good work, we should have a sponsorship deal scored before the summer break." Isabelle turned directly to me, squinting her eyes. "That means no Sassy Dubois this weekend, got it, Georgia?" As much as I wanted to complain about the toddler treatment, I knew it wouldn't be fruitful, so I opted for a sweeter approach.

"Yes, yes, I'll do my best to quell the beast inside of me." Truthfully, this was probably the best news I'd heard since winning Barcelona.

"Good." Isabelle frowned, and I suspected she didn't completely believe me. A well-deserved sentiment considering my track record. "Now, remember, we have the Italian Drivers Association event tonight. You will be attending with Luca. A car will pick you up at seven p.m. Do *not* be late. I took the liberty of having a dress sent to your room."

"I'll be there with bells on." I ignored Isabelle's frown. "Now, if you don't mind, I have plenty of race footage to review." Feeling a sense of undeserved accomplishment, I strutted out of Isabelle's office and toward my driver's room to talk strategy with my engineer.

The day flew by in a blur of VIP meetings and photo shoots, leaving me feeling as if it had ended before it even began. At four p.m., I made my way back to Luca's car and sank into the passenger seat. I opened my mouth to say something, only stopping when I caught sight of the tense frown and creased lines on Luca's face. Unlike the usually chipper Luca I was used to, this Luca said nothing as he drove us back to the hotel in complete silence.

When we finally reached our suite, I opened the door to my bedroom and saw it. Laid across the bed was a sleek black dress, the kind that whispered scandal with every sway of fabric.

Silk. Low-cut. High slit.

"Fucking, Nora." Opening my phone, I immediately dialed my press officer, intent on giving her a piece of my mind. She answered on the second ring, almost like she was expecting my call. "Care to explain the dress *Isabelle* had sent to my room?"

"Isn't it just so gorgeous? You are going to look stunning." Nora had her sickly-sweet voice on, the one that told me she was loving this far too much.

"No way I can wear this! There's going to be sponsors there tonight!"

"Exactly. What better way to secure a Maison de Klotho sponsorship than you making headlines with a sexy black dress designed by them?"

Before I could argue, the line went dead.

With no backup plan, I showered and then slipped on the dress, smoothing out the ruffled edges. To be fair to Nora, she was right, it was certainly a statement piece. With a long slit up the side and a sweetheart neckline, this dress was sexier than I was used to, but a part of me loved how it hugged my curves. We spent so much of our time in team polos or sponsored athletic dresses filled with corporate logos. It was nice to get dolled up, nice to feel glamorous for once.

The moment I stepped foot into our shared living room, Luca greeted me with a piercing wolf whistle from where he was lounging on the sofa. His eyes were heavy with exhaustion, but his face was relaxed, especially with the possessive smirk on his lips.

"What did I do to deserve this honor?" He was clearly pleased with himself as he took in the dress, starting at my neckline and not-so-subtly lingering on the slit at my thigh.

"Ready to go?" I asked, trying to ignore his heated gaze.

"Almost." He pushed off the sofa, grabbing a small navy box from his bag. "I have a gift for you first."

"I don't really wear—" I began to argue.

"Just open it," he said with an exaggerated sigh.

Inside, nestled in velvet, was a delicate silver necklace. A thin chain, and dangling from it, a single charm: a lightning bolt.

I stared at it. "Seriously? Your racing logo?" Luca had adopted the lightning bolt onto all of his helmet and clothing designs.

My words were dripping with sarcasm, but Luca's smile didn't falter. Even if it was beautifully designed, the idea of wearing my competitor's emblem around my neck irked me to no end, and my annoyance only grew as I met Luca's beaming, eager gaze.

"Designed it myself, *amore*. Don't want the other drivers getting any ideas when they see you in this dress tonight. I've seen how your *friend* Éliott looks at you." Luca's voice was cocky, but I didn't miss the hint of jealousy in his voice.

Deciding to ignore Luca's comment, I grumbled, "Whatever. Be quick and put it on then. We're going to be late." Realistically, everyone would expect me to be wearing *something* of Luca's.

Taking the necklace from my hands, he motioned for me to turn around. His rough fingers grazed my shoulders, adjusting the delicate chain around my neck. The cool metal rested against my skin, and I knew my cheeks were blushing at how intimate the moment felt. Luca's fingers lingered on the clasp, his touch sending electric tingles through my body. I tried to play it cool, keep my face the epitome of stoicism, but I knew he could feel how much the soft caress of his hands was affecting me.

"*Bellissima.*" His voice was low and warm, like honey sliding over silk. We both gazed into the mirror. I was admiring the delicate lightning bolt glinting at the base of my throat, but Luca's eyes were somewhere else entirely—fixed on mine. There was a kind of heat in his gaze that felt heavier than the weight of the necklace. When he finally pulled away, his absence left a trail of goosebumps down my skin.

-

After a short drive from the hotel, we arrived at the Drivers Association dinner. Crystal chandeliers dripped from the high ceilings, casting a soft glow over the opulent space. The air was filled with the gentle hum of chatter as drivers, sponsors, and VIPs mingled, their voices blending with the soft classical music playing in the background. The Italians never spared any expense when it came to their parties.

Spotting the bar, Luca tugged me behind him like a toddler whose mother was on a mission. I started to object when Luca handed me a champagne flute, but as I noticed everyone staring at us, I couldn't find it in myself to refuse.

A little liquid courage never hurt anyone.

"Well, well, look who it is? If it isn't Hermes's *number two* driver." Anthony's voice drawled behind me, and I glanced at Luca, who was gripping his glass so tightly it looked like it could shatter at any moment.

Lacing my fingers with his, I leaned in toward Luca and whispered loudly enough for Anthony to hear, "Luca, I think Hermes's *number three* driver is trying to speak to us." To my surprise, he turned to me, the frown on his face completely wiped.

How bad would it be if I punched the smug grin off Anthony's face?

Luca's eyes looked like he was contemplating the same question, but before I could tell Anthony to piss off, he glanced at our intertwined hands.

Anthony's smirk widened, clearly unfazed. "Nice to see the two of you are still going strong."

"Jealousy doesn't look good on you, Anthony," I bit back.

A familiar voice chimed in. "You might want to keep your eyes to yourself." Edward approached, a glass of champagne in both hands. "Luca once threatened to crash my car if I asked Georgia out on a date. Be a shame to see all that Texan oil money splattered about the track—there's enough oil on it as is." Edward was always one to get in a quick joke, an admirable quality.

Anthony grabbed his drink from the bar, taking a moment to look both directions before leaning in closer to Luca. "Let's hope your speech doesn't go as horrifically as your driving."

Luca's hand slipped from mine as he balled his fists, stepping forward. But Edward slid between them like a well-practiced bouncer, holding up a hand. Anthony snickered as he walked away, swaggering off to his table at the back.

"He's not worth it, Luca," Edward whispered finally, nodding for us to both take our drinks.

"Fucking hate that guy."

"Anthony is a moron who will never get a Hermes seat. Just ignore him." Luca nodded as he grabbed his glass and took a sip, but I could see the hurt in his eyes, could sense the frustration.

"Let's find our table, hmm?" I suggested, and Edward gave me a small hug, before giving Luca's arm another tight squeeze.

We settled into our seats, and while the others at the table—Henri, Isabelle, a few engineers—chatted animatedly about next year's specs, I watched Luca. His fingers trembled against his napkin, and he kept rubbing his palms against his trousers like he couldn't dry them fast enough.

I intertwined our fingers, smiling at him. "Your speech is going to be great, Luca."

"I don't know why they asked me to give a speech," he whispered back, not bothering to look at me. "I'm not a champion like my father."

"Not yet." Luca ignored my encouragement as his eyes darted around the room nervously. His grip on my hand was shaky and clammy, and he let go abruptly so he could wipe his hands on his pants again. Gently, I let my hand rest on his thigh, tracing soft circles. He glanced at me, eyebrows raised in question.

I'm not entirely sure why I felt responsible for helping Luca overcome his anxiety about the upcoming speech. Maybe it was because I had experienced similar intense media pressure before and knew how debilitating it could be. Or maybe it was because after Miami and the podcast taping and this morning's car ride, I was starting to genuinely *like* Luca more and more, and I couldn't bear to see the charming Luca Rossi everyone loved crumble under the pressure. He didn't deserve to feel this way.

And then, an idea hit me. Wild. Ridiculous.

Fuck it. I'm doing this.

Excusing myself, I quickly made my way toward the restroom, purse in hand. When I entered the stall, I slid off my purple lacy thong, a huge smile on my lips as I thought back to when Luca called me boring.

See if you think I'm boring now. I smirked, stuffing the panties in my purse with a little too much enthusiasm.

Exiting the bathroom, I looked left and right, as if someone was waiting to interview me on my underwear status, and then cautiously started to make my way back to my table.

"At least now you can picture one person in the audience naked. I hear that's good for pre-speech nerves," I whispered, sliding the lace thong discreetly into the inside pocket of his jacket.

He blinked at me. Then his mouth twitched as his hand slid into his pocket. His eyes went wide with disbelief, and no small amount of delight, as a grin crept onto his face.

When his name was called moments later, Luca rose, adjusted his jacket, and walked toward the stage with a swagger that was pure Rossi. Gone was the trembling hand, the bouncing knee. He grinned, took the mic, and gave the room a master class in charm.

He spoke about his time karting as a little boy on the Monza track and gave the Hermes F1 Team a heartwarming thank you.

Then, instead of exiting the stage, Luca paused. He'd left a copy of the speech on the table earlier this evening, and I knew the Hermes thank you was supposed to be the end of it.

"And last, but definitely not least, I want to thank Team Valkyrie."

Isabelle stiffened beside me.

Now where are you going with this one, Rossi? I thought to myself.

Luca smiled as if he was also amusingly surprised by the words coming out of his mouth. "Thanks for hiring me a racing coach," he chuckled.

Isabelle waved him off with her hands.

"Now, I know everyone here is wondering what's it like to date one of the most talented drivers in the paddock." His eyes locked with mine before he continued. "And fortunately for you, when I'm done with this speech, you can ask Georgia herself."

The crowd let out a few laughs, and Luca smiled at me from the stage.

"But in all seriousness, Georgia, thank you for pushing me. For believing in me. And thank you to everyone here tonight. I very much look forward to seeing all of you from up on the Monza podium on Sunday. Thank you."

The crowd's response was electric, and as Luca walked off the stage, various people stopped him on the way back to his table, wishing him luck for the weekend as they snuck in a photo.

I'd seen a dozen versions of Luca Rossi over the years—cocky teammate, smug rival, tabloid bad boy. But this version? The one who let me see his fear, who stood in front of the entire industry and thanked me?

I didn't know what to do with this version.

There was something about watching Luca confidently up there that filled me with an unexpected warmth. Luca had always oozed confidence, but this confidence was different.

He might think his charming, sly Cheshire cat smile was attractive, but there was nothing sexier than watching a truly confident man give the speech of his life. I wasn't sure if it was the couple glasses of wine or lack of underwear, but all of a sudden, I found myself wishing that I could turn my dream from earlier this week into reality.

Chapter Twenty-One

Luca

Georgia had single-handedly calmed me down and given me the confidence I needed to own that speech. The little stunt she pulled with the underwear was so shocking, especially from Little Miss Prim and Proper, but it left me feeling more impressed with her than I cared to admit. From the moment I felt my *surprise* in my jacket pocket, all I could think about was how much I desperately wished it had been my teeth that had removed her thong.

And it wasn't just the teasing. Georgia noticed things—things I'd always thought I kept to myself. The bounce of my knee when I was nervous. The way I fidgeted before big moments. All my life I had been a closed book when it had come to my feelings, but in just a couple of days Georgia had somehow managed to not only open that book but read between the lines.

So as soon as we could make our exit, I called for a taxi and ushered her in, muttering something about an early start. Considering it was only Wednesday, the excuse was a bit weak, but she followed me anyway, her cheeks still flushed from the applause, her eyes sparkling in the dim cab light.

"Feeling a little cold over there," I whispered, loving the blush that crawled up her chest.

"You offering to warm me up?"

Her voice was husky and low, and a mischievous smile played on her lips as she leaned in closer to me. My hand found her jaw, thumb grazing her cheekbone as she licked her bottom lip, and I swore the world stopped spinning for a second.

"Alright folks, we're here!" the cab driver called out.

We practically jumped apart, murmuring awkward thank yous before bolting into the elevator. Neither of us said a word, tension pulsing like electricity between us.

As soon as the suite door clicked shut, she started, "Luc—"

But I didn't let her finish, crashing my lips to hers.

To my delight, Georgia grabbed fistfuls of my shirt, pulling me closer as I wrapped my arms around her waist. Her lips were soft, but her kiss was hungry—urgent. Her body melted into mine, and everything around us faded until there was only heat and her and now.

Fuck. Georgia is a phenomenal kisser.

But I'd learned that from our kiss in Barcelona. Immediately, my mind wandered to what else she was good at. I pressed her back against the wall, hands skimming the hem of her dress, desperate for more. I was a man starved, and in that moment, Georgia's kiss was the only thing that could quench my hunger.

Breaking away, we both caught our breath as I rested my forehead on hers. Words seemed to fail us in that moment, the silence stretching between us as we stood there.

"What was that for?" Her voice was all but a whisper and I attempted to regain some composure.

"I think you know what that was for," I hummed. *For how incredible you were tonight.*

"Don't suppose there's any chance I can get my underwear back?"

I pulled the scrap of purple lace from my pocket, letting it dangle from my fingers.

"And give away my good luck charm?" She reached for it, but I held it just out of reach with a grin. "You want it back?" I teased. "You'll have to earn it."

I placed it back into my jacket pocket before taking a seat on the couch, patting my lap. I loved how her eyes narrowed at me, loved how she crossed her arms with pursed lips as she studied me. I could see the wheels in her head turning, could see her deciding on whether or not to call my bluff.

Georgia stalked toward where I was sitting on the couch, and before I could frantically add a "just kidding," she straddled my lap, her dress hiking up her body. When she reached for my belt, I raised a soft, questioning eyebrow, but Georgia just licked her lips in anticipation. As she unbuckled it, a soft moan fell from my lips, and she grazed her hand along my waistband, a silent question of consent. Without hesitation, I eagerly nodded, watching Georgia's hand as it slid into my boxers, palming my already hard and aching cock.

Grabbing the edge of my pants, she instructed me to lift, letting my cock spring free as my pants slid down.

Then she sank to her knees. Her tongue ran a slow, deliberate line up my shaft, and I choked out a curse.

"Oh fuck," I gritted out. "That feels—"

Her lips wrapped around me, her pace torturously slow. One hand stroked my length while the other gently cupped my balls. I buried my hands in her hair, pulling, needing something to hold on to.

"Stop teasing, *amore*," I demanded.

She continued to work me, her hands gently massaging my balls in a steady rhythm. As I started to get closer, my moans got louder and louder. Both of my hands were now tight in Georgia's hair, grabbing and pulling.

"Fuck, *amore*, such a good girl for me. Taking me like this."

I tapped her shoulder to warn her I was close, but to my delight Georgia didn't stop. Just kept going, deeper, until I came hard, her name on my lips.

Clutching my chest, I gasped for air as I gazed at Georgia's flushed face and tousled hair, feeling completely spent. She wiped the corner of her mouth with the back of her hand, then stood slowly, her eyes locked on mine as she reached into my jacket and plucked out her underwear.

"I'd say I earned this, wouldn't you agree?" Before I could answer, Georgia sauntered back to her room, looking awfully proud of herself.

Chapter Twenty-Two

Georgia

Sunday morning, I woke up before my alarm, likely from the anticipation of today's Grand Prix. The high from the drivers' dinner—and everything that happened afterward—had carried us both through the weekend. I'd topped Friday's free practice sessions and taken pole in Saturday's qualifying. Luca was right behind me in P2.

After the gala, I expected things to be weird between us, but to my surprise, they weren't. I'd contemplated bringing it up, but the moment never felt right.

Still, I could tell it lingered between us, unspoken but present. The way his gaze held mine too long. The way he bit his bottom lip like he was keeping words in. Based on Luca's heated gaze and the subconscious biting of his bottom lip, I figured he was probably having the same debate.

And if I was being honest? I liked having the upper hand for once. I liked the way he looked at me, like he was still thinking about me on my knees.

Because God knew I was thinking about having him on his.

And based on his blown pupils and the desire lingering in his eyes, I suspected he would have returned the favor if I hadn't waltzed out of the room. But I'd stupidly let my pride stop me. In the moment, it felt more fun to tease Luca, to show him that I wasn't as boring as everyone said—but now? Now I had spent all weekend debating how to get myself alone with him in between our hectic schedules.

A loud noise from the living room caught my attention. A thud, then something like a muffled curse. Curious, I cracked the door open just enough to peer into the suite. Luca was sitting on our living room couch, his head buried in his hands. He was rocking back and forth, muttering under breaths that were barely audible.

I shut the door quietly. It seemed like a private moment, and as much as I was dying for a cup of coffee, I didn't feel as though it was right to invade his personal space.

When the bathroom door closed, I took that as my cue and tiptoed out into the living room, making my way to the suite's kitchenette so I could brew my much-needed coffee. As I carefully poured hot water over my ground beans, I noticed Luca emerging from the bathroom, holding his shirt in his hands.

Was this man genetically opposed to wearing clothing indoors?

I opened my mouth to make a joke about this being a shared living room where shirts were necessary, but before I could utter a word I tripped over my own feet, and a pained scream escaped me before I caught myself on the back of the sofa.

Absolute idiot, Georgia.

Luca turned. His eyes were red and puffy, slightly sunken in. The vibrant gleam I usually saw in them dulled to something tired and heavy. Thinking back, I realized I'd never seen Luca cry, not even after his first win several years ago. His face was always a picture of stoicism, like one of Michelangelo's sculptures.

He mumbled a quiet, "Morning," before disappearing toward his bedroom, and the lump in my throat grew.

I hesitated only a moment before calling after him. "Luca!"

He paused in the doorway. I wasn't sure if I should bother him, but I thought back to what I always needed in moments like this. Anxiety was common in the racing community, and I understood what this home race meant to him, the pressure that he was under. Everyone he loved most in the world would be there today, watching him. Expecting him to put on a show that would make Italy proud.

I lifted the carafe. "Want some coffee? There's enough for two here."

Luca's eyes flickered up to the kitchen and then down to his toes, but much to my surprise, he nodded, taking a seat on the sofa. Handing him a cup, I sat down next to him on the plush maroon couch, letting the silence fill the room as I watched the ripples in my coffee.

Should I say something? Sometimes just having someone near me was enough to calm my anxiety. I knew this more than anyone, how comforting it was to just sit next to someone when the world felt so impossible and heavy on your shoulders.

After a few more minutes of sipping our coffee in silence, Luca finally spoke up. "I'm surprised you take your coffee black."

"I would never insult a coffee roaster by adding cream and sugar," I gasped, pretending to feign offense, although I was slightly offended on behalf of coffee everywhere.

That earned me a small chuckle. He took a sip, hands wrapped tightly around the mug. "You feeling okay?"

Luca's eyes darted to the window, before settling on the floor. "Just a lot on my mind. After yesterday's qualifying, Henri had to take a penalty, so he's starting at the back of the grid."

Which meant today—for the first time—Luca would be the number one driver at Hermes. He would finally get the prioritization he deserved. But it also meant expectations. The kind that crushed you before you even got behind the wheel.

"I've never had so many eyes on me," he said. "Family, team, fans… Italy." He swallowed. "No Italian has won Monza since my dad. And now they all think I might."

Words kept spilling out of him, as if the load on his mind lightened with each passing breath.

"Sometimes I feel like it's all too much. It would just be easier if someone crashed my car, so I wouldn't have to face the possibility of completing the race but not making it on the podium. The possibility of disappointing my father."

I smiled at him softly, taking a moment to process and appreciate his vulnerability. "The only person that you can let down this weekend is yourself," I said finally. "You don't owe anyone anything, including your father. You drive for *you*, and only you. You're going to drive this weekend with all the passion you have for your country, and I think it'll translate into something you'll be proud of. You have immense talent. If you want this win, then fight for it today."

"I just—"

"No," I cut him off. "You're many things, Luca, but you're not a coward."

A faint smile ghosted across his lips.

"Plus, you have a real opportunity to come *second* in this race, assuming that pesky driver starting pole doesn't run you off the track." He actually laughed, the sound low and real.

We sipped in silence again for a few more moments. A strand of hair fell over my face, and Luca reached over, brushing it back, fingers lingering against my cheek. His lips slowly parted as if he was about to speak, but he said nothing, his eyes instead flickering down to my lips as a familiar spark of butterflies surged. My breath caught as he closed the space between us.

Wednesday's gala had been teasing and fun, fueled by one too many champagne glasses from each of us as we both fought to dominate the other. But this? This was something else entirely.

His lips hovered over mine, our foreheads brushing. Luca's thumb traced the corner of my mouth like he was memorizing it. The sun was rising outside. Warm light spilled across the living room floor, and for a moment, the entire world fell away.

All I saw was Luca. The one behind the headlines. The one who made me laugh. The one who got it, who understood the pressure, the performance, the fear.

I liked *this* Luca sitting next to me. Leaning in, I found myself drawn to the charming dimple on his left cheek. Our lips were now only inches apart, and I couldn't deny the growing desire to feel them against mine.

"Georgia, you there?"

Loud banging on my hotel room door caused us both to jump, startled by the interruption. His cheeks were flushed pink, and he looked a bit embarrassed by our near-kiss.

Groaning, I got to my feet and cracked the door open. "Lily? You alright?" Lily and I were close, but it was unusual to hear her knocking on my door at seven thirty in the morning.

She nodded timidly as she fidgeted from side to side, biting her lower lip. It wasn't until she entered that I remembered Luca was sitting on the sofa—*shirtless*—wearing some skimpy, soft athletic shorts as pajamas, which became evident by the cheeky smirk on Lily's face.

"Oh," Lily snickered quietly. "Am I interrupting something?"

I gave her a withering look, one I hoped communicated *Not one word of this in the garage, or I will sabotage your car.* She gave me a sweet smile and plopped herself into the nearest chair.

I poured her a cup of coffee, trying to ignore the way her eyes kept flitting back to Luca. Such a flirt.

After handing her the cup, I sat down next to Luca, closer this time. Possessive, petty, but I didn't care. He might be a fake boyfriend, but for now, he was *my* fake boyfriend. Lily gave me a quick, bemused smirk.

"Luca, I finally listened to the podcast," she said, taking a sip. "It was very funny. Although, I think Nora might murder you for the ending. Not exactly the part of the relationship they want to be made public."

Luca chuckled, pleased with himself. "Glad you enjoyed it."

"So, Lily, I appreciate the visit, but seven thirty is a little early, even for you." Lily was a notorious early riser. She loved to watch the sunrise before a race, claimed it gave her serenity before a Grand Prix.

She shrugged. "I know. I couldn't fall back asleep this morning. I just feel like the last few weeks haven't gone as well as I'd hoped, and I'm nervous for today."

Lily was a phenomenal driver and incredibly talented, but managing a Formula 1 car at the young age of twenty was hard for anyone, man or woman. I often reminded Lily that she shouldn't compare herself to me. I'd won F3 and F2, and then I'd gone on to race open-wheeler cars in Japan and America.

Experience came with age, and I knew my teammate would get there.

"You know this, but I'll say it again. It takes time to get used to a Formula 1 car. Isabelle picked you for a reason. All you need to do this weekend is put your head down and drive with that hunger that got you a racing seat." Lily's mouth curved upward, her eyes brightening as she took a sip of coffee.

If my job as a driver didn't succeed, there was potential in a job as a therapist.

"Wisdom comes with age, as my father always says," Luca added. "I've no doubt that you have several World Driver's Championship wins ahead of you, Lily. *Probably* more than this one will win." He ruffled my hair, and I swatted his hand away, scoffing.

"And *definitely* more than Luca." He feigned a look of hurt.

Lily stayed for another twenty minutes, finishing her cup of coffee, before returning to her room to get ready for the day. As soon as she left, I heard a ding on my phone, a text from Lily lighting up the screen.

Lily:
Why have you not had some angry hate sex with this fine man yet?

Lily:
Or was that what I was interrupting this morning?

Georgia:
A classy lady never tells.

I set my phone down, but the smile stayed. Across from me, Luca raised an eyebrow.

"You gonna tell me what that was about?"

"Not a chance, Rossi. Now get dressed. I've got a race to win."

Chapter Twenty-Three

Luca

"Luca, are you listening to me? Race starts in one minute. Get your head together," my race engineer griped into the radio.

"Ready," I huffed back in the affirmative. At least as ready as one could be before the biggest race of their season.

The radio beeped in again. "Right, you're in second behind Georgia. Keep diligent with your tires, you'll be able to pass her soon enough."

"Roger."

My car idled on the second spot of the grid, and I looked up toward the five lights as my lungs filled with fumes from my engine. This was it. If I was going to win a race this season, this was my chance.

"*Good luck getting around Georgia.*" My father's tone this morning felt like a knife in my back, but I tried to push it out of my mind as I glanced at the starting lights.

I exhaled once, slow and controlled. My eyes flickered toward Georgia's car ahead of me. She wasn't going to hand this to me, and I didn't want her to. I was going to *earn* this win. She might have had compassion for me this morning, but she was fighting for dominance in the World Driver's Championship.

The five lights blinked out.

Unsurprisingly, Georgia had an excellent start, and for the first quarter of the race, we stayed in position as we slowly pulled away from the other drivers. Even though Georgia drove like she had a rocket ship underneath her, as each lap passed, her tires were starting to give out, and surprisingly, I was starting to gain on her.

Tire management had never been either of the Dubois twins' specialty.

Just as I was starting to feel comfortable in my pace, dust exploded in front of me.

"Shit!" I cursed, jerking the wheel slightly as Georgia's car spun out ahead, a wild 360 that kicked up dirt and debris. By some miracle, she corrected and kept going, but it was enough. Enough for me to slip past.

How close was third place behind me? What if he didn't see her?

My heart panicked, and I quickly checked my mirrors. In a split second, Georgia was back in the race, her car quickly accelerating, attempting to regain her position.

I hit the radio button. "All okay with Georgia?"

"Yes," my engineer replied calmly. "Head down. Only thirteen laps to go."

While I knew Georgia would be furious about her mistake, this had given me the opportunity to get out in front of her. For the first time all season, this was my race to *lose*, and as my dad liked to say, "*They don't ask how you won, just if you won it.*"

Lap after lap, Georgia gained on me, but I fiercely held on, defending my position. I could hear her engine growling just behind me, feel her closing in.

By the final lap, she was practically glued to my rear wing. Georgia was just over a second behind me. Her pit stop had gone better than mine, and even with her small mistake she'd driven with such precision she'd managed to make up almost all the lost time.

Georgia lunged her car again as she attempted to pass, and I knew by the final turn, she would probably have me.

And then it hit me. Back at the go-kart track, we'd discussed the racing lines she liked to do when sneakily passing. "*The thrill of taking an unexpected racing line to surprise someone, to pass them. It's the most thrilling part of racing.*" There was only one spot at Monza where I knew I could take her, and it was coming up.

"Alright, Luca," I encouraged myself. "You can do this." My car went flying into the last corner, and I drifted off the racing line, breaking early as I defended her aggressive lunge. The move blocked Georgia's attempt to overtake. As expected, Georgia hadn't anticipated my car being there and was forced to back off. I could almost imagine her cursing under her breath, her face furious like it was after my karting victory.

"Fuck, yeah!"

Only the final corner remained. For the first time in over a year, I could taste victory. I was going to show Hermes that I was worth the investment, that I could also be a winner. The checkered flag waved frantically as my tires skidded over the finish line, beating Georgia's car by mere inches. The cheers and roars of the crowd were muted by the thrumming in my ears.

I had finally done it.

Monza was mine.

"That's P1, Luca!" Francesco yelled into the radio. "What a race! First Italian to win since your father! You've made your family and Italy proud."

Tears burned my eyes as I choked out, "*Grazie* to the team!"

With shaking hands, I parked in my assigned spot and turned off the engine. Stumbling out of my car, the weight of my victory settled in my chest. To my right was Georgia in the P2 spot, on top of her car doing her classic window-washing dance as her mechanics cheered her on. She would be disappointed that her win was lost purely on driver error, but still, P2 was an excellent result, one all the other drivers on the grid would gladly take—all except for *me*.

"*Congratulazioni!* I am so proud of you, son!" My mother grabbed my face, bringing it to her lips as she kissed my cheek.

Then my father. He pulled me into a large hug, our first this season. I pulled back, gazing into his excited green eyes that were filled with pride. Watching my parents celebrate together, I felt like a little boy again. All of my frustration and anger this season had made me forget how amazing it was to stand next to my parents, joy lighting up their faces. We hadn't celebrated a race win in well over a year.

"This is a great win for you and for Italy! It should really get your reputation back on track," my father announced. "This is exactly what we needed!"

And just like that, the magic cracked. A win would never be just a win with him. Forcing a tight smile, I gave my parents a quick kiss on the cheek before making my exit toward the interview area.

A light touch on my shoulder startled me. Turning, I saw Georgia grinning, radiant, her hair windswept and her cheeks flushed with adrenaline. Without a word, she threw her arms around me. I held her against me, appreciating the moment of genuine, unguarded affection.

"Congratulations, Rossi, a race well won," she whispered. "Not that you should get used to it, I'll be back next week."

Laughing, I went to put her down, but then I felt it: her lips against mine.

The kiss was nothing like the one we'd shared in Barcelona, or even the one after the gala. It was the kiss I'd wanted to give her this morning. Commanding and urgent, fueled not by champagne, but by all the emotions that had been building between us this week. Cameras flashed all around us, capturing the intimate moment, but I didn't care. My hands cupped her face as she wrapped her arms around my neck, pulling me closer.

When I finally pulled away, I rested my forehead against hers. "Until next time, *amore*." She just grinned as she waltzed confidently toward the interview area, my eyes following her form.

Next to me, I heard Edward whistle loudly. "And to think, three races ago you wanted to have her banned from F1?" Edward teased. "Might just get my thousand euros after all."

I couldn't help the grin tugging at my lips. Edward was much closer than he realized.

Chapter Twenty-Four

Georgia

With Luca's taste still on my lips, I marched myself over to the cooldown room, not ready to face what I'd just done—or why I'd done it. Nora told me to sell this relationship, and what girlfriend wouldn't kiss their boyfriend if they had just won their home race?

Obviously, that was 100 percent the only reason I kissed Luca.

It definitely wasn't because, in that moment, Luca had the most kissable face I'd ever seen. Or because I felt so much pride and joy for him, I just couldn't help myself. Or because I was so pissed for my driving mistake that a kiss from Luca was all I could think about to relieve my anger.

Nope, not a single one of those reasons was true, I concluded.

After the cooldown room and a champagne-soaked podium ceremony, I was shuffled into my least favorite circus act of the weekend: the winner's press conference. We were supposed to clean up before these post-race press events but based on how much champagne was oozing out of Luca's clothes, it was clear the Hermes team had kept on partying. There was no other way to describe it: Luca looked like the cat that had got the cream.

"Welcome to our Monza winner!" the moderator announced.

Sweat clung to the back of my neck as I mentally prepared for the topic everyone was going to want to discuss, my disastrous spin that had ultimately lost me the race. My throat tightened as anxiety slowly started to take over my body, like a python circling its prey. More than anything, I hated discussing my racing errors. I knew I'd fucked up.

The media knew it. The team knew it. The fans knew it.

Remembering Luca's earlier advice on body language, I straightened my back, trying to make myself look taller and more confident.

"Let's start with Luca," Michael Clifton began. "Luca, congrats on a riveting win here at home for you. How does it feel?"

"Incredible. Just… unimaginable. This has been a dream of mine since I was a child, to win at Monza in a Formula 1 car just like my father. And now I've finally done it."

Despite my own disappointment, watching Luca gush about his victory, I felt nothing but pride and excitement for him. Even though I'd lost, something about watching him win made the hurt sting less. Losing didn't matter as much when it was to someone you cared about.

And I did care about Luca.

"Tell me, when you saw Georgia spin in front of you, what were you thinking? Were you slightly relieved, knowing that your main race competitor was going to lose time?"

Luca's jaw ticked, goofy grin immediately dropping from his face. "No, my first thought was: *Is my girlfriend okay?* You never want to win because another racer puts themselves in potential danger. We're competitive, but ultimately, there are only twenty of us in the world. I know many of you find this hard to believe, but we're also friends. Once I knew Georgia was okay, I put my head down and focused on *my* race." I threw Luca a small, appreciative smile. Concern for our fellow drivers always came first.

Next came my turn. "Georgia, you almost had Luca at the end. Tell us, what happened in the car today?" Exhaling a breath, I attempted to steady myself as I straightened my back and uncrossed my legs.

Become the bear, Georgia. You're the scary one.

"I made a mistake," I said evenly. "It caused a spin. Luckily it was minor, and I recovered quickly. I'm happy with second. It puts me in the lead for the championship." The steady tempo of my voice surprised me, and I gave myself an internal pat on the back as I stared down the journalist with a confident smile.

"Sure, you're a few points ahead of Henri," another journalist chimed in, "but aren't you worried mistakes like this will keep you from winning the championship?"

He stared at me with a sturdy face, clearly unhappy that I had mentioned my lead. The frustrated part of me wanted to stand up and throw my water at the journalist, but since Sassy Dubois was meant to be left at home, I opted for a steady, calming breath.

"That applies to all of us," I said cautiously. "Even champions. A mistake happened this race, yes, but I'm not worried about the next race until I'm in the car again." I knew it was a good answer because I saw Nora flash me a thumbs up, a rarity at my press conferences. I looked over to Luca, and he just slightly nodded, straightening his own back in a reminder for me to regain my posture.

"Sure, champions don't make these mistakes *every race.* That's evident by previous championships." I wanted to desperately roll my eyes at his stupid comment. "But, so far, you've made three mistakes in the last six races. How do you plan on controlling your emotions in the car when you make these mistakes? Or is there some, perhaps, monthly reason you're being emotional...?"

Did he just imply that I'm on my period?

The world went red, and the conference room might as well have been on fire with the amount of steam leaving my body. I might be a predator on the track, but these journalists truly were the vultures of the paddock.

"What the fuck is wrong with you people?" I stood, mic clutched tight in my hand. "What do you want me to say? That I plan on making a small mistake every weekend? That I can't wait to lose the championship?" I threw my hands up in the air, my frustration growing with each word. "Or do you want me to say, *Of course I'm going to let my emotions dominate my driving.* I have a reliable car. I have talent." I started listing off items, pointedly showing the journalist each finger. "I get on podiums—"

A hand touched my shoulder, warm, grounding. I turned to see Luca's eyes steady on mine, quiet pride softening his features.

Pausing, I took a moment to scan the room. The flurry of reporters stared back wide-eyed, their notepads clutched, cameras pointed, and Dictaphones aimed directly at me.

"You know why I'm going to win the championship? Because you've all spent the last several races pissing me off. So, thank you, truly, for giving me another reason to win each week."

I dropped back into my seat, pulse thundering. Not a single journalist dared ask me another question. Isabelle was going to be pissed, but I couldn't find it in myself to care.

Outside, the rush of media buzz still swirled around us, but I barely noticed. Nora met me with a look that was half disappointment, half restraint. I just stormed past her, knowing I couldn't say anything to make this mess better. We made our way to the Valkyrie garage where Isabelle was waiting in her office.

She didn't say hello, instead motioning for me to come inside. Her furrowed brows and deep frown just about said it all.

"What is wrong with you?" Isabelle hissed. "Seriously, Georgia?"

"I don't know," I answered truthfully.

She rubbed her temples. An uncomfortable silence engulfed the room, like dark clouds before a storm. "When are you going to learn to ignore the journalists? They are rubbish. You *know* this. Why give them what they want?"

"When are the journalists going to learn to treat me like a respectable racer?" I snapped.

"When you show them that you are one."

Isabelle was definitely a believer in *When they go low, we go high*. I rather preferred *Revenge is a dish best served cold*.

She sighed. "This is working, Georgia! We have an important meeting with Maison de Klotho next week. They're keen to talk about a bigger promotion, maybe even a three-year deal. But we need to keep up the good appearances. Something I need you to remember whenever you get yourself plastered onto a headline."

"When do I get to *defend* myself?" I felt incredibly small and defeated.

"When we have enough money," she stated.

"It's not fai—" I stopped myself before I could even finish the words.

Since when was being a female athlete ever fair?

Isabelle was right. Every time I stood up in front of the journalists and said something snarky, I did more than give myself a bad name; I gave the team a bad name. It didn't help our vision of getting more women into Formula 1.

"I'm sorry," I whispered. After today's second place, I was now leading the championship, and yet I felt more dejected than ever.

"I thought Luca was supposed to be helping you with these press conferences," Isabelle grumbled. Luca had been helping me, but I was too embarrassed to admit that to Isabelle.

"We'll have him do some more training in Monaco," Nora said, taking out her phone to check her texts. "Matteo just told me that Luca will be waiting for you by his car. Do us all a favor and drive him back to the hotel. He's had quite a bit of celebratory champagne." I glanced at Isabelle, who still had a blank look on her face, and nodded before exiting the office.

Chapter Twenty-Five

Luca

Even though Georgia was deathly quiet, she couldn't hide the tears that started to fall down her face. The press conference had been a disaster, and my idea to joke through the conference had done nothing to sway the journalists' ire. I reached over and gently rested my hand over hers on the steering wheel. At my touch, she broke, shoulders trembling as a sob escaped her lips.

"Pull over, Georgia," I demanded softly. She shook her head no, and I made the request again. "I mean it. Stop the car." This time, she complied, pulling over to the side of the road in front of a cafe. Hands gripped tightly on the steering wheel, she stared out of the windshield, refusing to look at me.

I clasped her hands in mine. Unbuckling her seat belt, I pulled her out of the driver's seat and across the gearstick, glad that we'd opted to take my SUV instead of the sports car today. Georgia settled into my lap and I softly rubbed circles up and down her back.

"It'll be okay," I whispered into her ear. "It'll be okay." I didn't know what else to say, so I continued to soothe her. It didn't take a genius to realize that this was about more than the press conference. There was still the rest of the season to drive for, and coming in second place was hardly a crying matter. Henri hadn't scored any points today, giving Georgia a small lead in the championship.

"No, it won't. I'm going to lose my seat," she whimpered, trying to get a hold of her heavy breathing.

"Isabelle fire a World Champion? I doubt it."

"I won't *be* a World Champion. The press made that clear. You and Henri are better drivers, and once the teams fix the reliability of your cars, I won't be on podiums. I won't win the Driver's Championship. If we lose this Maison de Klotho sponsorship because of me, the team won't forgive me. They won't have to because we'll be out of money." The reality was, Hermes could give me a literal rocket ship, and I was still convinced Georgia would beat me.

"One outburst doesn't erase a season of top finishes," I said, brushing the hair from her cheek. "And you and Lily? Come on. No brand is walking away from that much brilliance and beauty."

That earned a choked laugh. She wiped her cheeks with the sleeve of her hoodie. "You're a terrible liar, Luca Rossi."

"And you're an ugly crier," I teased, gently poking her in the side. "A face as beautiful as yours shouldn't have tears on it." Cupping her chin, I forced her to look up at me.

There was an easy silence between us as I continued to stroke her back, watching her wipe away her tears. I knew I shouldn't have enjoyed holding her when she was in this state, shouldn't have enjoyed how perfectly she fit on my lap, but I couldn't help how good it felt to be there for her. Comforting Georgia filled a piece of my heart that I didn't know was missing.

She liked to make snide remarks here and there about me dating models or influencers, but the truth was, none of them compared to her. With her wavy dirty-blonde hair and sapphire eyes, she took my breath away. Throw in her hilarious wit, infectious laugh, and undeniable intelligence—Georgia Dubois was a catch.

It's why I had asked her out all those years ago.

But then I'd let my pride, and anger, get in the way. I summoned up some bravery and asked her out, only to let my deflated ego win in the end. I'd accidentally overheard my father's conversation with her agent the morning before our date as he offered to be her racing coach in F2.

Truthfully, the pain of that conversation still haunted me, and the more I thought about it, the more I considered how that was the beginning of the breakdown in my relationship with my father. Even back then my dad was enamored by Georgia. Listening to him offer his services away to a potential rival cut deep, and while she'd surprisingly ended up turning him down, a small part of me hadn't let that jealousy go.

Over the past few years, I'd grumbled about how similar Georgia was to my dad, comparing her fierce ambition and aggressiveness on the track, but the more I got to know her, the more I saw that, unlike my father, Georgia's ambition was rooted in her *mission.* It wasn't at the expense of not caring for others. In fact, sometimes it felt like the opposite. Lily, Henri, even Éliott—they all came to her for advice and comfort, comfort that she provided to them without question—and now that included me as well.

My stomach soured as I considered how I'd judged her with the same lens that I judged my father. My father always dove straight into planning, had always been one to bulldoze over me when I just needed him to listen. But Georgia had done nothing but surprise me. I hadn't expected her to be so open with me this morning. Hadn't expected her to just sit and listen to me complain and vent.

But she listened diligently, and with the sort of patience one could only expect from a saint.

"I should get us back to the hotel. We've got your winner's celebration tonight." She hopped back into her seat, buckling her seat belt without looking at me. "Sorry I ruined your winner's press conference."

I leaned forward and touched her hand, wrapping mine around it before she could shift into gear. "Never apologize for standing up for yourself, *amore*. Never."

She gave me a small, tired smile, one that didn't quite reach her eyes, but I held on to it anyway. The rest of the drive back to the hotel passed in silence, but the kind that felt warm, steady. The kind where words weren't needed.

And in the quiet, I knew something had shifted between us.

Something important.

Something real.

Chapter Twenty-Six

Luca

As soon as nine p.m. hit, Georgia and I made our way into the hotel lobby, immediately spotting Henri and Lily by a large limo that Henri had booked in celebration for my race win. Georgia hadn't said anything more about her fight with Isabelle, and judging by the way Henri casually greeted her, either she hadn't told him, or he was pretending not to know.

When we arrived at the club, Éliott greeted us with his typical eager golden-retriever energy that irked me to no end.

"That was a solid race today, Georgie!" He brought her into his embrace, and I reluctantly let her go, my eyes drifting to Henri's best friend. "And congrats, Luca! Winning at home is an absolute dream. Let's hope we get to see it next week with one of our favorite twins." Georgia lightly punched his shoulder, batting her eyelashes at him a bit too much for my liking.

"I'm gonna go catch up with a couple of the other drivers, let me know if you need something!" Georgia yelled over the music. Before I could protest, she disappeared into the crowd.

I stayed back, making the rounds with Edward and Lily, but my eyes kept drifting to the back of the room where

Georgia was now perched beside Éliott in a booth, her hand on his arm, her head thrown back in laughter. I couldn't help but feel an unwarranted ache in my chest as I watched her lean into him, giggling away at whatever joke he was telling. She looked so comfortable with him, so relaxed. A staunch contrast to earlier today when she was sobbing in my car.

I fought back the urge to interrupt their conversation, attempting to shove down the petty part of me that wanted to tell Éliott to piss off before stealing Georgia back to our hotel room where I could have her all to myself. After our kiss earlier today, I couldn't stop thinking about how desperately I wanted to drag her to my bed. Opting to listen to the angel on my shoulder, I headed to the bar for a refill.

"I gotta say, Luca, you're a better man than me. When Georgia and I were dating, I was always annoyed about how close she was to Éliott," Anthony sneered, grabbing my shoulder in a pretend bout of compassion.

"I don't know what you're talking about." Leaning back against the bar, I took a sip of my drink as I spared another glance at Georgia whispering into Éliott's ear.

"Well, they did go on that *one* date. You know that, right?"

Ah, so the comment she'd made outside my driver's room in Miami was starting to make sense. Anthony had a hook into me, and while I should have told him to piss off, something stopped me.

"So, how are things going with your new *relationship*?" He'd clearly made it his mission tonight to wind me up about Georgia, and to his credit, it was working.

"Why?" I said coolly. "Feeling jealous?" My tight smile did little to mask my irritation.

"Just surprised you're her type."

I cocked an eyebrow. "And what do you suppose is her *type*?"

"Winners."

"Explains why *you* broke up," I said, taking a gulp of champagne as I frantically looked for Edward to save me from this exchange.

He laughed, completely unaffected. "Probably explains why Georgia and Éliott didn't get past date one, even if Henri constantly encouraged it."

The casual dig sliced deeper than I expected. I knew Henri had a complicated relationship with me, and I knew he loved Éliott like a brother. But the idea of him wanting Georgia with someone other than me, someone he approved of, felt like salt in a very open wound.

"They're just friends," I insisted, but the words rang hollow. My mind raced, replaying every moment I'd seen Éliott and Georgia together.

Come off it, Luca, I convinced myself. *If she liked Éliott, then they'd have kept dating.*

Anthony leaned in with mock sympathy. "I don't know. They look a little close to be *just friends*. Do you actually think Éliott would say no if she gave him another shot? I always figured that was why he hung around so much. Probably hoping for a redo."

Honestly, Anthony had me there. It was hard to imagine any man not being attracted to Georgia. The laugh, her smile, the cute way she drank her coffee in the morning. She was so unique and different from anyone else I'd dated before. I glanced back at the two of them laughing together, a wave of unease and heaviness settled in my chest.

"Well, it's a good thing I plan on being her last boyfriend."

The comment tasted bitter, and I hated myself the moment it left my mouth. Per this arrangement, eventually Georgia and I would break up. She wasn't mine to keep. And then Anthony's taunts would be justified—everyone's taunts about how Georgia was too good for me would be justified.

"Sure, mate, good luck with that," he chuckled. "When Georgia finally decides to stop trying to fix you, give me a ring, yeah?"

Anthony smugly patted me on the back before traipsing back to his table. Trying not to let the envy consume me, I turned my attention to the bar and motioned for the bartender to come over.

"Buy me a drink?" The silky, smooth voice caught me off guard, and I looked up to see a woman with dark brown curls and red lipstick standing next to me, a casual smile on her face. Without waiting for my answer, the woman ordered a cocktail.

As the bartender made our drinks, I awkwardly chitchatted with her as I glanced at Georgia and Éliott's table, noticing that Henri and Lily had now joined them. Watching them all converse, it was so easy to imagine how Éliott would fit into Georgia's life. He was a rising star at his own F1 team and lived an incredibly private life. He was perfect for her, not me, some washed-out driver who was known more for his paddock parties than his wins.

Glancing up, I caught Henri's eye. He gave me a look, one of those silent, judging glances I knew too well, before whispering something to Éliott, who turned toward me with a confused frown.

Great. Now they were talking about me.

I could practically hear the conversation: *Look at Luca, already flirting with someone else. Can't keep his shit together for one night.* My teammate started to slide out the booth, and I knew that Hermes's golden boy was about to give me a lecture on my behavior.

Anthony's smug words echoed in my head. *When Georgia finally decides to stop trying to fix you…*

I slammed my drink back and set the empty glass down with a hard clink. Fuck this. Henri may not consider me worthy of his sister, but as Anthony said, Georgia dated winners, and tonight?

I was the only winner in the bar.

Without a word, I left the brunette at the bar and pushed my way toward Georgia's table, forcing a cocky grin onto my face.

"I hope no one minds," I said as I reached them, "but I think it's time I dance with my girlfriend."

Georgia blinked up at me, startled, as I took her hand without waiting for an answer. I could feel the weight of everyone's stares but I didn't care. Not right now.

I didn't just want to dance with her. I needed to remind her, and maybe even myself, that I was the one she'd kissed today. That I was the one she'd cried on, confided in. That I was the one she was going home with.

As I pulled her into the crowd, I swore I'd make sure she remembered that, too.

Chapter Twenty-Seven

Georgia

"What… Luca!"

A strong hand wrapped around my wrist and forced me toward the DJ. Luca's fingers curled around my hips, pulling me toward him with a sense of urgency. He pressed his forehead against mine, breaths mingling as we danced in the middle of the crowd.

"Sorry, *amore*, just felt like dancing with my beautiful girlfriend," he whispered into my ear. His admission surprised me, and I cocked my head to the side.

"I thought you'd be off with Edward, trying to see who could down the most glasses of champagne."

He grinned, the corners of his mouth curling with boyish charm, but his eyes, those deep brown eyes, were focused solely on me. There was something unreadable in them. Something vulnerable.

"Without my good luck charm? Never!" His smile couldn't hide the slight disappointment behind it. As Luca attempted to give us a twirl, his feet stumbled before catching himself, and I couldn't contain my belly laugh at his ridiculous smile and gleaming eyes. "It's nice to see you laugh again," he said with a wide grin.

"Oh?"

"You were so sad earlier, and it made me feel sad." The way he said it, soft, almost shy, made my chest tighten. "I don't like seeing you cry."

"Because I'm such an ugly crier," I teased, thinking back to his earlier joke.

He shook his head slowly. "No, *amore*." His lips just barely touched my neck as he whispered into my ear. "I hate seeing you cry, because it breaks my heart to see someone who deserves so much happiness not get it."

My breath hitched. The club around us buzzed with laughter and clinking glasses, but in that moment, we were in a world of our own. The way his hands held me, the way his voice dropped into something private and soft, made it hard to remember this was supposed to be fake. The sincerity in his eyes, the tenderness in his touch as we danced, it felt *different*. Inexplicable.

"And then when you didn't stay by my side tonight..." His voice trailed off. "I thought maybe you were regretting our kiss from earlier today."

A knot twisted in my stomach. Had Luca wanted to hang out this evening? After my outburst earlier in his car, I decided to give him space so he could relax and enjoy the night with Edward. Luca deserved to celebrate this victory with his friends, without the added pressure of our "relationship," but as I studied his expression, I wondered if maybe I'd misread the situation.

"Regret our kiss?" I smiled. "Judging by all the attention you keep getting tonight, I'm glad I showed everyone who Luca Rossi is going home with tonight."

My eyes flicked toward the brunette at the bar who had spent far too long trying to flirt with him. Watching him ignore her and march straight toward me like I was the only one who mattered, it set my insides on fire. After everything that happened with Anthony, it was nice to feel chosen.

"You didn't need to kiss me to do that, *amore*. You're the only person I want to go home with tonight." The words hit me harder than they should have, his breath warming my cheek. Maybe it was the champagne. Or the soft lights. Or the way he held me like I mattered. But something inside me cracked open.

For years, I'd buried that night he stood me up. Brushed it off. Told myself I misread his interest. Back then, I was fresh off F3, and he was this untouchable F1 prodigy who flirted with me like we were equals. I'd said yes to dinner so quickly it was embarrassing. But he never showed. No text. No call. Just a social media post from some club in Monaco.

He never reached out to me to explain. But he didn't need to.

What was it that Luca had said in the elevator? I was the *boring* twin. That much had been made clear by several of my previous partners. I was boring "Sassy Dubois" who competed in a man's sport.

What was sexy about that?

But now? Here he was, holding me like I was anything but boring.

He leaned in, slow and deliberate. His lips hovered just above mine, giving me the space to decide. I closed the distance without hesitation. Our mouths met softly at first, the kiss unhurried, searching. He tasted like whisky, his hands gentle as they cupped my face. With a smile on my lips, I pressed back with a bit more force before Luca pulled away to gaze at me through his hooded brown eyes.

Was that an adorable, shy smile on Luca Rossi's face?

"What do you say we head back to the room and grab a nightcap?" he murmured, brushing a loose curl behind my ear. I nodded, threading my fingers through his as we made our way back to the booth.

"Right, we're leaving folks!" I announced. "Got to make sure this one gets back to the room in one piece." I quickly grabbed my purse from Lily.

"Don't lie, *amore*," he smirked. "She just wants to get me back to our room so she can turn our *track fight* into a *late night*." No one missed the not-so-subtle wink he'd given Éliott, who to his credit just looked amused.

"In your dreams, Rossi."

"Don't you mean in *your* dreams?" Lily quipped with a smirk.

Luca immediately perked up, and I shot Lily a dirty look, before shuffling Luca into the taxi waiting for us outside. There was no doubt about it, Lily was the absolute worst at keeping secrets.

Unsurprisingly, within five minutes of getting back to the hotel room, Luca was asleep on the couch, the champagne and beer finally catching up with him. Chuckling, I grabbed the throw blanket from the end of his bed and gently draped it over him. On the coffee table, I set down a glass of water and a packet of painkillers for the inevitable morning headache.

For a moment, I contemplated how just two months ago I'd have done anything to get Luca thrown off the F1 grid.

But this wasn't the same Luca Rossi who'd ditched me for a night out. Wasn't the reckless driver who tried to throw me under the bus in front of the media.

This was a man who'd held me when I cried and who celebrated with me when I got on podiums. He'd surprised me all week, from karting and banter to the podcast, to his honesty in the car and that win at Monza.

Over and over again, I'd peeled back layers of Luca I hadn't expected to find. And somewhere along the way, something shifted. I wasn't just tolerating Luca anymore, wasn't faking anything for the media or sponsors.

I was starting to like Luca Rossi.

Hell, I was starting to like him a lot.

Chapter Twenty-Eight

Luca

The Tuesday before the Monaco Grand Prix, Georgia and I were scheduled to make an appearance at the local children's hospital. It had been a few days since our night out in Monza, but I found myself missing her more than expected.

The teams had agreed that it would be best for me to stay with Georgia instead of the team hotel, which was fine by me. I'd spent half my life in hotels, and it would be nice to see her thrive in her own home.

Georgia had left a key for me with her door attendant, and after letting myself into her apartment, I was greeted by Éliott Simon, casually sipping a cup of coffee on Georgia's couch, no Georgia in sight.

"Éliott, surprised to see you here," I snapped with more annoyance than necessary.

He lifted his mug in a mock toast. "Nice to see you too, Luca. I'm staying with Henri this week… or is that not okay with you?" I deserved his sarcastic and condescending tone, even if I didn't appreciate it. He motioned for me to take a seat across from him on the sofa. "So, how have things been going?" He studied me intently over the rim of his Valkyrie coffee mug.

"Fine."

I leaned back and stared at the clock, willing Georgia to hurry up. Talking to Éliott was akin to watching paint dry—though, if I were being fair, that probably had more to do with the fact that I was jealous of their closeness.

"Sounds like you and Georgia have a fun day scheduled today. You know last year I went with her to the charity event, it was a great experience. She's incredibly generous to give up so much of her time for the hospital, especially during such a busy week." Éliott shot me a pointed look.

Nodding, I kept my expression neutral as I considered why Éliott was hawking Georgia at me, as if I didn't know how special she was.

"Very glad I get to spend some personal time with her," I responded smoothly, before adding, "just the two of us."

Truthfully, I was thrilled that I had an entire afternoon of Georgia to myself. So much of our time was spent at the paddock with our teammates or with friends, and now I would finally have a moment to see Georgia in her element—without any distractions.

Éliott's mouth curved slightly as he looked back at his phone, like he knew something I didn't. "Well, at least you can't bail on this one."

My blood ran cold as I stared at Éliott.

Fuck. I hated that he knew.

The look on my face must have betrayed my shock, because Éliott let out a short laugh.

Before I could respond, the sound of a door opening caught our attention.

"Luca, you made it! Glad the key worked." Georgia emerged from her bedroom, already dressed for the charity event, her hair pulled back in a loose ponytail. She wore a navy-blue polo and black jeans that fitted her curves perfectly.

Éliott checked his watch. "Ah, shit, I'm going to be late for my VIP meeting."

At ten a.m.? I snickered to myself. No chance he had a VIP meeting this early, but I appreciated Éliott making himself scarce.

"Georgia, an incredible host as always." Éliott smiled, giving her a kiss on each cheek. "Go easy on Luca today, yeah?" Éliott's eyes lingered on Georgia like there was an unspoken understanding between them.

Georgia chuckled, playfully punching his arm. "We'll all catch up over dinner?"

"Deal."

The moment the door closed, Georgia wandered to the kitchen. "We still have fifteen minutes before we need to leave. Want some coffee?"

"Sure, thanks."

While Georgia started the coffee, I took a moment to take in my surroundings. To my surprise, the walls were completely covered in paintings—paintings of the tracks, the Valkyrie car, former teammates. Set in the center above her TV was a painting of Henri and Georgia, the two of them dressed in their respective racing suits, both of them wearing cheesy grins with a thumbs up. Everywhere you looked there was a painting of something involving racing, and I couldn't help but smile.

When we started this stunt, it felt like she was pretending to be a carbon copy of my dad just to annoy me, but if this showed me anything, it was that her love of all things motorsports was real.

She handed me a steaming mug and sat beside me on the couch. "That one," she said, nodding at the Henri painting, "I made for our birthday. Henri has one too."

"You're seriously talented." The word talented didn't feel like enough.

"Thanks." She smiled bashfully. "Apparently, someone told the world on a podcast that I painted, so now Valkyrie have been hounding me to send them some artwork for their social media channels."

"What a jerk." I winked. "You should send him some artwork as payback."

Georgia scoffed, taking a sip of her black coffee. "So, I chatted with Isabelle this morning. Valkyrie met with Maison de Klotho yesterday. The meeting went better than expected, and we've secured some more funding. She mentioned that you reached out to them and offered for us to do a joint photo shoot together?" Georgia looked surprised.

"Well, I figured a model shoot with the most beautiful girl in F1 wasn't a terrible way to spend my summer break," I teased. Blushing Georgia really was starting to become my favorite Georgia.

"Thank you, Luca. I mean it. For Miami… and offering to do this photo shoot. I'm sure that helped sweeten the deal." I loved the way she was looking at me, eyes soft and filled with appreciation. It filled my chest with so much joy and warmth. I'd do anything to keep Georgia looking at me like this.

"So, you ready to head to the hospital?" I asked, finishing my cup of coffee as I pulled my sweater over my head.

"Let's do it."

The crisp morning air accompanied us as we made our way through the narrow streets and toward the hospital. Everywhere we turned our faces were plastered on billboards, banners, even on the sides of buildings. As we approached the towering hospital in the heart of Monaco, its glass facade glinting in the sunlight, a coordinator greeted us with an eager smile.

"Good morning!" Georgia called out, grabbing the woman in for a hug. "So good to see you again."

Extending out a hand, the coordinator crooned, "And this must be Luca. I'm Nancy, your assistant for the day."

"Morning."

After a few more pleasantries, our coordinator led us through a labyrinth of hallways, the sound of children's laughter echoing in the distance before we finally reached a large, brightly lit conference room. I trailed behind Georgia and Nancy as they led me through the expansive room, my eyes scanning over the various pieces of artwork hanging from the walls. Stopping at one of the drawings, I noticed a crayon artwork of what looked like a little stick-figure girl standing next to a dark blue car, with another figure standing next to her.

"Me and Georgia," I whispered aloud, reading the caption. "Nice picture, looks just like you." Georgia's smile was so wide her eyes crinkled at the corners.

"All year the kids from the hospital send me artwork, so I always ask the staff to display them before the events. They love seeing their art on the walls. I can't always respond to them, but this way they know I got it."

I nodded, observing Georgia as she slightly fixed the crooked drawing. She was at ease, and it felt like a stark contrast to the Georgia that roamed the paddock with a face full of serious determination.

"So, um, what's the plan for today?" I asked.

"Our meet-and-greet starts in ten. We'll let the kids hop into the pretend Valkyrie Formula 1 car, get some photos with them, sign some pictures. They're very excited you're here this year!"

"Oh?" Considering we were in Monaco, I'd expected the kids to all be Team Valkyrie.

"Oh, yes! Yesterday I saw a parade of LR52 shirts and hats all over the hospital." She winked at me.

Walking over to the Valkyrie model car they touted around for events, Georgia motioned toward it.

"Wanna hop in?" she teased as I ogled the dark blue exterior. Valkyrie had one of the better paint jobs, although that perhaps had something to do with the lack of sponsorship logos all over it.

"Think Hermes would fire me," I chuckled.

"Coward," Georgia taunted, knowing full well that I would immediately have to prove her wrong. Luca Rossi was many things, but as Georgia had reminded me before Monza, I wasn't a coward.

"Fine, but don't be alarmed when Valkyrie gives me your seat because I look better in the car than you do." A wry smile on my face, I threw a leg over the side and hopped into the tiny cockpit, struggling to get comfortable as my broad shoulders squeezed into the seat.

"Good grief, is this car made for toddlers?"

Georgia snapped a couple photos, and I had no doubt I'd be hearing from Edward about this one later. "You look like Buddy from *Elf* when he's trying to fit behind those desks."

As I stepped out, I heard a soft, small voice from behind me. "Excuse me, Mr. Luca?" A small boy with a bright purple Hermes cap was standing there when I turned around. Smiling, I bent down, taking the pen from his hand.

"Want me to sign your hat, little man?"

"Hand it over, Pierre," his mom urged. I ruffled his thick brown hair before taking the hat from him, signing my name on the bill. "Would you like Georgia's signature as well?"

"Ew, gross. No girl cooties!" Pierre giggled as he snatched the cap from my hand, proudly displaying his prize. Georgia was beaming at the mother, who was silently whispering an apology, but she just shrugged it off with a large smile, laughing away as she was passed a hat from a little girl.

"You're great with kids," Georgia whispered as she leaned into me, waiting for the next set of children to arrive. We took a seat behind the small table, and I grabbed the water bottle that had been left out for me.

"Do you do this often?"

"I like to visit whenever I have a break. Less now that I'm traveling so much," she lamented. "But it's always a joy to come back here, to see the smiles on their faces." Her eyes glistened with genuine affection. "These kids, they're warriors, you know? They fight battles every day that most adults can't even comprehend. And if I can bring them a moment of happiness, then it's all worth it."

"Who knew Georgia Dubois had such a soft side? This is truly incredible, Georgia."

I watched her interact with another little girl, her warmth and kindness shining through in every interaction. In the paddock Georgia was so fiercely guarded, and I loved seeing this more relaxed, warm part of her shine.

Over the next two hours, we signed countless posters, hats, and pictures, listening to their stories and answering questions about racing. Some of them dreamed of becoming professional drivers themselves, while others were simply in awe of how fast our cars went.

"Alright, Luca, last one and then we can head off." Georgia was smiling, but I could see a hint of sadness on her face. She really did love it here.

As the little boy approached, I bent down, giving him a wide smile as he announced, "I want to be a racer just like you, Luca!"

"Oh, yeah?" I chuckled, grabbing his Hermes hat.

"Yeah! You're my favorite racer ever! I'm going to win Monza, too. My dad's Italian and he said you're one of the best racers Italy has ever had, even better than your dad! My dad isn't a racer, he's just an accountant."

I perked up, flashing him a grin. "Your dad says I'm the best racer on the grid, huh?"

"Oh no, he says Georgia's the best on the grid." The boy said the words with such sincerity and honesty that I couldn't help but throw my head back in a laugh as his mother, embarrassed, hushed her son. Georgia let out a snicker behind me.

"Well, I can't argue with your dad there!" I finished signing the cap and handed it back to his mother, before signing a Hermes cap for the boy's father as well.

"Thank you," the boy's mother whispered. "He always talks about how he wants to be like Luca Rossi when he grows up." Staring into her eyes, I kept waiting for the *just kidding* but as the woman continued to stare back at me, I knew that she was serious.

"Keep chasing your dreams, hmm?" I said, ruffling his hair one more time. "And one day you might just find yourself standing on that Monza podium." The little boy nodded, waltzing off to get a photo in the model Valkyrie car. I turned back to Georgia, who was gathering her things.

"Want to walk to the paddock? I need to grab a few things," she asked.

"Yeah, I'd love a walk."

As we pushed through the heavy glass doors, the cool evening breeze greeted us. It felt nice to be outside, especially on such a beautiful day.

"So, did you like today?" she asked.

"It was really fun, Georgia. I haven't felt that relaxed in a long time, to be honest. Who knew I was someone's favorite racer?"

"I did," she said firmly, her voice overflowing with sincerity. "I did."

"You keep your work here so private. You should tell people about this charity. It's so good for the kids."

Georgia shook her head. "I don't do it for fame, Luca. I do it because I love it. Because working with these children, it's an honor. They've been through enough, and I don't want to use them for my PR gain."

"Like you're using me?" I'd meant it to be a joke, although Georgia's expression told me I was about as funny as a comedian at a funeral. "Sorry, too soon," I added, appreciating Georgia's forgiving laugh. "You know, there's a balance between showing off versus showing who you are. This charity, these kids, this is something you love to do. Celebrities are always talking about their charities, and yes, I'm sure in a big part to make themselves look good, but think of the good it does for the charity. The money and awareness it would raise could really help make a difference." Her expression softened, and she looked at me with a mix of gratitude and contemplation, but she said nothing, and I knew that was the end of the subject for today.

As we walked through the streets of Monaco, the sun began to set, casting a warm, golden glow over the bustling city. We walked the next half-mile in mostly silence before finally arriving at the Valkyrie garage. Since it was Tuesday, the paddock was mostly empty, barring some mechanics and logistics people setting up. The drivers and fans weren't expected until Wednesday and Thursday.

I followed Georgia into her driver's room, loosening my sweater, when I froze. "Um, Georgia, why is there a hamster in here?"

"Oh, that?" she shrugged casually. "That's just a little gift I got Edward."

"Georgia Dubois, you know Edward hates hamsters, rats—all rodents!"

"Exactly." She pulled out a Wilmington garage mechanic outfit from her closet, unrolling it in front of her.

"I'm sorry," I chuckled in disbelief, "are you going to dress up as a mechanic, sneak into the Wilmington garage, and prank Edward?"

Who was this Georgia standing in front of me?

"Oh no, *we're* going to dress up as mechanics and sneak into the Wilmington garage," she laughed, pulling out a second outfit. "You guys are always pranking each other, figured it was my turn."

"Absolutely not!" I scoffed in disbelief. "You're out of your mind. I can't sneak into my old team!"

"Wow, and to think you once called *me* boring." She tsked, shaking her head in disappointment.

Little Miss Goody Two-Shoes Dubois did not just call *me* boring.

"Come on, Luca. Don't turn into a coward on me now." Georgia really did know how to push my buttons.

"Fine."

Incredibly pleased with herself, Georgia grabbed her mechanic's outfit, slipping it on over her polo and jeans as I did the same. Grabbing the hamster cage, which was now disguised by a small blanket, we made our way out of the garage and toward Wilmington.

When we approached, Georgia casually waved at the security guard standing by the entrance to the offices. Before he could recognize us, we quickly opened the doors and snuck through. I glanced over at Georgia, who seemed surprisingly composed, and I almost felt embarrassed that *I* was the nervous one.

Spotting Edward's room, I scanned the empty hallway, knowing most people would be out since it was starting to get close to dinner time. I nodded to Georgia that the coast was clear and she hopped into the room with me hot on her heels.

"I feel like it shouldn't be so easy to break into another team's garage," Georgia chuckled as she looked for a spot to place the hamster. Before I could answer, I heard Edward's voice down the hallway.

"Fuck!" I whispered to Georgia.

"Quick! In here." She ran toward the closet, and we piled inside, Georgia silently shushing the hamster like it, too, was part of this fiasco. As soon as the closet door closed, I heard Edward's footsteps as he entered the room.

"See you tomorrow!" he called out.

A crash made us jump. Georgia's shoulder pressed against my chest, the hamster cage wedged awkwardly between us. Her breath was warm on my collarbone, and I glanced down at her in the dim space, her lips parted in silent laughter.

"Damn it. Where is this thing?" Edward grumbled, and I silently prayed that whatever he'd lost wasn't in our hiding place. I flashed Georgia an annoyed look, but she just continued to smile as she shook her head at Edward's mumbling commentary to himself. She nervously licked her lips before wrapping her hands around my arm for balance, gripping the cage tightly. Here I was, trapped inside my best friend's closet holding a hamster doing what was probably one of the most ridiculous pranks yet, and all my body could think about was how soft Georgia's hands felt wrapped around my muscles.

Finally, Edward let out a triumphant "Aha!" followed by the sound of the door shutting behind him. Georgia burst out of the closet, stifling a cackle.

"Fucking hilarious," she whispered, carefully placing the hamster cage on Edward's desk, along with a note. "Right, ready?"

I shot her one last disbelieving nod before opening the door, peeking through the small crack. "Coast is clear, let's get out before someone catches us." Georgia followed me out of the room and down the hallway, both of us taking care to keep our steps light as we silently walked past the offices.

The moment I stepped outside, I grabbed Georgia's hand and started running toward the Valkyrie entrance. Georgia let out a squeak but kept up with the pace. We ignored the strange looks from her mechanics as we sprinted our way to Georgia's driver's room.

"Edward is going to kill us. I cannot believe you convinced me to do that!"

Georgia shimmied out of the mechanic's uniform, shoving it into her closet, before motioning for me to do the same.

"Edward is never going to know, and even if he does, he deserves it for all of those pranks he's pulled on Henri over the years." She grinned. With her dimples making an appearance on her already flushed cheeks, Georgia looked beautiful as she basked in the satisfaction of her prank.

"If I didn't know better, I'd say you've been holding out on me, tricking me into thinking that I was hanging out with the *boring* Dubois twin."

"Just like you tricked me into thinking I was going to win that karting race?"

I stepped closer, crowding her gently against the doorframe. One arm braced above her head. With the other, I reached up, trailing my fingers lightly under her jaw.

"There's a lot more to you than meets the eye, isn't there?" I whispered. Our bodies were flush against each other as I towered over her.

Her breath hitched as our eyes locked. Slowly, I leaned in, and her lips parted slightly, like she was daring me to close the gap. After Monza, I'd gotten another taste of her, and over the last week, kissing Georgia again was all I'd thought about. I edged closer, my lips just barely ghosting hers, when I heard the unforgivably loud ring of my phone, breaking the spell that had taken hold of us.

She cleared her throat, cheeks flushed, motioning toward the phone. "You, um, gonna get that?"

Of course, it was Edward calling. "Ed, what's up?" His tone was seething with annoyance. "A hamster? Weird, why would your team principal get you a hamster?" It was nearly impossible to hold in my laughter as I listened to Edward's franticness on the other side of the line.

I pressed the speaker button on my phone as Edward's voice boomed through. "I grabbed my wallet from my driver's room, got to my car and realized I'd forgotten my keys. I walked back in and then all of a sudden there was a hamster in my room!"

"Well, you've always wanted a pet."

"I'm going to fucking kill my team principal. He left me some ridiculous note, too," he grumbled.

"Keep me posted on what Arthur says, yeah?"

I probably should have felt worse, but considering he'd once told security that I was an intruder after I'd forgotten my pass at the hotel, I figured this served him right.

As soon as I hung up the phone, Georgia was doubled over in a fit of laughter, tears streaming. "Fuck, he's going to be so mad."

"Nah, he's a good sport!" I said finally, watching Georgia chortle away, speedily checking her messages to make sure Edward hadn't texted her. "Look, I gotta go back to the garage, but I'll see you at dinner?"

"See you then, Luca."

I turned to leave.

"Oh, and Luca, not a word of this to Henri!"

I nodded, although when I felt a large pillow hit the back of my head, I knew she didn't believe me, which was fair.

If I had it my way, the entire world was going to know about the Georgia I had met today.

Chapter Twenty-Nine

Luca

Wednesday evening was Georgia and Henri's live recording of the *Home Stretch* podcast, and I was glad that Edward had offered to tag along, especially since he had no idea who had pulled the little prank on him earlier.

Georgia and I had done some prep in her condo, and even though she claimed she didn't feel ready, I had every bit of confidence in her. This was Georgia's time to shine, her time to show the fans that she was more than *just* racing.

Watching her up on stage, I hated seeing the darkness in her eyes, the stiffness of her shoulders as she sat down, clearly uncomfortable in front of all these people. I flashed her a large grin, a small reminder that she was ready for this.

"So, Georgia," Josh, the presenter announced, "we've been very impressed with your F1 season. You're a few points ahead of your brother in the championship. Tell us, why do you think you have what it takes to win?"

"Dedication." Georgia tapped her fingers a few times on the table before continuing. "I know I can do this. I've never had a training regime this intense, and I feel like this is the fittest I've ever been. I'm so incredibly fortunate to have a world-class strategy team at my fingertips. Plus, I've got the fastest car on the track." She winked at Henri, who just flipped her off from across the table.

"Tell me, Georgia, what would it mean to win Monaco?"

"I've wanted to be a Formula 1 champion since I was a little girl. I want to show young girls all around the world that they can compete in Formula 1, and there is no better place to do it than to win one of the crown jewels of motorsport. If I win this race, I will be the second driver to win the Triple Crown of Motorsport. I won the Indianapolis 500 last year and the 24 Hours of Le Mans a few years before. It would mean the world to me to win this honor in front of my home crowd." Henri gave her shoulder a brotherly squeeze. "It's why I help organize this charity event at the local children's hospital. Racing is such a big part of this community, and seeing the kids fall in love with Formula 1 is so incredibly special."

A sense of satisfaction swelled when Georgia mentioned her charity. After the event, photos had been circulating of the two of us, but Georgia had never really discussed her work publicly. Besides the photos, she'd been so private about her philanthropy. It was these genuine pieces of Georgia that I so desperately wanted the fans and sponsors to see.

"Oh, I've been wanting to ask you about all of those cute photos I saw on social media from various parents."

Come on Georgia, you can do it, I silently urged her on.

"The charity puts on an event before the Monaco Grand Prix. This year we were able to get Valkyrie's model that we use for VIP photo shoots, and the kids got to take photos sitting in the car. It's really sweet, very fun." She smiled.

"What a lovely idea!" Josh gushed. "We'll have to get the information from you, Georgia. I'm sure our supporters would love to contribute."

Georgia's face lit up with a radiant smile. "I'll be sure to share it."

"Well, it's going to be an interesting race this weekend, I dare say! Georgia, not to change topics here, but rumor has it the women of the paddock have a reason to hate you," the presenter crooned.

"Oh? Didn't realize you packed the room full of journalists?" Georgia quipped, earning her a genuine laugh from the audience. Even they were starting to notice the bullying that Georgia was experiencing each race.

"Oh, come on now, we all saw that kiss you and Luca shared at Monza. I have a lot of friends, but I don't think I've ever kissed any of them like *that*. So, tell us, how did Luca Rossi manage to snag the heart of everyone's new favorite driver?" Georgia's eyes widened, and I knew she was trying to suppress a sarcastic laugh.

"Well, you know, Josh, Luca can be pretty convincing when he wants to be." She cast me a wink and a kiss, much to the audience's amusement. Edward just snorted next to me. "But in all seriousness, it was just sort of sprung on me."

I had to fight to hide my grin at her subtle truth.

"Well, we really are happy for you both. Now, it's no secret you've had a bit of a tough time with the media and fans. Your team is new, and as a community, we can be a bit tough on newbies."

Sure, that's it, Josh. Even Henri couldn't suppress his laughter at Josh's comment, poorly covering his smile with the back of his hand.

"But I think you've been painted a bit unfairly. Tell me, Henri, what is something the audience should know about your sister?" Henri's eyes were glowing with eagerness, and I immediately knew what story he was going to share. He'd caught me laughing in my driver's room this morning, and after very little persuasion, I'd finally let it slip.

"Oh, Josh, I'm worried if I tell this story, Georgia might get banned from a certain competitor's garage." Josh leaned in as if he and Henri were two schoolgirls gossiping at the lunch table.

Noticing my eager face, Georgia butted in, "I don't think this is a story anyone wants to hear."

"Nah, I think it's a good one!" I yelled, urging Henri to continue. Georgia shot me a stern look, but I just continued to sweetly smile at her. This was the Georgia everyone needed to see. The hilarious, silly Georgia that hid behind her strict persona.

"Nonsense!" Josh just put his hands up as the audience booed her.

"So, Georgia thought it would be hilarious to sneak a hamster into another driver's room. She bought it a nice cage, even added a mini Formula 1 car to its home. She dressed as a mechanic and somehow made her way into the other driver's room, placing the hamster on the desk with a note about it being a gift from the team principal. The only problem? Georgia apparently didn't close the door to the cage all the way, and about an hour later, the team principal opened his bag to find a hamster burrowed in his expensive Armani briefcase."

Suddenly I heard a gasp next to me, and I knew the moment it had all clicked in Edward's mind. "It was YOU that left the hamster in my room!" Edward was now standing, his finger pointed toward Georgia, but before I could defend her, a large grin formed on Georgia's face as she proudly waved off Edward's disdain. The crowd erupted with laughter at the two of them, and I flashed Georgia another knowing smile, urging her to continue.

"It was Luca's idea!" she lied, and I shook my head no, wagging my finger at her.

"Oh, no, Dubois, this one was all you!" I called out. Edward flashed her his middle finger, his head shaking with laughter. He was always such a good sport.

"I'll get you back for this one, Dubois!"

Once the crowd had settled down, Josh shook his head in disbelief. "So, tell me, what happened to the hamster?"

"Apparently, after an hour, they were able to catch it and return it to its home." Henri grinned. "I hear it was quite the model during some VIP photo shoots at Wilmington today! He's got a sweet mansion, a nice toy car inside. It's won the jackpot."

"Well, who knew the Dubois family had such a prankster in their midst!" Josh announced. "I dare say, this has been a great podcast. You have both been an absolute delight, and we look forward to seeing you both on the podium this weekend!"

As soon as the taping ended, I met Georgia at the end of the stage. "Nice little interview you gave there!" I grabbed her and pulled her into a hug, kissing the top of her head as she rolled her eyes.

"Can't believe you betrayed me like that," she quipped, but before I could defend myself Edward arrived with a tray of shots from the after-party bar.

"Absolutely not!" Georgia protested. "We have to be in the paddock tomorrow!"

"Come on, Georgie, you've already broken your 'no alcohol' rule. What's a teeny, tiny harmless shot? Plus, you owe me after that *story*." Edward winked, although Georgia still looked completely unconvinced by his charade.

"Geez, no wonder they call you the boring twin." I stuck my tongue out at her, and to my surprise, Georgia grabbed a shot and downed it like the fucking champion I knew she was. The group of us drivers erupted into applause as Georgia tried to hide her gagging. The look on Edward's face was priceless, eyes wide with utter disbelief dancing on his face.

"There you have it, ladies and gentlemen. Never underestimate Georgia Dubois!" I announced.

Chapter Thirty

Georgia

On the Monaco Grand Prix Sunday, my arrival at the paddock was truly madness. Fans flooded the streets, pressed up against barricades, shouting, cheering, and waving flags in every direction.

"Wow, Monaco really does show up for a race, huh?" Luca laughed. To be fair, I was shocked at the number of Valkyrie flags waving in the wind. Surrounded by a countless sea of blue, I was touched by the strong turnout for both me and Valkyrie.

"Morning, G!" Mel greeted. "Ready for the race? I know we're starting second today, but I have a good feeling about this."

A feeling I didn't remotely share.

Starting second in Monaco felt more like a death sentence.

I hopped into the cockpit of my car, settling into the tight space as I checked my water and radio. After yesterday's tense qualifying session, Henri just managed to squeak out pole, leaving me starting second. Overtaking was damn near impossible on this track, and the fact that the only person who knew this track as intimately as I did was starting in P1 made my heart sink into my stomach.

Mel leaned over the halo, grinning down at me. "Let's show these boys how Monaco is won."

This was the tenth time I'd sat in my car this season, but there was something different about this moment. It was almost dreamlike, as if I were watching it all unfold from outside of my body.

As the formation lap ticked down and I pulled into my grid slot, my eyes locked on the lights above. My pulse quickened, each light igniting in sequence until they all vanished.

I launched off the line, holding tight behind Henri as we darted into the first corner. The buildings blurred around us as we weaved through the tight twists and hairpins of our childhood city. He had the edge, but I stayed close. Henri might have started this race from pole, but unlike my brother, I had something special: a woman-run team with a point to prove. Monaco wasn't about raw speed. It was about strategy. Pit stops. Timing. Precision.

Half the race flew by, and Henri was still leading. My only real chance was in the pits. If I could nail my stop, I might leapfrog him.

But when I dove in for fresh tires, the left rear stuck.

Three seconds went by. An eternity.

"Fuck. What happened?" I snapped into the radio.

The response came, frustratingly calm. "Just keep driving. We'll make up the time."

Just keep driving? What else was I going to do?

"We'll need a fucking miracle," I bit back. Mel proceeded to respond to me, but I ignored her.

Lap after lap ticked by. Fifty. Fifty-one. Hope started to dwindle.

And then, on lap fifty-two, Henri dove into the pits for softs. But Hermes flubbed the stop. A fumbled tire gun.

Henri came out behind me in P2.

Suddenly, I was leading.

Narrowing my focus, I cruised through the next several laps with unnerving precision, driving within millimeters of the barriers. This was my race to lose and no *man* was going to take it from me.

Eight laps to go. Then six. Then two.

The car hissed as I turned into my last lap.

"Mel. Noise. Why?"

"Debris stuck in the floor," Mel confirmed.

"Fuck. What do I do?"

There was a pause. "Remember when we went to that stupid fair in Paris?"

"How is this fucking relevant?" I bit back.

"We went on that silly go-kart track, and you were so mad you qualified behind me, so you just blocked the way for everyone like an absolute menace."

"Yes?" *How was this the time for that story?*

"Now's your time, G. Be that menace we all know and love."

Mel didn't have to ask me twice. Feeling the debris lodged in my car, I slowed down my pace and did something I'd never thought I'd have to do. I started to drive in the middle of the road, not caring about the racing line. For once in my life, I didn't need to be faster than Henri.

I just needed to be in front.

The streets of Monaco were tight, almost impossible to pass. I could see his car swerving, trying to find an opportunity to get around.

But this was Monaco, and the only person who knew these narrow streets as intimately as I did was behind me. I adjusted my line, started driving defensively, right in the middle of the street, cutting off any sliver of hope Henri had for a pass. Monaco's streets were barely wide enough for one car, let alone two. He tried the inside. He tried the outside. But I gave him nothing.

As soon as the checkered flag came into view, I launched my car with all the might and power of a Valkyrie, like my car *was* a warrior from the Norse legends of old. Henri's car was gaining, our cars almost touching as he made one last attempt to get past me. But it was too late. The waving of the black and white flag signaled the end of the race.

And I was officially a Monaco Grand Prix winner.

Every emotion I'd felt in the last year, all of the pain and suffering from the journalists, the teasing about my dedication to the sport, faded away. Every ache and sacrifice I'd buried deep burst free as tears streamed down my cheeks. I let out a half-choked sob, unable to contain it. The roar of the crowd faded into a blur, replaced by a single truth echoing in my chest: we'd done it. Not by luck. Not by accident. But through grit, precision, and a team that never once gave up on me.

We *deserved* this win.

The radio clicked on. "Georgie, this is Isabell—" A pause. "No, this is the *entire* Valkyrie team speaking. Well done, love, well done! Also, that's third place for Lily. Double podium at Monaco, couldn't have asked for a better race from you both. I'm so proud."

My scream into the radio was raw. "Fuck yes! This trophy belongs to the team. You believed in me when no one else did." I paused, taking a moment to wave at the crowd. "This win is for every little girl who is told she can't compete with the boys. Let this be a lesson to those who want to keep women out of motorsports. We're here to *stay*." I carefully maneuvered my car into the P1 spot before eagerly jumping out of my car, flailing my arms in my classic window-washing dance.

Henri barreled into me first, sweeping me into a tight hug, "I'm so proud, Peaches!"

I caught Lily's eyes and barely had time to open my arms before she jumped into them, legs wrapped tight around my waist, squealing into my ear.

"You did it!" she cried. The moment I set her down, I saw my brother pull her into his embrace, his arms wrapped around her as she buried her head in his chest, too overwhelmed with excitement.

My eyes darted around the bustling crowd, searching for Luca.

And then I saw him. That familiar swagger, that impossibly wide grin. Luca swooped in and dipped me backward, his lips finding mine in a passionate kiss. I felt like Cinderella being kissed by her Prince Charming as Luca held me so tight I could feel his racing heart.

"Go and celebrate, *amore*. I'll give you your real prize later," he whispered, lips brushing over my ear. Part of me wondered how large of a fine I would be given if I missed the winner's press conference and dragged Luca straight into my bed to see what kind of prize he was offering.

After the podium ceremony was complete, I made my way back to the garage to prepare for the media circus. For the first time in the history of my Formula 1 career, I wasn't feeling overwhelmed with crippling anxiety. My car could have caught on fire, and I'd still be full of this inexplicable joy. Nothing could ruin the magic of winning Monaco.

A knock pounded on my driver's room door. "Come in!"

Isabelle stepped inside, setting a small gift bag with blue tissue paper on the coffee table. "This is for you."

Opening it, I pulled out a Valkyrie team polo, giving Isabelle a confused look.

"Look at the back." She grinned. Flipping over the shirt, I immediately understood why she was beaming with excitement. Isabelle had taken my team polo and embellished it with the phrase "*Triple Crown of Motorsport*." The words I'd wanted to say since the beginning of my career.

24 Hours of Le Mans. Indy 500. And now Monaco. They were all mine.

Gazing up at her in awe, tears started to pour out of me. This shirt must have taken weeks to create.

Even before I believed in myself, Isabelle had never faltered.

"Th-thank you," I whispered. She flashed me a lovely, pearly-white smile. With the way the season was going, I might have enough Isabelle smiles collected to fill up both hands.

"Wear it to the press conference, Georgia. Wear it and remind those journalists that a lioness has arrived, and she has a bone to pick with them."

–

At the after-party I stuck to just a few drinks. I fully intended on remembering every part of my Monaco win. Luca, surprisingly, had also decided to drink less. Ever since the kiss after the race, he'd been acting aloof. Instead of being his normal, boisterous self, he was quiet as I got ready for the party. It felt unnerving. Even at the bar, he was attentive when I needed him, but mostly kept to himself.

Truth be told, I was feeling annoyed. I'd won the Monaco Grand Prix, my home race, and for some reason, Luca had decided *this* was the time he was going to give me the space I had been craving. Instead of grabbing me and giving me my prize, he'd kept his hands to himself all night, and if I was being honest, I was disappointed.

Was this how Luca felt back in Monza after his win? Suddenly, I was starting to understand how he felt.

It was infuriating watching Luca and Lily sit at the bar, innocently chatting away about their races. Green envy slowly crawled up my spine as I watched the two of them. Just as I was about to march up to Luca and demand he give me that prize he promised, I heard a voice call out behind me.

"Georgia, wait up!" Turning around, Anthony smiled at me.

Christ, not now, Anthony.

"Hey, um… so…" I shot him an impatient look as I spared a glance at Luca and Lily chatting a few tables over.

"Spit it out, Anthony."

He recoiled at my snapping but swallowed before continuing regardless. "Congrats on today. That was an amazing race from you."

I forced a smile, trying to act polite despite my irritation.

Shifting uncomfortably, Anthony slid his hand through his hair. "Look, Georgia. I know things have been… complicated between us." Understatement of the year. "But seeing you up there on that podium today, living your dream, it made me realize how much I missed you," he sighed. "Here you are winning the Grand Prix you've been dreaming about, and all I wanted to do was congratulate you. I just, I'm sorry, alright?" I stared back at

Anthony in disbelief, mouth wide open. "For before, you know? For not believing in you."

"Uh huh." I wanted to kick myself for not being able to say something—*anything*—better than that. "And this sudden change of heart is because…?"

Anthony lightly laughed. "I know, I know, why would you believe me now? Look, I feel bad for what I said before, and for what I said at the bar. I guess… I'm not really over you." I felt like I'd been punched in the gut. "You don't have to say anything back. Seeing you with Luca back in Barcelona, I guess I wasn't able to handle the truth."

No way was he being serious.

"The truth being?" I asked cautiously.

"That Luca's right. That you deserve better than me. I couldn't handle all of your success, and I was an ass about it, but that doesn't change the fact I miss you, you know? I miss our late-night conversations, our fun road trips."

"You sure have a hell of a way of showing it," I said dryly. "Honestly, Anthony, I'm sort of struggling to believe you right now."

He cut me off. "I know, and I deserve that. Look, I know you have to get back to your friends, but I just wanted to let you know." Stunned into silence, all I could do was stare at him while I attempted to process Anthony's unexpected confession. He reached for me, but before he could grab my wrist, Luca suddenly appeared by my side, a discernible frown on his face. Arms wrapped around my waist in a possessive hold as Luca narrowed his eyes at Anthony.

"Is there a problem here?" Luca's voice was laced with a subtle threat.

Anthony's eyes widened in surprise, clearly taken aback by Luca's sudden appearance. "No problem," he stammered. "I was just congratulating Georgia on her win."

"Yes, well, thanks, Anthony," I said flatly before turning to Luca. "Ready to go?"

He quirked a questioning eyebrow but nodded, letting me drag him into the cab I'd hailed outside of the club.

The ride to my apartment was silent. Truthfully, I didn't know what to say or think about Anthony's confession. It was unlikely that this sudden change of heart was genuine, but a part of me wanted to believe the apology anyway. I'd held on to my hate and anguish for so long, and yet watching Anthony apologize to me, it felt unfulfilling.

I didn't need his apology to feel whole anymore.

His opinion of me didn't matter. Whether the apology was genuine or not didn't matter. At this moment, the only thing that mattered was Luca. He was the only person I wanted to spend tonight with, even if it felt like he was ignoring me. The moment the car arrived, we quickly shuffled into my living room, and I was feeling more and more annoyed with him.

He padded over to my fridge, grabbed a bottle of water, and turned back to me, smiling slightly. "Well, what a good day. Night, Georgie." And with that, he waltzed into his room and shut the door.

Why was I fuming? Not for any decent reason I cared to admit. I marched over to my guest room and flung open the door, not sparing him a knock. Inside was a shirtless Luca staring back at me. His eyes conveyed a look of innocent shock, but the ever-so-slight curl of his lip told me otherwise.

"What was that all about?" I demanded.

"Hmm?" he asked casually, setting his water down at his bedside table.

"You!" I yelled back, starting to raise my voice. "You spent the whole night ignoring me by, like, *not* ignoring me."

Good grief, Georgia, you can do better than that.

"I thought you'd want your space," he responded easily. "Didn't want to overcrowd you."

"Why would you think I'd want space from my boyfriend?" I gritted back.

"*Fake* boyfriend," he added quietly, and he almost looked disappointed as he said the words. His smirk grew into a full-blown grin, and my throat tightened with embarrassment.

I felt like a criminal that had been caught red-handed.

"What is it you want me to do, Georgia?" he asked, slowly inching toward me. His eyes were dark, pupils blown as he watched me like a hawk. "Hmm?"

What did I want Luca to do?

I stepped back, but he followed. When my back hit the wall, his hands came up to cradle my face, his eyes burning into mine. His lips brushed mine, featherlight. I tried to keep my eyes focused on his, but it was next to impossible, not as he snaked his other hand around my waist and pulled my entire body flush with his.

I wanted to say *something* back, but I was frozen while I contemplated what I wanted. Luca chuckled as he watched me try to form words, his knowing smile growing larger by the second.

"Oh, *amore*, I'll let you get away with not answering me this time as a reward for winning today, but next time I ask you a question, I expect an answer. Only good girls get rewards." Goosebumps shot down my body as I felt his warm breath on my neck. Luca's lips met mine in a passionate kiss. I wrapped my arms around his back and pulled him closer.

His hands traveled down to my thighs and tapped them gently, inviting me to jump up and wrap my legs around his waist, which I happily obliged. Luca turned on his heels and swung open the door, making a beeline for my bedroom. I sunk into the softness of the bed as he pinned me down.

I was a panting mess as he pulled off my top. Looking up at me, he asked if he could continue by removing my skirt. Without hesitation, I nodded in desperate agreement. This was my race win, and I was going to enjoy my spoils. Luca's lips curled into a mischievous smirk as he hooked his fingers around the waistband of my skirt and pulled it down in one swift motion. I was about to protest, but before I could, his mouth was trailing soft kisses up my leg.

I felt his mouth get to my thong, and he pulled it aside, placing gentle licks around my core—everywhere except where I desperately needed him most. He slipped a finger under the fabric and tugged. My legs draped over his shoulders as he worked his way back up, his slow kisses sending shivers down my spine. My whimpers grew louder as he reached the top of my thighs.

"Luca, stop teasing," I demanded. All I heard was a chuckle, but to my surprise, he gave in. His tongue slid up the entrance to my clit, and I sucked in a breath. I started to squirm from the pleasure, and I felt Luca's hand press down on my hips, keeping them in place as he stopped my movements. Unconsciously, I had begun to grind on his tongue, hoping to get some additional friction, but to no avail. Luca had me locked down, and damn if it wasn't making me even more turned on.

Luca began to pick up the pace, working me like he was a starved man who had just been presented with a feast. His tongue moved quickly and forcefully and then gently and slowly, sending waves of pleasure throughout my body. He continued this pattern, driving me to the brink of ecstasy. And when he slid a finger inside of me, I couldn't resist any longer. My pants and moans were uncontrollable.

"Fuck, so much better than my dream..." Luca stopped, his dark eyes looking up at me with a grin so wicked, it'd give just about any movie villain a run for its money, but before I could protest, his mouth kept working me until my toes began to curl. I let out the most animalistic sound as Luca sunk a second and then a third finger into me, sliding them in and out, hitting that sweet spot each time. With a few more thrusts, I was coming hard and fast. Shock waves of pleasure were coursing through my body. Luca helped me ride out my waves of pleasure as he licked up everything I had to offer.

As soon as I came down from my high, I started to catch my breath. Opening my eyes, I saw Luca hovering above me, a huge fucking smile on his face. He gave me a quick kiss on the lips before standing up and slowly backing away from the bed.

I noticed the large bulge in his pants, and just as I was about to propose that I could help him with that, he uttered, "Tonight's about you, *amore*." And then he smiled a wicked grin, adding, "Plus, now we're even," with so much arrogance he might as well have been the winner tonight.

I blinked. "Wait, what?" Speechless didn't justify how I was feeling. Luca put on a devilish grin, turned around, and left my bedroom.

Even? I stared at the door, still catching my breath. It certainly didn't feel like we were even. If anything, it felt wildly, unfairly, tilted in his favor. Tonight, Luca had given me exactly what I'd been asking for—space, control, a reprieve from the pressure of our relationship—and yet somehow, he'd still left me wanting more. Left me craving him.

His touch. His mouth. His praise.

And now here he was, walking out of my bedroom with a smug grin that said he knew exactly what he was doing. I wasn't sure if I was impressed by how well his cold shoulder worked to get under my skin—or annoyed that I had fallen for it like a complete buffoon.

Both. It was definitely both.

Georgia: 1. Luca: 2.

Chapter Thirty-One

Luca

I woke up the next morning to my phone buzzing on the bedside table.

Henri:
A few of us are coming over this morning to surprise Georgia with a celebratory brunch.

Luca:
Sure that's a good idea?

Henri:
Are you saying I don't know my sister?

Definitely was going to ignore that loaded question.

My body felt like it had been hit with a ton of bricks. After I walked out of Georgia's room, I hopped straight into the shower and desperately finished myself off. It wasn't nearly as satisfying as Georgia's mouth had been back in Monza, but it was the only thing keeping me from going back into her room and ruining her a second time.

Seeing her like that—open, trusting, wrecked from my touch—would have to be enough. For now.

This game of cat and mouse had been building between us for the last two weeks, and I'd gone into the room expecting to make her see stars all night. But as I watched her reach out for me, I realized I didn't want our first time together to be in a drunken haze. Or just a heat-of-the-moment decision fueled by a desire to one-up each other.

In that moment, I knew I wanted Georgia to choose me. Admit that she wanted this as much as I did, and so I decided to play it cool. Tell her that we were even, even if it was far from the truth. We weren't even.

Not even close.

This little game of cat and mouse we were playing? She was winning. I couldn't stop thinking about her, her scent, her voice, the fire in her eyes when she was annoyed. Georgia's imprint was all over my mind, my heart. I couldn't stop thinking about her, her touch, her lips. She was dominating, and in just a short period of time, I had become a pawn in her master plan to overtake my heart.

Another buzz.

Henri:
Be there in 30. I told her to be ready for a coffee date.

Luca:
And instead, you're going to bring several uninvited people into her home?

Sometimes it felt like Henri didn't know his own twin. If my social battery was close to zero, I knew Georgia's had to be empty. But if there was one thing Henri liked to make clear, it was that he knew *his* "Peaches" the best, everyone else be damned.

Deep down, if I admitted it to myself, I knew it was partly why I wanted her to like me so much. Like a petty teenage boy, I secretly loved how much Henri despised us dating, even if it was fake.

Just as I dropped my phone on the bed, it rang again, and my father's name flashed on the screen. "Morning, Luca. Did I wake you?"

Of course, he expected me to still be asleep because of last night's celebration.

"No, I've been awake for a while now, but I have brunch with Georgia soon. Why?"

"Some good news! Matteo landed you a photo shoot with Helios before the Austrian Grand Prix. Probably the best sponsorship news we've had all season. You're doing a great job at selling this, son—"

"But?" I cut him off, knowing what was coming next.

The back of my neck prickled. "You and Georgia have had a lot of success these last few weeks, but there's uncertainty with Hermes and your contract. It still hasn't been renewed and we're about to start summer break. Anthony's father has really been pushing Hermes, mentioning bigger sponsorship deals if they put Anthony in your seat…"

"What? A win in Monza wasn't good enough for them?"

"Luca, we need more than one win. Hermes needs money. Real, hard-earned sponsorship deals that might fall through if they keep you. I need you to pick up the pace on this." I knew one win wouldn't be enough to convince Hermes to sign me, but hearing it confirmed out loud made my heart sink.

As I sat on the edge of the bed, dragging my hands down my face, something clicked. A card I hadn't played yet.

"You know, Dad," I said nervously, my hand unconsciously rubbing the back of my neck. "I wanted to ask you something. What if Georgia joined us on the yacht during summer break?"

There was a beat of silence before he responded, too eagerly. "Now that is a great idea! Frankly, I told your mother the same thing last week, but she went on and on about not bothering Georgia on her one break this season. Great thinking, son. She'll fit right in with the family!"

"I'll ask her."

Without saying goodbye, my father hung up, but I knew he was pleased, even if we had different reasons for wanting Georgia on that yacht. Part of me felt bad that Georgia would have to spend the summer break with my family, but my selfish side was incredibly excited to have alone time with her.

No racing, no Henri, no expectations.

Venturing out of my room, I noticed Georgia sitting on the couch with a cup of coffee, reading the latest issue of JOULE magazine. No doubt prepping for our upcoming interview and photo shoot that Nora had organized.

Was there ever a moment she went into something unprepared?

Dressed in a dark blue blazer, jeans and a silk shirt, Georgia looked ready to go out. She had no idea that in just a few minutes, Henri was going to burst through her front door, followed by a parade of several uninvited guests. I cleared my throat, and she glanced up at me, a small smile forming on her lips.

"Morning," she said cheerily, taking another sip of her coffee. Her shoulders were stiff, but her face was the epitome of calm and collected, like she was daring herself to act as normal as possible.

So, we were going to ignore last night then. That's fine. Two could play at that game.

I flopped down onto the opposite couch. "Sleep well?"

Georgia ignored my question as she continued to flip through her magazine, but the creeping blush on her cheeks and dark bags under her eyes told me she had slept about as well as I had.

"So… I know we haven't really discussed summer break," I started, and Georgia tilted her head, interest flickering. "But I figured the media are going to expect us to be seen together. I was thinking, if you don't have any concrete plans at the start of our break, I always hop onto my family's yacht to spend time with them before my training camp. Away from prying eyes and fans. You should come. We can get a few strategic photos. I'll do my best to keep my mom from fangirling too much."

Her brows lifted. "You want me to join you on your family's yacht?"

I nodded coolly, not wanting to scare her away with my eagerness. "If I can tear you away from your simulator for a week?" I teased. "We can just relax, spend some time together without any distractions…" My voice faded off as I watched Georgia's unreadable expression.

She set the magazine aside, her fingers tapping nervously against the rim of her coffee cup. "Are you sure? I mean, don't you want a break… from *us*?" The last part came out as a whisper, and I could see her confidence waning.

Reaching out, I grabbed her thigh, giving it a soft, reassuring squeeze. "What? Never! Plus, it'll be nice to beat you in a jet ski race. Gotta get my wins in when I can."

"Alright, I'll come, but you better bring your A game, Rossi."

An entire week of just me and Georgia with plenty of time for us to get to know each other. Maybe even have a redo of the date that I'd messed up all those years ago.

As we sat there, discussing our plans for the upcoming summer break, a sudden commotion from outside caught our attention.

And so it begins, I laughed to myself, feeling a tad guilty that I hadn't let Georgia in on the secret.

A knock at the door rang out, drowning out the soft music from her stereo. Georgia yelled for Henri to come in as she returned once more to her magazine. I kept my eyes trained on her, not wanting to miss her priceless expression when she saw a group of hooligans walk into the apartment.

And she did not disappoint.

Henri threw open the door, and in walked Henri, Éliott, Edward, and Lily with what looked like twenty balloons and six bags of food from Georgia's favorite restaurant and bakery.

If looks could kill, hers would have slaughtered the entire paddock.

But just as quickly as she could, her face turned to the biggest, lightest, most cheerful composure I'd ever seen from her.

Guess some of my media training was working. I grinned to myself.

Henri lifted her off the ground, swinging her around the living room like a rag doll. "Surprise!"

"Wow, um, I didn't expect this," she stuttered, shifting her eyes to me in an accusing glare.

"What a lovely surprise your *brother* had," I said, smiling innocently. "All by *himself*."

Henri's face lit up, and I reached out to give him a congratulatory pat on the back. A sly smile crept across Georgia's face, her eyes widening with understanding at the subtle implication of my tone.

"Starting to look like a circus in here," Georgia grumbled under her breath.

Henri called us all over to the table, taking a seat next to Georgia. Before Éliott could sit on the other side of her, I grabbed the chair. Judging from his side-eye, I could tell he was slightly annoyed. I put my arm around the back of Georgia's chair and she shot me a look, but I just smiled as I shoved a croissant into my mouth.

Petty? Maybe. Satisfying? Absolutely.

Brunch blurred by in a haze of croissants and forced small talk, except with Edward, who was showing me the latest pictures of Arthur, Wilmington F1's new hamster.

Henri tapped me on my shoulder, motioning for me to join him outside.

"You got a minute?" he asked casually, although he looked nervous. Nodding, I stepped away from the table, following him to Georgia's balcony.

"What's up?" I asked, leaning on the balcony railing, my eyes drifting off to the view of the water down below.

"So, I—uh—" Henri looked uncomfortable, shifting his weight. "Look I have to ask. What's going on between you and my sister?"

Fuck. Not really the topic I wanted to discuss with my teammate. His hazel eyes were full of concern. There was no escaping this conversation. Playing dumb was obviously the only tactic here.

"What do you mean?"

He gave me a disapproving look. "Come on, Luca. The kiss yesterday after she won? You dragging Georgia to the dance floor in Monza? This morning you put your arm around her, even though literally no one besides her close friends are here. Plus, I see the way you look at her." Henri paused, likely rethinking his next words before continuing on. "The way you and Georgia have been all snuggled up this weekend, it's making me concerned."

"Concerned?"

He sighed, raking a hand through his hair, frustrated that I wasn't catching on. "Look, Luca, I'll just spit it out. Me and you, we've always been honest with one another, so here's the truth. I can see my sister starting to fall for you."

My heart did a traitorous leap, but I forced a scoff. Stuffing the rush of happiness back down, I worked on keeping my face neutral. Henri had already proven today he didn't know his sister as well as he thought, why would this be any different? There was no way Georgia was falling for me. Not after I broke her trust all those years ago.

Henri could tell I didn't believe him. "She falls hard and fast, Luca. After Anthony, I don't want to see her hurt again. This might be a fake relationship to you, but I'm worried the lines between fake and real will begin to blur for Georgia."

"And dating me would be so bad?" I hated how pathetic I sounded.

"Luca, come on, mate, you've *never* been a serious dater. You've made it clear you don't want anything serious for at least another few years. Georgia isn't like that. She doesn't do *casual*. She needs someone willing to commit." I could tell Henri was trying to be nice about it, but the tone of his voice was almost pleading, and it was making my blood boil. How dare he assume that he knew what was best for both of us?

"Like Éliott?" I scoffed.

"I don't know why you always have it out for Éliott." He crossed his arms, leaning against the balcony wall.

"I don't have it out for Éliott," I corrected, annoyed. Even if it was a tad true. "It's just—" I paused, struggling to find the right words. Georgia and Éliott's laughter could be heard from the balcony, and I tried to ignore Anthony's annoying voice in the back of my mind. "He's clearly into your sister."

"Considering you two aren't *actually* dating, that shouldn't be a problem." Henri looked at me skeptically, his hazel eyes bearing into mine. "Which leads me to my point. I don't want you to lead her on. Georgia wants something real, something long-term. Plus, my teammate *actually* dating my sister? I mean, would you like me if I dated *your* sister?"

Truth was, I didn't like Henri at all right now, and the thought of him dating anyone I knew made me want to punch him. My fists clenched at my sides and my jaw tightened as Henri's words stung me like a slap in the face. Based on his tone, he clearly didn't know I'd asked Georgia out all those years ago, or this conversation would have been a lot worse. A small silver lining in this nightmare.

Henri was still looking at me, still clearly wanting an answer to his earlier question. "So, is there something going on between you and Georgia?"

I exhaled slowly, jaw tight. Was there something going on with us?

No. Yes. Sort of? After this week, I knew what I wanted, but it had become very clear that Henri didn't think I was good enough for his sister.

I stood there, weighing my options. One wrong move, and he'd find a way to blow this whole thing up before it even started. I just needed time—time to show Georgia that this was more than a performance. That she was starting to mean something to me. And summer break would give me that chance.

So instead of giving him the truth, I did what I did best and deflected.

"The only thing going on, Henri, is that I'm playing the role Hermes asked me to. Now, if you don't like that, I suggest you take it up with our team principal," I retorted, with a bit more malice than intended. My hand landed heavily on Henri's back as I pulled him close, forcing a smile onto my face. "But don't worry, *mate*. I'll be sure to keep my irresistible charm and good looks in check during our summer vacation. I mean, your sister is *much* too intelligent to fall for a man just because he has a yacht off the coast of Spain, right?" I grinned.

Without looking back, I marched inside, knowing full well that Henri was now contemplating how he could get himself invited to our mini vacation. The image of

Georgia and me intimately hanging out on my personal yacht now etched into his mind.

Good.

Chapter Thirty-Two

Georgia

The last race before summer break, Belgium, had gone better than expected. I had another win under my belt, and a slightly bigger lead in the championship.

As promised, Luca and I had agreed to do a photo shoot with Maison de Klotho and JOULE, a fashion and lifestyle magazine, at the start of summer break, a photo shoot I'd been dreading. Even if it was nice to finally see the fruits of this fake relationship unfold, I hated knowing that I had to spend all day being interviewed, poked, and prodded by strangers.

But it would be worth it. This was a huge moment for Valkyrie—and for me. Finally, we'd be front and center of an international magazine, and the team deserved this, which was the only thing keeping me going at the moment.

Well, that and knowing that in just a few days I'd have Luca all to myself on his family yacht. When he'd asked me after Monaco if I would join him, I was secretly quite pleased. Of all the things I was learning about him, my favorite was that he knew how to have fun and relax. After a stressful first half of the season, I realized I didn't want to spend my four-week break on the simulator practicing all of the upcoming races. I just wanted to *relax* for once.

And if our yacht trip also led me to the possibility of Luca and I having a little *fun*, then I wouldn't mind that either.

When we touched down in London, a glossy black limousine waited for us on the tarmac, complete with a chilled bottle of champagne tucked into the armrest. Luca poured us both a glass, watching me cautiously.

"To suffering through coordinated outfits and incredibly cheesy questions," he said, raising his glass.

"To pretending to like you for the camera." I clinked mine against his with a wink. I practically downed the glass. Liquid courage never hurt anyone, right?

Luca mock laughed, pouring me another. "How you wound me with your lies."

When we arrived, a Maison de Klotho staff member called out to us. "Good morning. I'm Lilah, your coordinator and escort for the day. Now, who is ready to have some fun?"

"Define fun," I muttered under my breath. Luca squeezed my hand, leading us both inside the building.

Polished marble floors, gowns in glass cases, and enough velvet couches to stage a Regency drama greeted us. The hallways were filled with various outfits that the clothing company had designed for celebrities and royalty.

After introductions with our stylists, Luca and I were shuffled into different changing stations to try on various pieces of clothing. JOULE had sent a writer to hang out with us during the shoot. As we got ready, Mark, our journalist, planned to sit and chat with us, to get to know who we were as people, not just world-class racers. He felt as though he could see the "real Georgia and Luca," his words, when we were interacting with each other on set.

"An emotional anthropologist." Also his words.

My first outfit was a soft pink silk number I would never be caught dead wearing on a Tuesday, but when I stepped into the studio, Luca was already lounging in front of the camera like some Italian Bond villain: dark suit, shirt undone just enough to be scandalous.

"Beautiful," he called out, not bothering to lower his voice. His eyes dragged down the length of my dress and then slowly back up to my face, where his smile went full smirk, probably a little too obviously. But I knew he wanted the journalist and photographer to catch that.

I felt a blush creep up my neck. "You don't look too bad yourself, Rossi."

Cameras flashed in my face, and I felt a sudden headache coming on, fueled by my growing anxiety. My palms grew clammy, and I wiped them on my dress before tucking a loose strand of hair behind my ear. Focusing on the patterned tile floor, I exhaled a steady breath to ground myself.

I felt a hand interlock with mine. Luca was still chatting away with the photographer, but he continued squeezing my hand just a little bit tighter. My shoulders relaxed, and I glanced up at the camera and smiled, trying to at least pretend to be involved in the conversation, even if I hadn't said a word.

Eventually, Luca was whisked away for his solo shoot, leaving me alone with Mark, whose "let's peel back the layers" energy made me want to peel off my skin instead. The gleam in his eye told me he wanted something, and my back stiffened up as I wiped my hands nervously on my dress.

"So, Georgia, that win in Monaco, quite spectacular! For Luca to win his home race, and then you to win yours. Wow, you really are quite the racing power couple right now." I gave him a polite nod, unsure if there was a question hidden in there.

Mark continued to stare at me like I was a mystery he was determined to solve. His eyes felt like they were piercing my soul, trying to read all my deepest and most private thoughts.

"Tell me, what does Georgia and Luca look like off the track? What's a boring Wednesday night like for F1's power couple?"

"We're like any other couple," I said simply.

"Oh, come on, I don't believe that for a second. What do you do for fun?"

What did Luca and I do for fun?

My mind immediately wanted to talk about the karting, but then I thought back to Luca's media training. *Maybe tell them something other than more racing?*

"We like to play chess," I responded finally.

Always bake a lie within a truth. A safe answer. Luca and my brother played chess all the time, and I liked watching Luca wipe the floor with Henri.

"Luca is an amazing player. We often try to sneak away and play in the garages when we have time. As for at home, we really do live simply when we're together. We like to go on walks or make dinner together."

"Oh yeah, anything fun?"

I nodded with an air of uncertainty, one I knew Mark would pick up on. Was I really about to say this?

Fuck it. Luca told me to joke with the journalists.

"I probably shouldn't say," I said, leaning forward like I was about to whisper a scandalous secret. "I wouldn't want to embarrass Luca."

"Oh, come on," Mark groaned. "You have to tell me."

"Well," I paused for dramatic effect. "My *Italian* boyfriend *loves* mac and cheese."

Mark gasped in horror, and I just nodded enthusiastically at him, enjoying the moment a little too much.

"From a box," I added in a whisper.

Luca approached, a mock-betrayed look on his face. "*Amore*, please tell me I didn't just overhear you telling Mark that I love *mac and cheese*." Giggling, I lifted my cheek up for a kiss, which he aptly provided.

"Your girlfriend was just telling us about how you guys make homemade pasta together in your free time," Mark added, no doubt looking for Luca's reaction to see if he would be surprised at that comment.

"Well, let's hope she told you off the record. I don't think my Italian fans would appreciate knowing I think boxed pasta is homemade," he quipped, winking at the journalist.

"A couple who cooks together, stays together, my mom used to say," Mark said cheerfully. "So, Luca, how is it dating your teammate's sister? Any arguments yet?"

Luca's lips twitched—just for a second—before he masked it with a charming smile. But I caught it, caught the slight uncomfortableness in his posture.

Had Henri said something?

"Honestly, no," he said with a refreshing laugh. "I'm almost surprised at how supportive he is of our relationship. Sometimes it seems suspicious."

"Oh?" Mark asked, his interest clearly piqued by Luca's last statement.

"He's just always asking about what dates we'll go on next and telling me about all the cute things Georgia sends him about me." I felt myself dying a bit inside, but I batted my eyelashes at him playfully, keeping the bit alive. "I once joked that Georgia must have a ton of skeletons in her closet, because why else is her brother pushing her on me?"

Mark snorted, scribbling that gem down. I tried not to look horrified.

"Henri didn't find it quite as funny," Luca added innocently.

"Alright, kids, let's finish strong. Time to get into the last rounds of clothing!" Lilah called out.

A stylist handed me the final look of the day, a tiny black evening dress with a plunging back. Luca was in another crisp designer suit, this one with his shirt unbuttoned halfway down, revealing his obnoxiously tan, sculpted chest.

"Lovely, lovely," Lilah called out, "but let's try something a little different. Have a little fun. Georgia, show us your back. Luca, hand on her lower back. Eyes on each other. Intimate. Romantic."

I felt Luca grip my lower back tightly and look down at me with those gorgeous brown eyes. He pulled me closer to him, my body now flush with his front, my hands on his chest. Suddenly, this photo shoot felt a lot more intimate than I had anticipated. I caught his eye, and instead of the smug grin I expected, he gave me the softest smile.

Then he leaned down, voice low and sinfully smug. "Why so shy, *amore*? You weren't this shy Sunday night."

I nearly swallowed my tongue while my brain short-circuited just long enough for the photographer to call out, "Lovely, Georgia. Much better, you look so relaxed."

My face flushed, my shoulders loosened. Luca Rossi, master of mind games. Luca knew exactly what he was doing. He'd seen the tension in my shoulders, the nerves in my fingers, and he cut straight through them with one devastating line.

Well, two could play that game.

I'm not sure what came over me, but all I wanted was to wipe that satisfied smirk off his face, and there was only one way I could think of doing that.

Luca froze for half a second. Then, he kissed me back like he'd been waiting all damn day for me to do it. His hands slipped lower, grazing the top of my ass, and the room erupted into delighted chaos. Cheering, clapping, camera shutters firing like fireworks. So much for subtlety.

And then, because Luca Rossi is incapable of acting normal for more than five seconds, he picked me up. Bridal style.

I screeched, grabbing at his lapels and praying to every deity that my dress hadn't ridden halfway up my back. He kissed me again, slower now, deeper. The kind of kiss that made time bend a little, that made the lights dim and the sound fade, like we were the only two people in the world.

"Alright, you two lovebirds!" Lilah called out. "That's a wrap!"

Luca set me back down, and I toppled as I tried to steady myself. My cheeks were undoubtedly flushed from the long make-out session—and the embarrassment of how public it was.

Had I just made out with Luca in front of all these people?

During the kiss, it didn't seem so terrible, but now I felt mortified. Luca smiled as he grabbed my hands, pulling them up to his chest.

"Sorry, Lilah, can't help myself sometimes. As Georgia likes to say, *it's in my nature*." He grinned, pulling my hand to his lips and giving it a kiss.

"You two are too much!" Lilah exclaimed, clapping her hands together. "I cannot wait to see how these photos look."

Mark, who'd been sitting by the photographer the entire time, stood slowly. He had the kind of look people get when they realize they've struck gold. His notebook was practically glowing in his hand.

"You know, I came in, trying to see if the chemistry was there between the two of you, you seem like such an odd pairing, but after today, I can really see that this is the real deal. Good luck, you two. I'll be sure to have several copies sent to your offices."

Had we actually survived that? I glanced at Luca, and he winked back, a triumphant look in his eyes. Our biggest test and we'd passed with flying colors.

Although the more I thought about it, somewhere between the teasing, the champagne, and the camera flashes, I suspected Mark wasn't the only one buying into this relationship.

Chapter Thirty-Three

Luca

I could tell Georgia had been nervous through most of the shoot. She was very good at working through her anxiety, but I'd learned how to read her. The stiff shoulders. The twitchy hands. The way she bit the inside of her cheek between takes. So I did what I could, kept the banter flowing, slipped in that little whisper about Sunday night just to make her squirm in my arms. She'd relaxed, just slightly, and I filed that away with everything else I'd learned about her lately.

And now, back at my London apartment, all I could think about was how good it felt to be near her when no one else was watching. About how excited I was to get her onto my family's yacht, itching to have some more private time with her so that I could finish what I started in Monaco.

She mumbled something about needing to change, disappearing down the hall. After I finished my shower, I slipped into my favorite set of sweatpants and a comfortable V-neck, heading back into the kitchen so I could prepare our dinner. Ironically, after her joke in Monza, I'd decided to make her a fancy mac and cheese tonight, a fact I was slightly embarrassed by since she'd told the journalist it was my favorite food.

I was stirring the sauce when she stepped out of the bedroom. And promptly gave me a heart attack.

Black dress. Hair half up, wearing the lightning bolt necklace I'd given her at Monza.

Shit. Did she think we were going out? Did she want to go out?

I cleared my throat and raised an eyebrow. "I know my cooking is pretty good, *amore*, but I think you might be a little too formal for mac and cheese." The look on Georgia's face was priceless. A general mix of shock, relief, then happiness. "I figured after the last two weeks you wouldn't want to go out to eat. I certainly don't."

"So, we aren't going out?" she clarified in a quiet whisper.

"Nope." I turned back to the cheese grater, hiding a grin. "Figured you'd be as tired of the cameras as I am."

"Oh." She vanished again, only to return with black leggings underneath her dress.

"So, I, uh…" She pointed to her leggings. "I forgot to pack a comfortable shirt. Only packed workout clothes and beach items. Do you mind if I borrow one?"

"Of course," I said, perhaps a little too excitedly, heading to my room.

Pulling out my deepest purple Hermes shirt, I tried to control my giddy excitement. I felt like a high-school boy whose crush had just asked to borrow his letterman jacket. The idea of seeing her in my shirt stirred something within me, and my chest felt tighter.

A minute later, I handed her the soft purple Hermes polo.

"Really?" she deadpanned. "This is the only shirt you could find? I'm not wearing your team shirt, Luca."

"I mean, no shirt is always an option." I winked.

Georgia groaned, but grabbed the shirt anyway and headed to the guest room. When she reemerged, my polo hanging loosely off one shoulder, her leggings clinging to her legs, I let out an involuntary whistle.

She scoffed, barely hiding a grin. "Absolutely no photos, Rossi."

"Spoilsport," I laughed, before pointing to my wine cabinet. "Want to open a bottle?"

She nodded, pouring us each a glass of Tempranillo from my collection. "Thanks for not making us go out to eat. I'm exhausted." I handed her a piece of grated cheese, which she took happily. "Plus, it's nice to see I didn't lie to the journalist today."

Georgia grabbed her wine and wandered into my open-plan living room, taking a moment to review each of my photos and trophies scattered across the wall. I watched her as she traced a finger along one of the framed photos of my dad and me from an old race of his.

I loved watching her here, in my space. Barefoot, wine glass in one hand, wearing my shirt like she'd done it a thousand times before.

It felt easy. Right.

"You know, I saw a clip recently of you racing Monster Trucks. Was that back in the US?"

Georgia smiled that beautiful big smile, nodding. "Sometimes I miss being in America. There was such a comfort in knowing what to expect. A comfort in knowing the team, the car, the crowd, even the journalists. There were no surprises in IndyCar," she whispered as she stared at the photo of me and my father. "I was just another driver, no different than the boys."

"But you've done incredibly in Formula 1. You look so comfortable in the car, and if I didn't know any better,

I'd say it was easily your third year in the sport. A real natural."

"Say that to all the girls, Rossi?" she joked.

"Just the pretty ones."

Her cheeks flushed, the freckles across her nose brightening. She rolled her eyes, but I saw the twitch at the corner of her mouth. The one that meant she was secretly pleased. I refilled her glass before motioning for her to take a seat on the couch next to me. Dinner was in the oven, and we had some time before it was finished.

"By the way, I read that engineering book you recommended to me," I confessed. "Figured if you could use it to beat Henri, then I could too."

She blinked in surprise. "Oh?"

"I meant what I said at the podcast back in Monza. You really are making me a better racer."

Georgia's cheeks turned a deep shade of pink, highlighting the small freckles scattered across her nose. Her blushes always melted my heart, and after each one, I found myself desperately looking for the next one. She looked embarrassed by my praise, but she had no reason to be.

It was all true. At the start of the season, it was impossible to picture myself on the podium again. But now? Now I had another winning trophy to add to my collection.

My dad had spent years trying to get me to focus on racing, and here was Georgia, convincing me to read engineering books after just a few months of getting to know her. That was the big difference between Georgia and my father in their motivations in encouraging me to love racing. My dad wanted to continue living his glory days.

Georgia wanted me to be happy and fulfilled.

"What kind of music do you listen to?" she asked, taking another sip of wine. "I notice you have a lot of records in your spare bedroom."

"I like a good mix of things," I said honestly. "I don't really have a favorite band, but recently, Bon Iver after seeing them in London. Beach House is pretty good, too. Saw them at a festival back in France."

She quirked her eyebrows, clearly surprised at my answer. "Didn't expect party boy Luca Rossi to have a secret love of indie music."

"There's a lot of things you don't know about me, Dubois."

She thought she had me all figured out, assumed that I didn't care about art or music or reading. But I was determined to show her a different side of myself.

"A man of mystery, apparently," she teased. A beat passed, and I saw something shift in her. The humor softened into something more reflective. She leaned forward, fingertips playing with the edge of her wineglass.

"There is something I wanted to ask you, actually."

Georgia nodded for me to continue.

"Several years ago, I overheard my father offering to be your coach. Why did you turn him down?"

She hesitated, her expression unreadable. "I wondered if you knew about that. Honestly? It was tempting. Your dad's a legend. But I didn't want to owe anyone my career. In IndyCar, people said I only got ahead because of Anthony's family. I wasn't about to start my F1 chapter with people saying I rode in on Michael Rossi's last name."

I nodded, understanding exactly what she meant. A luxury I didn't have, but would have loved. "You wanted it clean."

"I wanted it to be *mine*," she said quietly. "And mine alone. Whether the reputation was failure or success, I'd own it."

"You've definitely earned your place here through your own talent and hard work."

Georgia smiled gratefully before taking another sip of wine. "You know, I was going to tell you during our dinner *that* night, but you never showed."

The guilt sat heavy. She didn't need to clarify which night. We both knew, had both been dancing around that elephant since Miami.

"I'm sorry I never showed, Georgia. I was young and stupid, and as terrible as this apology sounds, I was jealous and angry at my father. And, somewhat you. After hearing his conversation, I felt oddly betrayed and instead of asking, I did what I do best, I ignored it."

She reached out and squeezed my hand. "I was hurt that night. Everyone had told me to stay away from you. But I wanted to see the real Luca. The one who wasn't just a headline or a smirk." She smiled softly. "The Luca I'm getting to know *now*."

Something cracked open in my chest at that. For a second, I couldn't breathe. Not because I was caught off guard by her kindness, but because I didn't realize how much I'd been waiting for her to say something like that.

This was the same woman who'd nearly shoved me into the barriers a few races ago. Who used to look at me like I was something to be scraped off her tire. And now she was sitting across from me, sipping my wine, wearing my shirt, and slowly letting me see all the parts of her that weren't for public consumption.

I raised my glass of wine to hers, feeling a warmth in my chest that had nothing to do with the alcohol.

There was a beat of comfortable silence before she shifted on the couch, tucking her leg underneath her, looking at me again, this time a little more serious. "Well, since we're talking about forgiveness..." She shifted in her seat, eyes flickering away. "Anthony apologized to me in Monaco."

"Oh?" I asked curiously.

She nodded, swirling the last of her wine. "Anthony's a lot of things—liar included—but he's not exactly a great actor. He looked pretty sincere. But honestly? It doesn't matter. I used to think an apology would fix something inside me. That it would make it all okay. But when he finally said the words, I realized I didn't need them. I'd already moved on. He doesn't get to live in my head anymore."

"I'm glad," I said, giving her hand a quick squeeze. "He doesn't deserve your time."

Noticing her glass was empty, I opened my wine cabinet. My fingers grazed over the labels of the wine bottles, searching for one of my favorites. As I poured us both a glass, Georgia leaned back in her chair, taking a sip before letting out a contented sigh. During the last few weeks, I'd finally caught a glimpse of the Georgia that Henri always raved about. As each layer pulled back, I was finally seeing the witty, charming Georgia that had her friends and family in a chokehold.

That now had me in a chokehold.

The oven timer dinged, signaling that our dinner was ready. "Shall we eat?" I asked over my shoulder.

She lifted her glass in response, her face beaming. "Excited to be the first customer of Chef Rossi!"

Laughing, I grabbed the two plates of mac and cheese, balancing them expertly in one hand as I ushered her back to the living room, setting them on the coffee table. "Dinner is served, *amore*."

Georgia took a bite, moaning softly as the gooey cheese and al dente noodles melded with the rich, creamy sauce. It had been a long time since I'd cooked for someone else, let alone enjoyed their company this much.

"So," Georgia said between bites, "if you don't mind me asking, how are things going with your dad?"

"Okay. After the Monza win I thought he'd be over the moon, that the win would give me some relief, but honestly? It's almost been worse. Like Monza showed him that I *could* win, and so now he expects it *every* race."

"Well, for what it's worth, Luca, I believe that you *can* do it. You're just as capable of winning the championship in that Hermes car as Henri is."

Her eyes had such a determination in them, so steady that I almost felt the self-doubt melt away. If Georgia had a superpower, it would be the ability to instill unwavering confidence in anyone she believed in.

"Hermes still hasn't signed my contract extension," I mumbled finally.

"There's still plenty of time. Summer break only just started. Have any other teams made offers?"

I laughed dryly. "Matteo said there's been a little interest, but I don't think I'm the most desirable driver on the grid right now."

Georgia just shot me a pointed look. "You're a Formula 1 race winner. Plenty of teams would be lucky to have you. If he gets a meeting set up with another team, you should go."

Trying to hide my nerves, I looked down at my slippers. "Maybe."

"So, are your parents annoyed that I have to join you on this break?" Grateful didn't begin to describe how I felt at her changing the subject.

"Not at all," I chuckled. "My mom's a huge fan of yours, if you couldn't tell by the Valkyrie shirt she wore on Sunday." Georgia's eyes lit up, undoubtedly pleased at my mother's choice of attire last week. "I'm sure if my dad got to pick my *actual* girlfriend, you'd be top of the list."

"Oh?" she questioned, intrigued by that answer.

"A talented race car driver who doesn't break the rules, get wasted at parties, or steal yachts? Pretty sure my father would happily swap the two of us." I didn't mean for the words to sound so pathetic.

Georgia tilted her head, a wry smile playing at her lips. "You make me sound so dull, Rossi." Georgia topped off my glass of wine, shuffling closer to me on the couch. Her presence felt like a warm blanket on a cold night.

The shrill ring of Georgia's phone cut through the quiet living room.

"That's odd. Why is Nora calling?" Georgia answered, putting it on speakerphone. "The interview went fine, Nora. So nosy."

"Georgia, is Luca there as well?" Nora's voice was low and serious, instantly killing whatever buzz we had left.

"Yes. You're on speaker," Georgia said nervously. "What's going on?"

"I've had some bad news. We've just been told that the *Daily Reporter* is working on a story about us. Fortunately, I went to school with one of their journalists, so she called to give me a quick heads-up."

Georgia's face went still. "Wha-what do you mean? What story?"

"They're going to publish an article at the end of summer break about your relationship with Luca. Our guess is they're going to accuse Valkyrie and Hermes of conspiring together, possibly by trading secrets, but we aren't sure."

"That's bullshit!" Georgia yelled.

My phone buzzed violently against the table. Dozens of texts from Matteo. This wasn't some absurd rumor, it was already moving. Georgia's hands were trembling, and I intertwined them in mine.

"We don't know who their supposed *source* is, but we're working hard to find out. Isabelle has retained a crisis manager, a close friend of hers who works in London. We're to meet at the Valkyrie Monaco offices tomorrow, we've booked you a flight first thing. Luca, Matteo is booking you a flight back to Hermes HQ. With any luck, it'll be a nonsense story that'll blow over after the Austrian Grand Prix."

I exchanged a glance with Georgia, and for the first time all evening, her confident blue eyes were filled with dread. Her jaw clenched, lips parted, like she was still trying to form the words to fight back. Georgia said a quick goodbye to Nora before hanging up the phone.

"My F1 career is going to be ruined," she sobbed, her voice cracking with every word.

I cupped her cheek, letting my thumb swipe away the tear trembling on her lashes. "No, it won't, Georgia. I'm here for as long as you want to keep doing this. I promise you that. Whatever is going to be said about us, we can fight, prove them wrong."

"Even if we break up at the end of the season, everyone is going to accuse us of this being a PR stunt! I can't force you to date me forever." She continued to cry into me as I kept rubbing her back, trying to soothe her tears.

"Georgia Dubois, I promise you, I don't care how long this takes." I wiped away a tear with my thumb, gazing deep into her exhausted eyes. "I'm not going anywhere."

Chapter Thirty-Four

Georgia

The flight back to Monaco was a special kind of hell. Sleepless, stuffy, and silent, except for the anxious loop playing in my head. By the time we landed, my neck was aching, my eyes were burning, and my stomach felt like it had been through qualifying laps of its own. Isabelle had reached out earlier this morning, reassuring me that her friend from London was the top expert in handling such situations. While the article hadn't come out yet, we knew we had to get ahead of this—and fast. So far, only the few individuals who were directly involved in the relationship between Luca and me knew about the crisis firm's involvement.

By the time I arrived at the Valkyrie factory, my nerves were practically vibrating. The fluorescent hallway lights felt extra aggressive, like they were daring me to have a meltdown under their glow. I made my way to the main conference room and paused outside the door. Through the glass, I could already see Nora scribbling frantically in her notebook, occasionally nodding at a woman I didn't recognize. When I entered the room, I cleared my throat and the three of them stopped their private whispering, and Isabelle waved for me to come in.

"Ahh, Georgia, good morning. This is Deborah. She's been retained to help us." Deborah was a staunch, gray-haired woman whose dark-rimmed glasses framed her large green eyes, which sat on top of an incredibly tense frown. It was hard to imagine her ever smiling, although if my entire job was to fix the mistakes of politicians and celebrities, I don't suppose I'd smile much either.

I shook Deborah's outstretched hand while Isabelle introduced the two of us. As I plopped down onto the old wooden conference room bench, the Hermes team's faces appeared on the large TV screen. Lily entered the room a moment later, offering a quick apology for being late.

"Thank you for joining us. I know this is your midseason break, and that you are about to go on vacation, so I will keep this concise and to the point. While we aren't entirely sure who leaked this information or what this article is going to say, rest assured, my firm is discreetly working on it. However, until we figure out how this was rooted out, we must continue to be a united front. It's business as usual. Georgia and Luca, I hear that you have a nice trip to Mallorca planned. After some discussion with Isabelle, I think it would be best to add Henri to the trip. Lily, too, if she's up for it. A strong show of unity before this goes live means we'll have some fun social media posts and footage to share when this *tabloid* drops about your relationship."

When I glanced at the large conference room screen, I could have sworn I almost saw my brother smile on the other end of the camera.

Did he want to come on this trip with me and Luca?

"Now, Georgia and Luca, we need to get some social media posts of the two of you going. The teams will work with you on what photos are best to share with the caption. I've sent some ideas over to Nora. Our strategy boils down to the following: we need everyone to believe, without any doubt, that Georgia and Luca are in love. Any potential accusations of cheating or PR stunts need to feel ridiculous whenever someone looks at these two. Now, any questions?"

A dark chuckle escaped my lips, much to Isabelle's annoyance. To be fair to the *Daily Reporter*, if the article was about Luca and my PR relationship then they'd written a truthful story. And yet, somehow, as I sat in the Valkyrie conference room staring at Luca's face on the screen, the insinuation that we *weren't* actually dating didn't really feel truthful either, because as each day passed, what Luca and I had was starting to feel… *complicated*.

Deborah's loud voice pierced through the air, dragging me out of my lull. "Obviously, it goes without saying, you'll need to extend this relationship timeline. Isabelle said the original arrangement was to potentially break up at the end of the season or when some sponsorship deals were made, but let's make sure it's pushed out to the start of next season at the earliest. Give us some time to weather this article."

"Oh noooo," Luca's face popped up on the screen as he interjected sarcastically, feigning annoyance, "another couple of months dating the most *beautiful* woman in the paddock, what a bummer for me." My cheeks began to burn as they turned a bright shade of red.

"Don't be silly, Luca, *we* aren't dating," Lily teased. Such a flirt. "Well, I think this sounds great. I've been dying to get onto Luca's yacht, so any chance to sneak in a visit to Mallorca is fine by me."

Deborah nodded at Lily as she motioned toward me, her painted fingernails now pointing my direction. "Any questions, Georgia?"

"When this article comes out, how are we going to manage our sponsors?"

"We'll cross that bridge when we come to it," Isabelle responded. "With any luck, this will blow over quickly. The JOULE article is meant to come out that weekend. I think it could work in our favor."

I gave her a skeptical smile.

She returned it with a small, tired shrug. We both knew there were no guarantees. Not when it came to Valkyrie and the media.

Chapter Thirty-Five

Georgia

Luca sat down on the deck next to me, both our legs now dangling off the side of the boat. "Here you are! Hiding from my parents, I see?" he teased, nudging his shoulder against mine. "Hope my family hasn't driven you crazy these last few days." He chuckled, brushing his fingers through his thick black hair.

"Probably not as much as mine is about to."

It had been almost a week since we boarded the Rossi family yacht, and to his credit, Luca hadn't brought up the impending tabloid article once. While I'd been quietly bracing for impact, he'd made it his mission to distract me with jet ski races, incredible meals, and long, sun-soaked days that made me forget we were supposed to be pretending.

A gentle gust of wind swept my hair into my face, but before I could reach for it, Luca leaned over and tucked it behind my ear. His fingers lingered just a second too long on my cheek, his smile lazy and soft and so unguarded it made my chest ache.

I was beginning to feel *almost* relaxed. Spending time with Luca and his family, enjoying the peacefulness of hiding from the media, had been a much-needed change of pace, but I knew this serene moment was about to be bombarded by my brother, Edward, and Lily.

"So, Henri have anything to do with why you invited Edward?" I prodded.

"Don't be silly, *amore*," he said, far too quickly. "Edward is a close friend, and I figured the more the merrier."

Liar. The truth was that Edward had this uncanny ability to ease the tension in any situation. He was an excellent buffer between Henri's competitiveness and Luca's desperation to reset and relax. After the intensity of last week, I couldn't blame Luca for wanting his best friend around—he'd been forced to accept mine.

As if on cue, I heard Henri and Edward's bickering from behind us as they approached the dock.

"Peaches!" Henri called out. "We were just discussing how today would be a lovely day to race jet skis."

"Well, hello to you too, Henri," I grumbled at my brother as Lily and Edward dumped their suitcases on the deck next to Henri's. Out of the corner of my eye, I saw Luca roll his eyes, but I kept my laughter to myself. Not even on the boat for a minute and my brother was already challenging me to a race.

"Henri, have you ever contemplated that not everything in life is a competition?"

Edward and Lily tried to stifle their snickering behind cupped hands, while Luca's lips curled up into a smile full of pride.

Did I just turn down a race?

"If it has an engine, we race it," Henri replied with the conviction of someone quoting scripture. "Unless, of course, you're scared I'm going to beat you."

Fucking Henri. He always knows how to get a rise out of me. I had every intention of *actually* relaxing this weekend, but after watching my brother's smug face taunt me, that option started to feel less and less appealing.

"Happy to show that I'm the better Dubois both on the track *and* on the water."

"Well, fortunately, the jet skis are fueled and ready to go," Luca's father announced. "There's only two of them, so you'll need to pair up."

"Right, Lily, you ready to take these guys on?" Henri nodded toward Luca and me.

Lily didn't even hesitate. "Let's show these losers who the real racers are!" She enthusiastically grabbed my brother's hand as she sat behind him, wrapping her arms around his waist. Lily and Henri had gotten closer over the last few months, but watching the two of them on the jet ski, giggling away as my teammate whispered something into my brother's ear, it was hard not to wonder if something more was developing between them.

Before I could think too hard about that, a pair of strong arms lifted me clean off the dock.

"Excuse me? Who said you get to drive?" Shifting to the front of the seat, I patted the spot behind me. "Maybe we should let the Formula 1 leader take this one."

Sitting down, Luca wrapped his hands around my waist, whispering, "Fine by me, *amore*. Any chance I get to be close to you is a win for me."

Luca closed the gap between our bodies as his grip tightened, pulling me flush against his chest. At the feeling of Luca's firm abs and hardening cock, my mind flashed back to the night of my Monaco Grand Prix win where Luca's hands were somewhere else entirely. His fingers started rubbing soft circles on my hips and under the life jacket, and I leaned into his hold, enjoying the feeling of Luca's lips ghosting my neck.

"You guys ready or just going to keep flirting over there?" Edward yelled, pointing to where we were meant to start the race.

He blew the whistle, and we shot off into the distance like bolts of lightning. Luca's warm breath danced across my neck, sending shivers down my spine. His lips were dangerously close to my skin, leaving a trail of incredibly soft kisses along my neck, making it almost impossible to focus on the water ahead.

Bastard was having way too much fun with this, I concluded.

Grinding my hips back against him was not the most responsible move as the person driving a jet ski at high speeds, but I couldn't help myself. His breath hitched and a low groan spilled from his lips, curling around the edges of my ear like a dare. I felt his hands slide lower, fingers ghosting just under the edge of my life jacket, stopping just short of where I was burning.

As I tried to focus on the last lap, I heard Luca whisper, "Now, now, *amore*, what's got you so distracted?"

"Maybe it's a certain someone behind me who can't keep his hands to himself," I shouted back over the roar of the engine and wind. I gripped the handlebar and tried to block out Luca's teasing fingers, his soft touch.

Before he could answer, Henri and Lily rocketed past us, water spraying in our wake.

"Looks like we know who the fastest Dubois on the water is!" Henri's voice boomed over the hum of jet skis, his gloating unmistakable even over the sound of the water. Henri was as much of a sore winner as he was a loser.

"He's going to be insufferable about this," I groaned.

"Well, then you should have been paying more attention," Luca whispered into my ear, and I elbowed his side. The vibration of our jet ski slowed to a purr, and moments later, we pulled up next to the boat that had been our home for the week.

"Alright, I think that's enough racing for me today. Lily, can I interest you in a glass of wine?"

Henri threw his head back in a loud, playful laugh. "Avoiding the rematch, Peaches?"

"More like saving myself from your inevitable sulk when you lose."

And, more importantly, my sanity from my brother's persistence.

"Actually, Georgia, I have something for you. Give me a moment." While Luca disappeared, Lily and I made our way to the front of the boat, settling into the tanning chairs that had been laid out for us.

Five minutes later, Luca emerged from the lower cabins.

"Got you a little something," Luca preened as he walked over to where Lily and I were tanning, a bright blue gift bag looped through his arm and a smoothie in each hand.

"Oh?" I made grabby hands at the bag, and Luca dropped it at my feet.

Tearing through the tissue paper, I froze. Inside was a travel-size watercolor set bursting with vibrant pigments, a sleek leather-bound sketchpad, and a petite wooden easel.

"Wh-what's this?" I asked, flipping through the empty pages of the sketchpad.

"I noticed you left your paints at home, so I asked Edward to pick up some supplies before he left. Painting relaxes you, and I want you to be as relaxed as possible on this trip because you deserve a break. Plus, you can't get a better backdrop than this!"

Luca wasn't wrong. The colors of the ocean and the sky blended seamlessly, creating a landscape that begged to be captured on canvas.

"Luca… I—um, I don't know what to say," I stammered. "Just… Wow. Thank you. These are incredible."

Tears pricked the corners of my eyes as I looked up at him, speechless with gratitude. My heart felt like it was melting in the best way. While packing, I'd forgotten to throw in my art supplies, and I didn't want to burden Luca or his parents by asking to pick some up before embarking.

Luca had a knack for picking up on the little details, such as my silly window-washing dance or my nervous ticks before an interview, that no one else seemed to notice.

"You even got my favorite brand of paints!"

Luca shrugged, bashful. "I may have gone snooping in your condo when I was with you in Monaco," he laughed, putting his hands up innocently. "Had to make sure you didn't have any *real* skeletons in your closet."

I playfully swatted his arm, unable to keep the grin off my face. "Well, I'll let your snooping slide this time, if only because I did the same last week." My cheek found its place against his chest, my arms now wrapped around his waist, and I let myself savor the quiet thrum of his heartbeat beneath my ear.

He tilted his head to kiss my forehead and whispered against my hair, "Maybe later you can paint me like one of your French girls."

"In your dreams, Rossi." I rolled my eyes, but I couldn't hide the satisfied smile that crept onto my face as I looked up at him.

"Fine with me. Based on what I heard in Monaco, sounds like I'd like what we do in *your* dreams."

So, he had noticed that outburst.

Fuck it, I did too.

"Hey, Luca, you can flirt with her later!" Edward called out, whistling at the two of us.

"For fuck's sake, Edward," Lily muttered behind her sunglasses with exasperation. "Don't ruin the moment!"

"Right, well, we're going to head off to get some snorkeling in, but you should be all set up here with my mom and the captain," Luca said. "Give us a radio if you need anything."

I grabbed his hand, giving it one last *thank you* squeeze, before Luca joined my brother and Edward on the smaller boat.

Lily slid closer. "Time to make these smoothies fun." She reached into her beach bag and pulled out a slim silver flask, tipping a generous splash of rum into each smoothie. "So, you and Luca looked awfully close on that jet ski. Don't think I didn't notice his hand on your thigh when we arrived. And those paints he got you!" she gushed. "You know Edward—"

"Edward is betting on us actually getting together," I cut her off. "So I've heard."

"Well..." Lily wiggled both her eyebrows suggestively.

I snorted, but the pressure behind her words lingered in my chest. I wanted to tell her. Wanted to spill everything about Monaco, about the kisses and the way Luca looked at me like I was his whole universe and not just a press strategy.

But I couldn't.

If I told Lily, Edward would know by sunset. And if Edward knew, the whole paddock would know by next Tuesday. They already thought we were *actually* dating. I didn't need to give Edward any more fuel to the rumor.

"There's nothing to tell. We needed to do this vacation, remember?"

"Oh, bullshit," she blurted out. "Sorry, Georgie, I just see the way Luca looks at you. Edward sees the way he looks at you. It's not the same way he looks at other people."

"Oh, that's ridiculous," I scoffed. "As long as I've known him, he's only ever had flings. We're both so focused on our careers. Luca doesn't need the added stress of a professional race car driver as a girlfriend. I'm not sure what everyone thinks is going on here, but Luca and I are just two friends having *fun* on a yacht."

Even saying the words, they felt *wrong*, and I took a sip of my smoothie to hide the solemn ache that had crept onto my face. We were just friends. Friends who flirted and occasionally kissed. Nothing more.

"*Sexy* fun?" Lily asked, and I shook my head, unable to hide my smile. No chance she believed me. "Look, all I'm saying is, I see how Luca looks at you. It's different."

"How much has Edward bet on us getting together? Must be a lot if you're over here hawking Luca at me. Did he offer to split the money?" Wouldn't have put it past Edward to drag Lily into his silly bet. She drew her lips in a tight line as I dodged her question.

"Fine. Believe what you want. At least tell me you're getting some on the side." Shimmying her shoulders, she licked her lips. "That man is just too fine for you not to be sleeping with him."

Now that, Lily *was* right about.

Chapter Thirty-Six

Luca

On the last night of our trip, my parents opted to have dinner on the mainland, leaving just the five of us on the yacht. As the sun began to dip below the horizon, a surprisingly strong wind blew through, offsetting the warm weather with a cold chill. I welcomed the cool sensation on my skin, as I had spent most of the day under the hot sun.

Lily and Georgia had opted to skip today's windsurfing in favor of painting on the boat. When we hopped back onto the deck, they were sitting at the outside dinner table, enjoying a glass of wine.

"You boys have fun today?" Georgia called out.

"Yeah, it was great," I replied, giving a nod to Henri and Edward who were trailing behind me, adding with a grin, "Edward here decided to compete with the fish for the most vibrant shade of red."

Taking a seat next to Georgia, she passed the bowl of fresh peaches over to me. "I asked the chef to pick some up for you, apparently the peaches had a great season this summer, and I remembered you liked them."

Taking a bite out of one, I grinned. "Well, I'm definitely a fan of their *taste*."

Georgia shoved me lightly with her shoulder, but the flush on her cheeks betrayed her amusement. I slipped an arm around her and tugged her against me, letting my fingers trail lazily up and down her arm.

"Got you a little something today." Digging in my pocket, I took out a large seashell that I'd found off the coast. "Thought you could paint me wearing it later."

She raised an eyebrow. "Oh yeah? You think it's big enough?" She pulled me closer before adding, "You know, to cover up your massive ego." Unable to contain my laughter, the rest of the group turned to watch the two of us.

"Only one way to find out, *amore*." To my absolute delight, Georgia winked at me before pouring another glass of wine.

After a lovely last dinner, the five of us opened another bottle of wine as the sun dipped below the horizon, causing the temperature to drop, and I felt Georgia shiver next to me.

"Here." I draped my Hermes jacket over her shoulders.

"Thanks." Georgia smiled at me, cuddling deeper into my coat. With her rosy cheeks, she looked absolutely adorable wrapped up in the oversize jacket, and I tried to keep a straight face as Edward wagged his eyebrows at me.

"The color purple looks good on you, Georgia," Edward teased.

She didn't miss a beat. "Well, the color red doesn't look quite as good on you, Edward, so maybe use some more sunscreen next time."

Taking a seat across from Georgia, Henri's gaze landed on his sister. And then me. His expression was unreadable to anyone else, but I knew he wasn't pleased with her new outfit. I suppose the only thing worse than seeing your sister in another driver's team jacket was seeing her in your teammate's—especially the teammate with a reputation like *mine.*

"Hey, Edward, mind if I take your spot for a bit?" Henri asked.

Not noticing my desperate plea, Edward got up, swapping with Henri as he continued to loudly discuss his next prank with Georgia and Lily.

Henri's jaw flexed, his voice tightening around the edges. "So, Luca," Henri whispered, "thought any more about what I said after Monaco?"

My lips formed a small grin as I nodded slowly, tightening my grip around Georgia's waist. She didn't seem to mind, still engrossed in conversation with Edward and Lily. Henri's frustrated eyes narrowed on me.

"Right, well, just remember what I said, hmm?"

"Sure thing, Henri, sure thing."

Henri and I sat in a tense silence, and I knew he was studying me carefully. Georgia and I had spent the better part of this boat trip flirting, and I wasn't about to apologize for that. Watching her relax on this trip made my heart burst with joy. All I wanted was for Georgia to feel that she had a safe space to escape the outside world, from this impending article and everything that went with it. I didn't care if it pissed Henri off. Georgia was the only thing on my mind, and seeing the pure anguish on her face back in London made my heart crack. I'd meant what I said, I would stick with Georgia until the end, no matter what happened in that article.

I wasn't leaving her until she told me she didn't want me anymore.

Standing up, Georgia gave her legs a good stretch as she leaned from side to side. "It's getting late! Think it might be time to head to bed."

"You know, I'm going to crash too," I agreed, giving Henri a *friendly* pat on the back. "Sun really takes it out of me."

Lily and Edward waved us off, both heading toward the bar for one last round, and Henri gave me a long, unreadable look. A muted glare. For a split second, I thought he might follow us. Instead, he just nodded once, his expression unreadable but cool.

A smart move.

Georgia was already ahead of me, the sea breeze catching the ends of her hair as she padded barefoot across the deck. When she reached her door, I moved to hold it open, leaning against the frame with what I hoped was casual charm. She smiled, kissed me on the cheek, soft, quick, and waltzed into her room like she hadn't just set every nerve in my body on fire.

Part of my heart—the part that thought maybe she'd invite me in—sank, but I knew she was exhausted.

I went to close the door, and she suddenly called out, "What are you doing? I'm just grabbing my paints."

She held up her sketchpad, then nodded toward my room.

"Well, we aren't going to get *my* room messy."

Chapter Thirty-Seven

Georgia

I had absolutely no intention of painting Luca. And judging by the way his lips crashed against mine the moment we stepped into his room, he was very much on the same page. We'd spent this entire trip dancing around each other, tiptoeing on some sort of gray boundary that we were both perhaps scared to cross. But I didn't want to just flirt with him anymore.

Tonight, I wanted more. Craved it.

His kiss was hungry, urgent in a way that made my knees weak. My painting bag hit the floor with a thud, forgotten, as I jumped into his arms. Luca caught me effortlessly, pressing me against his chest as he carried me straight into the bathroom.

He grabbed his jacket, tugging it off my shoulders. "Fuck, *amore*. I almost don't want to take it off. Fucking love seeing you wear my colors." I slipped from his hold and watched his lips part in protest, then, slowly, I unzipped his team coat and let it fall in a puddle on the floor. My sundress joined it a moment later.

"I think I know of a way to make it up to you."

Warm steam rose around me as I stepped into the shower, still in my bikini, the water cascading over my shoulders. Luca didn't need any more invitation. He was behind me in seconds, his hands already sliding over my wet skin, his mouth finding mine in another bruising kiss.

"Need to get you all clean, before dirtying you up again," he whispered, grabbing the body wash. His hands moved slowly over my chest, down my hips, then to my thighs. He knelt in front of me like I was something sacred, trailing kisses up each leg, pausing to press his lips to every freckle. Every mark. Every part of me. I loved watching Luca on his knees as he lavished kisses up my legs, paying attention to each freckle.

"So perfect," he murmured.

When he stood, his body pressed against mine, trapping me gently against the tile. His gaze held mine, chaotic and soft all at once, his forehead leaning into mine as his hand cupped my cheek. Feeling his arousal pressing into me, I swallowed hard. His full lips were just inches from mine, and I felt a gentle hand caress my cheek.

"You are so beautiful," he said softly, his forehead resting on mine. "So incredible. Mine." Compliments had never been easy for me, especially not in moments like this, but something about the way Luca said it, like I was the only woman that had ever mattered, made my throat tighten. Luca really did have a way of making you feel like you were the center of his world when you were with him.

I kissed him then. Soft at first. Then deeper, until I was wrapped around him, clinging like I'd never get enough. He lifted me effortlessly, my legs around his waist. His lips trailed down my jaw as I tilted my head back, breathless and reeling. When we came up for air, I found myself looking down at him. His pupils were blown, and he licked his lips like he was a cat about to toy with its prey.

"As much as I want you in the shower, *amore*," he growled, voice rough against my neck. "I want to worship this body with the respect that it deserves."

Luca carried us out of the bathroom and tenderly placed me on his bed. I knew I was soaking his sheets, but I didn't care. All I saw, all I felt, was Luca. His kisses, his hands, the reverence in his touch. He trailed light kisses down my neck, eliciting a soft moan. I flipped us, straddling his thighs, placing slow kisses down his chest. Smiling as his breath caught with each one.

"Stop being a tease," he demanded, grabbing my hair.

"So greedy," I teased, licking the tip of his cock just enough to make his hips twitch. His dark eyes and half-lidded gaze told me if I kept teasing, I was going to regret it later.

I took him in slowly, hollowing my cheeks just right. He let out a raw moan, one that made heat pool between my legs. With slow movements, I began to move up and down his shaft, enjoying each moan as it escaped his lips. Like I had done at Monza, I took him deeper into my throat, using my hands to stroke the part of him that didn't fit. My fingers roamed down to his balls, giving them a gentle squeeze, and Luca grabbed my hair even tighter.

But just when I found my rhythm, Luca's hand tangled tighter in my hair, guiding me off him. His mouth was on mine a second later, kissing me like he needed to feel everything all at once.

"As much as I love your mouth, this time I want to finish inside of you." He groaned and kissed his way down my body, fingers slipping between my thighs. When he found how wet I already was, he stilled and looked up at me. "Oh, *amore*, are you this wet from sucking my cock?" His voice alone nearly undid me.

He slid two fingers inside, curling them just right, expertly hitting the same spot that had made me scream in Monaco. His thumb grazed my clit with maddening precision, and by the time he added a third finger, I was writhing beneath him.

I was so fucking close.

And then, he stopped.

I let out a frustrated noise and opened my eyes to see him smirking down at me.

"Sorry," he said, sucking my arousal off his fingers with an exaggerated wink. "I couldn't help myself. Needed a taste."

I could have died in that moment, watching Luca suck my juices off his fingers.

The bed dipped as he climbed onto it. His lips pressed against my skin, starting with my stomach and then moving up to my breasts. He lavished attention on each one, his tongue swirling around the peaks until they were hard. I gasped softly, threading my fingers into his damp hair, tugging gently as he kissed his way back to my mouth. Reaching for the bedside table, Luca grabbed a condom, smoothly sliding it onto himself.

"You ready, *amore*?" He asked softly, hunting for my consent which I gladly gave with a breathy yes, pulling him closer.

He eased into me carefully, taking his time, and even though his fingers had stretched me earlier, nothing quite prepared me for the full reality of him. My hands gripped the sheets, breath caught in my throat, until I felt him still, buried deep, giving me space to adjust.

"You okay, *amore*?" he asked softly.

"God, Luca, I need more," I begged, wrapping my legs around his waist.

He started to move again, slow and steady, drawing out a delicious ache that curled my toes and made my hips chase his. But it wasn't enough. Not even close.

"My fucking good girl." The words sounded like utter filth, and I loved every one of them. "Fuck. You take me so well." The more he whispered dirty praises into my ear, the more I wanted to be a good girl for him.

"Luca... faster..." I panted.

He smirked against my throat. "Ask politely."

Cocky bastard.

"Pl-please."

"Please, what?"

Did he expect me to beg for this? Torturously, Luca continued to move in and out of me at a snail's pace.

"Please, Luca." I tried to sound forceful, but my words came out as a pathetic plea, much to Luca's delight. "Fuck me harder."

"That's my good girl," he purred.

His pace changed. Fast, deep, relentless. My hands flew to his back, nails dragging down his skin as I cried out. Every thrust hit the exact spot inside me that made my vision blur.

When his hand slid down and began to circle my clit, I shattered. Each thrust hit that spot inside me that drove me wild. Soon enough, I felt the coiled tension snap and I couldn't hold back anymore.

My body clenched around him as I came, a strangled cry escaping my throat. I tried to muffle the sound, palm pressed against my lips, but Luca tugged it away.

"I want this whole fucking boat to know that you're mine."

That was it. That was all it took. With one final thrust, he groaned my name, spilling into the condom as his forehead pressed against mine.

For a moment, the only sounds in the room were our ragged breaths and the soft whir of the ocean breeze against the windows. He stood and padded into the bathroom, returning with a warm towel, cleaning me up with gentle hands. I tried to sit up, but he tugged me down again, guiding my body onto his chest.

"I-I can go, let you get some sleep."

"Oh no you don't, *amore*. You promised me a painting." Luca grinned, pulling me closer to him. "But since you're probably quite tired from that incredible workout I just gave you, I can settle for some cuddles instead."

I crawled higher up his body, draping myself across him like a blanket. "Who knew F1's notorious bachelor was such a cuddler?"

He chuckled, stroking a lazy hand down my spine. "And who knew F1's most dominant driver was such a good girl in bed?"

"Don't let it go to your head."

"What? Me?" Luca playfully gasped. "I can't help it. I have an amazing woman in my arms. What's not to gloat about?"

His words tugged at my heart. With the majority of my past dates, it had been the opposite. They didn't want a dominant, confident woman who was more talented than them in their bed, but here was Luca, ready to boldly proclaim it to the world. Snuggling with him, I couldn't help but feel a warm sense of comfort and security.

We drifted into silence, bodies tangled. "Thank you, Luca," I whispered. "Thank you for this week. It's been amazing. Just what I needed."

His smile was quiet, but it reached all the way to his eyes. “Me too, *amore*. Me too.”

Chapter Thirty-Eight

Georgia

I was jolted awake on Friday morning by a low, rhythmic noise behind me, something between a sigh and a sleepy groan. For a moment, I wasn't sure where I was. My body was warm, too warm, and the air was full of a scent entirely unfamiliar but deeply comforting.

I blinked my eyes open.

I was still in Luca's bed.

We were still tangled in his bed, his arm looped tightly around my waist, his body molded perfectly to mine. And very much hard against me. Memories of last night surfaced.

I want this whole fucking boat to know that you're mine.

I knew he'd probably only meant it in the heat of the moment. Still, my heart wanted to believe the words held weight outside this cabin. Because the truth was, wrapped in Luca's arms, warm and safe, I wasn't sure I wanted this to be temporary anymore. What we'd built this week didn't feel fake. It felt maddeningly, frighteningly real.

Being in bed with Luca like this, it all felt too easy. A nagging voice told me it shouldn't have felt that way, not with someone who wasn't officially mine, even if I was starting to wish he was. I couldn't shake off the conflicting feelings stirring inside me, especially since it had been so long since anyone had made me feel this way.

I glanced at the clock. Five thirty a.m., which meant the sun was just about to rise. Since I was already awake, I decided to take advantage of the opportunity. I turned slightly, trying not to wake him, but the moment I shifted, the arm around my waist pulled me firmly back.

"Leaving without a good morning kiss?" Luca's voice was full of sleep.

"Cuddles not enough for you, I see?" I teased.

He nuzzled into the crook of my neck, his stubble dragging deliciously against my skin. Luca draped his arm over me, and he pulled me flush against him, giving me a small peck on the lips. His hands trailed down to my center, his fingertips lightly grazing my upper thighs, and I knew he could feel how wet I was from just his teasing.

"What's got you so wet, *amore*? Have another *dream* last night?" I rolled my eyes, but I didn't push him away. Not when his hand was slipping between my legs, brushing against the most sensitive part of me. A soft moan escaped before I could catch it.

"Luca," I warned, but it came out far too breathy to be taken seriously.

His other hand slid beneath the hem of my shirt, his shirt, technically, cupping one of my breasts and rolling my nipple between his fingers. He pressed his hips against my backside, and I could feel just how ready he was.

"I mean," he murmured against my shoulder, "if you want me to stop..."

Instead of answering, I guided his hand lower, pressing him exactly where I needed him most.

"Didn't think so." He grinned, kissing the top of my shoulder.

His fingers slid inside me, slow and steady, and I gasped, arching into his touch. The spooning position only made everything feel more intense: his lips tracing my neck, his chest flush against my back, the warmth of his breath at my ear as he whispered softly to me.

"You're so fucking beautiful like this. Ruining me, Georgia Dubois. I swear."

My eyes fluttered shut. His fingers worked expertly, curling just right, stroking that place inside me he'd apparently memorized. My body tightened, pleasure building fast, and I clutched his wrist to steady myself.

"Oh my god, Luca. Don't stop."

"I wasn't planning to."

My moans grew louder, and even though part of me remembered we weren't alone on the boat, I couldn't bring myself to care. Luca's name spilled from my lips like a prayer, over and over, until the orgasm crashed through me, fast and hot and impossible to contain.

"So fucking hot," he whispered, voice thick with want.

As I panted through the aftershocks, he reached for a condom in the drawer beside us, tearing it open with one hand.

"Think you have another one in you, *amore*?" I nodded, still out of breath from the last orgasm.

I could barely form a coherent answer, so I just nodded again, catching my breath. He kissed my temple as he positioned himself behind me again.

"So dominant on the track," he murmured as he eased in, slow and careful, "but so willing to be a good girl for me in bed." I whimpered at the stretch, full and overwhelmed all over again. Luca groaned into my shoulder as he bottomed out.

"Fuck, you feel unbelievable."

He started to move, slow and deep, each thrust making my breath catch. One of his arms wrapped around my waist, the other hand finding my clit again. The sensation built too quickly, my body still sensitive from the last orgasm.

"Let go for me again, *amore*. Let me feel you fall apart."

I clung to the sheets as another climax crept up on me, this one even more intense. The way he touched me, like I was his and he was desperate to prove it, unraveled me completely.

When I came this time, I cried out his name without shame.

"God, I've wanted this… wanted you for so long," he said, his thrusts losing rhythm, his voice raw.

A few more frantic strokes and he let out a guttural groan, emptying himself with a deep shudder. His arms tightened around me, holding me close even as we both collapsed back onto the pillows.

We stayed there for a moment, our bodies tangled, breaths slowing. He pressed soft kisses to my shoulder, then my neck, then the curve of my jaw.

Eventually, he turned me to face him. His dark eyes softened, but something unspoken swirled beneath them, like he wanted to say something and couldn't quite figure out how.

"I meant what I said, Georgia. Being with you… you bring me this peace that I've never felt before." Rough hands cupped my chin, and Luca leaned in for another kiss. His soft sincerity caused a devastating flutter to erupt in my stomach. We both lay there peacefully, enjoying the company of one another for a little while longer.

I looked at the time, and not wanting to miss the sunrise, I sat up.

He whined, trying to pull me back into his bed.

"I'm going to watch the sunrise," I murmured, starting to slide out of bed.

"No, *amore*. Just a little while longer," Luca groaned, trying to reel me back in with one heavy arm. His hand grazed my hip like it was reluctant to let me go. "It's warm here. And soft. Stay."

"You can, of course, join me if you can bear to get out of bed." As light started to peek through the blinds, I heard Luca groan, a confirmation that he was not a morning person, unless sex was involved.

"'Tis so cold without you," he hummed, although I could see him close his eyes, already giving in to sleep.

I crept out of Luca's room, scanning the hallway to make sure no one had decided to emerge for a pre-coffee stroll. I darted into my own room, slipped into leggings, then headed toward the bow of the yacht.

The golden edge of morning light was just beginning to kiss the water when I saw him.

Henri. Standing at the front of the boat with his arms crossed, holding two mugs of coffee like he'd been waiting for me.

"Hey!" I called out, jogging a few feet. "You hogging all the coffee on this boat?"

Henri let out a small, audible exhale as he passed me a mug. His expression immediately changing as soon as his eyes landed on my shirt.

Shit. I looked down to see I was wearing Luca's Hermes shirt, the one he'd let me borrow back at his apartment.

"Wearing his shirt now, too, I see." Henri took a contemplative sip of coffee, motioning for me to take a seat next to him. His voice was full of disdain as he pointedly ignored my LR52 shirt.

I winced. “Luca let me borrow it a couple weeks ago.”

Henri didn’t respond to my admission of guilt, his lips in a tight, thin line. His lack of words spoke volumes. He was clearly unimpressed with the choices I’d made last night.

“I heard you sneak out of *his* room this morning.”

“I’m sorry…” I started, but Henri shook his head.

“You don’t need to apologize, Georgia. You’re an adult with the freedom to do what she wants. I just don’t want to see you get hurt.” Henri’s shoulders sagged, avoiding eye contact. He scuffed his shoe against the ground, a defeated expression on his face. It was if he was weighing his options, trying to decide what to say to me. “You think you know Luca. But I know him better.”

“I know what I’m doing.”

“Do you?” His voice was sharp. “This is Luca Rossi, F1’s notorious playboy. More one-night stands than race starts, something I’ve witnessed for the last couple of years as his teammate. And here you are, hopping into his bed each night.”

I stilled for a moment, leaning back as I crossed my arms. “Excuse me, I am not hopping into his bed each night. And even if I was, it’s none of your business who I sleep with.” I didn’t appreciate the subtle hint of what my brother was trying to say.

Henri turned to face me fully. “I’m not saying that it is,” he sighed, “I’m just… worried he’s using you to get back at me. Or at least, prove that I’m wrong.”

Get back at Henri? They might not be on the best of terms as teammates, but this felt dramatic even for him.

Henri was the number one driver, he'd won the Hermes battle for power.

"Back in Monaco, I asked Luca to stop leading you on. And before you say anything," he held up his hand, "I see the way you look at him, Peaches. You've never been good at hiding your feelings, and you've never been someone to have casual sex. You've practically been all over each other this trip." Henri's face pinched with guilt, but he held firm. "I asked him not to mess with your head. And of course, he got pissed. You know Luca, he hates being told what to do. Especially by me. And now I'm worried this is his way of proving he can cross that line just because I drew it." He exhaled slowly, running a hand through his hair. "He's *never* been a serious dater. Hell, he still brings up Éliott like it's a game. Like he's testing the waters. He's told me himself he doesn't plan to settle down until he retires from Formula 1. After your winner's brunch, I asked about his intentions, and he said he was just playing the role Hermes had asked of him."

The words hung in the air, heavy and sharp.

I pressed my fingers to my temples, trying to ward off the pressure building behind my eyes. His voice was calm, his tone even, but every word chipped away at the fragile little hope I hadn't even realized I'd been nursing.

Henri grabbed my hand, sincerity laced in his voice. "Look, you both did this for a reason, and I think you need to think about what's going to happen when Luca finally lands that contract. I've heard rumors of his agent shopping him around to other teams."

His words stung, but there was some truth to his warning. Luca's reputation preceded him, and I knew better than anyone not to get emotionally invested in a dead-end situation. But something about our time together—the way Luca's eyes softened when we were together, and how he held me close, whispering into my ear as we laughed away at silly jokes, it was easy to forget that maybe they were just that, nice moments between friends having casual sex. It didn't mean that Luca was falling in love with me, even if I was falling for him.

It didn't mean Luca wanted a commitment. Hell, Henri had basically just confirmed this wasn't anything special.

I'd been the one to initiate last night, not him. He hadn't done anything wrong. We hadn't agreed to be anything but friends. Contemplating the sincerity of my brother's voice and concerned eyes, I couldn't dismiss the nagging feeling in my heart. I put on a brave face, forcing a smile.

Henri's voice broke through my spiraling thoughts. "Plus, Georgia, and I can't believe I'm saying this to my biggest rival, but you don't need any more distractions this season. You're winning the championship right now; don't let anything distract you from that, especially not Luca. You've got to put 100 percent out there."

I forced a hollow laugh. "Henri, It's just some fun, okay? I'm fine."

I knew my words fell flat. With each passing second, more disappointment started to creep in, and I hated myself for it. Being mad at Luca wasn't fair because we weren't *actually* together. I was the one who had initiated sex, and I didn't have a right to be angry at him. But deep down, I couldn't shake off this feeling of frustration and stupidity, because I had started to let my heart wonder *what if*.

Henri was right. Between the championship battle and Luca's history with relationships, I needed to keep my heart in check and my mind focused. The fake dating was enough of a distraction from the racing, I couldn't imagine what real dating would look like. I needed to slow whatever it was Luca and I were doing down.

We had a two-week break after this vacation, during which we would both be completely absorbed in our respective training camps before the second half of the season started. While I was fucking annoyed Henri had butted into my business, he was right that after just a couple months of knowing Luca, I'd let my heart run wild with possibilities.

I'll talk to Luca before the Austrian Grand Prix, I resolved. *Tell him I need a little space. To slow down. He'll understand.*

Even if the thought left a bitter taste in my mouth, even if my gut twisted with something that felt a little too much like heartbreak, I knew what I had to do. Because I wasn't going to lose the championship over a guy who might never be mine.

No matter how badly I wanted him to be.

Chapter Thirty-Nine

Luca

A few hours after Georgia left, I finally crawled out of bed, quickly packing my suitcase. I moved slowly, still riding the high of last night and this morning. I was going to miss this trip more than I wanted to admit. Even with Henri's permanent scowl, Lily's meddling, and Edward's nonstop commentary, the past week had been nothing short of perfect.

All week I'd been so worried about crossing the line between flirting and something more with Georgia, but the moment she stepped foot in my room last night, I knew she felt the same as me. Knew that she, too, couldn't resist the constant pull and electricity that had been building between us for the last few weeks.

I left my suitcase by the door and headed to the breakfast lounge, drawn by the sound of quiet voices and the scent of fresh espresso drifting from the galley. Georgia and Lily sat together in the corner booth, heads together as they chatted away.

Despite knowing I shouldn't eavesdrop on their conversation, my curiosity got the best of me. Every part of me wanted to hear Georgia bragging about the incredible sex we'd had.

Because it had been just that: *fucking amazing*.

"So, have a good night last night?" Lily asked, leaning over the table in anticipation.

Georgia let out a soft groan. "Oh God, did the entire boat hear?"

After the text I'd received from Edward this morning, I was worried that Henri had heard. He wasn't exactly thrilled with me right now.

Lily laughed, taking the cup of coffee from Georgia's outstretched hands. "I'm just glad you took what I said to heart! I knew Luca was into you, but no one listens to meeee…"

Georgia put her hands up. "Whoa, getting ahead of yourself there. It was just sex, Lil. Nothing more."

I took a step back, shoving my hands in my pockets. *Had I heard that right?*

"Oh, come on, Georgie," Lily said, voice rising slightly, incredulous. "There's no way it was *just* sex. The way you two loo—"

"Lily, for fuck's sake, there's nothing going on between me and Luca. We had sex, and it was fun. I wish everyone would stop making more of this than it is," she snapped.

Lily blinked, stunned into silence, her mouth parted in disbelief. I stood just out of view behind the corner of the galley wall, the words ringing in my ears. My heart felt like it had just been thrown to the bottom of the ocean.

Fun. That was all it had been?

I stepped away, careful not to make noise, slipping out toward the front deck with my head down. Each step felt heavier than the last. I kept my gaze fixed on the teak wood planks beneath my feet, trying to ignore the burn spreading through my rib cage. Last night had meant something more to me. Having Georgia in my arms, laughing away with her as she joked and chatted about our day, it felt so different than any other relationship.

I tried to reason with myself, reminding myself that I shouldn't be offended by her comment, that the intimacy of last night and this morning had been just two friends flirting, nothing more.

After all, I'd let her down before when I'd stood her up. I'd given her every reason to doubt that I wanted more, that this was more than a game. Especially with this reputation that I dragged behind me like a curse.

Did I really think a yacht vacation was going to fix five years of a bad reputation and an abandoned date? Georgia saw us as friends, which was a hell of a lot better than where we'd been two months ago.

I gripped the railing, the salt air stinging my eyes more than I cared to admit.

I couldn't force her to see what I felt, not if she wasn't ready. And I couldn't keep chasing something she wasn't ready to give. Something she might never be able to give to someone like me. Anthony had made it a joke. Henri had made it a warning. But they both saw what I was too afraid to admit: I might not be what she needed—or wanted.

I needed to give us some space, I decided. Let her breathe. Let myself breathe.

Training camps would keep us apart for the next two weeks. After the Austrian Grand Prix, I'd figure out what was left. *If* anything was left.

I turned to head back to my room, but paused when I saw my father walking toward me. He looked about as happy as I did.

Fuck. Matteo had finally told him.

I'd begged my manager not to tell my father my big secret, the one I'd been hoarding to myself since the beginning of this vacation, because I knew it would ruin this trip.

"Luca Michael Rossi, you have some explaining to do," he demanded, grabbing my arm as he pulled us closer. There would be no hiding from this inevitable conversation.

"Dad—" I searched for the right words to explain myself, but he didn't wait for me to continue.

"What the fuck is this I hear about you possibly signing with Rennen F1?"

The wind whipped off the sea behind us, filling the tense silence between us. "Dad, I know this is a big surprise for you, but I've been considering a few options for my future."

"I won't have my son racing for a rival team," he spat out.

"I owe it to myself to explore all my options, and Rennen is offering me something that Hermes can't."

My father scoffed at my defiance. "And what can't Hermes offer you? They're the oldest racing team on the grid. They're legacy. Our legacy."

I took a step back, letting his words settle. "A chance to win the championship," I said calmly. "A chance to show everyone that I'm more than Michael Rossi's washed-out son."

"You have a spot at Hermes, but you're throwing it all away for some empty promises from Rennen?"

"Except I don't have a spot at Hermes."

His eyes narrowed. "We're working on that..."

"No," I snapped. "I'm tired of this. I'm tired of being the disappointment, the mistake, the second choice. I want to prove myself, and Rennen is my chance to do it."

At the beginning of this trip, I hadn't decided if I was going to take the offer. Part of me had still clung to the hope that maybe Hermes would come through. But as I looked into his cold, furious eyes, I knew. I couldn't wait for a seat that didn't feel like mine.

I couldn't live under the weight of his legacy anymore.

Matteo had warned me: *Rennen's offer wouldn't last forever.* They were willing to take a chance on me. Not the son of a legend. Not the washed-up second driver with too many headlines and too little faith.

Just me.

I met my father's gaze and straightened my spine. But as I gazed at my father's angry eyes, I realized that I needed to take this leap of faith and finally break out of his Rossi legacy chokehold.

"We finalized the terms in London before the yacht," I said quietly. "The contract's ready."

All that was left was for me to sign.

And this time, I wouldn't hesitate.

Chapter Forty

Georgia

As expected, on the Thursday before the Austrian Grand Prix, the first race post summer break, the *Daily Reporter* released their article. Nora had explicitly instructed me not to read it, which I had listened to for all of one hour, if only because I was too terrified that if I read it, then this nightmare would actually be real. Some irrational part of me still believed that if I didn't acknowledge the article's existence, it wouldn't exist—would never haunt my dreams.

But as I sat down on my driver's room couch, staring at my face on the home page of the *Daily Reporter*'s website, I knew that wasn't the case.

This nightmare was real.

To make matters worse, it had now been two weeks since Luca and I had gotten back from Mallorca. Two weeks since I had seen or heard from him. Between our two midseason training camps, I knew we'd have very little time to speak after the vacation, but I hadn't expected such glaring silence.

Watching the notifications from friends and family pour in, I just continued to stare blankly at my phone screen, hesitant to tap the link. Every piece of me wished that Luca was here in my room to help me face my fears.

Each notification built up a new panic, a new anxiety, and by the number of texts that were flooding through, I knew I couldn't let this sit unread anymore.

SHOWMANCE? F1 star Georgia Dubois accused of "PR stunt" with fellow driver Luca Rossi

Despite public displays of affection, leading female F1 driver Georgia Dubois and alleged boyfriend Luca Rossi's relationship is a "PR stunt" according to sources close to the pair.

Documents shared with the Daily Reporter claim the relationship was set up by Valkyrie F1 Racing to help "boost Georgia's sponsorship prospects." According to the insider, Dubois is using fellow F1 driver Rossi's famous racing family to get funding for her Valkyrie seat.

It was similarly claimed during her IndyCar days that Dubois participated in the same stunt with fellow driver Anthony Walker. A review of Dubois' sponsorship records proved she accepted money from her now ex-boyfriend's father's company, Walker Industries.

Avid viewers have equally speculated that during recent races Dubois had been allowing Rossi to pass her on track, a move seen when she "spun" in Monza that allowed him to win his home race. According to expert engineers close to the F1 leadership, the spin was "clearly intentional."

The insider said: "It's really a shame because the F1 community believed that they were finally getting a female driver that deserved to be in this sport, not one that slept their way into it.

> "We all want a female driver, but not if it's achieved by cheating," they commented.
>
> Dubois and Rossi are due to appear at the Austrian Grand Prix this upcoming weekend. What will the FIA do about this incident?
>
> Check back for more updates and click here for our in-depth investigation.

By the time I finished the article, I was gripping my phone so tightly that my knuckles were white. My heartbeat thundered in my ears, drowning out activity in the garage. The words on the screen blurred together, forming a sickening concoction of disbelief and anger. I tried to manage my shallow breathing as I processed the magnitude of what I had just read.

They had accused me of *cheating.*

Because how could a woman ever be successful in a man's world without help?

"Hey, Georgia, you got a moment?" Lily's gentle voice drifted through the door, barely audible over the ringing in my ears. She hesitated before knocking again. The door creaked open, and I didn't bother looking up. She didn't wait for permission, just came in and sat beside me, reaching for my trembling hand. Her palm was warm against my cold skin.

"Georgia, what's going on?" Panic was laced in her voice.

"These journalists..." I finally whispered, "I'm done with them. *All of them.* They're going to rue the day they decided to mess with Georgia Dubois." My hands shook as I clenched the phone.

"Fuck, Georgia. Nora told you not to read the article!"

"Have *you* read it?" I shot back.

Obviously, she had.

Hell, I knew by the end of today, everyone in the paddock would have read it. Lily said nothing. Her gaze drifted to the window, her silence answering for her.

"I knew it would be *bad*, but I never thought it would be *this* bad."

"It's not *that bad*," Lily offered weakly.

My face might as well have said *fuck you*.

"They accused me of cheating! What could be worse than that? Luca has only finished ahead of me twice this season. Twice! I win my races fair and square."

Lily opened her mouth again, but I held up a hand, shaking my head.

"And for them to bring in IndyCar. Just ridiculous. I *earned* that spot. Saying I bought my seat with sponsorship money? That's how racing works! That's how it *has* to work. Cars don't run on magic and fairy dust. It's why I'm in this mess to begin with. Cars aren't free! The idea that I dated Anthony for clout is laughable. He was a loser. I had more fans than he did."

With each passing second the growing pit in my stomach churned even deeper into anger.

"You know, Lily, I'm going to be this year's Formula 1 champion. And no journalist, or executive, or steward is going to take that away from me."

The sobs came without warning, hot and silent at first, then louder, the kind that wrack your shoulders and make you feel like you're coming undone. Lily pulled me into a crushing hug, arms wrapped around me like a life raft in a storm.

I clung to her, letting myself fall apart for just a moment.

When the silence finally returned, I exhaled shakily and looked up, my face blotchy and wet.

"Feel better?" she asked softly.

"… sort of." I sunk my head into my hands.

"You can't let these journalists win, Georgia. You know the truth. The women on this team know the truth. And most importantly, all the little girls who watch us race? *They* know the truth. Men are never going to stop trying to take away our success. Our wins. It's up to us to not let them have that power. You're going to win this race. And the next one, and then? Then you're going to win this championship. We set out with a mission, and articles like the one published today? That's why we're here."

I put my head in my hands, rubbing my face in frustration, before whispering, "When did you get so wise?"

Lily flashed me a bright smile, before finally standing up, lending me her hand so I could do the same.

"We signed up to achieve the Valkyrie mission, Georgia," she announced. "They're only attacking us because the mission is succeeding, but it doesn't matter because we're here to stay."

My phone buzzed violently in my hand, startling both of us. A text from Isabelle lit up the screen, followed immediately by an incoming call.

"Hi, Georgia," Isabelle said softly. Hearing my sniffles, she didn't wait for me to respond. "I assume you didn't listen to our instructions and that you've read the article?"

What did she think I was going to do?

"Yes," I mumbled.

"Oh, Georgia, they aren't worth your time." There was a long pause on the other line before Isabelle continued, "I need you to meet me at the FIA offices in an hour. I know you have strategy meetings, but I had them rescheduled. Giovanni wants to see us."

Well, fuck.

Before I could respond she added, "It's not as bad as it sounds."

No chance she believed that. I certainly didn't. As much as Isabelle wanted to dissuade my worry, the moment I read the cheating accusation, a trip to the FIA leadership offices was inevitable.

After a quick lunch and another pep talk, Lily left, and I made my way to the director offices where Isabelle was sitting outside Giovanni's door, a stern expression on her face.

I dropped into the seat beside her and lowered my voice to a whisper. "You used to work for Giovanni, back when you were an engineer at Hermes, right? Maybe that'll help?" I tried to sound casual, but the tension made it come out brittle. Before becoming President of the FIA, Giovanni had been the Hermes team principal for many years.

And it showed. Objectivity was not his strong suit.

She snorted under her breath. "Just let me do the talking. We'll be a calm, united front. He may look scary, but he's nothing more than a wet blanket."

The receptionist stood up, motioning for us to join the FIA President in his office. Giovanni was a staunch Italian man with large round glasses that made him look a bit more like a cartoon character than the leader of the governing body of motorsport. As he watched us, he wore a frown on his face, although Isabelle had told me he was always like that—including at his own wedding.

"Good morning." Once we were seated, he cleared his throat and began. "So, in light of the article that came out this morning, the FIA wanted to touch base with Valkyrie to make sure we are on the same page." A heavy silence hung in the air as he paused, no doubt preparing himself for our reactions. "To be clear, the FIA does not condone two teams conspiring to get more sponsors. Or to get ahead, for that matter."

"Valkyrie—" Isabelle started.

But Giovanni cut her off with a single raised hand. It wasn't a gesture of deference; it was a command. One meant to silence.

The change in Isabelle's face was instant. Her eyes narrowed dangerously as she balled her fists at her sides, and she looked like she might lunge forward to slap him across the face. Before this meeting, she'd coached me on staying calm, composed.

But now? Now she looked ready to burn the entire building to the ground.

And I'd be lying if I said I wasn't rooting for it.

"Most importantly," he added. "The FIA does not allow drivers to *collaborate* in any way."

Isabelle said nothing as she continued to stare him down. Giovanni leaned back in his chair, studying Isabelle for a moment before returning his attention to me.

"So, do we know why this article from the *Daily Reporter* was released?" His brows drew together, creating deep lines on his forehead, his mouth twisting into a frown.

Isabelle didn't miss a beat. "Do we know why *trashy* tabloids write *trashy* articles?" Isabelle scoffed. "Because it's in their nature."

He clenched his jaw, before leaning forward in his seat. "After this accusation, I'm obligated to look into Georgia's spin at Monza. Several teams have requested a formal investigation. If Georgia is passing Luca engineering secrets or spinning on purpose—"

"Wait a min—" I started.

Isabelle cut me off. "Investigate, Gio. We're always happy to take some free engineering advice. Be sure to have that '*report*'"—she added exaggerated air quotes with both hands—"sent to my office."

"The FIA is taking this seriously, Isabelle. We investigate every accusation of cheating, even if it comes from a newspaper. You'd do well to show some respect. And concern." His hands gripped the sides of his leather chair.

"You can't actually think I'd share my racing secrets with Hermes, Gio? Even you aren't that stupid." Standing up, Isabelle set her left arm against her hip. "You're lecturing me on taking this seriously? You have just told me that the FIA is investigating *my racer* because a *tabloid* published an uninformed, misogynistic article about her. Not even a monkey would take this seriously, and quite frankly, Gio, I am embarrassed for you and the entire FIA operation. You have dragged me in here with the intention of wasting my precious time."

When Giovanni said nothing, Isabelle slammed her hands down on the director's desk, leaning forward so that her face was no less than a foot away from his wide eyes.

"How about this: I'll take this seriously when you answer me one question. Where the hell is the Hermes team in all this? Hm? You really think we'd be able to pull off all of that supposed *cheating* alone? You know *receiving* engineering secrets or help on the track is *also* cheating."

Giovanni's silence said everything. Isabelle raised one perfectly arched eyebrow, the question lingering like a loaded weapon between them.

"Don't tell me only Valkyrie was called to your offices?" The taunt in her voice rang throughout the entire office.

"Hermes weren't accused of—"

But Isabelle lifted a single finger, cutting him off. "Save it. You can investigate my team all you want, Gio. You can drag Valkyrie's name through the mud. You can try and scare off our sponsors, but that isn't going to stop me from beating your *precious* Hermes. Nothing will stop me from beating *you*."

The way she said "you" made me think there was more to this grudge than the newspaper article and investigation. There was history here. Deep, dark history that likely only a select few knew about. I almost enjoyed the tiny inkling of defeat in his eyes, but to be fair to him, arguing with an angry Isabelle was next to impossible, something he'd likely learned many years ago when she was his employee. Isabelle had never told me the real reason why she'd left Hermes, but judging by the animosity between them, it was clear their split wasn't as amicable as everyone believed.

He tapped his fingers together like a man grasping for composure. Then, begrudgingly, he turned his attention to me. His mouth twitched, but it was clear that he'd already lost control of this meeting.

"Georgia, anything to add?" he said finally.

"No," I smiled sweetly. "I try not to comment on men's poor behaviors."

Giovanni cleared his throat, adjusting his tie like it was suddenly choking him. "And so, I am to believe that your relationship with Luca is all above board? That you're both wildly in love?"

"I—um—" The question hit me harder than I expected. My fingers twitched against my thigh, the soft fabric of my suit digging beneath my nails. "Yes." Isabelle placed a comforting hand on my shoulder as I continued, "My relationship with Luca… It's changed me. He's thoughtful. Kind. *Infuriating*. He drives me insane and calms me down in the same breath. And he… he sees me. Not as the boring, bossy female driver. Not as someone to fix. Just… me, the girl who loves to race." I turned to Giovanni, locking eyes with him. "Luca Rossi is special, Giovanni, and that's why I'm with him."

He studied us both for a moment, his gaze so piercing that it felt like he could see right through me, like he could read my every thought and emotion. But it didn't matter. Even if he could, I'd meant every single word. There wasn't a lie in sight.

My life was immensely better with Luca in it.

"Valkyrie has earned its success, Giovanni," Isabelle added. "No investigation will change that."

"Alright then." Without another word, Giovanni dismissed us. The meeting hadn't gone as expected, but I wasn't necessarily disappointed with the outcome.

When we stepped outside, Isabelle pulled me into a tight hug. "Let's focus on this weekend, okay?"

I nodded, grateful for Isabelle's unwavering support. "Thank you for that, Isabelle. I'm sorry—"

"Don't you dare apologize, Georgia," she said gently, grabbing my shoulder with a tight squeeze. "Not to me. Not to any of those men. This weekend, do what you do best, and everything will work itself out."

I pushed down the nerves that threatened to bubble up.

"Right, I need to head over to the VIP area. You should head back to the hotel, Georgia. Have you even checked in yet?"

"No, I haven't had time, but I need to head back. There's a dinner organized by Edward."

"Great. Try to enjoy tonight, yeah? Maybe even sneak in one glass of wine."

I managed a laugh, giving her a mock salute. My phone pinged, and I opened it to see a text from Luca.

Luca:
Heard you got called into Giovanni's office. Totally unfair. You okay?

Georgia:
Thanks. Yeah, I'm fine. Got to watch Isabelle scream at Giovanni, so it wasn't all a loss.

Three dots appeared on my screen, and it felt like seconds had turned into hours as I waited for Luca's response.

Luca:
I've got a busy week this week, so I won't be at the hotel much, but I didn't want you to hear this from anyone else. It releases later this evening.

As I clicked on the screenshot of the press release Luca had attached, my heart burst into a million mixed emotions.

Well, fuck.

Chapter Forty-One

Georgia

Formula 1 driver Luca Rossi has officially signed with Rennen F1.

The racer had been linked to several teams, but has now landed a contract with Rennen, the third-place team in the Constructor's Championship.

After the retirement announcement of their team leader, Rennen has been looking for an experienced driver to fill the position.

Emotions soared through me too quickly for me to pick just one. Each reread of the press release left me feeling more and more confused. Luca had signed with a new Formula 1 team?

The morning of our last day on the yacht, I could see a staunch change in Luca's demeanor. The happy-go-lucky, relaxed Luca that I had come to enjoy had turned sour. It had been two weeks since Mallorca, and all I'd received were these casual text messages. At first, I blamed our grueling midseason training camps. We were all exhausted, running on discipline and adrenaline. But deep down, I knew it wasn't just that.

Luca was never one for complete silence, and his lack of words spoke volumes.

Something had shifted between us. Something I couldn't name. Maybe Henri had been right all along. Maybe Luca had gotten what he wanted—press coverage, sympathy, a glossy image—and now he no longer needed this. No longer needed me.

And even though I'd agreed with myself that I was going to tell Luca that I needed more space, now that all I had was space, I knew it wasn't what I wanted.

My head buzzed like white noise. A thousand conflicting thoughts spinning around at once, but underneath it all, one emotion floated to the surface: sadness. Pure and heavy. He'd achieved what I so desperately wanted for him, an opportunity to step out of his father's shadow.

He'd done it. He had finally broken free of his father's legacy. Stepped into a spotlight of his own making. The thing I wanted most for him had come true.

And I wasn't there to celebrate with him.

"Earth to Georgia." Lily's voice rang beside me, breaking through the fog of my thoughts. I blinked, realizing I'd been standing outside my hotel room, key card poised uselessly in front of the door. Lily cocked an amused eyebrow. "You planning to camp out in the hallway?"

She and Nora had driven us to the hotel, with me staring silently out the window the entire ride, the press release echoing in my brain like a bad chorus. I hadn't mentioned Luca's impending press release, but I knew by tomorrow morning the entire paddock would be talking about it.

"I've heard the suites in this hotel are so nice!" Lily stood behind me, practically breathing down my neck.

"Well, don't forget I have a roommate," I said dryly, giving Lily a furrowed brow to remind her why I had a suite in the first place.

As the door swung open, my breath caught, hard. I gasped so loudly my phone slipped from my fingers, clattering to the hallway floor. Nora and Lily rushed in after me like a herd of stampeding wildebeests.

And then we all froze.

The entire suite was bursting with flowers.

Everywhere I looked were roses, lilies, tulips, daisies. Soft whites, delicate pinks, blush-toned orchids. Like a botanical garden had exploded in the middle of the hotel room. Bouquets covered every surface: the desk, the dresser, the vanity, the nightstand. Not a single inch of counter space was left untouched.

"Oh. My. God," Lily breathed, spinning around in a full circle like she was trying to take it all in at once.

Turning to the coffee table, I noticed a gift bag with a blue bow at the top. A note was attached to it.

"Open it! Open it!" Lily and Nora chanted together, both of them jumping up and down like children on Christmas Day.

My Dearest Georgia,

I hope this helps focus you on the race this weekend. I don't know what will be in this article, but I do know that it doesn't matter. Your determination and passion have always been your greatest assets, and I have no doubt they will carry you to a second-place finish this weekend. ;-)

P.S. Please wear the items in the gold tissue paper on Sunday to celebrate my race win. Under your racing suit is preferable.

Your Luca

"Why am I going to cry? That is so sweet!" Lily wailed.

My hand trembled with uncertainty as I untied the satin ribbon and reached into the bag, pulling out a small jewelry box. Inside, a glimmer of silver caught my eye, and I carefully lifted out a charm bracelet featuring three charms: a lioness, a Formula 1 car with a blue diamond, and a crown with three spires on top. No one said a word as we all stared in awe at the beautiful piece of jewelry.

"Oh my god, he's *definitely* in love with you!" Lily gasped.

"Lily!" I scolded, putting the bracelet back into the box. "That is not true."

Nora leaned forward, peering into the box as I set it down carefully on the table. "I sort of have to agree with Lil on this one, Georgie. You don't make a personalized charm bracelet for someone you *aren't* in love with."

Heat rose in my cheeks. I crossed my arms, trying to deflect the growing knot in my throat. "If Luca was so in love with me, why has he barely spoken to me since Mallorca? He just likes to give extravagant gifts. I'm sure it's just for promotion. Like this." I reached up instinctively, touching the dainty lightning bolt charm that still hung around my neck. "Luca gave me this lightning bolt necklace back in Italy."

"So, what you're saying is, he's been in love with you for a while," Lily chuckled.

"For fuck's sake, he's not in love with me."

Desperate for a distraction, I dumped the gold tissue-paper-wrapped gift out of the bag. Mindlessly, I tore the paper open, revealing a purple lingerie set. My cheeks burned with embarrassment. Nora just shook her head in amusement, still sporting a huge smile.

What was Luca playing at?

"I suppose this is the moment I should remind you that you need to wear your fireproof underwear on Sunday," Nora snickered.

"So, let me get this straight." Lily held up the lingerie like a piece of evidence in court. "Luca buys you jewelry and lingerie, takes you on a sexy yacht vacation *and* you're having sex. How is this not *actually* dating?"

"Because dating requires feelings," I grumbled.

"Well, then I guess it's a good thing that he's *in love* with you!"

"Don't you two have somewhere to be?" I was practically shoving them toward the door when the front entrance to the suite opened with a soft click.

Luca and Edward strolled in, mid-laugh. Luca looked freshly showered and relaxed, wearing a crisp white shirt with his signature chain peeking out beneath the collar. The two of them didn't notice us at first, chatting away about a cross-promotional photo shoot they had just done, which, by the look on Edward's face, had gone very well.

The second Luca looked up and spotted the contents of the room—flowers, gift wrap, the open jewelry box—his entire body stilled. His smile faltered, slipping away like a wave retreating from shore. For a second, confusion clouded his expression, followed by realization.

And then nothing. A wall. His trademark grin vanished, replaced by a flat, unreadable frown.

Never thought I would miss that Cheshire cat grin.

"Luca… umm, hi," I half-whispered as he stared at me. Silence settled over the room, thick and awkward.

Edward pointed toward the gifts on the table. "Ooo, what's this?"

"It's nothing," Luca cut in. "Just some promotional stuff I got Georgia a few weeks ago."

I flashed Lily an "*I told you so*" look, before dumping the items back into the basket. Even though I was right, it didn't stop my heart from cracking, and I tried to blink away the tears that were forming. Edward shot Luca a frustrated glance, which Luca pointedly ignored. I stuttered out a thank you, and Luca just curtly nodded as he walked over to his room, throwing his bag onto his bed.

"I've got a few things to do, but I'll meet you all at the dinner tonight," Luca announced. Not waiting for an answer, Luca slammed his door closed.

-

At first, I thought it strange that Edward was organizing this dinner for Henri, Lily, Luca, and me, but after reading Luca's press release, I knew why. As soon as his contract with Rennen was announced, my phone blew up with messages. Lily had sent no fewer than five texts filled with question marks and exclamation points, while Henri wanted to know how long I'd known. I didn't respond to either of them. I figured they could ask Luca themselves at dinner.

It wasn't like I had the answers anyway.

As promised, Luca met the four of us at the restaurant, which fortunately wasn't too mobbed with tourists. I'd secretly hoped that I'd have a moment in the hotel room to ask him about his move to Rennen, but every time I went to knock on the door, I chickened out. After his coldness earlier today, space felt safer than rejection.

"Hey! Look what the cat dragged in!" Edward called out to Luca. Taking a seat at the table, Luca thanked Edward for the glass of wine before quickly ordering with the waiter.

"Sorry I'm late. Had to finish a call," Luca apologized.

Lily leaned in. "So, Luca, I see you signed with Rennen. Why such a big change?"

"It just felt right, I guess," he said with a shrug, swirling his wine. "It'll be nice to get a fresh start."

"Well, sounds like a good move then." I tried to give him a smile, soft and genuine. But Luca just gave a small nod, barely meeting my eyes, before taking a sip of wine. Seconds later, he excused himself to the bathroom, leaving a lingering silence behind him.

Leaning over, Edward grabbed my wrist, admiring the charm bracelet. "Wow, Luca did an amazing job with the design."

"I'm sure the Aphrodite Jewelry's sponsorship team gave him a few pointers."

Edward shot me a confused look.

Edward's voice dropped, serious now. "Luca did this by himself, Georgia."

"I mean, I'm sure he helped, but Aphrodite sponsors both of us—" I started before Edward cut me off.

"Georgia," he said sternly. "Luca designed these charms himself and ordered the bracelet without any knowledge from the sponsorship team. I saw the designs on his phone before summer break."

"Wh-why?" I whispered, my voice cracking like thin ice.

"That's for you to ask him."

"Well, maybe if he'd stop ignoring me, I would," I bit out.

Edward gave me a pitying look that made me want to sink under the table. "Look, Georgia, you and Luca will have to work this out between the two of you, but here's what I can say. Don't give up on him. Not yet. He might appear to have a laissez-faire attitude, but deep inside, he's just like you, trying to live up to all the pressure that's been mounting on him. I'm not sure what happened between you two in Mallorca, but give him a chance to explain when he's ready."

Before I could respond, Luca returned, sliding silently into his seat. I tried to catch his eye with a small wave, but he didn't look up. His focus went straight to his plate, his fork moving mechanically as he picked at his food, eating in silence for the rest of the meal like he wasn't even in the room with us.

By the time we made it back to the hotel, the sun had long since dipped below the Austrian skyline. Outside the front doors, a crowd of fans buzzed with excitement, their eyes scanning every car that pulled up. We were used to this by now. Fans always found the hotel, no matter how quiet the team tried to be.

Guess it's their lucky night, I thought grimly, tightening my jacket.

I pushed into the hotel lobby, taking a few selfies while I attempted to maintain the happiest face I could muster. A deep, unsettling voice called out to me.

"Feeling guilty yet for taking a spot from a driver who *deserves* to be here? How's it feel to be a diversity hire?" My body stiffened at the taut, and I quickly scanned the crowd for the source. Lily and Henri spun around, scanning the faces, but Luca beat them to it.

"Come over here and say that to her face!" he demanded.

The crowd's murmuring quickly turned into a tense silence as Luca locked eyes with the offending fan. With a single hand gesture, he summoned the man to step forward. The sound of phones clicking pulled me out of my haze. No doubt this would be all over social media tomorrow.

Luca's eyes burned as he pointed directly at the man. "Come on. Let's hear it again." The guy stood still, stunned. His mouth opened but no words came out. Luca looked like a man hell-bent on destruction, ready to burn anything in his path. The man was deathly still, his eyes wide and mouth hanging open. After a few moments of silence, I finally found my voice.

Thrown insults had never rattled me, but something about Luca dragging me in front of this man, refusing to let me hide from it—*refusing to let me shoulder it alone*—it sparked something in me. My spine straightened.

"Cat got your tongue?" I taunted.

The man sneered. "I said what I said. Why would they lie?"

"Because cash is king, darling," I said coolly, "and these journalists know they can con idiots like you into buying their lying *trash*."

The man finally backed away, his shoulders slumped and his lips moving in silent frustration as he disappeared into the bustling crowd. Shaking my head in amazement, I glanced around at all of the cameras filming me, and I couldn't help but smile.

As the hotel staff began clearing the lobby, I turned to Luca, my adrenaline still thrumming. Without thinking, I grabbed his hand, pulling him closer to the elevator and away from prying eyes.

"Th-thank you," I whispered.

He looked at me, then cupped my chin, tilting my face toward his. "You shouldn't ever back down from a fight, Georgia," he said finally. "And I know that sort of goes against everything I've been teaching all season. Hell, even the purpose of *this*." He motioned vaguely between us. The fake relationship. "But I don't know if backing down is the right thing anymore. Not after that article. You should fight back. You should be *loud*. You're stronger than all of them, and you should face your critics like the champion that you are. You're incredibly special. And unique. And strong. You shouldn't back down from the press, because they're wrong about you." His voice faded, and he looked away from me. "Just like I was."

I didn't know what to say, so I just stood there, dumbfounded. Luca rubbed his face, threading his hand through his thick waves.

"In the press conferences this weekend, just be *yourself* this time."

My chest ached with all the words I wanted to say. All the questions I still had. But before I could respond, Lily's voice called out behind me and I turned.

"Are you ready to go upstairs, Georgia? We have an early start tomorrow."

I put my hand up, asking her for a minute, but when I turned back to Luca he was already making his way over to Edward. As the elevator doors closed behind us, I watched him return to Edward's side, a nightcap waiting for them at the bar.

His words ran deep in my chest.

Maybe Luca was right, I contemplated. *Maybe I had been approaching this all wrong.*

If watching Isabelle take on Giovanni today taught me one thing, it was that backing down was no longer an option.

Chapter Forty-Two

Georgia

I pulled into the track before dawn on Sunday morning, the sun only just beginning to bleed gold across the peaks. The air was crisp, almost too clean, like the universe was daring me to breathe deeply when all I wanted to do was scream. A few engineers milled around like ghosts, half-awake with coffees in hand, and the silence clung to everything like a film.

After a quick strategy meeting with Mel, I walked outside of the engineering office to see Nora and Isabelle waving at me ecstatically, both of them looking like they'd won the lottery.

"It's here! It's here!" Nora gushed, holding up her phone as she waved it around erratically. "The JOULE article is out, and it's amazing!"

Fuck. With everything else going on, I had completely forgotten about the article.

Nora hurried me into the conference room, with an insistent Lily trailing behind. Nora already had the article pulled up on her laptop, and she all but shoved me into a seat, gesturing for me to read the glowing paragraph she'd highlighted in bright yellow.

> It was not hard to see that Georgia was extremely nervous during the photo shoot, which I found to be

interesting considering the public life she leads. As I watched Georgia nervously navigate my questions, it allowed me to see how someone like Luca complements her. His infectious laugh and ability to turn anything into a joke truly is a wonderful complement to Georgia's quick wit and cheekiness. It's hard not to have a smile on when you're around Georgia and Luca. There was a genuine warmth and connection between them that shone through in every shared glance and inside joke, and as I continued to watch them together, I couldn't help but feel privileged to witness such an intimate moment unfold between them.

Lily pointed to one of the photographs. "You know, for a couple that's meant to be fake dating, you sure do look real."

I didn't answer. Couldn't.

The photo of the happy couple staring at me from the screen seemed to mock me as I contemplated how we were nothing like what was described in the article. It felt like staring into someone else's life. Someone who had it all figured out. Someone who wasn't standing in a white-knuckle tug-of-war between what she felt and what she feared. And my heart ached as a certain realization set in.

I wanted this article to be true.

As I had got to know a deeper side of Luca, I'd realized that there was so much more to him than I'd thought. Luca's cocky, devil-may-care attitude was just a mask, something worn to protect himself.

Like I was doing now.

"The fans have just been loving this article. I was on the phone earlier with a few of our sponsors, and they're interested in having you and Lily feature their products. Such great news!" Isabelle smiled.

Considering the mess of the *Daily Reporter* article, this felt like being thrown a life raft after going overboard. Nora was doing a little dance in the middle of the conference room, jiving to the invisible music in her head. I let out a small huff and a chuckle at her antics, glad she was pleased. My eyes met Nora and Isabelle's expectant gazes. I attempted to conceal my nervousness with a forced smile, but Isabelle only saw through it.

"Georgia, did you hear me? This is very good news." Isabelle's earnest voice pulled me out of my lull, but this time I couldn't feign a happy face. Couldn't stop the tears from falling down my face. Isabelle sat next to me, the four of us in complete silence, barring my sniffling.

"I'm fine," I said finally. Isabelle reached over and grabbed a tissue from the box on the coffee table, gently handing it to me.

"You're clearly not fine." Her voice was gentle and sincere, but I couldn't bring myself to meet her eyes.

"I just didn't expect it to affect me like this," I admitted, my voice shaking. "I thought I could handle the scrutiny, the fake relationship, but after reading this article, it just… Sorry, I don't know why this article got to me so much."

"Georgia, stop apologizing for things that are not your fault," Isabelle said firmly. "I didn't realize you felt this way. The whole point of this was to improve our publicity, but not at the expense of your mental health." She paused, taking in a deep, steady breath before calmly letting it out as she watched me sniffle away on my sofa. "I mean, with Luca joining Rennen, our agreement will end soon."

After a few more moments, Lily chuckled as a wide grin stretched across her face. "You know what, I call bullshit."

"Lilian—" Isabelle started, but to my surprise, Lily cut her off.

She straightened up, fixing me with a look so intense I half-expected her to leap across the table and shake the truth out of me. "You know what I think. I think you have real feelings for Luca," she accused, wagging her finger at me. "That's why the article affected you so much."

"Wha—have you not been listening to me?" My voice shot up half an octave, tight with frustration.

"This article shows how good things could be between you and Luca, how good things *are* with you, but you're scared Luca doesn't feel the same way. I think all that crap about you and Luca just '*having casual fun*' in Mallorca was exactly that: complete and utter crap." I furrowed my eyebrows as I downed the rest of my coffee, desperately looking for all the reasons that Lily was wrong.

But Lily was right, and I fucking knew it.

She stared at me intently, as if I were a ticking time bomb, questioning if she had pushed me too far. I squeezed my eyes shut, trying to compose myself despite the chaos inside my head.

"You do realize that it's okay to *want* this, Georgia. It's okay to *want* to be with Luca," Lily said finally.

My gaze was met with large, comforting smiles. If love and support could be summed up in one facial expression, it would be theirs.

"But what if Luca doesn't feel the same?"

"But what if he does?" she countered. "You won't know unless you tell him how you feel."

Isabelle leaned in, compassion in her eyes. "You know, Georgia, I never told you this, but I was glad the photo that started this fiasco was with Luca. If I'd gotten to pick, it still would have been with him. I knew he'd give you something *more*. Knew he'd challenge you. Luca wouldn't back down from a fight. Or your attitude. You would get as good as you gave with him. Luca reminds me of my first love. I hated that cocky Australian driver when we first met. He thought he was God's gift to aerodynamics, but as time went on, I saw a different side of him, and I fell in love… There's more to Luca than meets the eye, Georgia."

Her words settled in my chest.

Maybe I had let my fears speak louder than my feelings. Maybe, in all my effort to seem composed and untouchable, I'd forgotten that love was messy, and wild, and brave.

I'd wanted Luca to chase me. To prove Henri wrong. But how could I expect him to fight for something I'd never actually said I wanted?

I had let my silence do the talking, and all it had ever said was: you're not enough.

I'd never made Luca feel anything but unworthy of my love, and I had to fix that.

"Nora, can you do me a favor?" I finally asked. "There's something I need you to grab."

Chapter Forty-Three

Luca

Qualifying had been a disaster. My lap times were sluggish, my focus nonexistent. My mind was elsewhere. When Edward knocked on my driver's room door, I could have hugged him just for existing. His easy presence had become something I leaned on more than I cared to admit. He didn't push, didn't pry. Just sat with me in silence, the kind that only old friends know how to make comfortable.

I was grateful, because these past two weeks had been hell. I'd been stuck in my own head, replaying every moment of Mallorca on a loop. Georgia's laugh as she steered the jet ski, the way she looked wearing my jacket, the sound of her breathless giggles echoing off the shower tiles.

And then the sound of her voice saying it was *nothing more than fun*.

I'd stuck to my plan. Given her space. Given us space. No texts. No calls. Just long, sleepless nights and a phone screen I couldn't stop checking. I'd picked it up a dozen times to tell her about the Rennen contract, but every message I typed felt wrong. Empty. Worse than silence.

But now, with the deal signed and announced, all I felt was the echo of her absence. A hollow pit where her voice used to live. The space I'd given her had become a wall. And I was the one who had built it.

God, I missed her. Not the headlines. Not the hand-holding for the cameras. *Her.*

Now it felt too late to say what I should have said back in Mallorca. That I was falling for her.

With the *Daily Reporter* article, we couldn't end the PR relationship just yet, but I knew this announcement was essentially the start of the end. Valkyrie was on the cusp of signing a large deal with Maison de Klotho, and now I had my new contract. With the cheating rumors, Matteo and Nora were already discussing ways to make our relationship feel more casual and less public. We might have to say we were dating, but it wouldn't feel the same, and by the end of the year, rumors of our breakup would undoubtedly be circling the paddock.

"Delivery!" I looked up as Matteo dropped a box just inside my room. "Francesco said someone dropped this off. Tried to ask who from, but he just waved me off in a huff. He's not exactly thrilled with me right now." My manager shrugged.

An understatement. Francesco was relatively pissed that I'd signed a new contract without negotiating with Hermes.

"Thanks, Matteo. See you for the final briefing?" He nodded, closing the door behind him.

"Ooh, who's it from?" Edward snatched at the box, but I pushed him back, opening the present. A sharp breath caught in my throat, and my vision blurred as I reached in and pulled out a painting.

"Is that…" Edward's mouth gaped open.

I felt a tear prick the corner of my eye. "The picture of me and my dad at my first karting win."

A folded note slipped out and landed on the floor.

Dear Luca,

Wishing you all the best in your new journey with Rennen. I couldn't be prouder of what you've accomplished this season.

Your Georgia

Tears stung my eyes, and I tried to blink them back, but it was no use. "I fucked up, Edward." I said suddenly, voice cracking. "I slept with Georgia in Mallorca, and it was incredible. It felt like we'd finally made a connection. But that morning I overheard her telling Lily that we were nothing more than friends, that it was *meaningless*." The words tumbled out of my mouth.

"Is this why you've been icing her out?" Of course, he'd noticed.

"Instead of talking to her like an adult about it, I opted for the easy way out. To ignore the comment and my hurt feelings, because I felt embarrassed. And stupid." My throat burned. "Éliott told me that he knew about Georgia and I's missed date. No doubt he's been reminding her of that. Couple that with Henri telling me back in Monaco to keep things professional, I'm sure they both warned her to stay away from me, that I was only after her for sex or a quick fling, because that's the reputation I have. The reputation I *deserve*."

Edward shook his head slowly. "Luca, that's not true…"

"You know I asked her out years ago? And I didn't show. I was pissed that my dad offered to be her coach. I let that resentment eat at me for years." My voice dropped. "I proved to her back then that I couldn't be trusted. That I wasn't good enough for her."

"Oh, Luca, is that what you think?" He leaned forward, giving me a brotherly hug. "You *are* worthy of love. If Georgia can't see that because of your past actions, then it's your job to show her with your current ones." He paused, then added more gently, "Tell me this, Luca. Why did you tell Georgia that the bracelet was a promotional gift? I know you made it yourself. I saw it on your phone."

I twisted my hands, rubbing the sweat onto my pants. "I know I should have told her. I just… I want her to wear it because she thinks it's beautiful. Because she *wants* to wear it. She deserves to have something special, something that reminds her that she's a champion. That when it comes to proving her worth to the sponsors or the fans, she's more than enough. Because Georgia Dubois is worthy of so much greatness."

Edward nodded slowly, a thoughtful expression on his face. "Then, Luca, that's what you need to tell her. On the yacht, Georgia might have said that to Lily, but that's because she thought she was sleeping with noncommittal, scared-of-a-relationship Luca Rossi. Show Georgia that she's wrong. Show her that you can be the Luca that she knows you are. The one you've been over the last few months."

I huffed out a shaky laugh. "You're a good friend, you know that?"

Edward grinned. "The best. Now come on, let's get ready for the race."

He was right, as usual. If I wanted Georgia to see me differently, I had to *be* different. I had to show her with my actions, not just my words, that I cared for her. That I respected her. That maybe, just maybe, I could be worthy of her heart.

After this race I would stop hiding from my feelings, and once we were standing on the podium together, I'd tell her how I felt.

Chapter Forty-Four

Georgia

After dinner on Thursday, I'd maybe seen Luca two or three times. He'd spent practically every waking moment at the Hermes garage or with Rennen for photos. Based on the unwrinkled bedspread, he hadn't even slept in our hotel suite last night. After my chat with Isabelle this morning, I'd picked up my phone over a hundred times, each time typing out a text only to delete it.

This was a conversation I wanted to have in person, and I was going to have it today.

After the Grand Prix, I would lay it all out on the table and tell Luca how I felt. No more avoiding each other. Our relationship was real, the moments we spent together were real.

"Georgia, you ready to hop in? Race is about to start!" Mel called across the garage. I threw her a thumbs up before pulling my helmet over my head and adjusting the microphone.

As soon as I was given the go-ahead, I started the car and made my way around the circuit, doing my best to warm up my tires during the formation lap. When I reached the P1 position, I idled the car, staring up at the familiar five lights that hovered above me.

"Just another day at the office," Mel cackled into the radio.

"It's good to be back."

As soon as the five lights went black, I launched my car forward. The first corner came fast, and I was too eager, too tight. I hit the apex late, and in that razor-thin window of error, both Henri and Luca swept past me in perfect synchrony. A Hermes double strike. I was now sitting in P3, with the fourth-place car creeping up in my mirrors like a predator on the hunt.

"Fuck!"

"G, Hermes cars are pushing, very good pace." I didn't need Mel in my ear to tell me that. Luca was in front, and I knew his pace was just slightly quicker than mine.

My pulse was ticking in time with every gear shift, and I could see it happening. Luca was pulling away. Just a tenth. Maybe two. But it was enough to get away from me.

I was about to push, to recalibrate my brake balance and go for it, but then the smell hit me.

Burning.

My eyes darted to the dashboard, searching for any warning lights or indicators, but everything looked normal. My heart began to race as I scanned the road ahead, trying to pinpoint the source of the smell.

"Mel, something is burning."

"Keep driving, it's not you." But I heard it, that tiny shift in her voice. The slight lift at the end. Like she was trying too hard to sound calm.

And then I looked to my side. Suddenly, my eyes were drawn to a terrifying sight. Luca's car was off the track and in the gravel, leaving behind a trail of dust and debris. Smoke—thick, oily, furious—began billowing from the rear of the chassis. The kind of smoke that stuck to your skin. The kind that signaled fire before your brain caught up. In my rearview mirrors, I could see the flames growing larger and more menacing as the car continued downhill.

My whole body went cold. "Mel, it's Luca!"

This can't be happening.

"Stay calm and keep driving. Yellow flag." Mel's tone was unnervingly calm.

"I'm going back." Panic crept in. Images of Luca's car on fire ran through my brain.

"Georgia, *do not* under any circumstances go to that car. The marshals don't need to put out two fires." My head knew that Mel was right, but my heart couldn't bear to listen.

"I'm not going to leave the man I love in a car that's fucking burning!" I screamed back into the mic.

There was a pause. A silence heavy enough to drown in.

"Is he out?" I couldn't stop myself from asking, from desperately hoping. Tears streamed down my face, and I was glad to be wearing a helmet so no one could see my despair.

Another beat of silence.

"Not yet."

I clenched the steering wheel so hard my hands felt numb. "I should have gotten out and helped. What if I lose him?" I choked out another sob. "What if I don't get to tell him how much I love him? I have to tell him, Mel. I have to."

The words just kept pouring out of me, spilling into the microphone. Not a bone in my body cared that the entire world had just heard me confess my love for Luca. I didn't care about the press, sponsors, or even what the FIA would think. All I wanted was to see Luca again. Cared only that he knew how much I loved him and his ridiculously adorable Cheshire cat grin.

"Georgia, this is Isabelle. He knows that you love him. He *knows*." Isabelle's voice was the definition of confidence.

Mel popped back on. "Red flag. Time to come in."

The moment I pulled into the pit lane, I ignored everyone. I refused to climb out of the car, even as engineers hovered nearby. I stayed strapped in, frozen, staring at the massive garage screens like they were life support monitors.

I just needed one image. One sign.

But the feed dragged on. Camera angles changing. Marshals still gathered. No sign of him.

Why was this taking so long? I closed my eyes. Tried to force in air through clenched teeth. In, out. Count to three. Again. But the panic was winning.

The sound of cheering cracked through the air. The camera was zoomed in on Luca.

He had gotten out.

The roar of applause rolled through the paddock like a wave as Luca was helped toward the ambulance.

"Luca is out, G," Mel whispered into my earpiece. "He's safe."

But the relief didn't come like a flood. It came like a quiet ache. The kind that lingered in the space left behind after a bomb has gone off.

Averting my gaze from the giant screens that now replayed Luca getting out of the car, I tried to shake off the horror from the last few minutes. The horror would likely stay with me for months, a constant reminder of how dangerous racing could be.

I sat in the pit lane, still strapped in, eyes forward, waiting. The announcement came a few minutes later: standing restart. I'd be in second, thanks to Luca's DNF.

I was so lost in my thoughts, lost in my breathing exercises, that I almost missed the radio turn on. An unfamiliar—*and yet familiar*—voice came onto the radio.

"You didn't have to set my car on fire to get second, *amore*. I'm sure you would have passed me anyway." His voice was gravelly, amused. Tired. I let out a strangled laugh, choking on it as fresh tears filled my eyes.

Luca had stolen Mel's headset.

"Fuck off!" I cackled into my radio, grinning from the flood of emotion.

"Oh, and Georgia," he said, voice soft. "I love you, too."

Finally, after all this time, we'd both had the courage to say it.

Suddenly everything around me felt a little more bearable. The race, the impending Maison de Klotho sponsorship. None of it felt quite as scary.

The sound of metal on metal echoed in the background, along with Mel's distant voice yelling at Luca to stay away from the Valkyrie pit wall.

"Sorry, intruders in our camp," Mel chuckled into the feed. "Alright, G. Race will begin soon with a standing start. You sure you're ready?"

"Let's do this." With each exhale, my heart rate started to return to normal. My knuckles finally unclenched, shoulders dropping.

It was as if new life had been breathed into me.

And after a successful restart, I was back into second place.

Chapter Forty-Five

Luca

"Have you seen my son?"

I perked my head up, recognizing my dad's commanding tone.

Fuck, he's going to be furious with me. With that sort of damage to the car, it would be unlikely I could race next week.

"Luca? Luca are you in here?" my father called out.

"I'm over here!" Looking up, I saw my father's panicked face. The moment we made eye contact, I could see him visibly relax. He took a moment to catch his breath.

"Oh, thank God you're okay." He let out a heavy sigh of relief. "Your mother has been frantically calling me. They wouldn't let me over to you. Fuck, I'm going to have words with Francesco next week. They need to up their quality controls."

"I know, I'm sorry. The car is going to be out of commission for a while," I whispered.

"The car? Luca, *fuck the car*, you could have been *killed* out there." My father's grip on me tightened, his voice filled with a mix of concern and anger. "None of this is your fault, son. Racing is dangerous, and accidents happen. What matters most is that you're safe." I leaned into his embrace, feeling the weight of his words.

"I know but the car might not be drivable next week." I shrugged. "It'll put me even further back in the standings."

"Then you'll get them the week after, Luca. What matters is that you're okay."

Who was this imposter standing in front of me? Where was the fire-and-brimstone racer who used to scold me for tenth-place finishes in karting? Who once made me run simulator laps until my knuckles blistered because I missed a braking point?

"I don't know, Dad, it's so many points to make up." My throat tightened as the words spilled out, bitter and hot. "I've let the team down. I've let you down…" A lump formed in my throat as tears welled up in my eyes. I hated disappointing my father. I'd done it so much this season, and with the Rennen contract, I knew he was furious with me.

He pulled back, just far enough to meet my eyes "Let me down? Is that what you think, Luca? No, son. I've let you down," my father admitted. "Instead of listening to you, trying to understand what you were going through, I doubled down on your racing because it's what my father did to me, and I'm sorry. Seeing you out there in that burning car… I'm not going to lie, if you told me today you wanted to quit, I'd be okay with it. I hated knowing that you were in that car because I forced you to be in it."

I looked away, down at the bandage on my forearm. The ache in my shoulder. The burn of soot still lingering in my nostrils. Had my father forced me?

Silence stretched between us.

I thought back to all of the amazing memories I'd had as a child, the races won, the trophies sitting on the desks at home, the fun photos adorning the walls of my apartment.

The painting Georgia had given me.

"When I was a kid, I wanted nothing more than to be like you, to race fast cars and be on the tallest podium step, but over the last few years, it's been hard to remember that dream. And then when I heard you offer to coach Georgia several years ago… the dream started to feel like a lie."

"Oh, Luca, I wish you'd told me about that. I only offered to coach Georgia because I wanted to give you an opportunity to have a new coach, get some fresh perspective. But when she turned me down, and you reaffirmed you wanted me as a coach, I figured I was wrong to offer it to her and let it go."

"Well, if I'm learning anything this week," I sighed, "it's that confronting your problems head on? Definitely the better option."

He pulled me into a tight hug. "Luca, I'm so proud of you. Your mother is proud of you. The more I think about it, I think it's good you're going to Rennen, getting a fresh start at a team where you can make your own legacy."

I nodded, throat too tight to answer. For the first time in years, it felt like I wasn't trying to earn my father's love. I just had it. Unconditionally.

"Now, what do you say we head to the Hermes garage and watch your girlfriend kick your teammate's ass?"

A slow grin curled on my lips. "Sounds like a plan."

As soon as I was given the all-clear, my father escorted me back to the garage so we could finish watching the race. Together. Just how we used to watch races when I was a kid.

It was lap sixty, and Georgia was finally able to take P1 from her brother, only for him to take it back from her moments later. Both of their tires were old, so it was down to driver skill to determine which Dubois would take home the victory.

The crowd was electric. Each time the two of them switched places, a new wave of screams tore through the grandstands. They hit the final straight side by side.

As Georgia and Henri reached the checkered flag side by side, I saw the officials hovering around their monitors, reviewing the footage of the race. For the first time this season, the finish had to be reviewed. My father and I held our breath, waiting for the final verdict.

Finally, they called it.

Georgia had won the race.

She parked in the winner's spot, launching herself out of her car. Henri was already there, pulling her into a hug.

Then, Henri looked toward me.. His eyes found mine across the crowd, and something passed between us. A moment. An understanding. He gestured toward me, subtle but unmistakable.

He was sending her to me.

Georgia's eyes searched the crowd, landing on me like I was the only person there. Her expression melted, relief, joy, disbelief, and then she ran. I barely had time to brace before she launched herself into my arms, knocking the breath out of me in the best way possible.

"Don't ever scare me like that again!" her voice muffled against my shoulder.

"I don't know, it did get you to confess your love for me, *amore*." She swatted the top of my head.

"Just shut up and kiss me."

She didn't have to ask me twice. My hands locked behind her back as I spun us around in a scorching kiss, laughter and cheers echoing from the team behind us. When I finally set her down, our foreheads remained pressed together, the world blurry around her eyes.

"What can I say? My heart burns for you so much my car caught fire." Georgia stiffened, shaking her head in disapproval. "Alright," I laughed. "Too soon." I gave her one last squeeze. From somewhere behind us, Nora was yelling for Georgia. "Go get that trophy, *amore*. Tonight, we'll celebrate properly."

Georgia reluctantly let go of my hand, shooting me a mischievous grin before disappearing into the crowd.

After years of pining. Years of being an idiot, of hating myself for the self-loathing.

No more. Georgia was *mine*.

Edward clapped his hand on my back. "Looks like you're gonna have to get yourself a Valkyrie polo."

"No need. I already have one. Bought it the day she signed."

Chapter Forty-Six

Georgia

After the podium celebration, Henri motioned for me to follow him. "So, you *love* Luca, huh?" He grinned.

"What if I did?" I asked cautiously.

"Then I would be happy for you, Peaches. Very happy." Henri laughed at my surprise. "He's good for you. And he seems to love you, very much. Which is good, considering after that JOULE article and your little outburst professing your love to the entire world on live television, it's going to be pretty hard for anyone to argue otherwise. Bet the *Daily Reporter* journalists are ready to crawl into a hole right about now."

At least that was one good thing to come out of today.

"Now, come on. Let's get this press conference over with, I'm dying for a beer."

We walked shoulder to shoulder toward the media center. Part of me suspected this was going to be brutal. Besides the early Thursday morning press conference prior to the article's release, I had managed to mostly avoid the media on Friday and Saturday.

But no more. As the race winner, I had to face them now. This was their last chance to get questions answered in a public setting. And yet, as I sat there with another Formula 1 race win under my belt, I didn't feel the same nerves that usually overcame me at media events. Sweat didn't drip down my hands as normal, and the trembling of my fingers was replaced with steady confidence.

The moment the Q&A was opened up to the floor, countless hands went flying into the air. Marcus from *Sports Broadcasting* stood up.

"Georgia, congrats on a great race. There's a rumor you were brought into the FIA offices earlier this week. Anything to report on that?"

So much for that meeting being confidential.

"Marcus, I think you know I can't comment on private FIA meetings," I replied, keeping my face even.

"Really? Well, reports say that the FIA is investigating you for cheating in Monza." I gave him an incredulous look. It was easy to expect this from the tabloids, but not from *Sports Broadcasting*, a company that had become the crown of British sports reporting.

A smile tugged at the corner of my lips. "If you have reports, then sounds like you don't need my input."

"So, are you denying it?"

These journalists really were like vultures, eager to tear into any shred of vulnerability they could find. I'd spent the season calling it the Lion's Den, but as I sat here now, I realized they weren't lions. They were vultures who fed off of the scraps from the racers—*from me.*

"I'm denying that it's any of your business." Nora was now waving at me in the background, motioning for me to quit the conversation, but I ignored her wild gesturing.

No more of this. Luca was right, it was time to face my fears, to do something different.

"In fact, I'm denying the whole *fucking* thing. If you all think you know me so well, well enough to write articles before even speaking to me, then why do you bother asking me these questions?"

Marcus may have been slightly discouraged by my question, but his next statement showed that he wasn't deterred nearly enough. "I'm asking because a serious allegation has been brought against you, and you have yet to say anything about it. Instead, all you've done is gallivant on a yacht and attend fancy dinners."

"That's enough!" a voice yelled beside me. Edward, who'd come in P3, was now standing, microphone in hand. "Press conferences are for us *drivers* to answer questions for the fans. You know, the people we race for."

"Don't you think the fans want to know if Georgia actually deserves to be in Formula 1?" Marcus fired back.

"Not as much as the fans might want to know why *Sports Broadcasting* hired such a lunatic to do their press interviews," I retorted. A ripple of stunned laughter went through the room. A petty thing to say—*and frankly, not the best quip*—but his unamused face told me my point had been made.

A murmur rippled through the press room, and for the first time, I noticed some nodding heads among the journalists.

"So, let me get this straight, you've been accused of cheating, and your response is to giggle about it?"

Unbelievable.

Henri bristled beside me, but I held out a hand, stopping him. This was my battle to fight. I'd spent the last several races hiding behind my friends and family, letting my anxiety get the best of me, but as I stared down at the broadcaster, I realized how little I cared in that moment. How little I cared about the press's comments, jabs, and insults.

"No, Marcus, my response is to laugh at *you*. All of *you*. You call yourselves journalists, but you don't have a shred of journalistic integrity. Let me ask you this: did you question why the *Daily Reporter* article didn't have a single bad thing to say about Luca?"

Silence. Not a shuffle, not a tap of a laptop key.

"Of course not, and I'll tell you why. Because you all know that attacking Luca, the son of a world-famous F1 champion, won't sell papers. No one would believe you. But attacking the woman you've berated all season? Well, that's fair game, isn't it?"

As I held their gazes, it seemed ridiculous that I had ever been afraid of them. They seemed so small and insignificant staring back at me.

"But—" Marcus went to interject.

"I'm not finished," I bit out. "You all have tried to bury me since Bahrain. You call it reporting. I call it misogyny." I scanned the room. "You want a statement? Fine. Here's one: I'm not leaving. I'm not backing down. I am going to win this championship, and then I'll win the next one. And the next one. And you can write that in your fucking papers. I don't care if you don't like me. I'm not here to be liked. I'm here to win. I'm not leaving Formula 1. *Valkyrie* isn't leaving Formula 1, so I suggest you all get used to it."

I could see some heads nodding. Some faces falling, and I took another deep breath, before standing up and stepping off the small stage.

"You've all held too much power over me since I started this season, but no more. From now on, in press conferences, I'll only be answering questions about my driving. You want to know what I do in my personal time? Tough. It's none of your business."

I turned to Michael Clifton, and I almost gave him an apologetic smile before stopping myself. He didn't deserve an apology from me. None of them did.

I set the microphone down in front of him.

"Georgia," Michael whispered, "you'll get fined if you leave now."

I half-smiled. "Then expect a check in the mail, Michael. Maybe use the money to get us some better journalists."

Nora was chasing after me as I walked out of the press conference. When I got to the garage, I marched straight into the team principal's office and took a seat in front of Isabelle, who just narrowed her eyes at me while motioning for Nora to shut the door. The office vibe felt like a showdown from one of those old western movies, the sheriff vs the villain, except I was no longer going to be the villain in my story.

"Damn it, Georgia. *Why?*" Isabelle finally lamented.

"Why?" I scoffed sarcastically. "Why do they get to treat me like garbage?" I demanded back. "Why can't I defend myself?"

"Because we're supposed to be burying this story, not giving them *more* reasons to bring it up!"

Isabelle was angry, that much was clear. She leaned back into her chair, resting her head in her hands and rubbing her eyes with frustration. It was rare to see Isabelle so defeated, and it felt like a kick to the stomach, but I wasn't going to apologize. Not this time.

"I just want this to go away for you, Georgia. I get it. You're young and ambitious, and yes, it's unfair that they treat you this way, but we need to learn to control the narrative, not feed into it," Isabelle begged.

I had spent the entire season backing down, letting journalists get away with their misogyny. Had spent these last few months hiding in the shadows so we could get sponsors, but the more I thought about it, the more it became clear that sponsors wanted someone *loved* by fans.

"To hell with the press. I don't care if this story drags on for ten years, Isabelle. I'm not going to sit back and let them treat me this way. I won't teach little girls that it's okay for male journalists to tear down female athletes. You hired me to win, to fight. So that's what I'm doing. And if I lose my racing seat, then so be it, because I'll lose it staying true to who I am."

I pushed back my chair and strode toward the office door. My hand closed around the knob—

Laughter.

A loud, unapologetic, delighted laugh.

I turned around in surprise. And there she was, my team principal, sitting behind her desk with her arms folded and a proud, almost defiant smile on her face. Not a hint of scolding. Not a flicker of doubt.

Only pride.

"Well, then, Georgie, sounds like we have some work to do."

Chapter Thirty-Seven

Georgia

Walking out of the Valkyrie garage, I felt an arm drape itself over my shoulders, drawing me in for a hug. I gazed up at Luca, who was sporting a cheesy grin on his face. He looked like he had just hit the jackpot, and in a way he had.

"Well, well, well, looks like I won my little bet," I heard Edward announce behind us.

"Who did you bet anyway?" I knew about Edward's annoying gamble, but I realized I didn't actually know who had bet for or against us.

"Georgia, I am *soooo* glad you asked." Edward held out his hand to Luca, who immediately went into his back pocket and took out his wallet, handing Edward €100 as he shook his head.

"I'll get the rest to you next week," Luca grumbled.

Edward smirked with satisfaction. "You see, Georgie, I bet Luca that you two would fall in love by the end of the season. Luca was so insistent that you'd never look at him again after he *rudely* ditched you all those years ago, but I knew better. I know a jealous woman when I see one." He threw me a wink, and I scoffed in response.

"I wasn't jealous!" The protest was weak—and untrue.

"Oh, please, the way you babbled on about Luca and who he was supposedly *dating* or what he was *doing* and 'how *annoying*' he was. You were *jealous*. Figured as soon as you got to know the sweet, soft Luca that I knew, you'd fall madly in love with him. Well, after he got his act together, of course. Which I figured you'd help him do."

Edward looked incredibly impressed with himself as he finished, literally patting himself on the back after putting away his prize money.

"And so, now I am a thousand euros richer, and you two will have lifelong happiness. A win-win for everyone." Without another word, Edward took off for the Wilmington garage, a smug smile still gracing his lips.

We had barely taken a step when a familiar sneer cut through the air.

"Well, look at that," Anthony snickered. "Still clinging to this little PR stunt, even after the article."

"That's a weird way to say congratulations to the race winner," I replied coolly, trying to step around him.

"You think you're so special, don't you?" Anthony sidestepped me, blocking my path. "Guess it's good you gave up at Hermes, Luca. With your abysmal driving today, I would have taken your seat anyway, but now I get to crucify you both on the track next year since the press isn't doing a good enough job of it."

I perked up, glaring at Anthony. *What did he just say?*

Then it hit me.

"You were the *Daily Reporter*'s source, weren't you?" Of course, that apology back in Monaco wasn't real. Anthony didn't have a genuine bone in his body.

Anthony's smirk was all the confirmation I needed.

"Why?"

He chuckled darkly, but before he could answer, I cut him off.

"You know what, Anthony? I don't care why you did it. It doesn't matter, because none of it's true. I'm done letting assholes like you think they have power over me. No more." I tried to push past Anthony, but he lunged forward, gripping my arm tightly.

"I guess batting your eyelashes as a pretty racer really does have its perks," he said coldly. "Hard to compete with someone who can sleep her way out of anything." My body tensed, but Luca stepped forward and stood directly in front of me, their faces only inches apart as he grabbed Anthony's arm, forcibly removing it from mine.

"Funny. From what I heard, you're the only person trying to sleep their way into F1, but you were so lousy, Daddy had to *buy* your seat." Luca's voice was just loud enough for the three of us to hear. "If you think for one moment that Hermes is going to give you my old seat, you're out of your mind. Can't imagine they're into racers willing to sell stories to tabloids."

Anthony's face twisted in anger, his fists clenching. With his other arm, he grabbed me again, trying to pull me close.

Luca was on him in a heartbeat. His hand locked onto Anthony's wrist, yanking it from me with enough force to send a message. "Touch her again, and I'll make sure no one recognizes that ugly face of yours."

Anthony staggered back, stunned.

"You know what, Anthony, I almost hope you do get Luca's seat next year. It'd be nice to beat you all over again, just like I did in IndyCar." With a smug grin, I turned on my heel, leaving Anthony behind us.

The walk back to Luca's driver's room was enveloped in comforting silence, hand in hand. And this time, it felt genuine. The gentle pressure of his fingers in mine was soothing. Luca opened the door to his driver's room. Not wasting any time, Luca pressed his lips to mine in a possessive kiss that made my entire body light up in flames. I tangled my fingers in his thick hair, releasing a contented sigh as our lips met for another kiss. He scooped me into his arms and carried us over to the couch where I straddled his lap, eagerly leaning in for another kiss, but Luca stopped me.

"I'm so sorry, *amore*." His forehead rested on mine.

"Luca—"

"No, let me finish. Please. I need to explain the last two weeks." His voice was low, rough, and earnest. "In Mallorca, I overheard that comment to Lily about us not meaning anything. Between that and stupidly letting Anthony fuel my jealousy of Éliott, I convinced myself that you maybe didn't want me. Or at least, that I wasn't good enough for you. So, I decided to give us some space, because I thought it would be best for both of us."

His voice cracked as I ran a hand through his tousled hair.

I cupped his chin softly, forcing him to look at me. "First of all, Éliott and I went on a single, awkward date when we were eighteen. We had such little chemistry, by the end of the date, I'd already set him up with another friend of mine. A detail I'm sure Anthony conveniently left out." I kissed the tip of his nose, watching relief flood onto his face. "Secondly, it's me who should be apologizing. I should never had said that, Luca, because it wasn't true. I'm sorry for making you feel not worthy enough. Henri approached me that morning, and instead of going to you, I took the easy way out and let my fear speak for me." I swallowed, my thumb brushing across his jaw. "Then the Rennen announcement came out, and I panicked. I didn't know where we stood, and instead of asking, I pulled away."

"No more doubting, *amore*." His lips brushed against mine, and my heart leapt at the certainty in his voice. "This is real."

"I know," I breathed, kissing him again, slower this time, letting it say what words hadn't.

"In fact," he murmured, "I have something to talk to you about."

"Mhmm," I replied, clearly not listening. My hands were already wandering, tracing the waistband of his jeans as I leaned in for another kiss, eager to taste every inch of him before our night got interrupted again. Luca grinned against my mouth, tugging me closer.

"You," he said between kisses, "are going to be the death of me."

I began working on his belt buckle with deliberate slowness, drawing a low groan from his chest.

But before I could make good on my distraction, there was a sharp, insistent knock on the door.

"Lovebirds, we have to go! You can have sex back at the hotel!"

"Ew, gross, no!" I heard Henri yell behind the door in disgust. I'd forgotten that Lily and I had driven together this morning.

I groaned dramatically and flopped back onto the couch, laughing as Luca scrambled to fix his belt, his face flushed and his shirt crooked. He looked adorably unprepared. When I opened the door, Henri and Lily were standing there like two drunk gremlins with bottles of champagne, both grinning like fools. It was clear from the looks on their faces that they had *definitely* had too much already.

"Come along, children," I said, grabbing my bag. "Back to the hotel before we get shit-faced tonight!"

The four of us crawled into my car, which was much too small for four people.

"So… Lucaaaa," Henri slurred, reaching over to the front seat. "Now that you're in love with my sister, we have some rules to discuss."

"Oh, shut up, Henri," Lily protested, pulling him back into his seat. "Leave the happy couple alone!"

"*Non!*" Henri's accent always came out thick whenever he was drunk. "I will set some ground rules!"

"I can only imagine what these will be." I grinned.

Henri had pulled out his phone, and my heart warmed at the fact that my brother had made an actual list. I wanted to protest, tell Henri to fuck off and put his phone away, but I felt touched that my brother had thought about this relationship. His protectiveness was shining through, and this time, it was endearing.

"Shhhh…" Henri shushed me, and I knew he was intent on continuing this list of demands. "No making out with my sister in front of me. For the rest of this season, no sex on the Hermes plane. That's a sacred place. Oh, and no sex when our hotel rooms are next to each other."

"Too late on that last one," I interjected, earning me a glare from Henri and a cheer from Lily.

"You break her heart, and I will make sure next race you burn with your car. Understood, Luca?" Luca huffed and turned around, only to see a very determined Henri with a frown on his face.

"Don't worry, mate. Your sister's heart is safe with me."

Once we arrived at the hotel, Luca and I didn't even pretend to play it cool. We made a beeline for our suite, abandoning Henri and Lily in the lobby with barely a wave goodbye.

The second the door clicked shut, Luca had me pressed against it, his hands gripping my waist like he never wanted to let go. His mouth found mine in a kiss so full of relief and hunger, it stole the air from my lungs. I felt like a drowning woman, and Luca was my life raft.

"Guess we won't be needing separate bedrooms anymore," I giggled into the kiss, letting Luca drag me to his bedroom in our shared suite. Luca threw me down onto his bed. He pulled his shirt over his head, and I took my time to admire his body.

"Are you going to be a good girl for me and finish what you started back at the paddock?" he asked with a cocky grin.

With eager anticipation, I nodded, instinctively licking my lips as I scooted to the edge of the bed. My fingers expertly worked their way toward his belt, slowly unbuckling it before gliding over the top of his boxers.

As I hooked my fingers around the elastic band, I effortlessly slid both his pants and boxers down his legs. Taking hold of him, I began to stroke with a slow and steady rhythm, causing Luca to gasp and place his hand on my shoulder for support. The way he responded to me, his body arching, the way he hissed my name, made heat pool low in my stomach. I loved the way I could make him putty in my hands with my touch. Loved the way he melted every time I sunk my mouth onto him.

I loved him.

Luca tapped my lips with his thumb, motioning for me to open, which I obliged.

"Fuck, *amore*, I'll never get used to how good you feel," Luca hissed.

I let him slide out of my mouth, running my tongue from the base of his cock to the tip, which earned me another raspy groan.

"Don't be a tease," he demanded, although his voice came out breathy and I smirked up at him as I repeated my teasing. His tip was leaking pre-cum, clearly aching to be touched. I let my lips wrap around him, increasing my pace as his hips started to buck. He slid in and out of me, and I could tell from his thrusts and heavy breathing that he was getting closer, and I grasped his balls with my free hand, gently massaging them.

Luca pulled out, grabbing my head back. "As much as I want to finish in your mouth, *amore*, I want to finish inside of you more."

Without hesitation, he jumped onto the bed and climbed on top of me. He wasted no time in removing my shirt, pulling it over my head to expose the purple lace bra that he had included in my gift bag a few days prior.

"Fuck, I knew this would look incredible on you." He leaned down to kiss each breast, paying special attention to each peak. Slowly, he slid the purple lace off before moving to my skirt, sliding it down my legs as I laid down on the bed, now completely naked before him. Luca's hands slid down to my core, and upon feeling how wet I was, he gave me a satisfied grin. His mouth started to work its way down, but I shot out a hand, pulling him back up so I could capture his lips in a passionate kiss.

"I need you, now."

"Well, then, *amore*, your wish is my command," Luca whispered, his voice husky and overcome with emotion.

Luca quickly slipped on a condom, before leaning back down. His cock pressed against me before he slowly entered me, eliciting a loud moan from my lips. It felt like he was filling a void in my soul. I had been so restless since we left the paddock, and the sensation of him inside me was like the air I had been craving to breathe.

He gazed down at me with tenderness, his lips meeting mine in a gentle kiss. He whispered in my ear, asking if I was alright. With a nod, I eagerly returned his affectionate kisses while Luca began to move inside of me. His thrusts were slow and deliberate, a change from when we'd been on the yacht. As he trailed kisses along my neck, he whispered "I love you" after each one.

Such a good girl for me. I love you so much. You take me so well.

The praises kept coming, and I was reveling in them, each one bringing me closer to my peak. Luca leaned back on his heels, pulling my body with him, and I was now straddling him as he held me in place, moving me up and down on his cock. The new position helped Luca get even deeper, allowing him to hit that magical spot with each thrust.

"Oh, Luca, this feels amazing. Fuck. Don't stop."

"Come with me." My nails scraped along his back as I rode the waves of sensation. When his hand found the space between us, I was gone. Luca followed with a groan, holding me tightly as he spilled into me.

Exhaustion flooded my body as Luca carefully placed me onto the bed.

"Stay right there," he whispered. He kissed my shoulder and disappeared into the bathroom. He cleaned me up, then tossed the towel aside and climbed back into bed, immediately pulling me into his arms.

We lay there, panting heavily, our bodies wrapped around each other. Finally, I tilted my head to look at him, brushing a lock of damp hair from his forehead.

"So, you had something to say earlier?"

Luca sat up, his face serious. "I've been thinking about this. Us. And I can't do this anymore."

My body went rigid.

"Relax, *amore*," he soothed, letting out a little chuckle. "I can't do this *fake* relationship anymore, Georgia, because it's too much for me. I can't wake up each day, feeling how I feel about you, without being able to call you mine. I love you, Georgia Dubois. I want you to be mine, 100 percent, every day. I want—no, I *need*—to be able to tell everyone that my heart is yours. That it has been for years."

Luca's words filled my racing heart. No one had ever said those words to me before, not with that level of conviction, with such emphasis and meaning. No boyfriend had ever looked at me the way Luca was looking at me now, like I was the most precious thing in the world, a rare diamond that he would treasure forever.

"Are you, Luca Playboy Rossi, asking me, Georgia Sassy Dubois, to be your girlfriend? Have I finally tamed the infamous Formula 1 bachelor?" I teased, giving his neck a soft kiss.

He laughed, pulling me even closer. "Oh, Georgia, you've owned my heart for much longer than you know. When I asked you out all those years ago, my heart was already yours."

Tears of happiness pricked my eyes. "When I'd read that you signed with Rennen, a part of me felt hurt that you hadn't told me. I felt like I'd lost you, lost our friendship, because you wouldn't need me anymore with your new deal. But then I realized that it was more than that, that I didn't want you to *need* me. I just wanted you to *want* to be with me."

"Lost me?" He gave me a quick peck on the lips. "I signed with Rennen because of you. I have *you* to thank for this move. You encouraged me back in London to think about other teams. You gave me the strength to stand up to my father, who has surprisingly come around. Seeing that painting you made me… it made my decision feel even more right. Thank you for everything." His eyes locked on to mine, the intensity of his gaze making my heart flutter. In that moment, I felt nothing but pride in his accomplishments.

"I'm so proud of you, Luca. And I know your father is, too. That's why I made that painting for you. You've been making your family proud since you were just a little boy, and you still are." He took my hand in his and placed a gentle kiss against my knuckle.

"I want to show the world that I can win races. That I can lead a team, and not because my dad was a famous racer. I'm worth a team's investment."

"You are worthy, Luca. We both are."

Luca ran his hands through my hair, before moving it to my chin.

"I'm so happy, Luca."

"Me too, Georgia," he laughed, sliding back down, his lips now ghosting mine. "Which is good, because you're stuck with me. Pretty sure if we break up, your brother might *actually* set my car on fire." His fingers slid through my hair, cupping my chin. "Your heart is safe with me."

"I love you, Rossi."

"Right back at you, Dubois."

We kissed, slow and deep, and for the first time all season, I felt like I could finally breathe. Like I was exactly where I belonged.

My phone buzzed on the nightstand. With a groan, I stretched over Luca's chest to check it.

"Ugh, Lily wants to know when we're leaving for tonight's party," I groaned.

Luca chuckled, brushing my hair off my shoulder as he nuzzled in. "Maybe we should set Lily and Henri up so they stop bothering us."

I snorted, my hands running through Luca's hair as I kissed him again. "Those two are much too competitive with each other. It'll be a cold day in hell before Lily and Henri ever date."

"You know, Georgia," Luca laughed. "I think I've heard that one before."

Epilogue

Georgia

"And the championship is ours! Fuck yeah!" I heard Mel scream into the radio.

"Georgia, congrats. You had a hell of a season, and this is a well-deserved win for both you and the team. Can't wait to do this again next year, love." I smiled at Isabelle's words. The softness of her voice was refreshing. I had a sneaking suspicion she might even be smiling.

"I am speechless!" I yelled back into my radio. "Thank you to the team. This one is for you ladies… for every last one of you. Thank you! Thank you to Lily for being the best teammate I could have dreamed of, an absolute star."

"You have outdone yourself today, Georgia," Mel called into the radio. "Today, you have shown every single little girl that they can turn their karting dreams into a dream of being an F1 champion, just like Georgia Dubois."

As soon as I hopped out of my car, my brother grabbed my helmet. "I am so proud of you, Peaches, *so fucking proud.*" I squeezed my brother and he quickly dragged the two of us off to our parents, who had made it to the fence. I immediately jumped into their arms as we hugged, not a single one of us wanting to let go.

I heard the officials calling for Henri and me to head to the cooldown room to get weighed. I searched the crowd for Luca, desperately looking for my boyfriend, who was seemingly nowhere to be found, but just as I was about to walk in, I felt an arm link around my waist, pulling me in. Luca grabbed my head and crashed our lips together, pulling my body as close to him as he possibly could.

"I'm so proud of you, *amore*. So, so incredibly proud of you. You never cease to amaze me." As I broke the kiss, I let him pull me once more into another kiss as the FIA official started yelling behind us.

I begrudgingly let Luca go, heading back into the cooldown room where water was waiting for me. It was only a few minutes before we were being pulled onto the podium for the celebration. I watched Edward go out first, giving the crowd a big wave. Henri walked out next. And then it was my turn.

The moment I had been waiting for.

I walked onto the stage, watching the masses of people who had gathered in Abu Dhabi to watch us race. To watch me win. I waved at them as I walked onto the top step, taking my trophy from the government official before setting it down so I could take my hat off for the Monaco national anthem.

As soon as the anthems finished, I picked up my bottle of champagne to spray Henri and Edward, but it was too late—they had beaten me to it, absolutely drenching me, and then Mel, who was the Valkyrie podium representative, with their two bottles. As soon as the bubbles died down, I took one more look into the crowd, giving them a final wave before stepping off the podium.

I walked back to the garage, trophy in one hand and a bottle of champagne in the other. Nora was the first to pull me into a hug, but it was short-lived as the rest of the garage crew started to come over, all of them demanding hugs, everyone wanting to see the trophy. I looked around for Isabelle, my eyes scanning the garage.

Nora saw my confused look because she leaned over and whispered to me, "In the office." I nodded and made my way to Isabelle's office, knocking on the door. As soon as I heard the words "come in" I opened it slowly, looking around the dimly lit room.

There in the corner was Isabelle, sat on her couch, a glass of what looked like whisky in her hands. I walked over to her and sat down before grabbing a glass and filling it up with whisky. We sat in silence for several minutes, both of us sipping on our glasses.

"Maison de Klotho called me earlier today, before the race. They told me regardless of today's outcome, it would be their honor to be our lead sponsor next year."

"Why didn't you tell me?" I gasped.

"Figured I'd tell you after you became a champion." But Isabelle's cheeky grin told another story. She had wanted that dangling over me as I raced, knew the pressure would push me even harder, and I grinned at that realization. In just a year, Isabelle knew me so well.

"I'm not going to lie, even after the FIA's statement clearing me of cheating last week, I wasn't sure this would come through for us."

"Nah," she said, brushing it off. "They never had a case. Just like the *Daily Reporter* never had a good story. You know, Georgia, it doesn't matter how much they try, they can't keep us out of motorsports." Isabelle leaned back in her chair, her voice softening. "Did I ever tell you the story of why I started the team?"

I shook my head no.

"When I was a young girl, I loved racing. Loved it dearly. I spent every weekend with my parents in Italy, karting with my brother. But as I got older, the karting got more expensive, and there was only enough money for one of us to continue. Even though I was more talented than my brother, my parents chose to continue funding his karting. Apparently, there was no hope I would ever be a professional driver. That just wasn't something in the cards for a woman, so my brother, who could barely win races, got to continue living my dream as I was forced to return to normal life."

I set my glass down on the counter, pouring both of us another round.

"It was that day I promised myself I was going to start an F1 team. I decided that I was going to win this championship somehow..."

"And now that we have... it almost doesn't seem real, does it?" I finished for her. I understood what Isabelle was feeling. Deep inside my soul, I understood. I had fought so long to be here, fought tooth and nail to stand on that podium and accept the World Driver's Championship trophy, and now that this day had arrived, it felt almost bittersweet. The illustrious dream wasn't so illustrious anymore. Isabelle smiled at me, her tears drying up as she took another sip of whisky.

"And now we've done it. Today, a female-run and -operated team did more than just win the WDC. We proved to the world that women should have an equal seat at the table in motorsports—from mechanics to leadership to drivers, we're here to stay."

"That we are, Isabelle, that we are."

"Next year is a new year, Georgia. New car design, new challenges. You ready to do it all again?"

"How many championships do I need to win to beat the current record of having the most titles? They have six, so I need seven?" I said with a chuckle, earning me a huge grin from Isabelle.

"Hmm… perhaps we should make it eight, just to be safe," Isabelle countered, a refreshing gleam I had come to know so well gathering in her eyes.

"Well, we have one down." I raised my glass as I stood up, clinking it with hers. "Here's to another seven championships, Isabelle."

Acknowledgments

This book was born out of my own experience working in a male-dominated industry. It was challenging—often lonely—and there were times I felt like I had to fight just to be heard. It was through that journey that this story began to take shape. A story about a woman who boldly walks into that kind of world and stands tall.

A world where she not only belongs—but wins.

Thank you to everyone who helped bring *Racing Hearts* to life.

To my agent: thank you for believing in this story from day one. Your guidance, tenacity, and fierce advocacy made all the difference. I'm so lucky to have you in my corner.

To my editor: your insight and care brought this story to life in a whole new way. Thank you for your incredible insight, your steady encouragement, and your ability to spot plot holes before I had the opportunity to insist they were "intentional." You helped shape this book into something far better than I imagined.

To my early readers and critique partners: you laughed, cried, swooned, and sent unhinged texts in the best way possible. Your feedback, fangirling, and tough love made this book better in every way.

To my family and friends: Thank you for your patience, your encouragement, and for pretending not to notice when I disappeared into my writing cave. Your love held me up when I needed it most. Your support means the world to me.

To my husband: there is no Luca without you.

To the readers: romance readers are a rare and magical breed. You believe in happily ever afters, slow burns, and the kind of love that's worth the wait. Thank you for picking up this book and letting these characters into your heart.

And to anyone chasing something that feels just out of reach—keep going. You never know what's waiting on the other side of the last page.